BLACKBEARD'S REVENGE
BOOK 2 OF:
THE VOYAGES OF
QUEEN ANNE'S REVENGE

JEREMY MCLEAN

POINTS OF SAIL
PUBLISHING

Points of Sail Publishing
P.O. Box 30083 Prospect Plaza
FREDERICTON, New Brunswick
E3B 0H8, Canada

Edited by Ethan James Clarke
http://silverjay-editing.com/

Cover Design by Kit Foster

This is a work of fiction. Any similarity to persons, living or dead, is purely coincidental... Or is it?

ACKNOWLEDGEMENTS

All the people who read the novel when it was pre-release, thank you for putting up with the spelling and grammar errors to help make the novel as it is right now. Extra special thanks to Ethan Clarke who read it twice to give me feedback and fix those spelling and grammar errors.

If you're in need of editing, check out his services at: http://silverjaymedia.com

Ethan also has a novel of his own:
www.amazon.com/dp/B00NP4U6KW
Spoiler: It's amazing.

DEDICATION

I dedicate this to my loved ones, without whom this wouldn't be possible.

TABLE OF CONTENTS

PROLOGUE

The sun sent a gift of heat and light down in waves upon the open sea. Storm clouds advancing from the east, and the growing winds, were the only reprieve from the scorching.

"Cap'n, there be a storm brewin'," the helmsman said over his shoulder.

A tall, well-built man sauntered up beside the helmsman, a distinctive snap sounding as he thrust his one wooden leg to the lumber of the ship. A pipe was in his mouth and he blew great puffs of smoke into the air, carried off by the rising winds. His dark, grungy, salt-and-pepper hair was held in by a tricorn hat and covered his wrinkled, piercing eyes. The hair did not cloud his vision as he peered at the clouds. The man let the sea air into his nostrils with an almost animal ferocity.

"Aye, but she be a storm of man, not the Lord." After taking another puff of the weed and eyeing the east, he turned his attention to the crew. "Hoist the sails! A guest is comin' and he's not the type to be left waitin'."

None questioned the peculiar message from their captain. The crew was fully aware of his perception and long since past wondering how he divined his knowledge. And, as if to reward their blind faith, a ship approached from the east.

The ship, a second-rate ship according to the British Navy's standards, flew no flag and carried no mark of distinction to any country or man. Nearly one hundred guns over three decks and with a crew of over seven hundred souls made the ship fearsome to behold. A ship so large should be hard-pressed to manoeuvre delicately, but it moved as deftly and gracefully as a swan in a pond. The second ship sailed next to the first ship so close they appeared as one from afar.

If the second ship moved like a swan, then the captain was a falcon. He gracefully jumped across the railings to the waist of the first ship. As he passed, the crew of the first ship removed their caps or bent their knees. The second captain paid the crew no heed and headed straight to the helm where the first captain still stood.

"Leave us, Bertram," the first captain ordered the helmsman. "These old sods need to have a conversation."

"Aye, Captain." Bertram locked the helm and left.

The second captain threw the first captain a bottle of aged scotch.

"You come bearing gifts?" The first captain asked, then took a long swig of the scotch while walking to the middle of the quarterdeck. "So, am I in the presence of the Lord of Gifts today? Or Stormbringer?" The first captain gestured wildly. "Benjamin perhaps, or Albert? The Red Hand, or the Golden Horn? Or what is it you're called these days? … John? … Jack?"

The second captain raised his eyes for the first time, showing his aged face. "What about in the presence of a friend?" The man smiled, showing more wrinkles. He was well groomed with short black hair and a few grey hairs peeking through. His eyes, though softened in the presence of a friend, were just as piercing, if not more so.

The first laughed heartily. "Of course!" He grabbed the second man and the two hugged each other tightly. The first eventually pulled away and held the second at arm's length. "You are always a friend, and always welcome."

The two sat leisurely and passed the scotch and weed back and forth. Once the introduction was complete, the crews lost their formality and reserve and mingled together, swapping stories and alcohol like best friends reunited.

When the weed was spent and the scotch, like the stories, nearly depleted, the first captain decided to start business. "So, Benjamin, what brings ye here? Not playing dog today, are ye?"

Benjamin laughed bitterly. "No, not today. I've arrived to ask a favour if I may be so presumptuous."

"Speak and it shall be done. You know I can never refuse the Golden Horn's will."

"Even if the Gold is tarnished?" Benjamin cast down his eyes.

"Tarnished Gold is still Gold, no?" the captain said with a laugh hoarse from age and too much pipe.

Benjamin's smile was melancholic. "I suppose so." He took another swig of the scotch before passing the bottle back to the captain. "Have you heard news of my successor?"

Despite the din of the two crews, despite the storm which now surrounded the horizon, despite all the noise, the word *successor* caused a hush to spread over the two ships. Those drunk instantly sobered, and those laughing became silent. All eyes turned, and all ears perked, towards the two captains.

"I never thought I would see the day." The captain opened the scotch bottle and finished the remainder in one great gulp.

"You know of whom I speak?"

The Voyages of Queen Anne's Revenge

"Aye, I heard 'bout a fledgling youngster causin' a stir in the New World and Old. Uses your old ship, fer God's sake, of course I know who yer talking 'bout." The old man laughed hoarsely. "Need me to show him how things were done in our age?"

"No, he's running errands right now. I need him to remain unspoiled before he's ready to hatch, but my sources tell me the Black Plague is moving on the boy as we speak."

At the mention of "Black Plague" the first captain held fast for a moment before solemnly setting the empty bottle on the deck with a clang. "That is bad news. The egg is liable to be broken if the Plague ain't stopped."

"Exactly. Thus, I am asking you to stop Plague. I am asking you, William Kidd, the Tsunami, to do this for me." Benjamin's nonchalant demeanour belied the gravity of his request.

The crews, mainly silent until then, began whispering amongst themselves on the events unfolding.

"You're askin' for a lot," Kidd replied.

"I would not ask anything of you I believed you could not accomplish."

"Aye, even at yer boldest, yer reasonable. So, what do ye want me to do? Kill him?"

"No, just keep him occupied until the egg is ready, or cripple him, whichever you prefer," Benjamin smirked.

"And how will I find this egg of yours to keep an eye on him?"

"I have someone on the inside. They can provide you with updates on his whereabouts."

Kidd nodded, rose and strode to the edge of the quarterdeck, overlooking the crew. "Ready yerselves, boys! Soon we see if a Tsunami can stop the Plague. By the Sound of the Golden Horn!"

"By the Sound of the Golden Horn!" The crews repeated, raising their glasses and bottles before drinking. The old hymn was the battle cry from the olden days when all the world's best pirates followed Benjamin Hornigold, and it meant Kidd's crew approved of the deal struck.

The two crews separated soon after, knowing full well a great battle would soon happen between William Kidd, one of the Pirate Warlords who fought in the War of the Horns, and Edward Russell, one of the Immortal Seven, the Admiral of the Black.

1. CATCH TWO & TWENTY

Six Weeks Ago

The guard kicked a large plate of food, or something akin to food, into the prison cell. The plate clanged as it skid through a slot at the bottom of steel grates and across the dingy stone floor.

The guard's lamp illuminated the food and the men in the cell. The prisoners closest to the grate—rough, filthy men—shielded their eyes from the faint light. Satisfied, the guard moved on, leaving the lamp in the corner opposite the cell, illuminating just enough to eat by.

The prisoners' bodies were caked with dirt, bones exposed due to lack of muscle and fat, and their beards and hair unshaven. Bruises covered their bodies from beatings, white and red disfigurement peppered their flesh from the hot iron, and long bloody messes covered equally long scars on their backs from the lash. Craven sinners rotting in desolation in their communal hell.

Despite their ravenous hunger, none dared to move. *He* hadn't taken his share yet.

A man of above average stature and build slowly rose. His once-tanned skin was now lightened by lack of exposure, his strong arms were thinner from poor food and exercise, and his wavy black hair and long black beard matted with grease. Though his form was diminished, his spirit was not. His eyes carried the same strength as a year ago, and kept the devils of the prison at bay.

Edward Thatch sauntered to the plate of food and took his share, along with some for two others. Edward took what he needed, then sat back down in the dark of the cell. After he was seated the frenzy began, the strongest and fiercest fighting for their pathetic morsels.

Edward handed a share to an old man, and another to a young boy. Together the three ate in reflective silence after the fighting in the cell stopped.

The prison was made of hard grey stone hastily assembled with no regard for comfort. The stones were misshapen and set haphazardly, making sitting and sleeping a chore. Water leaked in from God knows where, causing an incessant drip, drip, sound every few seconds which lent to the dank atmosphere and stagnant smell. No fresh air could creep its way down to the basement and through the sweat and odour from thousands of days of compounded sweat and faeces.

"Can you tell me another story, Edward? Please?" the boy asked, as he had almost every day before.

The child's small frame belied his imaginative and intelligent mind. He was not yet aged enough to grow facial hair, but the blond hair on his head was long and shaggy from the years he'd spent in the dungeon. He was born in this prison and protected by his mother until she died. He had heard stories about the sun and sea and the outside world, but never saw them firsthand.

"Perhaps later, Edmond. A year has passed since I last laid eyes on the sun and my beloved. I feel I need time to reflect." Edward slowly ate the mouldy bread and gruel.

"Now, are you referring to the vast and untameable ocean, or your beloved Anne?" The old man on the other side of Edward spoke up.

The grey-haired gentleman possessed a beard longer than Edward's, a sharp nose, and keen eyes not yet dulled by his old age. When Edward arrived, the elder was nearing death's door, not having the strength to fight for his portion of food and relying on leftover scraps. Edward fought for the old man, and now he had a little skin on his bones and more strength to lend to his wisdom.

Edward chuckled at the old man's penetrating question. *Maybe both, Charles.* Edward's mind drifted to Anne, his love. The last time Edward had seen Anne was after he was captured and forced into the brig of a battleship. A fleet of warships from the British Navy descended on Edward and his group of pirates aboard his ship, the *Freedom*. The fleet was there to 'save' Anne, the daughter of the Queen of England.

Anne's father was gracious enough to take Edward but freed his crew as a last request. And, by Edward's estimation, it was only due to Anne's pleading to her mother that he was imprisoned instead of being executed. During his prison term, Edward had had a hard time deciding which would have been the worse fate.

Another man, large in stature but too thinned by malnutrition, also laughed, but haughtily. "That's all ye have left: stories. No use thinkin' bout them no more. We ain't leavin' here, least of all a little shit as you."

Even through the long hair and beard the man showed his yellow and grungy teeth in a sneer. His face and body were square in appearance, and in his prime he might have taken the appearance of a wall when standing.

He sat with his hands draped over his knees as he gestured to their surroundings. "This is the hell of hells. No one sent here will ever be let free because of our 'crimes against the state.' Any who think we's gonna be leavin' here is a sorry sod indeed."

"No one asked you, Simon." Edward, sitting cross-legged, turned his scornful gaze to the middle-aged man. Most would flinch and think twice about what they said after Edward's stare, but not Simon.

"Yea, well I's tired of hearing talk about the outside. Talk of the like is no use to us here. Jus' brings back bad memories."

"There's no harm in allowing the boy to dream."

"There's always harm in dreamin'. See where dreamin' got you. We all heard the story: You wanted freedom, so ye fought against the marines and ye ended up here. Nothing good never came from dreamin'."

"You're wrong, Simon. The realisation of the dream was the cause of our downfall. If I hadn't tried to achieve my dreams then I wouldn't have ended up here, but because I did this is the inevitable cause. And if you only dreamed of your revolution, instead of being a fool and lighting a bomb, you wouldn't be here."

Simon rose from his seated position and Edward followed suit, meeting him in the middle of the small cage. "Who're you callin' a fool, you dunderwhelp!"

At Edward's six-foot-four height, the top of Simon's head barely reached Edward's chin. "Careful what you say, Simon. I might break your other arm this time. Remember how long the first one took to heal?"

Prisoners in other cages whispered amongst one another at the beginnings of the fight. Several in Edward's cage also goaded the two on. The guard heard the commotion and smacked his club against the bars.

"What did I tell you twos 'bout fighting? Stop this nonsense or the both of ya get ten lashes."

Edward and Simon didn't turn their attention to the guard, but both knew he would follow through on his threat if they didn't sit back down.

"You heard the man, Simon. Sit down before you're hurt," Edward said.

Simon spat on the ground before turning back and sitting back against the wall. Edward nodded to the guard and he too sat down again.

Before the guard moved on, a noise echoed down the dark hallway near the stairs. The guard ran to investigate, his keys and weapons clinking and clanging as he moved. When the guard reached the foot of the stairs, he jerked back with muffled "Oof!" and dropped to the stone floor with a crack, knocked unconscious, or dead.

A dark figure jumped on top of the body and started rummaging around for something until another, taller figure stepped out of the stairwell.

All the prisoners with enough strength pressed their faces against the iron bars to catch a glimpse at what was happening.

"Hurry up, Princess," the taller one scolded. "We need to be outta here before they're done pissin'."

The first one grabbed the keys off the belt of the unconscious guard and turned to the taller one. "You think I'm not aware, Sam? Who was the one who created this plan? Now we need to find Edward's cell, so help me search."

Until now, Edward had had merely a passing interest in the event. One or two ill-formed attempts at escape happened during his year of imprisonment, and both failed. But the keywords *Princess, Sam,* and, of course, *Edward,* piqued his interest now. He also felt sure he'd heard those voices before.

Edward ran to the cell bars. "Anne?" he yelled.

At the calling of the name, the two figures snapped their heads around and ran over to Edward's cell. The small one passed the keys to the tall one and grabbed Edward's outstretched hands.

Edward could see the face of the one he loved in the faint light. Anne's curly red hair glistened from under her hood, and her ocean green eyes glittered from newly forming tears. She kissed Edward's palms and held them close to her face as if she were trying to impart, or take, every bit of warmth she could.

Despite Edward's dark reverie, he could not help but be brought out of his gloom and into Anne's light. She was as an angel in front of Edward. Every second felt like eternity as if to accentuate the horribly long time Edward and Anne had been torn apart, and yet eternity was not enough.

"What are you two doing here?" Edward finally asked, pulling himself back to earth.

Sam, working the keys one by one, spoke first. His straight black hair and smooth, pretty face had not changed in the year since parting. "We're here to save ya, mate! This be a prison break." Nor had his confidence bordering on arrogance changed either, apparently.

"Oh, is that why you stole the keys? I assumed you would become a guard for a moment." Edward's comment was full of sarcasm. Sam stared at Edward with eyes as cold as stone at midnight before continuing with the multitude of keys. "I mean *why*. Why are you both here?"

"Is not the action and reason the same? We wish to see you free, my dear, sweet Edward."

Edward pulled away from Anne's soft cheeks and sat back down against the back of the cell. "You had better leave before someone catches you then. I'm not leaving."

"What d'ya mean yer not going?" Sam said, losing his place with the keys out of shock.

"I think the words are fairly clear, are they not? I do not wish to join you, so please leave, unless you want to become a cell mate."

Sam turned to Anne and threw his hands up in the air, exasperated. "What now, Princess?"

"Work the keys, I'll handle this," Anne instructed with gritted teeth. "Edward, as much as I'm sure you've grown accustomed with your new surroundings, your family and I went through much trouble to be here, so, please, forestall any objections and join us."

"Why bother when the end result will bring me back here sooner or later?"

"So you believe what we are doing is futile? You believe freedom is futile?"

"I've enjoyed a lot of time to think here, Anne, and despite my bitterness over what has happened, I see no future for me on the sea. If I escape here, I will be hunted down and imprisoned again, or worse, killed. If I am captured at present, then what else can be done to me?"

"You feel there is no future for you? For us?" Anne held Edward's gaze, but Edward turned away. "No, I do not," he replied. "At least, not one ending without pain."

Anne's face fell. The sound of hastened footsteps at the stairs caught Anne's attention, so she ran to the edge of the stair opening with a knife drawn. When a large, well-built man emerged, Anne threatened him with the knife, but then lowered the weapon and began speaking with the man in hushed tones. Edward was not able to make out who the man was because of the little light, but judging from the closeness Anne shared, and his build, Edward had an idea.

The man walked over with Anne at his side, and when he reached the cell he lifted his hood so Edward could see his face. "Now what is this I hear about not wanting to leave?"

In front of the cell a man of Edward's age, twenty or one and twenty years, stood tall and large. He was shorter than Edward, but more toughly built, especially being well fed. His straight brown hair was tied back, and his strong jaw, like his crossed arms, were set as stone.

"Henry! You, as well?" Henry, Edward's childhood friend, had joined Edward on his first flight of freedom as whalers before they were accidentally branded pirates.

"Yes, I am here, as are two others of the crew. And John is waiting for us with horse and carriage as well. Will you stop being foolish and join us now that you are fully aware of the gravity of the situation?"

Edward crossed his arms in mirror to Henry, in direct defiance. "No. As I told Anne, I do not see the point in being captured again. I'm choosing to end the cycle here. Leave me be before you are forced to join me in my torment."

Henry considered Edward's words for a quick moment before laughing almost too loudly. Edward thought Henry to be mad, and from the looks on Anne and Sam's faces so did they.

"Apologies, Henry, but I do not see the humour in this situation," Anne said.

Henry looked at Anne, but pointed to Edward. "He's lying," Henry proclaimed. "You would have noticed if you'd known him as long as I. He's still acting chivalrous for our sakes. He's been so long here he doesn't think anyone can escape, and wants us to leave before anything happens."

"I'm not lying, Henry. You don't know me as well as you think. Run while you still can."

Anne nodded, the three ignoring Edward's pleas. "So what do you propose we do?" Anne questioned with one hand in the air, palm up.

"We force his hand." Henry sat down on the stone, folding his legs to get comfortable.

Anne grinned and joined Henry, and Sam shrugged his shoulders and made a sarcastic comment before sitting as well. The three faced the cell, watching Edward with nonchalance bordering on indifference.

"What are you doing? You must make haste before the guards find you."

The trio didn't move an inch, their bodies and faces becoming as the stone in the prison itself.

Edward stood up. "I don't want to go with you, don't you see? We are no longer friends, comrades, or family."

None responded despite the biting remarks Edward made.

The noise of several footsteps sounded against the hard stone stairs, signalling guards on the way.

Edward jumped to the bars, gripping them hard until his knuckles turned white. "You must flee, now!"

The three did not react, and simply gazed at Edward, calling for action with their eyes. Sweat trickled down Edward's face when two armed guards descended from above.

The guards, their muskets pointed at the three, shouted orders to clasp their hands behind their heads. Henry, Anne, and Sam all relented to the orders, and then rose at another command. One guard guided them away in front, with the second forcing them forward with his musket.

The three were about to be resigned to a fate Edward would not wish upon any, their freedom stripped and their spirits ripped from pain and anguish.

Deep down, in his heart of hearts, no matter what Edward said, he wanted to be free as well. For most of his life, Edward suffered an oppressive, unloving step-family, so even when he was branded a pirate and chased across the Caribbean, even when the world was at its bleakest, he was still free on that ship with those he cared about. Because of the consequences of his decision, his heart and mind struggled for and against the freedom he desired.

But today... today, the heart won.

"Take me with you! I want to be free with you, my family!" Edward shouted, his words resounding across the floor and then some.

Anne, Henry, and Sam smiled.

The guards were momentarily distracted by Edward's outcry, and the three took that chance to strike.

Anne spun around, gripped the muzzle of one guard's musket, and thrust it upwards. The musket smashed into the guard's nose, breaking it. As the guard clutched his nose, taken aback by the blow, Sam jumped around Anne and punched the guard square in the jaw, knocking him unconscious.

Henry held the other guard in a headlock. The guard dropped his musket and struggled to pull Henry's massive biceps away, but it was no use. The guard elbowed Henry in the ribs again and again. Henry endured as long as he could, but lost his grip and the guard broke free.

The guard pulled himself away and drew a deep breath. The man was about to cry out for his comrades on the upper floor when Anne whipped out a knife and flung it at the guard. The knife hit the man in the back of the head, his cry turning into a grunt as he fell to the floor dead.

With the guards dispatched, the trio ran back to the cell together, Anne and Henry grabbing each of Edward's arms in a desperate embrace.

Henry beamed at his best friend in all the world. "Let's set you free, brother."

2. GAMMOND CASTLE

"That's the key. Yes, that one," Edward confirmed, guiding Sam to one key among the multitude.

"How can ya tell? They all look the same!" Sam said, but he did not doubt the validity of Edward's statement, as he stuck the key into the lock.

"I've been here a year. I had to occupy my mind somehow."

Sam turned the key and it opened with a click. He pulled back the door and all the prisoners tried to rush out at once. Sam and Henry pushed the door closed again as Edward tried to calm them and keep their rabid grasps from his friends.

"What are you doing?" Edward yelled above the clatter in his cell. "Quiet!" Edward commanded, silencing the prisoners.

"We cannot take them with us. We can escape with you, and maybe one other," Anne explained coldly.

Edward considered Anne for a moment. Anne must have planned his escape for months, maybe even the whole year since he was imprisoned. Edward glanced at the boy Edmond and the old man Charles. *I can't leave them.*

Anne placed her hand over her eyes in frustration and shook her head. "I didn't plan for this. What do you suggest?"

"We free all the prisoners. The storm will be too much for the guards to handle. Besides, I will not leave without my belongings. The warden has my sword at his hip, so I will kill him and retrieve it."

"You would kill an innocent man?" Henry said in shock.

Edward turned his back, revealing the scars of previous beatings. "You think an innocent man could order people to do this?" Edward glanced at his cell mates, all of them itching to leave. "We do not have the time to argue, we lost too much from *my* stubbornness."

Anne sighed. "Fine, let us free them all."

As Sam was readying to open the door once more, Edward turned to the group of cutthroats and revolutionaries of varying ages in his cell. "You will all wait until the other prisoners are released. If we all leave as one then we will overwhelm the guards. They will stand no chance if we work together."

11

"For once, we agree on sumthin'," Simon declared. "If any try to skip before we are ready, I'll be breakin' their legs."

Sam opened the door, and instead of the rush as before, the prisoners left in an orderly fashion, warily glancing at the leaders of the escape when passing. Edward moved to the back, where Edmond and Charles sat motionless, but wide eyed.

"Today you will realise your wish, Edmond," Edward said, making the young boy smile. "Let's move, old man." Edward lifted Charles up and pulled the old man's arm over his shoulder for support. Edward carried Charles to the door, where Sam, Henry, and Anne waited. "Here, Sam, help this man, will you? I'll take the keys."

Edward and Sam swapped their cargo, with minor grumbling from the latter, and Edward took his first step from the cell that had been his home for a year. He left the cell to embrace his friend, Henry, and his love, Anne. The embrace was short, but more than sweet.

"I take the geezer and they get hugs. A little unfair, ain't it?" Sam asked no one in particular. "No offence, old man."

"None taken, my boy."

Henry and Sam guarded the stairs with Simon while the other prisoners were being freed.

"Anne, I will need your help with one prisoner. He's almost as stubborn as myself, and I think you're the only one who can convince him to leave here." Edward stepped to the cell opposite the one he was in and unlocked the door, letting all those inside out, save one who didn't move.

"Who?" Anne asked as she joined Edward in the cell. She studied the figure of a man not unlike Edward. The prisoner had the same shaggy hair and long beard, a trademark of those present for an extended length of time. Anne's eyes widened when the man looked up at her. "William!" Anne ran to William and knelt down, placing her hand on his cheek. "I thought you had been executed!" She embraced William tightly for a second. William had been Anne's protector, her confidant, and a great friend.

Edward left them to their reunion as he freed the prisoners from their cells.

"Not quite, Your Highness. By the grace of your mother, Queen Anne, I was spared the guillotine and the noose."

Anne scoffed lightly at his remark. "Then, by my grace and Providence, I shall rescue you from this crucible. We will escape from here, together." Anne grabbed William's hand and tried to lead him away, but he didn't budge. "What are you doing, William? We must make haste!"

"I am sorry Anne, I cannot. I will be of no use to you."

"What are you saying? Do not tell me your time here has made you weak."

William turned away; he could not face those eyes. "Prison has made me more aware of my faults, and I must atone for my weakness. I failed in my charge, and this is my punishment."

Anne reared back and slapped William hard. "All the more reason you need to be my protector! Fulfil your broken oath to me, not as royalty, not as your princess, but as my friend. Your punishment will be to keep me alive and regain your lost honour!" Anne rose and turned to the cell door. "Don't think you can take the easy way out because you feel you failed my uncle." Anne strolled away, leaving William with her words.

William's mouth was wide open. He rubbed his cheek where Anne had slapped him. After a moment he clenched his teeth and rose to his feet. Without saying a word, he joined Anne outside. Anne grinned to herself.

Edward finished unlocking the cells, and a total of fifty-eight criminals were ready to fight, comprised of thirty-five men and twenty-three women, eleven mentally ill whose minds were on the brink, and sixteen elderly and children.

"Do you know where the armoury is located?" Edward asked Anne.

"Yes, up the stairs and across a hallway," Anne replied.

"Take those who can fight to the armoury, and keep the elderly and children away from combat as much as possible," Edward commanded as he went the opposite direction of the stairs, instead heading deeper into the prison.

"Where are you going?" she asked.

"I am freeing more prisoners," Edward replied, jangling the keys as he travelled further into the darkness.

Edward had heard stories of those trapped in the deepest level of the prison. The prisoners said to be the worst devils in existence, or at least British existence, were sent there. Some considered these in league with Satan and practitioners of dark arts.

Edward thought they were just stories conjured by an overactive imagination, but upon seeing those in the darkness he had his doubts.

The stench of disease and filth hit Edward, and the smell was so vile he could scarcely breathe. He inspected the room, and could see the grates of eleven cells in the square room, five on either side and a large one at the back. Edward could feel the intense scrutiny of beady eyes, which caused his skin to crawl and itch uncontrollably.

Blackbeard's *Revenge*

Edward tried the keys on the closest cell. When he opened the door the prisoners rushed upon him, knocking him to the ground. Most ran away up the stairs, taking their chance to escape, while three lashed out at Edward viciously.

"Stop, stop I say! I am here to free you!" Edward yelled, but repeated himself another two times before the attack stopped.

"You mean to free us? Why?" one of the three asked.

"I cannot escape on my own."

Another tall man laughed. "The boy means to use us as decoys, methinks. No matter, this will be a golden chance, let us seize it." And without further deliberation, nor a helping hand to Edward, the three left.

Edward rose and began opening the cells once more. None attacked Edward like the first time, but some appeared on the verge. As the prisoners passed, Edward pondered what horrible deeds these prisoners could have committed.

Coming out of the second cell, a hunched-over, shifty-eyed man was being led by a pregnant woman. The man was muttering something under his breath about Poseidon and Davey Jones, but Edward could not catch the rest.

In another cell, three men passed by in tandem. The first man had no ears, the second's eyes were bandaged, but the third seemed perfectly normal. The second man thanked Edward for all three of them, stating the third's tongue was cut out.

In yet another cell a large woman with a missing eye and arm passed by with six other men following behind. The men seemed to fear falling behind the woman, but also afraid of leaving with her. After a few threatening leers from the woman, the men followed compliantly.

Several men and women were disfigured and diseased with leprosy and boils, as well as odd ailments and afflictions like frostbite. Many had also descended into madness, or were committed because of madness, so Edward decided to keep his distance.

Edward left the large cell in the back for last. He could see a man with a mask made of some type of metal. His hands and feet, unlike those of the other prisoners, were bound to the ceiling and floor respectively.

"Hold a moment, friend. I will free you in but a moment," Edward reassured him, to no response.

Edward first freed the man's limbs while examining him. The mask the prisoner wore covered the whole face, but slits left the eyes, mouth, and nose exposed. Edward found no visible signs of fusing, and the mask looked like one continuous piece of metal. *How is this possible? How was this affixed to his head?*

After Edward freed him the man stayed motionless, but whispered something under his breath. "What?" Edward asked.

The man glared the coldest malice at Edward. "The mask."

Edward inspected the mask once more from all angles, but couldn't find a spot for a key, no lock, no seam to work. "I see no way to remove the mask."

The man grabbed Edward and slammed him against the stone wall. After a moment, the man released Edward, screamed in anger and left the cell. "Anne, you will pay for this!" the man in the metal mask yelled as he quickly jumped up the stairs of the prison.

He must have meant Queen Anne. Who was that man? Edward shook his head. *No time to dwell.*

Edward ran back up the steps to the level of the prison his former cell was on. Anne, Henry, Sam, Charles, and Edmond were waiting for Edward. As he drew closer to the stairs, the sounds of battle could be heard echoing against the stone.

Anne noticed Edward approaching and stepped towards him. "I showed the prisoners to the armoury and things are escalating quickly."

"If ya thought it hell down 'ere, Thatch, ya'd best see upstairs," Sam cackled.

Edward ran up the stairs to the main level of the castle, his companions following closely behind, and found himself in the right corner, farthest from the drawbridge. If a castle could be called plain, this one qualified. The castle had a bailey in each of the four corners, with one large open courtyard in the centre, and a tall keep at the back. The perimeter had high curtain walls, making interior and exterior defence easily manageable.

The castle used to be owned by William III before his death, and ownership fell to his successor and sister-in-law, Queen Anne. Not wishing to bring unpleasant memories of her brother-in-law's death, Queen Anne converted the castle to a prison. The Queen quickly filled the prison castle with political prisoners, dissenters, and other enemies of the state.

Edward and his group stationed themselves behind stone columns and a waist-high barrier around the inside of the bailey. From above, on the curtain walls, guards popped in and out of cover trying to shoot the escapees with muskets. Below Edward, on the main level, the fifty-plus escaped prisoners fought off guards attempting to enter from the courtyard on Edward's left as well as guards rushing down the stairs on Edward's right. The prisoners raided the armoury to better fight the guards on the curtain wall.

"How is the best way to the keep?" Edward shouted over the gunfire, yells, and curses uttered from the unstable men he'd freed.

"The safest way is through a door at the top of this bailey. There isn't much cover on the baileys, but the walkways along the walls are thin so we cannot be overwhelmed with numbers," Anne yelled back. A bullet ripped into the stone column Anne was standing behind, so she ducked down further.

"What of our escape?" Henry asked. "We cannot use the latrine hole anymore."

"The way out is through. There are two release levers for the drawbridge in the front baileys. Both need to be thrown for it to be lowered."

"Then we 'ave no choice but to split up." Sam forcefully pushed Charles, the old man, down below the stone wall to avoid the bullets.

"First we need to acquire weapons, and then move to the top level," Edward said as he drew a deep breath and plunged into the chaos.

Edward dashed from column to column, ducking below the waist-high stone wall when he needed to pass between. Edward slowed down as the concentration of bullets increased, eventually stopping at the right corner of the bailey. Sam, Charles, Henry, and Anne were all following behind.

When Edward glanced back to make sure his friends were unharmed, he had to do a double take. "Where's Edmond?" The expressions on the faces of his companions told Edward they did not know the answer. Edward shifted his gaze rapidly until he saw the boy running between the fighting prisoners.

Edmond carried several weapons in his arms and more draped over his small frame. As Edmond's gaze moved to the sky a stray bullet hit near his feet, causing him to stop short. Edmond toppled over, fully exposed for the guards to see.

"Edmond!" yelled Edward. He took a quick glance from behind his cover before running out to save the boy. Edward bobbed and weaved through the mess of prisoners and bullets raining from above. Edward's heart beat like waves before a storm as the surrounding sights and smells invigorated him.

The stench of body odour and disease from the prisoners was lessened with the fresh outside air and mixed with the familiar smells of gunpowder and blood. All that was missing was the salty ocean air Edward so missed, instead being replaced with the fresh grass and newly tilled earth of the countryside.

Edward reached the young man in a flash and, after taking Edmond over his shoulder, grabbed the weapons and brought the boy back to safety. Edward dropped the weapons and plopped Edmond down below the stone barrier.

"What were you thinking, Edmond? You could have gotten yourself killed!"

Edmond's eyes filled with tears. "I saw the sun, Edward, that's why I fell. It's so beautiful."

Edward peered past the column he was hidden behind and saw a sliver of the sun through the opening of the bailey.

"You are right, Edmond, the sun is beautiful. But you have yet to see the sun as it sets and rises upon the sea. Now that... that is a sight to behold. You must be careful, or you won't live to see it. Understand?" Edmond nodded, wiping his tears away.

Edward grabbed a musket and a sword from the pile of weapons and signalled to his comrades to take their pick. While his friends equipped themselves for battle, Edward searched among the prisoners. "Simon!" Edward yelled. After a moment, Simon's eyes found Edward, and he ran over.

"Whut is it, you git? Can't ye see we're a tad busy here?"

"I am well aware," Edward answered. "We need to reach the top level of this bailey and split into two groups. There is a lever at the front of the castle to release the drawbridge. I want you to lead half the people on this side, and I will lead the others to the opposite side."

"You lead the way, and I'll make sure these rats follow." Simon started to rise, but Edward stopped him.

He handed the keys for the prison cells to Simon. "Take these and free the prisoners in the front bailey. We'll need their help."

"The bastards'll make good shields," Simon asserted with a heartless laugh.

Edward ignored the comment and peered at his crewmen, who nodded to his silent question of their readiness. Edward rushed for the stairs to his right with his friends following behind. Four prisoners were at the foot of the stairs, stopping the guards from descending, but their own ascent also prevented by those same guards.

"We're at a stalemate here, and the more time we waste, the sooner reinforcements will arrive. Does anyone have any ideas?" Edward asked.

"I 'ave one," Sam answered. "I need a bag of powder." Sam handed Charles to Henry and took a bag of powder from the young Edmond. "I learned this on the last ship I was on," Sam explained as he cocked a pistol and set it in the bag full of gunpowder along with musket balls.

"The crew turned on the captain, and 'e was holed up in his cabin, so 'e made a few of these to clear out the chief bastards outside his door. When you 'ear the boom, run up the stairs." Sam took the bag and hurled it up the length of the stairs.

Once the bag landed, the shock caused the cocked gun to release, striking the flint and exploding the powder in the bag. The explosion didn't hurt anyone, but the pieces of the gun and musket balls flying from the bag certainly did.

Edward's crew and four prisoners ran up the stairs and shot down those hurt by Sam's makeshift grenade. After, the prisoners attacked the guards now exposed along the curtain wall walkways. The only guards left were those on the opposite side of the bailey, and the reinforcements advancing across the walkway between the southeast bailey Edward was on and the northeast one where the drawbridge lever was.

Edward and his crew moved to the curtain wall of the bailey. When Edward rose from cover he could see through the opening in the bailey to the lower level where the majority of the prisoners were still fighting. The keep, where the warden was, was between the south baileys, rising high above the rest of the castle.

"Anne, are you able to kill those guards on the other side of the bailey?"

"Consider it done." Anne turned to William, they nodded to each other, and William ran to the south end of the bailey, knowing what to do without words.

Anne and William went into a sprint across opposite ends of the bailey's walls. When they reached the end, where the guards stationed themselves along the west wall, they both pulled out twin pistols.

Anne turned to face the line of guards. The guard's eyes widened. Anne let loose her pistols. The guards rose, but a moment too late. One bullet hit a guard in the back, the other bullet pierced the leg of the second.

William used his momentum to drop and slide into the walkway. William shot his pistols. Two guards fell. One guard was left with a musket in hand, ready to shoot Anne. William jumped up. The guard aimed. William plucked a musket from a dead guard's hands. The guard pulled down on the trigger. William shot the guard in the back. The guard's arms flew out. The bullet hit the stone on the wall two inches left of Anne's ear.

William dropped the musket and ran to Anne's side. She rose and thanked William as Edward and crew joined them in front of the walkway to the keep.

With the guards removed, the prisoners were able to move more freely, and, having heard the plan from Simon, the captives moved up the stairs to the top of the bailey. Edward waved a group of them across to the entrance of the keep. Reinforcements along the roof of the keep were being kept at bay with well-timed, albeit ill-aimed, musket shots.

In front of Edward were large double wooden doors with reinforced iron latticework and large iron hoops for handles. Edward pulled on one, but it wouldn't open. "The door must be barred. How will we enter?" he asked the group of twenty behind him.

"Watch out!" Anne yelled as she pulled Edward away from the doors.

A stone larger than Edward's head, beard included, fell to the ground with a loud crack. Ten feet above the double doors was an opening for siege defence, covered by a square wooden board on hinges.

Edward stroked his long beard. "That will work. We need someone to open the door from the inside." Edward turned to the prisoners. "Were there any ladders in the armoury?" The group shook their heads. "What are we to do then?" Edward questioned, mainly to himself.

"We make our own ladder," Anne declared. "Firstly, keep muskets on the opening and fire if it moves in the slightest." A few of the men complied. "Five of you move in front of the door and get down on all fours." Anne's words were met with confused expressions and tilted heads. "Now!" she commanded. The order was immediately carried out with minor backtalk. "Four more, climb on top and balance yourselves in the same position."

As the human ladder was being made, the guard throwing rocks poked his head out to attempt another throw, but was forced back by a few musket shots. Anne helped more prisoners onto the pyramid until just one man was on the top. After some time, the shaky masterpiece of filth was completed.

"Beauty," Sam said with his usual snark. "Now what, Princess?"

"Boys, you can stop firing." Anne climbed the pyramid.

Once at the top, Anne knelt down and kept a keen eye on the opening. When the guard pushed open the board to throw another rock out, Anne leapt into the air and gripped the wooden board. With a deftness all her own, Anne used her momentum to jump into the opening and kick the guard back into the keep, closing the wooden barrier behind her.

The men who formed the pyramid fell from the force of Anne's jump. "Ready yourselves, men! When she busts through that door we are storming that keep," Edward proclaimed.

Various muffled noises could be heard from behind the stone and woodwork of the keep. Screams of fighting, falling, and dying, and shots from guns and muskets filtered through the stone to the ears of the prisoners. The noises started from the spot Anne entered the keep and made its way down to the double doors.

As the noises grew louder, the prisoners grew tense with anticipation. Grips were made firmer, sights steadier, and wills steeled.

The door shuddered with a sudden whack, causing some to jump, then the sound of wood and iron scraping was heard. With another swift crack, the double doors burst open and a guard fell backwards through them, unconscious.

Anne ran across the threshold, bullets following in her wake. She gripped her left bicep with her right hand, and blood dripped in a thin stream from her forehead down her cheek.

Edward ran to Anne and held her against his diminished frame. "Charge!" he yelled.

The prisoners with Edward ran into the thick of battle, catching the guards unawares. The mass of greasy-haired and dirt-caked people yelled as they travelled up and down the spiral staircase in the first part of the keep.

"Are you well?" Edward asked of Anne, still gripping her tightly.

"Yes, I am fine Edward," Anne replied, pushing him away. She released her right hand and examined the wound, which was still seeping blood.

William too examined both sides of the wound before ripping off a strip of his tattered shirt and wrapping it tightly over Anne's forearm. "The bullet cleared through the other side, so you will not require surgery."

"Good. Now, Edward, we must quickly retrieve your belongings from the warden and free more prisoners to our cause."

"Agreed, but are you sure you're well? Will you be able to continue?"

"I will manage. Let us secure your freedom."

Edward, his musket in hand, advanced into the spiral tower heading up the right side of the staircase. The sounds of battle could be heard from below, and silence above. Upon moving to the next level, Edward was met with seven prisoners and, thanks to Anne's efforts, three unconscious guards.

This level had several arrow slits and weapon stores for a siege, as well as the wooden opening Anne used to enter and a large pile of rocks. Another staircase led to the roof, with arrow slits along the wall. To Edward's right, the west door leading to the warden's office stood undisturbed.

"Beyond is the warden's dining chambers and holding chamber for new prisoners. A stone enclosure on the left is the warden's office."

"Yes, I remember well when I was first brought here. That was the last time I saw the sun and the sea." Edward approached the door and touched the ring-shaped handle.

"Wait!" Anne yelled. "What are you doing? Guards are no doubt beyond the door, waiting for someone to open it."

"Yes, of course I considered that, Anne," Edward said, puffing up his chest.

Anne smirked, her brow raised.

"Alright, I didn't," Edward admitted, his head held down in shame. "But this is the only way through."

"Yes, well, we should force the guards to fire at nothing, then retaliate when they are reloading." Anne turned to the group of prisoners standing around. "Clear out of the way unless you want to be shot." The men complied with Anne's request without a word. Anne, William, Sam, Charles and Edmond all moved to the sides.

Anne nodded to Edward, and he waited for the company to assert their readiness. Edward swiftly opened the door and pulled until his back was against the wall. A barrage of bullets flashed past, lasting for all of two seconds.

After a silent moment, the prisoners retaliated and shot the guards in the room. Many were behind cover of one piece of furniture or another, but three foolish enough to be in the open were the first to fall. As Edward was about to take his shot he saw a man sticking a linstock into a large cannon.

The iron cannonball burst from the cannon, clipping a prisoner on the chin, snapping his neck, before crashing into the wall of the tower and sending stone chunks flying.

Blood splattered on Edward's face before he kicked the door closed, and bullets rained on it for a full minute. Edward looked at the dead man's body, blood draining from his neck and pooling on the stone. Edward didn't want to think on how that easily could have been him. "Did anyone get a good look at the room? We need to disable the cannon before the guards reload."

Above the sound of the guns being fired, the prisoners shouted descriptions of what they saw. "Near abouts twenty men, less three." "Table 'n chairs." "Tapestries." "A chandelier," Anne yelled last.

"What's a chandelier?" Edward asked.

"A chandelier is a large decorative candle holder hanging from the ceiling."

"How large is it, where is it situated, and what is holding it up?"

Anne closed her eyes to picture the scene. "The size is five to ten feet at its widest, located in the centre of the room above a long table with marines on either side, and held on an iron chain with a metal clasp."

"Do you think a musket shot could break the clasp?"

"I suppose so."

Edward turned to William and handed him his loaded musket. "Can I count on you? I know taking the time to aim is a big risk, but you're the best shooter we have aside from Anne."

"Hey! I resent that," Sam ranted, his and William's rivalry apparently still intact after a year of separation.

William, always sparing in his use of words, simply nodded, providing as firm an answer as any man could give. Edward did not doubt William's ability to complete the task in the slightest.

"Once the chandelier drops I want you to run in and shoot every last one of those guards. Understood?" Edward's question was met with loud grunts, which he took for agreement. Edward held the handle and, with a swift tug, pulled the door open.

No blast of bullets came as before, and in that second of hesitation William took his chance. He rolled forward and landed on one knee with his musket aimed high. He took one short but deep breath as his eyes locked onto the metal clasp holding the chandelier, and his arms followed immediately afterwards.

William shot his musket. The guards returned fire. The clasp of the chandelier broke, and the ostentatious candle holder fell. The seven guards around the table looked up a second too late. The crystal and gold smashed the table, sending shards of crystal and pieces of wood everywhere. The ends of the table shot up in the air, hitting a guard on the chin. The table collapsed to the ground with a thud.

Edward jumped into the room, using the confusion to his advantage, and let loose a pistol shot, hitting a guard in the stomach. The guard manning the cannon left his station and slashed at Edward with a sword. Edward jumped out of the way and kicked the man in the groin. The man doubled over and fell to the floor. Edward drew his sword and thrust it into the guard's back. The man let out a painful gasp of air before a death rattle.

When Edward turned around, the room was cleared. Bodies of guards littered the floor, their weapons strewn about, but three of the prisoners had also died.

Edward saw the large table split in twain, with one half upended from the broken chandelier. Opposite where Edward had entered, a door led to the west side of the castle. The warden's room was on the left wall, the wooden door closed.

Edward gave the door a kick. The door shook from the force, but didn't open. With the exertion from fighting, Edward was already out of breath and sweating.

"Sam!" Edward leaned on a chair. "Get the door, would you?"

Sam settled Charles in a chair. "Ye may be me captain, but I ain't yer servant."

"Open the door, Sam."

Sam, pistol in hand, reared back his leg and thrust it at the door. The door busted off its hinges and fell into the room. Sam entered the room, pistol forward, but he couldn't see anyone.

"I think the warden jumped ship." Sam laughed.

Edward entered the room. Boxes, shelves, and barrels full of prisoner belongings filled the walls. Papers, weapons, clothing, and other miscellaneous oddities plagued the small room, demanding space. A table in the centre of the room was full of peculiar items as well, with a lit candle and stacks of papers with quill and ink to the side.

"I didn't see the warden running," Edward said as he glanced about. "He's mad, but not a coward."

"Right you are, my boy," a voice rang from behind him.

Before Edward could react his golden sword was pulled in front of him and racing towards his neck. Edward's instincts kicked in and he grabbed the arm holding the sword, stopping the advance. Edward's other arm was bent behind his back, and the person attacking him forced Edward into the corner of the room.

The warden of the castle prison, Warden Balastiere, was the one now holding Edward's life in the balance. "I caught ye, caught ye good I did," the warden taunted in a manic, crazed voice.

3. THE GREAT ESCAPE

The warden rested his head on Edward's shoulder.

Sam, Anne, and Henry instantly tensed with the sudden turn of events and pulled their weapons on the pair. Those in the dining chambers approached to catch a glimpse of the scene unfolding. Edward stood stock still, the warden at his back, his hands held up to stop his friends from shooting.

"Get off him!" Henry yelled.

The warden laughed and shook his head wildly like the madmen he imprisoned. "No, no, no, that won't do. Cannot do that. No. I'm the warden, see? I issue orders here." The warden's breath was hot on Edward's ear. "I tricked you. All these years, playing the fool in front of you prisoners, for this payoff. You would not believe the delight I'm feeling…"

The thunder from Anne's pistol rebounded in the small room. The bullet sped through the warden's forehead. He collapsed in a heap off of Edward's back.

The crew and prisoners first glanced at the source of the sound, then to the warden as he fell, and then back to Anne and the smoking pistol. Everyone stared at Anne with shocked expressions, most notably Edward.

"What?" Anne said with a shrug. "He kept prattling on and on. We do not have time for such nonsense. And besides, the hostage trick is old." Anne turned and left the room. "We have what we need, let's move on."

Edward took one last glance at the warden, silently thanked Anne for her marksmanship, and returned to the dining chamber. "Right."

Anne ran to the west wall and kicked the door open. The west keep tower was a mirror image of the one on the east side. Weapons, stone stairs, an opening with rocks to throw, all there save for guards to use them.

"The guards must have been called down to the bottom of the keep or to the east side as reinforcements," William surmised.

Anne examined the western side of the castle through an arrow slit. "The bailey is clear too."

"That makes it easier for us." Edward headed down the stairs.

Edward, Anne, Sam, Henry, Charles and Edmond, and the remaining three prisoners out of seven, all ran down the stairs to the east side's set of identical double doors. The muffled sounds of gunshots and shouts could be heard from below, a small reminder of the battle being fought in the castle prison.

Edward pushed the doors open slowly on the off chance Anne missed something. A slight breeze was blowing across the castle walls imparting cold air on the small group as they trekked silently across the walkway.

The group moved into the depths of the west side of the castle to where the remaining prisoners were kept, and met no resistance along the way. The west side of the castle was eerily quiet, until they descended into the prison hold.

Through some sort of transference, the prisoners on the west end knew something was amiss. They were yelling and hollering obscenities so fierce and foul that Edward cringed. He could make no distinction between the mentally competent and unstable.

Edward did not spend any time dwelling on the situation. He took his golden sword and began slashing at the locks and bars. They cracked open with the force of the mysterious golden blade. The metal of the cutlass was far superior to the iron locks and bars.

Even so, Edward was in a weakened state, and after a few locks were broken his arm was tired from the strain.

"Here, let me take over," Henry offered. "You rest." Henry took the golden sword and continued freeing prisoners, eventually descending steps to do the same for the more dangerous ones.

Edward sat down, leaning against the wall of the prison, and closed his eyes whilst rubbing his arm. As much as he detested the prison, he felt oddly tranquil against the familiar stone wall.

A hand caressed his shoulder. "We're almost there, Edward," Anne said, her words bringing Edward strength.

Edward kissed Anne's hand. "I'm already there, Anne."

A flood of the oddest criminals ran up the steps, most notably a man both taller than Edward and larger in build than Henry, a hulk of a man with long chains dragging behind him from his arms and feet. A smaller man was atop his hunched shoulder, guiding the large man forward.

Henry returned from the deep soon after the large man passed by. Edward rose back up from his rest. "Ready?" Henry asked, offering the golden cutlass back to Edward. He accepted the weapon and nodded.

When Edward, Henry, and Anne returned to the main level of the bailey they could see the freed prisoners raiding another weapon storehouse on the north end of the courtyard. After loading up on weapons, some headed up the stairs, while others advanced to the inner courtyard through the east door. Sam was sitting down, munching on salted meat with nary a care in the world, beside Charles and Edmond.

Edward strode up the stairs and his crew followed soon after. Despite Edward's ragged appearance he was the image of a fearsome sea captain in his familiar black leather coat that reached to his knees and a tricorn hat.

"Forward, men! Release the drawbridge so we are rid of this prison!" Edward yelled to as he pointed his golden sword. The prisoners responded with hoots and hollers, and followed him to the north of the castle.

As Edward made his way across, the guards in the courtyard fired at him. Edward ducked down, but continued moving forward, while other prisoners retaliated.

Edward could see in the courtyard a wide open space with stables for horses, stations for the guards' quarters, and wagons of supplies. In the centre was a large fountain surrounded by a cobblestone road for horse-drawn carriages. Everywhere in the courtyard prisoners were fighting with guards, either out in the open or behind cover taking pot shots at each other. The courtyard was a mess of bodies, but Edward knew the prisoners outnumbered the guards.

Guards flew up the stairs of the northern bailey and met the prisoners as they reached the end of the walkway. Edward ducked below the bailey's inner curtain wall while the prisoners with muskets shot at the few guards and continued on.

Edward was about to descend the stairs, but noticed Anne climbing the outer curtain wall with a rifle. "What are you doing, Anne?"

Anne ignored Edward for a moment and searched the north-west field in front of the castle. When Anne found what she was seeking, she took a few deep breaths and fired the rifle.

"I signalled our transportation," Anne stated, jumping down from the curtain wall. "In the event we cannot escape as originally intended, the cavalry will pick us up." Anne dashed to the stairs and started her descent.

"Who is in this cavalry?" Edward asked, following Anne.

Anne turned and grinned. "You'll see."

In the lower level, the guards were being beaten to death by the prisoners. The security was lax, and Edward suspected the guards were spread too thin to gain control again.

Edward handed his sword to Henry to free the last of the prisoners in the northwest bailey before he followed Anne to a small alcove with the drawbridge lever. When Edward and Anne reached the alcove, the sudden dismay over what they saw sent chills down their spines and a wave of hopelessness washed over them.

"The lever is broken," Anne observed.

The wooden lever was cracked at the base and the mechanism underneath completely broken apart. One of the guards had had the forethought to break the lever sometime in the middle of the escape.

"Is there a moat? We could jump in and swim across."

"No, the moat was considered unnecessary and dried up after the castle was turned into a prison. We could take the original exit through the latrine hole, but I am afraid the old man Charles would not make the drop without injury and the hole is too small to carry him."

"What about rope?" Edward offered.

"I saw none in the armoury." Anne paused in contemplation, her hand on her chin, biting her thumb. "There is no other way. Someone must climb over the curtain wall and shoot the chains holding the drawbridge in place."

Edward ran his fingers through his hair. "Now the question is who."

"I can!" Edmond offered with glee, and without waiting for an answer he ran up the stairs of the bailey.

"No! Edmond, wait! It's too dangerous!" Edward yelled after him, but the young boy paid no attention.

Edward and Anne ran after Edmond, who was already at the top of the steps as they reached the bottom. As quickly as Edward and Anne could manage, one being physically weak and the other injured, they ran up the stone steps to the top of the castle. Edmond was atop the wall and making his way to the middle where the drawbridge was.

"Edmond, get down from there," Edward commanded.

"I'll be fine, Edward!" the boy asserted with the bravado natural to youth.

Edward let out a grunt of frustration and climbed the curtain wall along with Edmond. Edward tried his best to catch up with the youngster and stop him, but the little one gained too much of a head start.

Edmond was at the middle of the curtain wall when he stopped and peered over the edge. From the corner of his vision, Edmond noticed Edward trying to walk across the edge of the wall to catch him, and when Edmond turned further he could see the sun.

The bullet ripped past Edmond's cheek. He lost his footing and fell over the curtain wall, heading to the rocky ground below. Edward leaped towards Edmond, his arm outstretched. Edmond extended his own arm in an attempt to make contact. The tips of their fingers touched and slipped apart, and Edmond continued to fall. Edward watched, the horror in his heart mirrored in Edmond's eyes.

Like a flame flickering as it is being blown out, grasping for life, Edmond's hands tried frantically to grab onto something. The boy's fingers found the drawbridge. Edmond held fast to a slight, overhanging lip of wood, either from a design flaw or the loosening of the mechanism over the years.

Edward let out a sigh on seeing Edmond's falling motion cut short. "Are you well, Edmond?"

Edmond, after a few breaths and a securing of his grip, laughed from the heart. "See? I told you I'd be fine." Edmond grinned. With Edmond's added weight, and the jolt of the fall, the slight opening of the drawbridge became larger. Edmond was able to see into the small gap. "I can see the chains." Edmond felt around his body while hanging from the drawbridge, but all his weapons he had been carrying had fallen to the ground. "Toss me a gun, Edward," the boy demanded.

Seeing no other way, Edward motioned for a pistol from Anne. She passed one on and he let the pistol fall into the outstretched hand of the young Edmond.

Edmond reached the pistol into the small gap only his hands could fit into and fired at the chain holding the drawbridge. The side Edmond was on lurched forward and the chain was severed. While Edward retrieved another pistol, Edmond moved inch by inch across the drawbridge to the other side. Edward moved as well, staying low to avoid being shot, and when Edmond was ready Edward dropped the pistol into his hand.

"Now, you must be careful because the drawbridge is going to—" Edward started to say, but he was cut off by the shot of the pistol.

The drawbridge fell to the ground with Edmond hanging onto the edge. The rocky moat and grassy edge were closing in by the second. Edmond turned his head to see where he was headed, the gut reaction overpowering the mind's knowledge. The thick and heavy wooden planks could easily crush the boy in two, and was nearing its promise. Edmond pushed away from the drawbridge with his feet, leaping backwards off the planks. He landed on his back, hard, and rolled away as the drawbridge crashed loudly in front of his feet.

"Edmond!" Edward yelled.

Edmond was on the ground, his small frame heaving with coughs and spasms of pain, but he was eventually able to give a thumbs-up. After a few seconds, Edmond rose from the ground and then began looking around.

What is he searching for? Edward pondered, watching the boy intently.

Before Edward could ask, his eyes caught something around the bend of the sloping road. Two somethings, in fact. They were carriages, each drawn with four horses, travelling at break-neck speed. The driver's and passenger's faces were obscured, but Edward had a fairly good idea of whom they were.

Edward ran back to the bailey, down the stairs, and into the courtyard with Anne following as the carriages raced into the castle. The drivers pulled the carriages around the whole of the fountain while firing upon the guards, save one passenger who threw knives and a spear. After closing the whole circuit the carriages stopped close to the exit.

Edward ran to the front carriage with Anne, Henry, and Sam still carrying his charge, Charles, behind him. The driver and passengers of both carriages pulled back their hoods, revealing their faces. "Herbert, Nassir!" Edward exclaimed.

The one called Herbert was a young man with glasses, and a strong upper body. In quite the contrast, his lower body was small and thin. He normally was in a wheelchair, navigating at the helm of the *Freedom* with unparalleled skills.

Nassir was a large, middle-aged negro with a shaved head and a thick African accent. His eyes were dark, and could contain boundless fury, but he was a kind man. He worked as carpenter aboard the *Freedom*, doing necessary repairs after each battle and in between. His experience was a valuable asset in keeping the ship afloat.

Edward's gaze turned to the second carriage. "John, Pukuh!" More comrades of his former life, arrived to save him.

"Captain," Herbert said, "your chariot awaits."

4. THE CHASE

Edward, Anne and William joined the second coach with John and Pukuh at the reins, while Henry, Sam, Edmond and Charles entered the first. As quickly as they arrived, and before any other prisoners jumped aboard, the carriages were sent back out the castle.

The sounds of battle cries, gunshots, and death throes could be heard a ways down the road before being overshadowed by the sound of the wheels against the earthy ground.

The carriages passed by small rolling hills with light grass and eventually into a forest with a wide road and well-worn path. Poplars decorated the entrance of the forest and quickly turned to birch and beech. The trees passed Edward's vision in a blur before he could catch glimpse of the branches.

Edward's face was beaming as he gazed upon the outside world for the first time in a year. *I wonder what the expression on Edmond's face is.*

"Happy to finally be free?" Anne asked, directing her question to both Edward and William.

"I am happy when you are, Your Highness," William replied with a slight bow.

Edward cringed. "William, don't bow until you shave. Being formal looks... odd... when you have a beard as full as mine." William ignored the comment.

Edward held Anne's hand. "I too am filled with joy, but I will not truly be free until I have the *Freedom* back," Edward said, referring to his ship. His free hand glided over his coat pocket, to the letter left by the previous owner. *No, not yet.* Edward moved his hand away.

"We have a plan to retrieve the ship as well. For now, we can rest until we return to the inn we reserved." Anne leaned her head back and closed her eyes.

"How is your arm?" Edward asked, leaning forward to inspect. The wound had long since stopped bleeding, but Anne's arm was caked with dried blood. Edward also noticed she was as pale as a summer cloud, and sweating.

"I will be fine. Rest, Edward," she insisted.

I will let Anne alone. She needs this more than I.

The Voyages of Queen Anne's Revenge

Edward opened the carriage door and peered outside. He stepped onto a metal lip covering the wheels, then closed the door. Edward carefully stepped up to the coachbox, where Pukuh and John sat.

Pukuh, a six-foot-four muscular Mayan warrior, sat stoically, staring at the road ahead. He was intensely tan with long, deep brown hair which swayed in the wind. His strong jaw and fierce eyes painted the pure picture of a fighter. War Chief of his Mayan city where his father ruled as King, Pukuh left with Edward to learn more about the world so he too could be King one day.

"Brother!" Pukuh exclaimed joyfully, pulling Edward in for a hug. After a few seconds Pukuh pushed Edward back and examined him, his mouth a hard line. "You look weak."

Edward laughed. "Nice to see you too. I assumed you would have returned home after what happened."

"In fact I did. The crew were defeated, body and spirit. Henry and Anne both brought most everyone back together with much difficulty. Some are still missing, but all here are loyal to the man who gave them *Freedom*."

Edward smiled. "Good to hear. John, how are you holding up?"

John, a plump man with glasses, held the reins of the carriage and focused on the road ahead, as well as on the companion carriage. John was of nervous disposition when stressed in conversation, but on the battlefield no man was as calm. John had joined Edward from the beginning when Edward wanted to be a whaler. He had called Edward's father captain once, on a whaling vessel as well, before Edward's father disappeared.

"Oh, right as rain Captain. We have you back, and now our *Freedom*'s all we've left to st-steal."

Pukuh's head shot up and he peered to the road ahead. "What's wrong?" Edward asked.

"We are soon to be joined by others," Pukuh replied, his brow low and his eyes and body shifting to see his unknown 'others.'

"More of the crew?" Edward asked.

"No, we are not to meet any on this road." Pukuh pulled out a spear but kept it hidden.

Edward leaned back and knocked on the door to the carriage. William opened the window of the door with a questioning expression. "Someone is approaching. Pass me a musket, if we have any. Prop open the door so I have some cover."

Anne opened her eyes, still heavy as they were, and rose from her seat. "No, we may be able to talk our way out of this. Get inside." As Edward complied, Anne pulled up the cushion and revealed a storehouse of weapons and clothes. Anne donned a red longcoat of impressive make.

31

The ride went undisturbed for several minutes until the horses slowed. The noise diminished as the carriage eventually drew to a halt, leaving the clop of the restless horses and the sounds of animals in the forest for them to hear.

Edward opened the window of the carriage and could hear people talking with Herbert. He started to rise, but Anne stopped him.

"Wait, Edward. I shan't need more than a moment."

Anne counted off the seconds in her head before she opened the door of the carriage and strode out in a huff.

What is she doing? Edward began following Anne, but was stopped by William.

"I believe it would be more prudent to let Her Highness handle this for now," William recommended, to which Edward yielded and sat back down.

"What is the meaning of this delay?" Anne yelled.

In front of Anne were thirty men on horseback, the local militia of the town closest to the castle, on horseback. They had no special uniform, but carried swords and an assortment of flintlock weapons at their hips.

"We stopped you because…"

"Because why? We are travelling a road passed by travellers every day? Because you assumed we were common merchants and wished to purchase our supplies? Out with it, man!"

The militia man was fearful that Anne was someone of importance, and if he knew the truth the conversation could be quite different. "The castle Gammond down yonder sent a raven telling of a riot needing reinforcements."

Anne rubbed her palm over her eyes and let out a heavy sigh. "Then what, pray tell, are you doing wasting time with us? Not only are you delaying our journey, but you are allowing criminals to run free in the prisons. Off with you before you ruin anything else!" Anne pointed to the road leading to the prison.

Edward, cupping his ear with his palm, listened to the whole conversation. *Anne's speech sounds too natural to be rehearsed. Remnants of her mother's influence, no doubt.*

The militia men were flabbergasted at Anne's commanding tone. Better than ask questions and provoke ire, the leader turned his horse and galloped off with his men following closely behind.

After passing, Anne lowered her finger, but kept the scowl in case any chose to glance back until she entered the carriage again. She let out a sigh and wiped her forehead to clear perspiration.

Once again, Edward considered asking Anne if she was all right, as Anne was uncharacteristically nervous, but he decided to let her alone.

"Take us away from here, John," Anne commanded.

The carriage lurched forward and before long they were back to the same speed as before. The trees passed in a blur from the window of the carriage, and the noise heightened with the wheels spinning on the rough dirt.

"That went well, I would say," Edward said to no one in particular. The comment, however, was rather short-lived.

A gunshot echoed over the rumble of the wheels and the carriage veered sharply. "They pursue us! Counter their advances!" Pukuh yelled.

Anne darted out of her seat and opened the compartment once more. She pulled out weapons and handed them to Edward and William. The men promptly opened the doors and leaned out, peering through the window.

Edward could see eleven men on horseback chasing them, with a newcomer leading the charge wearing the uniform of a guard from the prison. *He must have told the militia to chase us, but where are the other twenty?* Edward glanced to the second carriage. Herbert moved the carriage to the other side of the road, Henry and Sam also aiming at the militia.

The guard fired the first volley, with the militia quickly gaining their wits about them. The bullets rained upon Edward and his crew like a torrent.

Edward shot his musket. The militia retaliated tenfold. Edward retreated into the carriage and gripped a pistol. The guard caught up to Edward's carriage and latched onto the door. Edward shot his arm and the man let go with a cry of pain as blood spurted from his fingers. Edward unsheathed his cutlass and slashed the man's throat open. The guard fell from the horse, clutching his mess of a neck.

The militiamen were gaining on the carriages. Henry and Sam kept firing, but, being farther ahead, their bullets missed the mark more often than not. Henry shot a man, felling him from his horse.

Two men jumped on the back of Edward's carriage. One climbed to the top while the other went around the side. Edward pulled a pistol out and aimed it at the man through the window of the door. The man grabbed the pistol and pulled it forward. Edward tried to pull his pistol back, but was too weak. The man slammed his fist into Edward's elbow. It snapped and he released the pistol with a shout of pain. The man grabbed Edward's arm and tried to pull him off balance. Edward stabbed through the door with his cutlass and impaled the man.

Meanwhile, William, on the roof of the carriage, was having similar difficulty. William's punches and kicks were slower than he was used to, and the power was a fraction of their normal ferocity. The only saving grace was that the man was more a brawler than a fighter.

The man threw wild swings, a variety of uppercuts and hooks aimed at the head and body. William blocked them easily and returned punches to the ribs and chin. The man pulled in close and clinched William, pinning him while delivering small punches. William was tiring quickly, his stamina running low, and needed to end the fight. William pushed the man off. The man was sent to the edge of the carriage, but stayed balanced and moved back to the fight. William dropped and kicked the man's legs out. The man fell like a lump, hitting his head on the edge of the carriage. William wrapped his legs around the other man's legs and spun over the side of the carriage. At the last second, William grabbed the door and hung onto the carriage while the man slipped off to the ground, unconscious.

William climbed back in as bullets swarmed on him. Edward was holding his left arm close as he fired a pistol at one of the militiamen trying to climb Henry's carriage. The bullet missed, five inches from its target.

Another horse galloped beside Edward's carriage. The horse moved like the wind, spurred on by its rider, to catch up. The man on horseback aimed a musket at Anne through the carriage's open door. William, the first to notice the imminent danger, leapt and covered Anne with his body. The rider fired. William jerked as the musket ball hit true. Pukuh threw his spear into the gunman's chest before he could reload.

Anne pushed William off and sat him down in the carriage seat. He coughed from the movement and blood spurted out onto the princess's coat and splattered her cheek. The bullet must have punctured William's lungs.

"My apologies, Your Highness."

"We cannot keep this up," Anne said.

"It is a flesh wound," William protested.

"No, it is not. We need to devise a new tactic."

Edward was about to offer a suggestion when a militiaman galloped up on the left side of the carriage. He had a pistol aimed at the group. Out of nowhere Pukuh kicked the man in the chest and swung into the carriage box. The man fell off his horse and onto a rotted tree which broke and fell on top of another man.

That leaves two men still pursuing us. We can make it.

"The men behind us were killed by Henry and Sam," Pukuh said, as if reading Edward's mind.

The three let out a collective sigh, but were well past worse for wear.

Again reading their expressions, Pukuh delivered mood-changing news. "Ten men are ahead of us on horseback, blocking the path. We will reach them soon." He held a spyglass, no doubt the catalyst to his knowledge.

Ten men on horseback waited in a line along the road, muskets pointed and ready to fire at the oncoming carriages.

When the prison guard had informed the militia of who the carriages belonged to, ten had pursued from behind while another ten must have rushed down a side road to gain ground and attack from the front, and the final ten were nowhere to be seen. Edward thought they might have moved on to the prison.

If the initial news lifted their spirits, then the second piece of information sent them back down doubly so. The three were silent while pondering what could be done to escape.

Edward considered the problem until an idea presented itself. "Do we have grenades?" he asked of Anne.

"Yes, twenty in each carriage."

"What about powder?"

"Three small kegs, again, in each carriage."

"Excellent." Edward leaned out the side of the carriage, still holding his arm close. The pain was dulled with all the excitement, but Edward knew it would be back later twofold. "John, take us up close to the first group."

"Yes, Captain," John replied, clutching a bloody shoulder with one hand while holding the reins in the other. He let go of his shoulder, pulled out a whip, and urged the horses to move faster and catch up.

"What do you have in mind?" Anne asked, having an idea of the wheels turning in Edward's head.

"I will explain when we are close to the other carriage." Edward, still leaning out of the door, watched as their carriage gained on the other, and Herbert, noticing the attempt, slowed their carriage down. When the two carriages matched speed, and Edward had gained everyone's attention, he laid out his plan.

John held the reins while Pukuh helped John into the carriage box. John had enough slack on the reins to hold them when leaning out the door. On the right carriage, Henry and Nassir helped Herbert into the carriage, with Nassir holding onto the reins in a similar fashion.

Sam pulled out all the grenades and the powder kegs and tied them together at the fuses into one large cluster. Anne did the same in their carriage.

John and Nassir whipped the horses, sending them racing towards the blockade. A few of the men, seeing no one in the coach seat, wavered in their focus. As the carriages approached without slowing, the men in the blockade lowered their aim and looked at each other as if wondering, "Are we going to move?"

Edward and company leaned out the sides of the carriages and fired upon the men, hitting a few and causing the others to move their horses away. After the carriages passed by, the militia followed in pursuit.

Edward and the crew moved out of the carriage box and to the front. They mounted the horses, with Nassir and Herbert, Edward and Edmond, and Sam and Charles all doubling up on one horse apiece. After everyone was safely on a horse, the harnesses on the animals were cut so they were not connected to each other or the carriages.

The carriages slowed to a stop while the crew escaped. The militiamen spurred their horses faster to try and catch up. As the militiamen were passing the carriages, the fuses on the grenades reached their end.

The blast of the grenades was deafening and blew the carriages apart, sending pieces of wood and iron flying. A piece of wood lodged in the neck of one man, another hit in a horse's stomach. A piece of the iron wheel pierced all the way through a young man's eye to the back of his skull, and iron balls left in the powder kegs punctured one man and his horse like a honeycomb. The blast itself tore a man's leg apart and killed his horse. After the ordeal, hardly any remained unscathed.

Edward looked back at the militiamen. Those unharmed ceased pursuing and helped their comrades, pulling the injured to the side of the road and away from the burning wreckage. Edward noticed his crew also glancing at the carnage.

Saved from the prison, Edward could finally start the plan to retrieve his *Freedom*.

5. REUNIONS

"So the *Freedom* is in Portsmouth?" Edward asked.

"Yes," Anne replied simply.

"Under heavy guard?"

"Most certainly."

"Well, bollocks. I suppose you have another plan?"

"Yes, of course. But we can discuss this later. Winchester is ahead." Anne pointed to the town ahead as she spoke.

The town of Winchester lay in front of them. The growing town was home to fifteen thousand souls and a large local militia whom Edward and crew already had the delight of encountering. Two roads crossed through the middle of Winchester. One, the main road, travelled alongside a small river leading north to London and south to the aptly named Southampton, amongst other locations, and the crossroads led west to Salisbury and east to the Gammond prison.

The square in the middle of the crossroads hosted a large market every day save Sundays, and shops and inns dotted both main roads, with the less reputable businesses relegated to side streets and back alleys.

Night was upon the crew when they arrived, and the only light was the moon rising and lanterns carried by the guardsmen. "Halt! Who goes there?" a militia man asked.

Anne jumped from her horse and ran to the man, nearly falling into his arms with tears in her eyes and hysteria in full force.

"Oh, heavens am I ever glad to see you, sir! My friends need medical aid. We were ambushed on the road, sir, by most foul brigands. We managed to escape with the help of your comrades on the road, but my friends were injured in the initial attack, so please let us through so we may find a surgeon."

"By Jove, my lady, yes. Bring your friends this way. I will show you to the nearest one."

The guard ran forward and Anne followed on foot, pulling the horse behind her. The crew were escorted five blocks down the main road to a normal home, by all appearances.

After a vehement knock, a light appeared behind the curtain and eyes could be seen glancing at the large company gathered in front of this man's house. "What?"

"Gelson, open the door. These people need your assistance," the guard yelled.

The door was opened without another moment's notice, and the man Gelson poked through. His hair and short bear was grey, though he was not an old man; his body was small but toned, and his wide eyes seemed sharp.

"Do you have any idea what time it is?"

"Come now, Gelson, these gentlemen and lady were attacked and need to be healed, and I need to return to my post. I trust you can handle things from here?"

"Yes, yes." Gelson waved the guard off, and the man walked back to the gate of Winchester. "You may leave your horses in the street, and enter when you are ready. I will gather my tools."

Henry, John, and Sam took the horses to the street next to the man's house while Anne and Edward helped William inside. Nassir carried Herbert, and Edmond helped Charles inside the home of the surgeon.

The room was wide open with no doors save the one for entering and exiting. The surgeon's bed was in the far right corner, sectioned off by short stairs and a railing separating the two levels. Cots and seats for patients were on the opposite corner.

Closer to the entrance, a desk stood at the front right, papers and notebooks strewn on top, with a large window showing the Winchester road. On the left was an operating table with dried blood on the floor nearby, an apparatus unfamiliar to Edward, and a similar window facing the road.

Edward lay William face down on top of the table. There was a faint smell of blood in the air, and something else Edward couldn't place his finger on like a lemon approaching decay: Sweet, lemony, but causing a sting in the back of the throat.

On the back left side of the room various tomes were on the floor, and strewn about a shelf and a desk. On the back right side, another shelf held jars of pickled animal parts, various liquids of unknown origin, and another desk with the surgeon's instruments on top.

In the middle of the room, for an inexplicable reason, two iron poles spaced about one metre apart were affixed ceiling to floor. The poles felt fairly sturdy and no amount of pulling or pushing made them budge, but none save Gelson knew their purpose.

The Voyages of Queen Anne's Revenge

Edward speculated that Alexandre, his surgeon while aboard the *Freedom*, would have loved Gelson's home. Alexandre was an eccentric man at the best of times.

"Thank you for your help. Mister Gelson, correct?" Anne asked.

"Please, call me Nathan. Now, what has happened to this gentleman?" Nathan inquired while walking to the operating table hosting William.

"He received a bullet in the back."

"Fascinating," Nathan commented, lifting up William's shirt and examining the wound. "And you?" Nathan turned his gaze to Anne.

"I have a bullet wound through the arm which needs stitching, and my comrade has a broken arm."

"And what of the gentleman unable to walk?" Nathan asked, pointing to Herbert.

Herbert laughed. "I don't think you can fix my legs, Mr Gelson, unless you're a miracle-worker."

"I will operate on this gentlemen firstly then," Nathan proclaimed while gesturing to William.

Nathan turned on the apparatus near the operating table. Pieces of metal and a yellowish liquid were in a clear bottle with a fire burning underneath. The steam from heating was then filtered through water and then to a tube with an opening at the end. Nathan positioned the opening of the tube over William's mouth and told him to breathe.

"What is that?" Edward asked.

"I call it funny fumes. Makes people laugh and oblivious to pain. I happened upon the recipe one day when I was testing a liquid toothache reliever. By itself, the liquid would burn the gums. I decided to try making the liquid a steam, and discovered the liquid produced a gas when in contact with the iron from my fillings which relieved pain."

The image of burning gums and teeth made everyone listening cringe, save an oblivious William who chuckled uncontrollably.

"See, funny fumes. Great for parties."

William had a smile showing at the corner of his lips and in his eyes. William smiling, and even laughing, was entirely foreign and uncomfortable for Edward to see.

Nathan took a thin knife and made an incision into William's back. He removed the pieces of the iron ball and sewed the wound shut without a peep from William. Henry and Sam held William down throughout, but it felt unnecessary.

Amazing. Perhaps this man is not as dull as I assumed.

"So how did you received such injuries? Do you happen to be street performers? Injuries such as these would seem to happen often by my reckoning."

Edward let out a sigh. *Perhaps not.*

"We were ambushed on the road by brigands in an attempt to take our horses," Anne replied, being the experienced confidence woman.

"Ah, how unfortunate. You should be wary at night, young ones, and keep your wits about you at all times. Consider me: I could spot a rogue any day."

Anne failed to completely suppress her amusement at this. "We will keep that in mind," she assured him as she replaced William on the operating table.

After Anne took hold of the fuming tube she closed her eyes as Nathan went to work. He sewed up the open wound and secured a fresh cotton bandage over it. After he was done, Anne removed the tube and opened her eyes, fully alert.

"Edward, you simply must try some of this!" she exclaimed, holding the tube. "My arm felt separated from my body and I could barely feel anything. What an incredible sensation." She took another whiff and began laughing uncontrollably.

"I think I will pass," Edward said, holding up his hand in protest.

"There is no need to operate on you anyway, my boy. Let me take a look at you." Nathan examined Edward's broken forearm, which was bruised and turning purple where the break occurred. "Yes, this does not need surgery. However, the bone is dislocated. If we do not fix the placement the arm won't heal properly." Nathan led Edward to the two iron poles. "Fully extend the broken arm and grip the iron bar. Then, push your shoulder against the opposite pole. Be sure to keep a tight grip."

Edward did as instructed. He closed his eyes at the pain shooting through his forearm. *What is the purpose of this nonsense?*

Edward received his answer sooner than he expected. Nathan reared back and punched Edward's forearm. Edward let out a scream which echoed through the whole home, and then fell, clutching his arm.

"Now your arm should heal properly."

"Dad damn you, you barnacle-covered son of a bitch!" Edward yelled.

Nathan laughed and shrugged his shoulders. Anne rushed over, dragged Edward to the gas machine, and placed the tube over his face.

Edward took deep breaths of the gas and his pain subsided. He closed his eyes and felt just as Anne described. His pain and arm were not part of his body, like he was floating in the air.

While in that dreamlike state, Nathan fastened a sling around Edward's arm. "I must tell Alexandre about this," Edward noted between deep breaths. "But knowing Alexandre, he will probably blow it up somehow." Edward laughed uncontrollably.

Later, Edward received instructions on how to recreate the gas, Anne paid Nathan, and the group left for an inn Anne had reserved. A few men of the militia and townsfolk still stalked the quiet streets in the middle of the night, making walking out in the open tempting fate, so Anne guided them through side streets to reach to their destination.

"So, speaking of Alexandre, why didn't we go to him for help?" Edward asked.

"Alexandre is at Bodden Town, and said to pick him up when we are ready."

"Tch." *That is something he would say.*

Edward and his group reached the back entrance of the inn without being stopped or spotted. They entered through the kitchen where those slaving over a hot fire glanced up and greeted Anne like they were the best of friends and didn't bat an eye at the odd troupe behind her.

The wafting smells of roasting meat and potatoes enticed Edward, William, Charles, and Edmond, and reminded them of the great hunger built over the time of their imprisonment. Anne's beckoning and the noises from the dining hall pulled Edward from the food and further into the inn.

He was not prepared for what would happen when he walked through the swinging doors of the kitchen to the dining hall.

At first, the noise continued as normal. The crew of the *Freedom* were jovially laughing, talking, pinching the servers, eating and drinking to their fill. But one person turned to see who entered and his jaw dropped instantly.

"Captain!"

A hush drew like a wave over the inn and all eyes turned to the entrance of the kitchen. In utter silence, the crew processed the face before them.

"It's the Captain!" "Edward!" "Blackbeard!" "Captain Thatch!"

The gathering in the large inn rushed to Edward and pulled at him all at once. Hands tried to grab Edward, or his beard; others hugged him and patted him on the shoulder. Eventually he was lifted into the air and carried around on a few of the men's shoulders. Edward was passed a drink, and cheers were shouted all around. Some had tears in their eyes, others the widest of grins, and still others were in shock over the whole affair, as if witnessing some dream.

Anne leaned against the wall of the inn, watching the crew with a wide smile on her face.

"Reminds you of old times, eh?" Henry asked.

Anne chuckled. "Yes, but there is still work to be done." Edward's face was full of joy as he greeted his crewmates by name, hugging or shaking hands. "Perhaps we can wait until tomorrow." Anne pushed Henry playfully. "Let's have some fun, yes?"

The crew were in high spirits and the festivities continued well through the night. Drinking, games, stories, and reunions were exchanged with the captain they loved so. William was also a source of much talking and greetings from the crew. Through William's calm exterior, Anne believed she could see happiness deep in his eyes.

The roast and potatoes cooked in the kitchen was served, along with a house ale. The smell of the ale overpowered the food, and thankfully the sweat from the crew as well.

Edward was also able to reunite with Nassir's son, Ochi, and Herbert's sister, Christina. Both had grown since Edward last saw them.

Ochi, now fifteen, had experienced a growth spurt and was almost up to Edward's shoulder, which is to say between about five ten and six feet tall. He resembled his father too, becoming broad in shoulder and with strong arms.

Christina, now sixteen, had grown out her strawberry blond hair, which framed her face and made her more womanly than before. Her brother had taught her how to sail a ship over the past year.

Edward was also shocked and delighted to hear that Ochi and Christina were dating as well. They were young, and of different colour, but the bond they'd developed on the *Freedom* and the year afterwards was strong. *They are happy together, and that is all that matters.*

Despite their injuries, the fervour of the crew managed to keep Edward awake until the last. But, as with every good thing, the revelry ended.

The following morning, Edward awoke with a terrible aching in his head, and his arm was pulsing waves of pain with each beat of his heart. His eyes slowly opened to the room he must have chosen at some point through the night. Anne was also under the blankets of his bed, opening her eyes after a long night of raucous behaviour.

Edward's mouth was dry, so he smacked his tongue to bring back some moisture. "Did we…?"

"No, we did not," she replied, knowing his stream of thought. "For one thing, our clothes are still on." Anne pulled the blankets off them both, revealing their dirty, smelly clothes from the night before.

"Right." Edward examined the room, noting the bottles of rum and glasses scattered on the floor. "For the record, I would enjoy remembering our first time."

Anne smiled as she snuggled closer to Edward. "I concur."

"So, I noticed only half the crew are here. Was this all you were able to gather?" Edward asked, his eyes closed and his left arm wrapped around Anne's shoulders.

"The rest of the crew are at Portsmouth, ready for when we arrive, where the *Freedom* is docked."

"And Jack is with them?" Edward asked of the American musician aboard the *Freedom*.

Edward remembered the last time he saw Jack. A demon from Jack's past had showed up, Admiral of the White, George Rooke, and Jack tried to kill him for retribution over something, but failed.

Anne opened her eyes, a sad expression on her face. "Jack... is having some issues."

Edward opened his eyes this time, darkness filling his mind. "Where is he?"

"In town. Jack has been at a tavern at least as long as we have been here, perhaps longer. I tried to bring him back, but I cannot bring him out of his pity." Anne raised herself up. "I think only you would be able to help Jack recover at this point."

"You may be right." *Jack, what happened? How could you fall so low?*

Edward recalled a conversation he once had with Jack. The man had explained how he was an addict, and the one thing which had brought him out was his love for a woman, but he never disclosed what happened to her. Edward knew the incident involved George Rooke somehow.

Edward rose from the bed and stripped. A piping hot bath, complete with rose petals floating in it, had been drawn by phantoms from the inn staff, which Edward took immediate advantage of.

After Edward lowered himself in, Anne rose and gathered his clothes. She took off the golden sword and left the hat on a seat, but took the coat, tattered shirt, and ripped pantaloons with her.

"I'll give these away and buy you a new outfit. I shall be back."

"Oh! Wait!" Edward yelled. Anne backed up, clothes in hand. Edward rummaged through the pockets until he found the ever-important letter left by Benjamin Hornigold. Without that letter Edward would not be able to follow the clue to the next key for the ship. "Could you set that on the table? Also, first the carriages, then the weapons, then the inn, and now clothes? Where are you acquiring all this money?"

"Some was donated by the crew." Anne took the letter and grinned devilishly. "And, when I left the palace this time, I... collected my inheritance early, selling it to a few merchants here and there."

Edward laughed. "You truly are a pirate at heart."

"It is the company I keep, after all. Spoils the bunch and all that," Anne said before passionately kissing Edward and leaving the room.

Edward took his time cleaning himself and thinking over his next course of action. *I want Jack with us again. He is a part of this crew and I'm sure he is equally missed by everyone else.*

The hot bath was more than welcome after the stay in prison. Edward washed away the grime from a year past in the rosewater. By the end of his bath, the water was well past clear and it lost its sweet smell.

Anne returned with new clothes and Edward knew what he wanted to do about Jack.

The clothes were very similar to what Edward wore before: white tunic, baggy pantaloons, and black leather coat. After cleaning the tricorn hat, Edward once again wore an outfit befitting the captain of a ship.

After Edward dressed, he pocketed the letter from Benjamin Hornigold and went downstairs, allowing Anne to bathe and change. A few of the crew were in the dining hall and greeted him. They too were feeling the effects of the night before, and ordered food to break their fast. Ham, fried eggs, and sausage were brought to Edward along with a cup of coffee and another of water.

The black liquid, bitter in taste, also brought memories of Jack to Edward's mind, coffee being Jack's favourite drink after a night of excess. The crew stared at Edward as he gazed into his drink, knowing what he was thinking.

The crew ate in near silence until more people joined the dining hall. By mid-morning the whole crew was out and being fed, talking and playing games of cards. When Anne entered the hall, fresh and rejuvenated by the bath, Edward talked with her about his plans to see if they coincided with hers.

Anne's red hair, still wet from the bath, glistened in the sunlight along with her oceanic green eyes. Edward could lose himself in those eyes like the sea he loved so. "So how long do we have to retrieve the *Freedom*?"

"Two months. The British Navy will start using *Freedom* as a marine vessel once all the paperwork is cleared."

"And what kind of travel time can we expect with a group this large?"

"Near one and a half weeks for travel to Portsmouth. Less if we split up, and we should. We'll stand out too much with this many people."

"All right then. Will you travel with the crew to keep them in line and set things in motion?"

"I'm fine with that, but are you expecting Jack to be resistant?"

"I don't expect any issues with Jack re-joining us, but we'll need him sober by the time we enter Portsmouth."

"I will stay and help," Henry said, walking up behind Edward.

"I be stayin' too," Sam added, walking down the stairs.

Edward cocked an eyebrow. "Why do you want to stay, Sam?"

"I 'ave a feeling somethin' fun is gonna happen." Sam said with a smirk.

Anne turned to Edward, fear in her eyes. "I think we should stay with you."

Edward laughed. "Don't let Sam's nonsense scare you. Nothing bad will happen." As soon as Edward spoke the words, he felt a chill from head to toe. *Suddenly, I have a bad feeling about this.*

"I will trust in you three then. Will you tell the crew what's happening?" Anne asked.

Edward nodded and stepped onto a small elevated stage at the front of the inn. He laid out the plan to the crew, leaving out the parts about stealing *Freedom* and anything which could implicate them to the inn staff. The crew made their objections and Edward simply stated he would be late by a week or two at the most to allow Jack enough time to withdraw the alcohol from his system. With the decision made, Edward descended the stairs and the crew prepared for departure.

Henry smiled widely. "I see your skills in public speaking have improved, my young apprentice."

"What are you talking about?" Edward said, exasperated.

"You spoke to the crew as if you had been speaking in public forever. You even answered questions without a hint of your nervousness," Henry said, referring to Edward's previous apprehension with public speaking, and Henry's attempts at helping Edward overcome his fear.

"Of course. I long ago lost any anxiety with speaking to crowds."

Henry wiped away a fake tear. "The apprentice... becomes the master."

Edward sighed. "Let's recover Jack." He stopped short. "Wait, I forgot one thing."

Edward sought out Charles and Edmond in the dining hall. The old man and the child were sitting together, eating with the crew.

"So, old man, this is it. You have your freedom now, so what will you do?"

Charles, appearing much better than he did in the prison, scratched his balding head. "I suppose I could head to Southampton, I have family who can support me."

"I will arrange for some of my crew to help you travel. Would it be too much to ask you to take Edmond along with you?"

"What?" Edmond yelled, rising from his seat. "I want to go with you, Edward. I want to have freedom on the open sea too!"

Edward pitied the boy, because he understood Edmond's desire. "I'm sorry Edmond, but you cannot join us. Especially for those reasons. You need to find your own *Freedom*. Just because my *Freedom* is on the seas doesn't mean yours is. I want you to join Charles and learn from him and then, maybe in a few years if you still feel you want to join us, I will allow it."

Edmond pouted and sat back down. "Fine."

Edward patted the young man on the head, then said goodbye to Anne and instructed her to escort Charles and Edmond to Southampton.

Henry waited at the door of the inn while Edward spoke his goodbyes to Anne. He watched with an unconscious frown on his face as Edward and Anne kissed. Anne ruffled Edward's wavy black hair and handed him a coin purse before sending him on his way.

"Ready?" Henry asked as Edward approached.

"Yes. Do you know the way?"

"Follow me," Henry replied confidently.

The two trekked through the streets of Winchester with the sun shining down upon them, allowing them a better view than the night before. The morning dew was still filtering in from the forest and carried with it the smells of fresh cooking from the market. The aroma mixed sweetly in Edward's nose before he could sense smells natural to the town, like livestock, horses, mud and moisture.

On the long cobblestone road, many were going about their business, some with child, some alone, and others Edward noticed were carrying notebooks. When Edward pointed out the many young men in similar uniforms, Henry mentioned Winchester College. The college was a prominent boarding school for boys, and accounted for much of Winchester's growth.

The Voyages of Queen Anne's Revenge

Halfway to their destination, Sam came running after them, offended that Edward and Henry didn't wait. The three then travelled further into town. Beggars frequently approached Edward to see if he carried coin, drawn by his dress. Edward kept his hands in his pockets at all times to protect his money and the letter, arguably the more important of the two, from being taken. They arrived at their destination well before reaching the square with all those delightful smells.

Henry stopped in front of a lively tavern and the three entered together. Inside, the place was packed with people even at this hour. There was loud music being played from a piano, and the people inside were equally loud in their festivities. The delightful smells of the town immediately fled in the face of the smell of sweat and ale inside the tavern.

Lounging on a couch in the corner was Jack Christian. Edward remembered a gentle Jack, with pleasing features of short brown hair, light hazel eyes, and fair, clean-shaven skin. However, this Jack was growing thick stubble, dishevelled hair, and his eyes were sullen with bags underneath. His normally fair skin had turned to a deathly pallor due to the drink, despite the appearance of euphoria on his face.

Edward didn't want to stay any longer than he had to, so he walked straight over to the man. "Hello, Jack."

Jack moved his whole body to see who called him. He didn't stand up, but he grinned and extended his arms. "Captain! You, you're here to see me, my brother," Jack said, his American accent distinguishing him from the British locals.

"That's right, and we're here to take you someplace special. Up you go." Edward took hold of Jack's hand and pulled him up off the couch.

"Special?" Jack asked listlessly, glancing back to the table full of booze in confusion and want.

"Yes, very special. Henry, Sam, are you going to make my injured self carry Jack?" Edward inquired, spurring Henry and Sam to take Jack.

The drunks at the table—his "friends"—wanted Jack to stay, but Edward and crew were able to tear Jack away after some coaxing. Some patrons and the barman eyed Edward and his companions suspiciously as they left.

Jack was carried out of the tavern and the four began the trek to Nathan the surgeon's house. Jack drifted in and out of awareness, asking questions of Edward a few times, but most were incoherent. The group elicited gaping from passersby as they walked down the main street.

When they reached the house, the door was quickly opened after Edward knocked. Nathan stood in the doorway. "Ah, I think I remember you. Patient of mine?"

Edward sighed. "Yes, we were here yesterday."

"What did I treat for you?"

Edward was dumbfounded, as the sling was still in plain view underneath the coat he wore. "Broken arm," he replied simply.

"Ah, yes, yes. Please, enter. Someone else need treating?" Nathan questioned, stepping aside to allow the group to enter.

Henry and Sam took Jack to the operating table and lay him down on it face up. "Our friend here is addicted to alcohol and God knows what else. We need him clean, and I understand the process can sometimes be rather... messy, without assistance."

"Well then, how interesting. I will see what I can do." Nathan used thick leather belts to secure Jack's chest, arms, and legs to the table.

"Are the straps really necessary?" Henry asked.

Sam laughed. "Have ye never seen an addict without the fix fer long? Jack old boy 'eres gonna be thrashin and screamin fer sustenance 'for long."

"I'm afraid your English-impaired friend is correct. Those symptoms are all part of the substances being removed from the system. There is not much we can do but provide comfort and ensure he does not die."

The door to Nathan's home opened loudly and three men stepped in. The man in the middle wore gentlemen's clothes of a puffy white neck tie, red blazer with gold buttons, a red long coat with gold trim to his knees, and pantaloons reaching below the kneecap with high socks. The two other men wore simpler clothes of white tunic and black vest, with long black pantaloons.

"What ails you gentlemen?" Nathan asked, approaching them.

"We 'eard some blokes was tryin' ta take away a man who owes me money, and I fancied seein' who had the gall," the man in the middle said. "The name's Thomas Blunes, and you must be the famous Blackbeard."

The man in red was a man of plain appearance in every other department. Average-sized nose, white teeth, brown eyes and hair, and medium build with a height just shy of six feet, and middle age made him indistinct. Edward reckoned Blunes craved attention, judging by his demeanour and flashy outfit.

"Oh, I am some dreaded man named Blackbeard, am I?" Edward feigned.

"Ye can play the fool all ya like, but the build fits. Not many so tall as you 'round these parts. And word has it Gammond prison suffered a riot the day 'afore, near the 'ole lot of prisoners escaped. Your name was all over the papers when you was jailed a year ago. Not much a stretch, truly." Edward tensed. "Don' worry, mate, I care not about you, until a bounty be on yer 'ead, that is." Blunes moved closer and pointed to Jack. "This man owes me a gambling debt, and I will be repaid before I allow him to leave Winchester."

Edward sighed. *Oh course he does. Why would he indulge in only one vice?* "How much?" Edward questioned, reaching for his coin purse.

"Sorry, mate, but I've arrived at an idea what will pay me back tenfold."

"What do you propose?"

"A fight. You 'gainst the reigning champ of underground fightin' in Winchester. Yer name is huge, 'specially with news of the escape. People will place bets on the man who kidnapped the princess, then you throw the match."

"In case you didn't notice, I'm injured. There won't be much of a fight."

"I'm sure you'll provide a good show until you lose, and besides, I only need yer name."

"So I lose this match and Jack's debt is paid?"

"I'm a man of me word. Ye do this and he's free to go with ye." Blunes extended his hand.

Edward took Blunes' hand and shook it, sealing the deal without hesitation.

Blunes went to the nearby table, removed some paper from his pocket, used a quill to write an address down, then handed the paper to Edward. "Two weeks, The Den, eight o'clock sharp. And be sure to bulk up to at least make the fight look good, ya?"

"Right." *This shouldn't be too hard.*

6. THE DEVIL OF THE DEN

During the two weeks, Edward began training with Sam and Henry, and was provided a diet regimen by Nathan which would help with stamina and muscle building. From Edward's lack of food in prison, he'd lost most of the fat on his body, so gaining back muscle was easy.

Edward simply returned to the basics so he could hold his own and make it appear as if he wasn't throwing the match. Early morning runs around Winchester, sparring with Sam, more running, sparring with Henry, and running again was the typical day for Edward over the two weeks.

Jack had a severely more difficult time. In the beginning, the detoxification was minor: Anxiety, yawning, but with difficulty to sleep, and sweating. But not long after, body aches, nausea, tremors, and even hallucinations set in. To Jack and his friends, combining those was like some sort of punishment from God himself. Edward and company tried their best to make Jack comfortable.

"Edward, please, this is cruel. You must allow me a little bit to take away the pain," Jack pleaded after a few days, tears in his bloodshot eyes.

"I am sorry Jack, you know I cannot. The most important thing I learned from being saved from prison is to wait and hope. If you hold out a little longer this pain will be gone and you will be back to your old self."

Jack could say nothing after seeing his captain's eyes. Jack closed his eyes to the pain and waited for it to subside. Throughout the detoxification, Jack never again asked for his precious alcohol.

At the end of the two weeks, Jack was through the worst and was cleared for release from the shackles. Nathan recommended constant supervision for the next while, and even afterwards not to let Jack alone when on shore.

Edward noticeably changed over the two weeks' training. Although he was not quite back to his old self, and his broken arm was still, well, broken, he was considerably more fearsome and would no doubt produce the effect Blunes desired at his 'Den.'

"Jack, you and Sam prepare some horses so we are ready to leave. Henry and I have some business to take care of and then we'll head to Portsmouth." Edward handed the coin purse to Sam and then left to the Den.

"You can count on us, Captain," Jack reassured Edward as he left.

Sam tossed the coin purse in the air. "So… want ta toss a few back with me, mate?"

Nathan and Jack both smacked Sam in the back of the head as he laughed at his own cruel joke.

Edward and Henry ran to the location Blunes wrote down on the sheet of paper, causing those in the streets to stare. After reaching the street, Edward and Henry travelled past a few worn houses until reaching a warehouse district. Edward continued walking until he found one with the number thirteen painted over two large wooden doors, matching what was written in the sheet. The warehouse resembled an old weapons manufacturing plant.

Edward and Henry walked up to two guards at the front of the warehouse. "Password?" one of the guards asked.

Edward took out the paper from Blunes, but there was nothing indicating a password for entrance.

"We were invited by Thomas Blunes, but he didn't provide a password."

The guards laughed. "Then it's simple: you're lying. The boss would have given you a password if he wanted you here."

"No, he certainly wanted me here. I am Blackbeard."

The guards were serious for a moment, then burst into laughter once more. "You? Blackbeard? What a joke."

"I'm telling you, I am Blackbeard and there is no password."

The guards stopped laughing abruptly. "What did you say?" one of them asked.

"I said, I am Blackbeard."

"After that."

"There is no password?"

"Tch." One of the guards opened the door. "Welcome to the Den, *Blackbeard*."

Edward shook his head as he went through the door. As he was passing he could hear the guards talk amongst themselves. "The boss really needs to make a new password." "I keep asking him what he wants the password to be, but he always says the same thing." Edward rubbed the bridge of his nose in frustration, and travelled further into the Den.

Edward entered and immediately noticed a table to his right with a young scantily clad woman sitting behind it and a guard standing behind her.

"What can I do for you gentlemen?" the young lady at the counter asked in a sickeningly sweet high pitch.

"I'm Edward Thatch, Blackbeard. I'm here for a fight."

"Changing rooms are behind me. Mr Blunes will call you when we're ready for you."

Edward thanked the woman and walked around the counter to a hallway. There was a door on each side of the hallway, so Edward opened the left door and headed in.

Inside, a man of Henry's build, six feet tall, wide, and muscular was sitting on a bench. He appeared to be Russian, from his prominent chin and eyebrows. When Edward entered, the man stood, his expression pure fury.

Another gentleman with a cotton towel around his neck looked Edward's way. "Blackbeard, I presume?" Edward nodded. "Your room is next door."

"Yes, thank you." Edward closed the door, the large man glaring at him the whole time.

"I'm guessing he's the person you are to fight," Henry surmised.

"Yes, I would say," Edward agreed as he went to the next room. "I would also say this fight will hurt."

"Yes, well, you're the one who decided to do something foolish again."

"Breaking into a prison is far more foolish than this."

Henry grinned and shrugged his shoulders.

The room they entered was plain in appearance with a low bench in the middle and a table with a rolled cotton strip for wrapping wounds, a wick for lighting, and a bucket of water.

A man standing in the middle of the room turned around. "Thomas Blunes," Edward pronounced. "To what do we owe the pleasure?"

"I need ta read ye the rules, and make a wardrobe suggestion."

Henry cocked an eyebrow. "Wardrobe suggestion?"

"More on that later. First: the rules. There are no rules. See? Easy. Fight with anythin' you can, make a good show, and throw the fight."

"And the 'wardrobe'?" Edward asked, wary of what was forthcoming.

"I have something flashy and fear-inspiring to make you stand out and make my regulars want to bet on you." After Blunes helped Edward with his image, he took Edward to the entrance hallway.

Edward wore a cloak and baggy breeches reaching to below the knees and thin shoes meant for manoeuvrability. His chest was exposed, which had filled out some since two weeks prior, showing his muscular abdomen.

"This won't work. I'll appear a fool."

"Nonsense. Remember, no smiling, jus' stare straight at the crowd," Blunes advised.

Blunes took a light to long strands of wick set in Edward's beard. The wick burned slowly and was meant for smoke, which surrounded Edward's face and lent him a ghastly visage.

After Blunes was satisfied, he pushed Edward forward and into the warehouse. On all sides a large crowd occupied the warehouse. Men and women of all stations stood arm to arm, shouting and jeering at the lack of a fight. Past them a large iron-barred cage stood in the middle of the warehouse, with guards holding the people at bay to allow the fighters passage to the cage.

Edward strolled forward, staring at the audience, the smoke wisping and billowing around his face. As Edward's eyes met the men and women, the silence his stare elicited spread like a wave around the crowd, starting at the entrance and making its way around. In the silence, Edward's gaze instilled fear. Some of the women wept, others fainted, and the men turned away, wiping sweat from their brows.

Blunes was beginning to sweat as well. "Tone it down, kid, you'll make them want to bet on the other fighter. Forget it, I can turn this around."

When Blunes and Edward reached the cage where Henry waited, the two stepped up to a stage, staring at the crowd below. "Ladies and gentlemen, tonight we are visited by a devil. He intends to show us the meaning of reaping what thy sows." Blunes lifted Edward's arm in the air. "The Devil Blackbeard arrived to take the soul of Hammons this night!" he yelled to the awed crowd. "As the dark messenger himself, Blackbeard knows the wages Hammons' sins must pay, and he will collect!"

Blunes continued to rile up the crowd as Henry, wearing Edward's coat and tricorn hat, examined and ensured the cotton bandage was tight around Edward's knuckles.

"I assumed you would be against this, Henry, but you never objected to the fight these whole two weeks past."

"Well, this seemed the only way to help Jack," replied Henry. "We certainly couldn't muscle our way out with the four of us. Besides, what's the harm in you being beaten to a pulp? You'll pay Jack's debt and learn your lesson in doing foolish things at the same time."

"I see no love was lost over our year apart."

Henry smirked and then took the wick out of Edward's beard as his opponent entered. He was met with jeers and shouts of damnation from the crowd.

"Looks as if Blunes' plan worked," Henry said, glancing at the muscular man and the crowd.

Blunes introduced the other fighter as Hammons the Hammer and brought him into the iron cage. Edward entered the cage, and the opening was locked behind him. Edward and Hammons were locked together in a prison for two.

Edward took in deep breaths. The smells of sweat, cheap ale, and blood crept into his nose along with the metal of the warehouse. Edward filtered away those senses, and focused on the man across from him.

Give them a good show.

A sharp ding of a bell indicated the start of the fight and Edward advanced towards Hammons.

Hammons took the initiative and rushed at Edward, fists flying. Edward pulled back and pushed the fists aside with his left hand, the good one. Hammons kept pushing Edward into his own pace from the start. Edward was backed into the wall of the cage. Hammons kept up the pressure and delivered blow after blow to Edward's head and chest.

Edward was having issues because of his injury. He had to block and jab with his left hand at the same time. *Damn this useless arm of mine!*

"Get off the wall!" Henry yelled, as riled up as the crowd.

Easier said than done. Edward kept bobbing and weaving, weaving and bobbing, blocking and jabbing, but he couldn't see a moment to escape the onslaught. Hammons reared back and delivered a right hook. Edward could easily see the fist approaching his temple. He pulled back, letting the wild swing follow through, then countered with a left cross.

The left cross, named for the fist crossing over the opponent's arm, was powerful because the opponent's momentum was used against him.

Edward's cross punch was brutal, and caused Hammons to trip and fall backwards. Edward jumped off the wall to the middle of the ring. The crowd turned wild.

Hammons quickly rose to his feet and continued his assault. Edward pushed back this time; he delivered jabs in quick succession to keep Hammons at bay. Hammons threw punches at Edward, but missed due to his poor reach.

By the time the bell rang once more, allowing the fighters a break, Hammons' lip was bloody and his eye was starting to swell.

Edward sat on a stool in the corner provided by Henry and drank some water. Henry wiped Edward's brow with a towel.

"Blunes wants another similar round and then you can start losing."

"Right," Edward acknowledged between deep breaths.

The bell was rung again and the second round began. The second round went much like the first, with Edward dominating the fight with quick jabs and a few well-timed crosses. Edward did end up taking a few hits; his ribs were hurting and his eye was feeling puffy.

That should be enough. Edward eyed Blunes as Henry cleaned him up and gave him water again. Blunes nodded.

"Don't lose too quickly, and protect the arm."

"Right." *I'll defend until the middle of the round, and then let Hammons punch me a few times.*

After the bell, Edward strode to the centre with confidence. Hammons ran up to Edward and delivered a right hook followed by a left hook to the body. The combination came so quickly Edward's instinct took over and he pulled up his arms to guard. The left hook hit his broken arm hard, and the jolting pain reminded Edward forcibly of Hammons' nickname: The Hammer.

Edward suppressed a scream. Whatever had been healed over the past two weeks was instantly wrought asunder from Hammons' punch. Edward's vision began fading from the pain, but he forced his eyes to stay open. He blocked an incoming punch from Hammons and fought back wildly.

Hammons stepped back and sneered at Edward's pathetic attempts. Hammons had known from the beginning Edward was injured, from Edward's plain-to-see bruise on his right arm to his affinity for blocking with his left arm.

Hammons took his time, working Edward over with lighter punches, whittling him down little by little. A jab here, an uppercut there, every hit meant to bring out Edward's weak and exhausted body.

The next round was like a blur. Edward was in too much pain to be able to fight back. He threw a left hook to Hammons' head, but he moved out of the way and punched Edward in the jaw, sending him to the back of the iron cage.

The sound of the crowd was deafening in Edward's ears, but loudest of all was a ringing noise which wouldn't quit. Sweat poured down his face, along with blood from a cut over his eye and a broken nose. Edward scanned the high walkway around the inside perimeter of the warehouse and saw Thomas Blunes, smiling.

Damn it, Jack. How did you rope me into this? Edward glanced at Henry. *I guess you were right Henry, I learned my lesson.* Edward's slow moving gaze turned to Hammons, who was stalking towards him, his massive arms ready to strike. *But I would do it again! Come on then!* Edward gritted his teeth and pulled up his heavy left arm in defiance of his weariness.

The two fighters were about to start again when screams rose from the entrance. The crowd was fleeing from something. Edward peered to the source of the noise and saw something worse than the beating he was receiving.

Twenty militiamen entered the warehouse on a raid and began arresting people in the crowd, with some of them heading towards the ring for the ultimate quarry.

Henry ran into the ring and pulled Edward out, helping him to stay up. As the two left the ring, crazed people running in front of them, they were met by an armed official.

Henry kicked him in the chest and the man fell over in a heap. Henry grabbed the official's gun.

Men and women crowded each visible exit. Edward noticed movement above on the walkway. Thomas Blunes was opening a window and jumping through, cursing as he did so.

"Look," Edward pointed.

Henry looked at where Edward was pointing, then glanced around. "Do you see any stairs to get up there?"

Edward tried to find stairs to the walkway, but he couldn't see any. Edward searched for another escape route and noticed a ladder near an exit at the back.

"There."

Henry followed Edward's outstretched hand, then rushed to the ladder, pulling Edward along in a near drag. They weaved through the crowd of people trying to run away from the militia, pushing and shoving those smaller than him out of the way.

When Edward and Henry reached the ladder, Henry pushed Edward up the steps. Edward's grip was feeble and the exhaustion of the match was settling in. He'd lost his boost of resolve from the last round and was running on empty. Edward climbed one rung at a time, trying to speed himself, but his shaking arms and legs made things difficult.

"Hurry Edward! They're gaining on us!" Henry yelled, pushing his friend further up. Henry let out an exasperated grunt and pushed Edward up using his shoulder. With the added help the two were able to reach the top of the ladder in less than a minute.

From the high vantage point, Edward and Henry could see the whole scene: The large iron ring in the centre with the crowd rushing to the closest exit, and some fighting against the local authorities. The militia barred the main entrance, and more slipped through the back, trying to block off all exits. Soon the whole warehouse would be blocked and the spectators suppressed at gunpoint.

Henry and Edward went to the open window Blunes had used to escape not moments ago. Henry helped Edward up and out of the window and then jumped up to start pulling himself through. The militia noticed and fired upon them, eliciting more screams from the crowd below. The bullets hit the window, causing the glass to shatter over Henry's head, and then he let out a scream.

Henry lost grip of the window ledge and began to fall. Edward grabbed Henry and pulled him back up inch by inch. Once Henry was high enough, he pulled himself over the edge and onto the roof.

Edward's eyes were focused again despite their puffiness. He lifted Henry's shirt and examined the wound on his back. "Good, the bullet missed the spine. Do you think you can walk?"

Henry pushed himself to his knees. "I think so. Help me up." He extended his hand and Edward helped Henry up to his feet; he was able to stand, albeit shakily. "How about you?"

"The danger has rejuvenated me; I'll be fine."

To Edward's left, a wooden board connected the warehouse to another building. "There!" Edward pointed. "Let's go that way."

Glass shattered as bullets ripped through more windows nearby, aimed to hit Edward and Henry. The two ducked down, glancing into the warehouse again. The militia were rounding up everyone they could and chasing after the escapees.

Edward moved forward, crossing the wooden plank with ease. Henry was moving slowly and he limped with each step. "Hurry, Henry!" Edward yelled. Henry shuffled across the plank, peering to the ground forty feet down. "Don't look down! Focus on me," Edward commanded. Henry trained his sharp brown eyes on his best friend as he took the last few steps across.

The militia were crawling through the window when Henry crossed over. Edward kicked the wooden plank over the edge and it fell to the ground below with a snap. More militiamen climbed to the roof and opened fire. Edward grabbed Henry and helped him move forward this time.

Edward and Henry hurried around the side of a rooftop entrance to escape the gunfire. Another plank led straight across to the next building. The two crossed once more and removed the plank so none could follow. The next building Edward and Henry were on had a flat roof and no discernible way into the building itself.

Suddenly, on the far building over, in front of the one Edward and Henry were on, a head popped up out of nowhere. When the person saw Edward and Henry, he stood up.

"Captain, this way!" Jack yelled, waving at Edward.

Edward, having no time for astonishment, moved to the ledge with Henry. Unlike the prior buildings, there was no wooden plank to bridge the gap.

Damn and damn again! Edward searched, but could find no other means of travel across. *I guess there's no other way then.* Edward pulled Henry back a fair distance, then pulled Henry up and over his shoulder, carrying him. The pain in his arm, as well as the injuries from the fight, flared, but Edward pushed it to the back of his mind.

Henry groaned in pain. "What are you doing?"

"I'm jumping across this ledge."

Henry considered what he wanted to say for a moment. "Please don't kill us," he pleaded, in no position to argue with Edward.

Edward bent his knees and focused intently on Jack. He took deep breaths as he tested his legs. Edward ran as fast as he could to the edge of the roof with Henry draped over his shoulder. He planted his foot down on the ledge, bent down, and jumped off. At the apex of his jump, Edward slowed and fell. He pushed Henry off of him at the last second. Henry fell and rolled onto the roof, but Edward slammed into the wall of the building and clutched to the edge for dear life.

Edward's grip was precarious at best, and his fingers were shaking with the effort he was pouring into holding on. Edward was already low energy, and this pushed him to the limit. One by one his fingers slipped. Before Edward and Henry were about to be wrenched from their perch, Jack grabbed onto Edward's hand and pulled him up.

Sam was on the roof as well, helping Henry into the trapdoor. Jack helped Edward move into the hole and shut it afterwards.

The four were in the attic of an abandoned building. A small lantern with a faint light illuminated the empty space.

"We should be safe here until things die down," Jack assured them, sitting down on the wooden floorboards.

"How did you find us?"

Jack scratched his head. "Well, I asked Sam and he eventually told me. We went to the warehouse and watched the match. After the militia arrived, I noticed you heading to the roof. I'm acquainted with the owner, and I knew the approximate location you would head to, so I entered this building in the hopes we could do just this."

Caught up with Jack's succinct explanation, Edward noticed Nathan treating Henry. "Not that I'm ungrateful, but, Nathan, why did you follow my crew?"

Nathan removed the bullet from Henry's back, then glanced at Edward before examining his surroundings. "I thought I was at home. Where are we?"

"You're... we're... never mind. We are at your home, in your attic."

Nathan was shocked. "I have an attic?"

Sam pulled Nathan back to Henry's open wound. "Focus, mate."

Jack stepped closer to Edward. "Captain, I want to thank you for your help over this past week. I can't thank you enough for what you did."

"I don't need your thanks, Jack. I know you would do the same for me. I need you to promise me this sort of thing will not happen again."

Jack was silent for a moment as the shadow of tears filled his eyes. "I'm sorry, Captain, but I don't know if I'll be able to keep that promise. I was in a dark place, and you brought me out, but I feel as if I'm on the edge... I need help to stay on the right side."

"Then we will all be there for you. The worst thing you can do is believe you are alone and without a family, Jack. I don't know the details of how you lost yours, and we're not a replacement by any means, but you have us now and always." Jack nodded, the tears flowing from his eyes now. "And I know not how the Admiral of the White is involved, but if you desire revenge, I will make it happen." Edward extended his hand to Jack.

Jack took Edward's hand firmly in grasp. "I will have his head, and then I will tell you my story."

"You've got a deal," Edward said.

7. THE PORTSMOUTH PILLAGING

"Do you know where we were supposed to meet?" Edward asked, a hood covering his face.

"Now, I knew I was forgettin' sumthing," Sam replied with a laugh.

"I know where we were to stay, follow me." Henry advanced his horse to the front of the line.

Edward and company reached Portsmouth in a week and a half. With their injuries, and taking care to avoid the authorities, they were forced to move slowly. There were a few scares along the way, and Edward refusing to shave his particularly massive beard, for which he was well known, didn't help.

Portsmouth was inundated with rain, the overpowering smell of mud and wet horses filling the air, but Edward could still smell a faint hint of the sea air. The horses' hooves clopped and splashed through the pools of rain. Being one of the busiest ports in England, Portsmouth didn't let the rain stop its commerce, and Edward had to guide his horse around the dense crowds.

Portsmouth had several dry docks for repair of ships, and most notably for warships. Because of its strategic position leading directly into the English Channel, Portsmouth also possessed one of the largest naval bases. Edward's ship, the *Freedom*, was being held somewhere in that dock.

Not much longer now, girl. We'll be out at sea soon.

The horses trotted slowly through the streets, over the cobblestone ground, along the edge of the Paulsgrove and Fareham Lakes, and stopped in front of a large inn. The name on the sign read "The Coast and Jib," with a picture of a triangular sail behind the words.

The group tied their horses at the stables in the back and entered the inn from the front. The pleasure upon leaving the wet outdoors and entering the dry indoors, with a crackling fire and the smell of roasting meat wafting from the kitchens, was immeasurable.

The innkeeper and bouncer stopped Edward and company as soon as they entered. "I am sorry, messieurs, this inn is filled with a party. If I am not mistaken the Cobb Inn and the Sea Wench have vacancies."

"We're part of the party," Edward assured the man.

The Voyages of Queen Anne's Revenge

Anne was sitting at a table in the dining hall drinking ale and laughing at one of the stories being told when she noticed Edward and the innkeeper talking, so she sauntered over. "Everyone, the captain is finally here!" she yelled to the crew.

The crew rose from their seats and crowded the entrance. The innkeeper and bouncer moved out of the way, knowing enough to see Edward was telling the truth. Edward walked into the inn, causing the same reaction as a few weeks prior. Everyone wanted to talk with Edward and ask him questions at once, not allowing him an inch to move nor a moment to breathe.

When the crew saw Jack, many hugs, smiles, and laughs were also brought his way. Jack returned them all in kind, the warmth of kinship strengthening his resolve to abstain from his vices. When he was offered ale or rum he declined politely and the crew, remembering their senses, switched to water.

The middle of the day still held the darkness of rain clouds overhead. The sombre atmosphere, and the ramifications from the night before, meant the crew had a somewhat quiet lunch, much to the delight of Edward, Henry, Sam, and Jack. They hadn't eaten much on the way to Portsmouth due to the clandestine trip.

"The date of departure for the *Freedom* was changed to five days from now," Anne said.

Edward was shocked by the suddenness and urgency brought on by the statement, despite Anne's calm. "Are we able to steal *Freedom* back by then?"

"Of course. Everything is prepared, we should be able to take the *Freedom* without a hitch. We have a diversion planned to help us out of the dock, but leaving the harbour is the problem."

"So, we don't have a plan for escaping the harbour itself? Far from being ready, wouldn't you say?"

"Rarely is anything perfect. We can only plan so much," William pointed out, sitting down beside Edward. After the month since being in prison, William was clean-shaven and resembled his old self. "Luck is also part of any plan."

"William! You shaved. Now I can look at you straight," Edward jested.

"Well, someone has to be presentable from this lot."

"You mean someone must be a pratter, right mate?"

William eyed Sam coldly, but he was unfazed. "You should do the same, Edward. It will make passing unsuspected easier," William suggested.

"No," Edward said flatly.

"Why not?" Anne asked.

Henry smacked his palm to his face and muttered, "Here we go again."

"I will not shave this beard because this is a symbol of what the marines and the government has turned me into. Blackbeard is now a name by which I am well known, and to take away the beard is to take away that name. I will use that name and this beard to strike fear into those who made me this way." By the end of his speech, Edward was standing and all eyes were on him. He sat down, embarrassed, and stroked his beard. "I will trim my beard, but no more."

Anne grinned. "I guess there is no way around it then. The beard stays."

"So, back to stealing *Freedom*, why can't we steal her after she's left the harbour? This harbour is filled with Navy ships waiting to attack us when we try to leave."

"The issue with taking the *Freedom* after she has left the harbour is twofold: Firstly, we have no idea where the *Freedom* is headed. Try as I might, I could not divine where she will be stationed. Secondly, ships are expensive. If we wanted to take the *Freedom* we would need a ship of our own, and of close rank to the *Freedom*. I still have quite a sum of money, but not enough for the size of ship we need. Not to mention if we did engage in a battle the *Freedom* would be harmed, and there is a chance we could accidentally sink her."

Edward nodded. "Understood. We leave tomorrow to take the *Freedom* then." Edward took a swig of some rum. "Anne, would you be so kind as to tell our distraction about the plans? I imagine they are in another inn?"

Anne moved from her seat. "Yes, our friends are at an inn down the road. I'll let them know." She left with William following her.

"Tell them I'll be over later to catch up!" Edward yelled to Anne as she left. Anne waved back to let Edward know she heard him. Edward finished his rum and approached the front of the dining hall. "Crew, may I have your attention please? I have an important announcement to make." The crew eventually ceased their jesting, story-telling, and rabblerousing to listen to Edward. "You've all journeyed a long way to be here, and I know all of you made sacrifices for this group of friends I have the pleasure of calling my family. I cannot tell you how proud I am to have you as my crew, as my brothers."

The men yelled a loud "hear, hear!"

The Voyages of Queen Anne's Revenge

"I am also proud to tell you tomorrow is a special day, so you'd best sober up and sleep well. Tomorrow, for the first time in over a year, we set sail!"

...

The sun was peeking out over the horizon, providing warmth to Portsmouth and offering good fortune for sailors. The previous rain washed away the filth and the clean smell of salty sea air breezed over the city.

Edward's crew travelled through the streets in the open, heading to the ports occupied by the marines. The only people up at this hour were other sailors heading to the wharf to fish or take merchandise from this port to another. Edward's group passed in a triple line behind William, the passersby staring at them with adoration in their eyes.

The crew were dressed as marines, with William dressed as their captain, and Henry beside him as a lieutenant.

William wore a more decorative outfit, not typically worn at sea, but one used for ceremonies. The coat was dark blue, almost black, with gold buttons along the front and gold trim. Underneath, he wore a white waistcoat which puffed around his neck, and on his head he wore a tricorn hat with matching blue colour and gold trim. Epaulets with his rank insignia were on the shoulder.

Henry wore the more traditional dark royal blue coat with gold buttons and gold trim. Beneath the coat, he wore a white tunic which was form-fitting instead of puffy like William's. Most of the crew wore something similar to Henry, but without the gold. Those in the back, who were supposed to represent the lowest ranked, wore civilian clothing, albeit cleaner than the crew was normally used to.

The inn was close to the port, so it didn't take the crew long to reach the wharf. It contained five ships, two in dry dock for repairs, two in open docks, and *Freedom* in an enclosed dock for supplying.

The costumes the crew wore were so well done that none questioned their appearance, despite its suddenness. William guided the group to the enclosed dock holding the *Freedom*. It was a large wooden structure with an open front leading to Fareham Lake.

The crew passed through a corridor which opened up to the closed dock. It was of simple and economical design, merely consisting of the dock itself surrounding the sides of the ship, and an open front for easy departure.

Blackbeard's *Revenge*

The *Freedom* was floating there, a fifth-class frigate with fifty-three guns and three masts, swaying with the rise and fall of the tide. The fortress home, made of Caribbean pine, was like a dream come true for its former—and soon to be current—crew.

Before setting foot onto the *Freedom*, the crew stopped for a moment to admire the beauty of their ship, their home. Some of them pushed Edward forward and he was jostled out of his silent reverie. He took a few tentative steps up the gangplank and onto the waist of the ship, listening to the familiar sound of his footsteps against the wood. Edward leaned against the railing as he examined his ship.

The main mast in front of Edward was broad and strong, with fife rail at the base, main top at the middle, and crow's nest at the top. Edward examined the stern section with the quarterdeck, holding the wheel, and poop deck above the stern cabin. At the bow, the *Freedom* had a forecastle deck above a bow cabin, facing the open harbour. Everything was as Edward remembered, bringing back the nostalgia of his previous adventure. Even the smell of the Caribbean pine mixed with the sea air and reminded Edward of the acrid gunpowder, the iron, the battles and adventures, and the lazy days at sea.

Edward turned to the crew with a wide smile on his face and motioned for them to board. The crew shared the same happiness over finally being able to return to their true home.

When Edward's back was turned he heard a voice ring out behind him. "What is going on here?" Edward ignored the voice and continued preparing the ship with the crew. *Stick to the plan. Regardless of who arrives, look as if you belong.* But that voice sounded so familiar.

"Henry?"

Edward's eyes widened. *How does this man know Henry's name?* Edward turned to see who had entered, and his jaw dropped at the sight. His best friend from his home island of Badabos, Robert Maynard, was standing there in a full marine uniform and holding a musket.

Robert had not changed in the almost two years since Edward saw him last. Blond curly hair, smooth features, blue eyes, five foot ten inches, medium build with a toned body. When Edward and Henry set out to be whalers, before being branded pirates, Robert began his training to join the marines.

The Voyages of Queen Anne's Revenge

When rumours started circulating around about a pirate named Edward Thatch, Robert had searched around for the truth of the matter, eventually ending up in Portsmouth just miles away from where Edward was imprisoned.

We can still salvage this as long as he doesn't see me.

As if hearing Edward's thoughts, Robert turned his gaze to meet Edward's eyes before he could turn away. The shock of recognition was painted on Robert's face when he saw those eyes. To anyone else Edward could have been passed off as someone else, but from Edward's and Henry's best friend, no disguise could hide them.

Knowing the futility of continuing the charade, Edward stepped down off the ship back onto the dock. He walked up beside William, who was still ranting at the marine in front of him and trying to salvage the plan.

"What are you doing, soldier? Return to your post and prepare this ship for departure," William commanded, oblivious.

"William, you can stop. This man knows who I am, and if I know him, he's already made his decision on what he is about to do. Isn't that so, Robert?"

William and Anne glanced at Edward and then at Robert with confused expressions.

"I always believed in your innocence, Edward. Always," Robert said, his back straight, but his eyes still in shock.

"Until now?" Edward asked. Robert didn't answer. "What say you forget what you saw, for an old friend?"

Robert's eyes filled with anger. "How dare you put me in this position, Edward? You too, Henry. If we were any bit friends you would know I cannot do what you request."

Edward closed his eyes and sighed. "I know, but our distraction should be here soon, and you need make a decision: Either cause your two best friends to be captured and imprisoned, or give us *Freedom*."

Robert, not having witnessed the transformation of his friend as Henry did, was even more shocked by the betrayal and devious nature of what Edward was doing. "What happened to you, Edward?"

"People such as yourself happened," Edward replied coldly.

The sound of a cannonball being fired rang out across the harbour. Robert, Edward and the crew turned their gaze to the sound. The distraction had started.

Edward used the opportunity and punched Robert hard in the face, knocking him to the ground. Several crewmen grabbed Robert and stuffed his mouth with cloth while tying him up. The utter hatred in Robert's eyes towards Edward and Henry was overwhelming. Henry turned away, but Edward stared straight at Robert. Edward would not recoil from what he was doing, what he was becoming. He owed Robert that much.

After Robert was tied up, Edward turned away. "Let's go," he commanded.

The crew boarded the ship, but Henry lingered, glancing back and forth between Robert and Edward. Eventually he too boarded the *Freedom*.

Robert writhed and thrashed on the ground. Rage filled his eyes as he struggled against the bonds. He eventually managed to spit out the gag.

"What happened to our promise, Edward? Henry? Weren't we to meet again when our dreams were fulfilled?" Robert yelled as the ship was pushed out. "What happened to being a whaler? What happened to your dream, Edward? Huh? What happened?" Robert screamed as he lay on his side, the bonds keeping their hold on him.

Edward, watching from the poop deck, replied, "Dreams change."

8. THE COST OF *FREEDOM*

Freedom was pushed out of the dock and into Fareham Lake. The wind was in their favour, heading southwest and allowing them to travel through the lake with ease.

"Set sail!" Edward yelled. The sails were let out and *Freedom* began moving. "Close-haul us south, Herbert. Let's help the *Fortune* and get out of here."

"Aye, aye, Captain!" Herbert replied, sitting in his wheelchair at the helm.

The men of the *Freedom* removed the marine disguises. Edward donned his captain's clothing, and William and Henry both removed their commanders' vests, leaving their white tunics on.

Pure pandemonium enveloped the docks. Citizens were clambering left and right, running out of their houses and trying to move as far away from the water as possible. The marines were trying desperately to man their ships, and failing due to the ship circling and firing on them in the harbour.

Edward's friends, the "distraction" he mentioned earlier, were pirates met long before Edward was imprisoned. On the right side of the other ship's black flag was a picture of a man holding the top of an hourglass and on the left the skeleton of Death held the bottom of the hourglass. The ship's name was the *Fortune*, and the captain's name was Bartholomew Roberts.

Edward and crew had met the giant Welsh Bartholomew and his crew after being caught in a particularly violent storm and landed on an uninhabited island. The *Freedom* had helped the *Fortune* out of a troubling situation with marines, and the crews became fast friends.

There, Edward and Bartholomew created the Pirate Commandments, a code each man on board must swear by and uphold. Bartholomew was a devout Christian and the idea for the commandments had struck Edward when he noticed the Bible Bartholomew carried.

In Fareham Lake, the *Fortune* was firing cannonballs at the marine ships in the harbour. *Fortune* was circling around to send another volley when the *Freedom* let out its sails. The *Fortune* fired all their cannons at the marine ships, and sailed ahead of the *Freedom*.

"Ready port and starboard cannons!" Edward commanded. When travelling south, port faced the marine ships. Starboard, however…

"Why are we firing starboard, Edward? There are no ships," Henry said, still in shock from what they had done to Robert.

"If we destroy those buildings, the soldiers who are about to show up could be slowed by forcing them to help the citizens."

"Those are innocent people, Edward! How can you justify attacking them?"

"Oh, so you are fine with attacking the marines then?" Edward said, his utter calm piercing Henry to the core. "And what about the prison guards? The thought of saving me was enough to justify killing them, so think of this as the same, and set your mind at ease." Henry was dumbstruck with Edward's cold comments, and ceased his objections.

The *Freedom* arrived at the first of two marine ships. "Fire!" Edward yelled. The cannons let loose on the marine ship at dock and at the buildings across the lake. The ship, a frigate like the *Freedom*, was blasted once more as the crew tried to board and counter. The buildings were hit directly, the cannonballs ripping through their feeble structure, sending them falling apart to ruin. The inhabitants nearby ran from the chaos screaming.

Henry knew some of those men, women, and children would die, and the realisation haunted his step. He could not move as he watched the anarchy unfold before his eyes.

The marines returned fire against the *Freedom*, and the second ship attacked the *Fortune*. A few of the cannonballs hit the *Freedom* directly, sending splinters of wood flying, and injuring some of the crew.

Soldiers entered from the west, opposite the marines ships, and also fired upon the pirates. Bullets rained down on the two crews, but they kept fighting.

Before the marine ships could be manned and the sails let loose, the *Freedom* and *Fortune* both passed by. The two ships, *Crown* and *Ruby*, quickly brought their crew aboard and lay in a pursuit course for the pirate ships.

The *Fortune* and *Freedom* were approaching a small canal before their exit of Portsmouth. Two obstacles stood in their path: At the mouth of the canal were the army's defence line of cannons and two dozen men, and to the west, the marine ships in dry dock, unharmed as of yet. The docks were filling with water and the ships were being loaded with men and readied to deploy.

Edward unsheathed his sword for display, standing with one foot on the quarterdeck railing and holding onto a rigging line with his other hand. "This battle isn't over yet, men! Let's show them what real men are capable of." The crew's morale was boosted and they shouted their agreement.

The scene, if gazed at from above, would be akin to a small skirmish, a light battle between a few ships and nothing more. But, when viewed from the harbour or on one of the ships, it was hellish.

The *Fortune* was feeling the brunt of the attack as it led the charge through the canal. The soldiers stationed at the small fortresses fired their cannons on the pirates, and the *Fortune* repaid them in kind.

The *Freedom* was passing the dry docks when one of the marine ships, the *Reserve*, left the dock and headed straight for *Freedom*'s stern. "Fire starboard!" Edward commanded. The bombardment didn't deter the *Reserve* as most of the shots missed or glanced off the front. "Brace for impact!"

The *Reserve* slammed into the tail of the *Freedom*, sending her off course. The jolt and resulting spin sent a few unlucky men of the crew to the floor of the ship. The two ships were then locked together side by side in the middle of the wide canal. •

The marines sent over grappling hooks over the side of the larger *Freedom*. Men in blue uniforms swung over on ropes to the enemy ship and attacked. The starboard broadsides of the two ships fired at will upon each other, opening holes, breaking cannons, and breaking bodies.

"Cut those lines!" Edward yelled as he used his golden cutlass to cut one of the grappling hooks off of the *Freedom*'s starboard railing.

Pukuh threw a spear at a marine swinging across. The spear hit the man in the chest and he fell to the sole of *Freedom* with a thud. Pukuh unsheathed a knife and ran to the starboard railing, jumping and rolling over and through pirates and marines, and cut one of the hooks keeping the *Freedom* pinned.

William kicked a marine in the sternum. The marine coughed once and fell over unconscious. William gripped the rope of one of the hooks and pulled with all his strength, bracing himself against *Freedom*'s railing. The hook went slack, and William threw it into the water with a grunt.

Anne, up in the crow's nest, aimed her powerful rifle at one of the hooks. The bullet hit straight through the middle of the rope. The twine unravelled and snapped with the strain.

Sam didn't pay attention to Edward's orders and jabbed at two marines with his cutlass, using the blade like a fencing sword. They deflected the blows. Sam took the cutlass in two hands and reared back to strike. The marines concentrated too hard on the jabs and were caught unawares. Sam knocked the swords away from the marines, bent his knees, turned the sword around, and swung the other way. He sliced open the marines' stomachs and they fell, dead.

The *Fortune*, noticing *Freedom*'s trouble, turned the ship around after destroying some of the cannon fortresses at the mouth of the canal. The second ship in dry dock, *Assistance*, was just emerging as the *Fortune* rammed her.

Herbert's sister, Christina, was watching the scene unfold and relayed the information to her brother. Being her clever self, she told Herbert to turn the ship hard to port. Christina could see what the *Fortune* was planning to do and how *Freedom* could help.

The *Fortune* pushed *Assistance* into the side of the dock. *Assistance*'s stern swung out and hit the other side of the dock. With the pressure of the *Fortune* on the other ship's bow and no way to move, the wood beams on the bow snapped.

Water immediately filled the hull of the marines' ship, and it began sinking with each drop. The crew jumped off and into the water, or swam out the hole if they could. The few marines at the broken bow jumped onto the *Fortune* and fought the pirates of Bartholomew's crew, but were easily dispatched.

The *Fortune* moved from the decapitated *Assistance* and its starboard broadside was now facing the tangled mess of *Freedom* and the *Reserve*. Herbert, under Christina's instruction, turned the ship hard to port, causing the *Reserve* to be parallel to the *Fortune*.

Bartholomew Roberts, seven feet tall, with burly arms and chest, smiled at the sight before him. "God is truly with us, and *Fortune* favours us this day, men! Fire starboard!"

The *Fortune* fired all her starboard cannons at the *Reserve*. The large iron balls ripped through the hull of the *Reserve*, killing, maiming, and destroying with each shot. With the *Freedom*'s volleys opposite *Fortune*, *Reserve* was sufficiently pumped full of holes. The *Reserve* took on water and after *Freedom*'s crew released themselves from the grappling hooks the *Reserve* retreated.

Freedom joined with *Fortune* and the two ships continued to the mouth of the canal. The *Crown* and the *Ruby* were in pursuit, damaged, but not as badly as the *Reserve* and *Assistance*. The enemy ships were far behind now, and being a weightier class than the *Fortune* and the *Freedom* they were at a disadvantage with speed.

The final obstacle was at the mouth of the canal. More soldiers and backup gunners had arrived since the *Fortune* helped the *Freedom* out. The gunners manned and aimed cannons along the harbour at the two ships.

"Forward unto *Freedom*!" Edward yelled, his cutlass high in the air, and the cry was heard across both ships.

Bartholomew repeated the charge, "Forward unto *Freedom*!" to his crew. Others among the crew chanted the simple but effective war cry. The two crews quickly became in sync with each other and the sound of the battle cry could be heard by the army at the mouth of the canal as the ships approached.

"Attack!"

Cannonballs flew through the air, bullets drove from their guns, men cried out, and pandemonium ensued. The two groups warred with neither side giving up, but the ones standing still were forced to lose. In a few short minutes the *Freedom* and the *Fortune* passed through the mouth of the canal and left the army behind. The cannons kept sounding off, and the marine ships kept pursuing, but the ships were too slow to catch up.

After the pirate ships passed the threshold, and they were a safe distance from the cannons and muskets, the crews of the two ships erupted in a cheer of unparalleled joy. Their captain, whom they went to such lengths for, was now free, and they were a family again.

Edward grinned as he turned his gaze to the *Fortune*. He saw Bartholomew Roberts on the quarterdeck of his own ship, clapping and smiling. Edward took off his tricorn hat and bowed deeply to the man who was, without a doubt, the sole reason they were able to escape today. Bartholomew returned the bow in kind.

The ships separated, as had been the plan from the beginning, the *Fortune* heading northeast to wherever the wind would take them. The *Freedom* was headed southwest, then back to the Caribbean, performing repairs along the way.

At least, that was the plan, before tragedy struck.

After they had separated from the *Fortune*, Anne ran to Edward with a grave expression on her face. "We have twenty-two injured and three dead."

"Poor souls. We will conduct a funeral service tonight in their honour. John?" Edward said, turning to the quartermaster. "Make sure the names of the men are written down so we may send their families some coin." John nodded.

"Edward, you should see the men," Anne suggested, pulling his attention back.

"Yes." Edward's face was solemn as he treaded to his fallen friends.

A crowd surrounded the bodies. Edward touched shoulders and pulled others aside so he could reach the centre. Edward mentally prepared himself for when he saw the bodies, but it was far worse than he imagined.

Nassir was knelt down, clutching a body, tears streaming down his face. The body was his fifteen-year-old boy, Ochi. He had taken multiple bullet wounds and died from his injuries.

The only sounds were the hissing wind, the flapping of the sails, and the slow sobs of Nassir. No one could offer words of consolation to Nassir; the crew could only watch the awkward spectacle and search for words which would never be uttered.

Someone pushed through the crowd to Edward's side. Christina emerged beside him to view the scene. Her eyes widened in disbelief at what she saw, and then slowly narrowed as the truth and shock sank in. The young man she had grown so close to was dead in front of her. She caressed a carved wooden rose around her neck.

Christina tried to take a step, her eyes focused on Ochi, the crew's focused on her, but she collapsed into Edward's arms. Edward eased Christina to the floor of the ship, holding her close as she watched Ochi's lifeless body. Tears fell silently down her cheeks, her fingers still on the carved rose.

Fingers quickly turned into a fist, and silence into screams.

9. RESOLVE

Nassir peered from his sorrow to see the crew around him, watching. He saw Edward and his eyes filled with rage. Nassir set his son down and rose up to his full height. "You are the cause of this!" he yelled to Edward.

Anne, beside Edward, took charge of the situation. "Nassir, please, how is Edward the cause of this? Did he shoot the gun?"

"No, but he caused the gun to be loaded. He is equally at fault for this!" Nassir pointed at Edward.

Edward gently pulled Christina off of him. Still in grief, anger was far from Christina's mind. "As Anne said, I did not kill your son. We are here today because of me, and I am partly to blame as my weakness caused these men to die, but none were forced to be here."

Nassir reared back and punched Edward in the face, sending him to the deck. "My son is dead and you blame him? Blame me?"

Despite Nassir's anger, Edward remained calm. He slowly lifted himself back up, but stayed sitting. "I am not blaming anyone but myself. I was merely stating that everyone is here of their own volition and knew the dangers. I do not believe I am the one you should be focusing your anger on. However, if this will help you ease your pain..." Edward closed his eyes, waiting for what was about to happen.

"Now you mock me?" Nassir punched Edward again and again, but Edward did not fight back. Anne, along with many others, could do nothing but turn away at the bitter display. Nassir's punches slowed and weakened until he gripped the clothing on Edward's chest and shook him. Edward hadn't moved since Nassir started. "Ochi, my son!" Nassir cried, sobbing into Edward's chest.

Jack pulled Nassir off Edward and embraced him silently.

Several minutes of agonising silence passed. Jack consoled Nassir, Anne consoled Christina, and the crew watched mutely, unable to help those who were hurting the most.

"We will perform a funeral service tonight," Edward whispered, rising to his feet.

"I do not want my son to burn. He will be buried in NiTalaa at my home of Calabar. If you do not take me I will go myself."

"We will take you, Nassir."

Henry emerged at Edward's call and, with Jack's help, Henry took Nassir downstairs to the crew cabin. Anne took Christina down as well, and she stayed with them for a bit. Edward went to the helm to tell Herbert the news.

Herbert was still unaware of what had occurred as the crowd, and his height disadvantage in his wheelchair, had prevented him from observing the scene. "What happened?"

"I'm sorry to be the one to tell you this, Herbert, but Ochi has passed in the fight."

Herbert's eyes, so similar to his sister's, at first held disbelief, but quickly grew wide with urgency. He abandoned the helm, climbed down to the waist, then crawled to the lower decks.

Edward manned the helm as some of the men returned to work and others wrapped Ochi's body. The earlier victory was marred by the tragedy, and morale was low.

That night the *Freedom* was let to drift and held a funeral service. The two crewmen who passed on were put in a small boat on the starboard side. Ochi was wrapped in cloth and placed on a wooden platform beneath the quarterdeck.

"We are gathered here to honour and remember the dead," Edward said. "They lost their lives defending us, and our being here is thanks to their sacrifice. They are gone, but we remain. Their dreams remain, their families remain, their regrets remain."

Christina and Nassir were at the front, holding each other, and Herbert was holding Christina's hand. Nassir dried his eyes, but Christina still wept for her significant other.

"We, as a crew, as a family, must fulfil their dreams, we must take care of their family, and we must fix what they regret, so they may rest peacefully." Edward stared intently at the crew. "Do you accept these responsibilities?" The crew responded with "Aye." Many of them had been part of the crew from the beginning and remembered a similar eulogy from Edward. "With your acceptance, these three will surely be able to rest peacefully."

Edward nodded to the crew stationed at the sides of the ship. Before lowering the boat, the Mayan Pukuh placed corn and a piece of jade in their mouths. Afterwards, he uttered a short prayer to his gods to tell them of the men's arrival. The corn was food for the journey, and the jade was the price of passage. The men lost their lives in combat, considered a sacrifice, and would be allowed into heaven in honour, according to Pukuh's beliefs.

The crew lowered the small boat into the water and threw in a torch. The bodies burned as others in the crew fired muskets into the air. Three shots and the service was done, but the fire lingered on.

The pain lingered on.

...

Over the seven weeks of travel to NiTalaa the morale of the crew was at an all-time low. Jack did his best to bring cheer with music, to no effect. The trip felt longer with the sombre and melancholic mood over the crew.

Ochi and Christina were but children, and to have them ripped apart was unbearable for the crew, but even worse to watch was the slow deterioration of Nassir. He spent every waking moment immersed in work on the ship. He worked alone, fixing as much as he could and restoring the ship to pre-battle condition. Through his constant work he took little sleep and as the weeks passed he developed bags under his eyes, and lost a dangerous amount of weight.

Christina did not have the benefit of a job to lose herself in, so she spent most of her days either sleeping or in the bow cabin weeping over Ochi's body. Anne and Herbert tried their best, but Christina was inconsolable.

Herbert too was troubled deeply by the loss, and by his inability to do anything to help his sister. Herbert had cultivated a great friendship with Nassir and Ochi through the past year, and the two were like family to him. He did not allow himself to feel grief, only empathy and sorrow over his sister's condition.

One day during the journey, Edward entered the bow cabin, mainly used for weapons storage, to pay his personal respects to Ochi. The small cabin was the only suitable location for Ochi to rest on the journey to Nassir's homeland.

Three cannons stood at the front of the curved cabin, and barrels of muskets on the sides. Spare hammocks for accommodations were also swinging in the air. On a pedestal of boxes, Ochi's wrapped body lay.

In front of the pedestal, Edward saw Pukuh kneeling down in silence. The noise of the door roused Pukuh and he turned to greet Edward with tears in his eyes.

"I'm sorry, Pukuh, I will return later."

"No, brother, stay. The dead should be mourned together."

Edward sat down beside Pukuh, a bottle of rum in his hands. He poured a little out on the floorboards of the *Freedom* and took a drink from the bottle. Edward muttered his own silent prayer, despite his not knowing anything about God, and then sat beside Pukuh in silence.

Edward stared at the wrapped body in front of him. The cloth was damp with decay, and the smell surrounding the body was foul and stung Edward's nose causing his eyes to water. Edward hadn't seen a body like this before.

The dead should not be kept in such a way. I wish we had another option, but I have to respect Nassir's wishes.

After a few moments, Pukuh broke the silence. "A father should never lose a son in such a way."

"Mmm," Edward mumbled in agreement. "If I was stronger I could have stopped them from dying." His gazed was fixed on the ground.

"Where death is concerned, strength has no part. All men die, this is fact. You say right when you say to Nassir his son chose to fight. The only choice we as men and women have is where we choose to lay our life on the line. Losing our lives in battle is tragic, but honourable. Ochi did what he could, and nothing more. You are the same. Trust in me, I felt the same before."

Edward contemplated Pukuh's words, then took another drink of the rum. "Thank you Pukuh." Edward left the room. *Thank you, but you're wrong, Pukuh. I will become stronger, and I will stop my family from dying. No matter the cost.*

...

When the *Freedom* reached NiTalaa, at the port of Calabar, the crew departed with Nassir to bury Ochi. Another service was held on the outskirts of town where the graves were marked with crosses made of tree branches. The crew took turns digging the grave in the hot overbearing sun.

Having no work to tend to his grief, and no exhausted sleep to take him away, Nassir mourned for his son once more. After the Calabar service, the crew left Nassir, Christina and Herbert alone at the graveside. The crew waited for hours at the dock before the three returned. Nassir wanted to talk with Edward, as did Christina. Edward spoke with Nassir first in the bow cabin.

The faint smell of decay lingered in the air, lending an eerie feeling in the small room. Nassir was haggard and tired. His usually well-groomed appearance was overtaken by stubble on his head and face. His well-rounded cheeks were hollow and his form diminished, the opposite to Edward's recovery from his stay in prison.

"I am staying in Calabar, Captain. I need to... think over things."

Edward opened his mouth to say something out of his gut reaction, but then simply nodded his head. "I understand. We'll call this a temporary leave to allow you rest. You will be returning, yes?"

"I will say maybe."

"We will return after a few months and see how you are feeling, how does that sound?"

Nassir nodded to Edward's suggestion and left the room, preparing to say his goodbyes to the crew. Edward followed and made the announcement. The crew became depressed but sympathetic for Nassir, and wanted to have a feast before he left, but Nassir declined. The ship set sail before night fell, the crew watching and waving to Nassir as he became smaller the more the ship floated away. Eventually, Nassir was no longer visible, and many in the crew felt they would not see him again.

Herbert and Christina stayed on the *Freedom*, and after their departure, Edward finally had his audience with Christina. Once more in the room filled with the faint smell of the dead taunting the recent victims of catastrophe with the sickening essence.

The beautiful girl was finally past the shock of the recent events, but was still visibly affected. Christina's strawberry-blond hair was dishevelled and her normally sparkling blue eyes were dark and bloodshot. Her frame was small and at the point of breaking standing before Edward.

"What did you want to talk to me about, Christina?"

"I want to be taught how to fight."

Edward could have expected a lot of things, but not this. "No," he said simply.

The young girl was on the verge of tears from frustration. "Why not?" Her mouth curled into a tight frown as her lip quivered.

Edward turned away from Christina; her grief-stricken face was too much to bear. How she had changed from the days when she and Ochi played on the ship. "Because I cannot risk losing you. Think about Herbert. What would he do if you were lost to him?"

"I am thinking of Herbert!" Christina shouted and anger seeped into her words instead of sadness. "Who else will protect him against those awful marines? I am the only one who has the right!" she yelled in her ire.

Edward heard the anger in Christina's voice, saw the rage in her sky-blue eyes. She reminded him of his love from his hometown of Badabos before he met Anne, Lucy. Edward could never say no to those eyes. Christina was breaking him. "There is more to what you are saying than you're telling me. If I am to approve this, I want to know the real reason you want to fight so much. I know why, but I want to hear this from you."

Christina crossed her arms. "I want revenge. I will make those bastards pay for what they've done. I want to make our enemies fear me the same as you."

Edward nodded, extending his hand. "I want the same."

Christina shook his hand, and the deal was struck.

10. THE BERMUDA GATEWAY

Two tragedies in a row took its toll on the crew's minds and many were fatigued. The loss of the crew members and Nassir leaving lowered morale, but time healed old wounds first. Mourning was over, and the crew learned to cope with the loss.

Edward felt a distraction was in order, so on their way to the Caribbean he decided now was the time to solve the next riddle. Most of the *Freedom* was locked by keys left scattered about by Benjamin. After each successive door was opened, another clue was found inside the room for the next key. The game Benjamin left, while trying, difficult, and sometimes deadly, was intriguing to all in the crew, especially Edward.

The remaining sections locked were a door on the berth deck, and two on the gun deck, one on the bow and one on the stern. The locked door on the stern gundeck was assumed to be the captain's cabin, but the others were a mystery.

Edward stood on the quarterdeck, leaning against the wooden planks at the stern. From his pocket, he retrieved the letter he reclaimed from the warden of Gammond prison. The simple white print was adorned with a golden wax seal of a classic hunting horn, the sign of Benjamin Hornigold. Edward touched the simple but elegant design before breaking the seal and opening the letter. The letter read as follows:

The Devil's Triangle
25° and Three Shots in the Dark
The Limey's Parallel Lights the Way

Edward pondered on the letter. *The Devil's Triangle sounds familiar, and twenty-five degrees could mean latitude, but three shots in the dark is a mystery and the final line is nonsense.*

"Herbert, what do you make of this?" Edward asked, handing him the paper.

Blackbeard's *Revenge*

Herbert set a wooden pole in the spokes of the wheel to stop it from moving while he examined the paper. Herbert adjusted his glasses and moved some hair behind his ear during his review.

"The Devil's Triangle is most certainly the Bermuda Triangle, an area between Bermuda, Puerto Rico, and Florida forming a triangle. The twenty-five degrees is a latitude point, and I imagine the three shots in the dark could mean cannon shots, or maybe gunshots. I'm not sure about the last line, though."

Edward took the paper back, reviewing it with cocked brow while stroking his beard. "Adjust our heading now, we will unravel the mystery of the last line on the way. Benjamin may have us on a fool's errand, but he was no fool. Whatever the last line means, it is of some import." Edward addressed the crew while Herbert adjusted the course. "Everyone, please move to the waist." Once the crew gathered, Edward explained. "As you all know, there are several locked sections of the ship, and we're searching for the keys." He held up the paper. "This next clue will lead us to a key, but we are having some trouble deciphering the final line." Edward read the line out to them. "Any ideas?"

Sam immediately spoke. "A Limey is slang fer British marines. 'Cause they bring limes aboard their ships."

"Good Sam, good. So what is the parallel of the British?"

"The French?" "Indians?" "Jews?"

Edward held up his hand to silence the crew. "French is the most logical parallel to English. So what is the light of the French?"

"The food?" "The language?" "The whores?" "The smell?"

Edward pinched the bridge of his nose. *This is getting nowhere.* "Alright, John, Anne, Henry, Sam, please join me in the meeting room. Jack, play us some soothing music please."

Those addressed replied with an "Aye, Captain!" and went about following the orders. The crew returned to work either swabbing the deck, fixing the trim on the sails, or other menial tasks. Jack pulled out his violin and played some upbeat and warm classical melodies.

With the relaxing sounds of music, ocean water lapping against the ship, and salty air blowing around the *Freedom*, the crew were settling into a better mood.

Edward and the ones he'd named headed to the cabin below the quarterdeck. Edward commanded the anchor to be dropped and Herbert to join them. Herbert climbed down and entered the war room with everyone else.

The cabin was lavishly decorated with a chandelier above Edward's head and red velvet carpet below his feet. On the sides of the room bookshelves held dozens of nautical books and a bevy of fiction to choose from. Windows at the back let in light and were augmented by oil lamps. Decorations of paintings, swords, and pistols were scattered about on the walls. In the middle of the room stood an oval table with expensive chairs front to back, and one ornate high-backed chair at the back in the middle.

Edward sat in the gold-trimmed, high-backed chair, and read the clue aloud. Afterwards, he ensured each one had a chance to examine the paper. "Herbert says the Devil's Triangle is another name for the Bermuda Triangle." At the mention of the Bermuda Triangle, Sam visibly tensed. "The twenty-five degrees relates to the latitude inside the triangle we need to be, and the three shots in the dark are assumed to be cannon shots."

Sam couldn't hold back any longer. "Captain, ye don't mean ta head ta the Triangle, do ye?"

"Yes, Sam, travelling to the Triangle was implied."

"The Triangle be dangerous. Horrible things happen to sailors travelling there," Sam claimed, uncharacteristically fearful.

"Well, with the name Devil's Triangle, I assumed..." Edward said with a smirk. "So, anyone have any ideas?" Edward tried to change the subject to something he considered more pressing.

The group offered suggestions on what they assumed the French light could mean, with the most logical suggestion being made by John. He supposed the parallel could be the Grand Royal Coat of Arms of France, but how that would light the way was beyond the group. After some time of deliberation, they decided to take a break and play a game of cards.

Edward, not one with much experience in games of chance, but a quick learner, put up a good fight. Sam was caught cheating and laughed it off. Anne and Henry had some playful banter and competed more against each other than the rest of the group. Herbert and John were by far the biggest winners, and Herbert was surprisingly competitive.

In the middle of the game, the door to the cabin opened and a gust of wind rushed in, the air of the sea invading the air of the old books and burning oil lanterns. The wind caused the paper and the cards to fly off the table. The group were trying to catch the cards when their eyes caught the clue flying away to the open door. They all lunged for the paper at once, but it escaped their grasp and flew to the door.

Christina was at the door, and she caught the paper before it flew off. She was wearing loose-fitting pantaloons ending five inches below her knees, a loose white tunic, and a leather vest overtop with the rose pendant showing. Her hair was tied into a ponytail, and she appeared decidedly better than a few days prior.

Christina peeked at the paper as she approached the table. Everyone was still piled on top of one another. "What are you doing?" she asked.

"Trying to catch that, thank you," Edward said as he took the paper back and folded it into his pocket.

Christina laughed as she circled behind Edward's seat. "Was that the riddle for another key?"

"Yes, and, as we've yet to find the solution, losing the paper would be devastating."

"You know, I'm really good at riddles. Would I be allowed to look?" Christina asked with a sweet grin.

Edward eyed Herbert, and Herbert nodded. "Alright, do you need to see the paper again?" Edward asked, reaching for his pocket.

"You mean this paper?" Christina was holding the riddle in her hands. She smiled coyly at Edward.

Edward smiled back at Christina's deviousness, and also at her happiness. Edward was glad to see Christina in good spirits.

Christina read the riddle over again as Edward explained what they figured out so far. Christina took a few seconds, then her face lit up. "What if Limey's Parallel means lemons?"

"Lemons?" Edward inquired, incredulous.

"Yes, parallel means side by side and lemons and limes go well together."

Edward, not wanting to dismiss Christina's suggestion outright, tried to reason with her and lead her to the conclusion herself. "So how would a lemon light the way?"

Christina touched the rose around her neck as she thought. "Ah, I know how! Don't move!" she instructed, and without any explanation she ran out of the cabin.

Anne and company peered at Edward in wonderment, almost asking him if he knew what was going on. Edward shrugged his shoulders and sat down. After a minute, Christina returned with a knife and a lemon.

Using the knife, Christina sliced a lemon open, threw one half into Edward's hand, and squeezed out the juice of the other half. Christina used her finger to wet the paper with the lemon juice. This piqued curiosity, so the others shifted closer to watch. Christina wet the whole of the paper with juice.

At first nothing happened, but after a moment the lemon juice penetrated the thicker stock paper and dots appeared on the paper. Soon, the whole paper was covered in small dots.

Edward picked up the paper. "Amazing! How did you know lemon juice would do this?"

Christina grinned at his adulation. "Well, I didn't. I read in an adventure book once about an ink which goes hidden after being written and the only thing that can bring the writing back is lemon juice. The scene stuck with me because of the ingenuity."

Edward laughed. "Maybe we need you to join us in more of these meetings." Christina smiled again even more widely. "Now let us see the familial combination in action. What do you make of this?" Edward handed the paper to Herbert.

Herbert too carried his joy on his face, delighted his sister was happy again. He scrutinised the paper at different angles to better see the dots. On the page, three circles surrounded specific dots, with a line connecting them in a triangle. In the corner, a time—one a.m.—was written in the mystery ink.

"I believe this is a star chart, with a time for when we can see them. With this, the latitude, and the location, I believe we deciphered the riddle."

"Excellent!" Edward left the cabin immediately. "Crew, we solved the riddle and are on our way to unlocking the next part of this ship," Edward yelled to the men. The crew cheered. "And we owe our thanks to Christina!" More cheers and hoots rose above the din. Christina and company left the cabin. Edward picked Christina up and held her on his broad shoulder. "Three cheers for Christina Blackwood."

"Hip-hip-hurrah! Hip-hip-hurrah! Hip-hip-hurrah!" the crew yelled, caught in the fever of praise to the young lady.

Christina was nearly in tears, but unlike in the past long while, the tears were not of sorrow, but of joy. She carried a wide grin as she sat on Edward's pedestal-like shoulder.

...

Another seven weeks passed as *Freedom* sailed to the Bermuda Triangle. Edward and crew resumed training with Anne and William. For most of the crew, having slacked in the past year, training felt like starting anew.

Edward also wanted Anne to do more personal one-on-one sessions with Christina. Anne was reluctant at first, but when she saw Christina's determination she quickly approved. Christina showed much promise, and her quick mind helped in her growth.

Henry, ever since the escape from Portsmouth, was downtrodden and lethargic most of the time. Edward could see Henry was angry as well. At first, Edward attributed Henry's mood to the loss of the crewmates and the general temper aboard *Freedom*, but Henry's disposition lingered as time passed.

Edward approached Henry when he was alone one day. "Henry, are you upset about anything?"

Henry smiled, but to Edward it felt hollow. "No, nothing at all, Edward. We're safe and we're free. What would I have to worry about?"

"You were rather distraught with our escape, as well as running into Robert. I am too, but you must understand, tying him up was for his benefit. If Robert let us leave, he would have been in as much trouble as us. If Robert ran off for help we either would have fought him on one of the ships, or been captured before we could leave. There really was no choice in the matter."

Henry kept that same smile. "Of course. I understand completely."

Edward considered Henry for a moment, skeptical, but unsure of what to say. "If there is anything you wish to talk about—"

"Yes, I will come to you," Henry said, cutting Edward off.

The trip carried on with Henry appearing less agitated, but whether mere acting or him actually coming to terms with his feelings, Edward did not know.

Sam, on the other hand, increased in uneasiness and agitation the closer the ship came to the Bermuda Triangle. Any little chop in the waters or high wind would trigger sweats, and the slightest loud noises caused Sam to jump.

Edward attempted talking with Sam, but all Edward could rouse out of him was, "Something... happened there, but you would not believe me." Sam would not say another word on the matter, but it was apparent that the travel weighed on him heavily.

When Herbert took the *Freedom* into the Bermuda Triangle, the rest of the crew became as agitated as Sam. Many of the older crewmates had heard stories of unbelievable happenings in the triangle, and their nervousness passed to the younger men. Even Edward couldn't help but be on edge.

Through various calculations, and compensating for magnetic variations in his compass, Herbert brought the *Freedom* to the specified latitude. The sails were furled and the *Freedom* was left to drift. As the night wore on, the wind deadened. The calm was eerie.

Herbert, using the star chart as a reference, guided the gunners to aim the cannons at the specified stars, which also happened to be in a triangle pattern. When the time indicated on the chart came, Herbert would command the gunners to fire.

The entire crew stayed awake for the event, all of them armed, eying the horizon, shifting at every sound. Sam had several weapons at the ready and was sweating profusely.

The night was cold, colder than normal due to the humidity in the air. Edward shivered and thought he could see his breath in front of him.

Herbert watched his overly complicated moon dial, which Edward had no chance of learning how to read, until the time was one hour past midnight. "Fire!" Herbert commanded.

With the slightest hesitancy, the gunners fired their cannons in the direction of the stars.

The crew tensed as the iron balls flew through the air. Edward gripped his cutlass, John and Anne aimed their rifles, William clenched his fists, Henry held a blunderbuss, and Sam held twin pistols with whitened knuckles. All eyes followed the cannonballs until the iron disappeared into thin air. Poof. Gone. Not even a splash sounded.

"Did everyone else see that?" *Or should I say* not *see that?*

Before any could respond, an unnatural fog emerged from where the cannonballs vanished. A great howling of wind ushered the fog around the *Freedom*, and soon the entire area around them was covered in pale white.

Edward shivered, partially from the cold night and partially from the supernatural spectacle. *What is this devilry?*

The fog shielded the crew's vision to twenty feet off the rail, and the howling gusts sounded like a woman's shriek. Even the most hardened man now carried a weapon in hand, and a sweat-soaked brow above the eyes.

While the crew was caught unawares, a ship struck the bow of the *Freedom* and jolted the crew. Men fell to the deck from the quaking, and shots were fired into the air. Edward ordered calm, and ran to the bow to see the ship.

The ship scraping along the side of the *Freedom* was a small merchantman, the name *Patriot* emblazoned on the side. It had no weapons, and the civilian crew on board seemed just as frightened by events as Edward's crew.

The merchantman did not slow as its port splintered *Freedom*'s wood. The ship eventually lurched to the side and separated from *Freedom*, then sailed off into the fog once more.

Edward's lips were a hard line, and his anger rose. "Hard to port! Follow that ship. It has some explaining to do," he snarled.

Before Edward's men could gain grip of their senses and take action, another ship came up beside *Freedom*, this time a sixth-class frigate with the name *Le Pandore*. It appeared to be in pursuit of the *Patriot*, but upon seeing *Freedom*, pulled up its sails and slowed itself as quickly as it could.

The crew of *Le Pandore* were waving as if greeting friends. Edward's crew lowered their weapons, but out of confusion rather than familiarity. Edward also noticed that the fog had dissipated, and the merchantman *Patriot* was almost past the horizon and out of sight.

Le Pandore turned around and eased itself up next to *Freedom*, then sent over grappling lines to hook the ships together. A gangplank was set for the crew to cross over, and the captain of *Le Pandore* was the first to step onto the *Freedom*.

The captain was a shorter man, a little over halfway between five and six feet, wearing a tall black top hat, a red vest with coattails, a white tunic with bow tie, and itchy grey cotton pantaloons. His face was of French perfection, and with high-set eyes and long chin and nose, he was handsome in his own way.

"Benjamin Hornigold, where are you, my old friend?" he yelled in a light French accent as he boarded the *Freedom*, searching but not finding the man he called out for. "This is no time for a prank, dear fellow, friends are here."

The sails flapped in the silence pervading the guest's declaration.

Sam, his mouth agape and stepping closer to the captain of *Le Pandore*, trembled at the sight of the man. He held out his hand like he was reaching for something too far away.

"Father?" Sam questioned, staring dead in the eyes of the captain.

The captain peered at Sam with a raised brow. At first, his expression was pure confusion, but it quickly changed to recognition and then shock.

"Sam?" he asked incredulously. The man ambled over to Sam, and Sam met him.

Sam held out his hand to shake, but the captain pushed aside his hand and embraced him. "It is good to see you, my son."

11. THE GHOSTS OF THE ISLAND BEYOND TIME

The crew observed the spectacle with mixed shock, confusion, and awe. No one knew what to make of the situation. When Sam and the mystery captain parted, Sam introduced him to Edward and the crew.

"Everyone, this is Dominique You, the Captain of *Le Pandore* and a man I call my father."

Dominique bowed with a flourish of his top hat. "A pleasure to meet you all. Though I am not Samuel's real father, I consider him my son, and I thank you for taking care of him." Dominique rested a hand on Sam's shoulder. "I thought we'd lost you, and I have many questions, but we can catch up momentarily. I am at a disadvantage, as I do not recognise the crew, but I know the ship intimately. Who, pray tell, is the captain?"

"This man here," Sam replied, pointing to Edward.

"Edward Thatch." Edward extended his hand.

Dominique took Edward's hand and shook firmly. "Might I also ask the year?"

Edward raised his brow to the odd question, but after what happened, he didn't know what was odd or not. "The year is seventeen-oh-seven."

"Ah, well I understand now. What Samuel here may have been reluctant to impart to you is the nature of where we are from, or should I say when? No matter. We are from the year eighteen-thirteen."

The *Freedom*'s crew laughed nervously at the statement, but Dominique was unfazed. He and his crew kept straight faces, and the laughter soon stopped and turned to awkward silence.

"Surely you jest?" Edward asked.

"Not so, Sam can attest to the truth of our words as well. He was part of my crew until the age of ten in the year eighteen-ten, yet now he is here before me at the age of twenty and some. That... fog we travelled through brought us here to seventeen-oh-seven."

"I fell overboard in a storm 'ere in the Devil's Triangle, and when I awoke I was in the year sixteen-ninety-six. That's why I am fearful of this place. Strange things happen."

To the crew, slack-jawed and bewildered, "strange" was a severe understatement. Even William carried an expression of pure disbelief plastered on his face.

Dominique laughed nonchalantly. "Yes, strange things indeed. Now, if you do not mind, can we continue chasing our quarry? I will stay aboard and we can discuss more while my crew leads the chase. Have your helmsman follow us."

Edward shook his head to clear the momentary confusion. "Yes, I believe further explanation is in order." Edward ordered Herbert to follow *Le Pandore* while Captain Dominique ordered his crew to continue pursuit. The grappling hooks were released and the ships were soon sailing once more.

Captain Dominique joined Edward, Sam, and the senior members of *Freedom*'s crew to talk in *Freedom*'s war room in the stern cabin. Dominique wanted to hear their story before he told his. Sam relayed what he had been doing the past eleven years and how he ended up on the *Freedom*, and Edward continued the story with a hint of Benjamin's game and the keys and their dealings with the British, while omitting certain sensitive details.

"Ah, well that explains this then," Dominique said as he pulled out a key from his pocket.

Edward's jaw dropped for the third time that evening. "Is that...?"

Dominique laughed. "Yes it is. I met Benjamin Hornigold one year ago in my time. Before he left he wanted me to hold onto this key, but never explained the meaning. When you meet a man such as him, and he asks you to keep something safe, you keep it safe."

"So, I guess Benjamin wants us to help you then?" Edward questioned, more to himself.

Dominique nodded. "I am chasing the ship the *Patriot*, which is carrying one Theodosia Burr Alston whom we mean to capture."

"And what is the purpose of capturing one woman?" Henry asked, wary of the supposed time-hopping captain.

Dominique paused, considering his words. "I hope you gentlemen understand if I keep the details light, as we don't know what could happen. Agreed?" Edward nodded for Dominique to continue. "In eighteen-thirteen, a war is raging between North America and the British Empire. Alston is a spy for the British, and because her father is the Vice President, the second in charge, of the North American colonies, she has access to sensitive information. Her father was arrested and suspected of treason due to her exploits."

"Hmm, the year has changed, but we have a common enemy." Edward rose from his seat at the head of the war room table. He extended his hand. "We will help you capture Alston, and you will give us the key we seek in return, agreed?"

Dominique returned Edward's gesture. "Agreed. The *Patriot* is heading to Charleston, and, as they are not aware of the mishap which has occurred with our date, they will continue as if nothing is the matter."

"How long will travel to Charleston take?"

"From where we are? A week at most."

"What happens when we catch this woman? What will you do with her?" Henry challenged.

Dominique had a crooked smirk as he glanced at his men then back to Henry. "If possible, we come back here to return her to my time and put her on trial. Is this acceptable to you, sir?" Dominique asked while mockingly bowing his head.

Edward held his hand up to silence Henry when he seemed poised to respond angrily. "This is acceptable," Edward reassured Dominique. "Now, we must hear all about your exploits in the next century, provided you approve?"

Dominique laughed. "I don't see the harm in talking about myself. I'm not so special. I would enjoy hearing more detail of this game you play as well."

Edward regaled Dominique with stories of their adventures and the trials left by Benjamin and how the *Freedom* arrived in the Devil's Triangle. During travel, Sam talked with Dominique and nearly spent every waking hour with him. He admired and looked up to the man like he was his flesh-and-blood father.

Although Dominique was an agreeable and cheerful man, Henry bore some misgivings about the whole situation. He kept a close eye on Dominique and tried to listen to all his conversations. After a few days of travel, Sam caught on to what Henry was doing and told him off, almost sparking a fight between the two. Edward would have none of it and met with Henry alone.

"Why are you bothering our guests, Henry?" Edward asked.

"I don't think we should trust Dominique."

"And why shouldn't we?"

Henry cocked his brow. "Do you really believe he is from another time? This whole story reeks of a fable."

"What about Sam, then? He confirmed the tale."

"Sam was but a boy when he was with Dominique. What if this is simply a jest which went too far, and now Dominique is keeping up appearances?"

"Why lie to us then?"

"To gain our trust, of course. He sees a familiar ship, but an unfamiliar crew, save Sam. Sam was a babe when he was lost, so Dominique thinks if he upholds the tale he wove years ago he will have an easier time getting what he wants from us. Dominique could have told us anything about the ship he's chasing, and because of Sam we are more likely to believe him."

Edward nodded, stroking his beard. "I do admit the story is hard to believe, but their story doesn't matter to me. Sam trusts Dominique, so I trust him, Henry. End of discussion."

Henry snorted. "In that case, don't turn to me when you find out we've been lied to."

"Good to know who I can rely on these days," Edward said as Henry walked out of the war room. *What is this mood he's been in recently?*

A crewmate knocked on the door to the war room, and after Edward beckoned him inside, he told Edward that Herbert wished to see him. Edward went to the quarterdeck to see Sam, Herbert, Dominique, and Dominique's helmsman. Sam had a pallor like none Edward had seen before.

"What is the urgent issue, Herbert?"

Herbert glanced at Dominique. "From what we surmise, our ships have been going in circles the past three days. We have not left the Triangle."

Edward's brow cocked. "How has this happened?"

"We don't know, my boy. Something about the air is foul, and I fear that this is the work of the Devil in his abode. Some force does not want us to leave."

Herbert ignored Dominique's ramblings. "I have been keeping a track of our movements each day, and we have been moving forward, but when I recheck our status on the morrow, we are somewhere different. The first day I chalked it up to a mistake I might have made, or a malfunction of my instruments, but Dominique's helmsman confirmed it.

"What do we do, then?"

Herbert shrugged his shoulders. "The one thing we can do is keep moving and hope whatever is the cause dissipates."

Sam wiped sweat off his brow. "Ain't there somethin' that can be done? Each day 'ere is like tightenin' a vice on our knickers. We go'n circles enough somethin' bad's gonna happen."

Dominique patted Sam on the head. "Fret not, son. We shall find a means of escape."

"Dominique is correct, Sam. This is but a temporary setback."

"Land ho!" a crewman screamed from the crow's nest.

After their eyes darted to the crewmate, all eyes scanned the bow for the land. Herbert and Dominique both pulled out spyglasses and peered into them.

"How...?" Herbert sputtered before dropping his spyglass and rummaging through papers on his lap. "We've been in this area before, and there was no island," Herbert commented. Beads of sweat formed on his temple and ran down his cheek, a physical indicator that Herbert was out of his depth and had no scientific explanation for what was happening.

Edward placed his hand on Herbert's shoulder. "Land us on the island, Herbert. I intend to find the cause of this mystery, one way or another."

Herbert nodded slowly. "Aye, aye, Captain."

The two ships approached the island, the wind picking up and almost guiding them straight for the beach. The island was surrounded by fog which blotted out the sun when they neared. When they were close, Edward could see a ship berthed at the beach, and he guessed correctly the vessel was the *Patriot*.

"I have a feeling we were not the only ones who became stuck in the Triangle," Edward commented to Dominique.

Even as the ships closed in on the beach, there was no activity upon the *Patriot*, and when the sails were furled and secured no signs of life presented themselves. The island itself was unpleasantly silent and barren. Edward could only see the beach of sand and flat grass for a hundred feet, then the fog became so thick it made a wall.

Edward sent a search party to the *Patriot*, consisting of Anne, Christina, William, and a few crewmates from both *Freedom* and *Le Pandore*, but they returned soon after with confused looks.

"There are none aboard, Edward. The ship has a ghastly silence within, as if the crew were plucked away in the midst of great activity," Anne yelled from shore.

"Thank you, Anne. Stay there, we will be searching the island next," Edward replied, then he turned to Dominique. "I will take some of my crew to the island. Could you stay in case something happens here? If we are attacked, we need at least one of our ships able to retaliate."

"I would be happy to oblige. I thank you for your assistance today, Edward. I know my son has been in good hands from the way you have offered yourself so fully to our cause."

"Sam is my family as well. When one of my family needs help, I will not hesitate to stand by him. I would do the same for any in the crew, no matter the cause."

"Well spoken."

Edward gathered the crew together and they set out in teams to explore the island. Edward and Henry, Anne and Christina, William and Sam, and John went into the island along with the majority of the crew, with Jack and Herbert and *Freedom*'s remaining crew staying behind.

Edward commanded the teams to remain at most ten feet apart due to the fog. As the crew walked further into the island they were still able to see the people close to them. Edward was walking with Anne, and Henry and Christina were ten feet ahead of them.

The grass was wet with dew and the smell of fresh rain saturated the surroundings. Aside from the crewmates talking, and the grass being trod underfoot, it was silent on the island.

"So, what do you make of this, Anne?" Edward asked.

Anne pursed her lips and gazed around at the fog and the unnaturally flat terrain of the island. "I am reminded of one of the first things I said to you: There are some things in this world that cannot be explained."

Edward nodded in recognition. "Yes, I remember. That was when you were still pretending to be a man to hide your identity. You were referring to the locks on *Freedom* being magical as an explanation for why they could not be picked, were you not?" Anne nodded. "So, you believe Dominique is from the future?"

"I don't think I'm the authority on what is happening, but I believe in the possibility. I have seen many things which, if I told you, you may not believe. What do you think of Dominique's story?"

"As with many of the wonders we have seen, I don't particularly care. Perhaps he is from the future, perhaps Sam, Dominique, and his crew were tortured into believing this fantasy, or perhaps they are insane. Our goal is this Alston woman, and that will bring us one step closer to the key I seek. That, and helping Sam's family, are all I care about."

"Perhaps that is the best way to think of this occurrence. If we cannot explain what is happening, what is the use in pondering over it?"

"Exactly." Edward smiled to his lover, but when he opened his eyes his happiness faded. His head darted back and forth. "Where is everyone?"

Anne spun around, searching for their friends. "Hello? Christina? Henry?" she yelled. Anne looked at the ground. "The fog is thickening, I can barely see the grass beneath our feet."

Edward joined in yelling for their comrades, but no matter how loud their plea, there was no reply. Edward and Anne were alone.

"Come," Anne commanded. She grabbed Edward's hand and pulled him into a run.

The two ran forward across the grass through the pale mist, yelling as they went. The island turned colder with each passing minute, but the exertion kept their bodies warm. The silence of the island became oppressive, with the only sounds being the soft crunch of their boots against the moist grass. They ran for what felt like ages, cold sweat passing down their faces and exhaustion taking over.

Edward thought he heard a voice behind him, a voice he hadn't heard in a long time, and the suddenness of it loosened his grip on Anne. Her hand slipped from Edward's, and she disappeared into the vapour.

"Anne?" Edward called. "Anne!"

"Hello, Ed."

Edward turned, the same voice from before beckoning him to its source. Edward saw the face of one he never thought he would see again, and it brought tears to his eyes.

"Dad?"

...

"Don' gimme that look."

William stared down at Sam, daggers raining from his pupils.

"Stop it," Sam commanded, to no effect. "Dad damn ye, William, stop starin' at me! Yer face is like a Catholic priest during a Sunday sermon: ye could make the most hardened man's sugar stick go limp with a glance." Sam waved his arms and turned to walk away.

William gripped Sam's clothes at the back. "I specifically instructed you to stay close to the others. We are now separated because of your ineptitude. Do not make the same mistake and go off on your own."

Sam pulled his clothes away forcefully and let out a sigh. "Fine, fine, dammit. I'm following orders now, your majesty." Sam cackled. "No... your majesty's dog."

William gave Sam another look, but this time Sam laughed it off and began walking again, with William following closely behind. The white wall on all sides seemed as much a physical barrier as a wall, shutting out most of their previous sight and sounds. William's

93

normally silent footsteps were as loud as a person talking, which made Sam's dragging feet deafening in the void.

Several times while walking gradually forward, William placed his hand on Sam's shoulder, but Sam kept shrugging it off. After a few occurrences, Sam snapped.

"William, put yer hand on me one more time and I swear…"

"Well, if you insist. I thought you could use the support, however, as I noticed the fog closing in on us."

"What?" Sam spun around, staring at the ground. As he confirmed what William said, perspiration formed on his forehead. "Dammit, dammit, dammit." Sam's eyes flitted back and forth, and he kept running his fingers through his straight black hair. After a moment, he looked William up and down. "How can you be so calm at a time like this?"

"I feel you carry enough hysteria for the both of us. Hold yourself together, man."

"We're goin' ta die here, in case ye hadn't noticed."

William placed his hands behind his back, straightening his spine. "If we were going to succumb to the fog, it would have happened already. We have been breathing it in since before we landed on the island."

Sam didn't have a response, so instead he paced around in a small circle, making audible groans growing in volume. As the grunts reached a crescendo he covered his face with his hands and wiped vigorously, finishing with a flourish.

"Why did ye join me anyway, mate?"

William arch his brow. "Could you repeat that?"

"Why did you come wit me when ye coulda went wit yer princess? We both know ye don't care fer me none, so why?"

William paused for a moment. "Contrary to what you may believe, I do not hate you. While we may disagree on methods of accomplishing tasks, we are part of the same crew. Camaraderie builds trust, trust keeps us working as a team, and teamwork keeps us alive."

"Do ye hear yerself, mate? Yer such a ninny I can't stand it. Git the stick outta yer butt sometimes, would ye?"

"The fog is touching you."

Sam jumped and circled around frantically until he noticed William grinning on the verge of laughing. "Oh, very funny, ye git. Come on, let's…" Sam paused, peering behind William.

William's gaze was drawn over his shoulder when Sam yelled, "I see a woman!" before rushing past William and towards the figure he'd noticed. William reacted just in time to begin running before Sam disappeared into the mist.

William could not see the woman Sam noticed, and because of the headstart Sam had, he could barely see him. William was fast on his feet, and routinely proved himself to be the most agile amongst the men aboard *Freedom*, but conditions were stacked against him: Thick fog which was becoming denser, Sam's natural agility, distance advantage, and changing his direction, all made William gradually fall behind. No amount of yelling for Sam to slow down helped, and Sam was beginning to disappear. First his arms, then his head, then all William could see was Sam's back.

William leapt into the air and reached for Sam, his fingers inching closer. The white smoke was overtaking Sam's clothes. William gritted his teeth as he fell. His fingers grazed the fold of Sam's tunic, and then William fell to the ground.

The force of falling caused William to close his eyes for a moment, and when he opened them again he was no longer surrounded by fog, and he could see Sam as clear as day in front of him.

William rolled over, rose to his feet, and a brick building greeted his eyes. After glancing about at the whole mansion in front of him, he recognised where they were. "London," William muttered.

Sam turned around, not noticing William before now. "How did we... what's happenin' right now? William? William!" Sam yelled, bringing William out of his stupor.

"This is Kensington Palace. Though I do not know how we have been transported here."

William and Sam examined their surroundings. To their left, a hundred feet away, was the palace itself, a two-and-a-half to three-storey mansion of red brick. The front of the building extended two hundred and fifty feet, and had several annex buildings on the sides going farther back. William noticed that fog surrounded the palace, allowing sight of the gates and perimeter, but not beyond.

"There she is!" Sam pronounced, pointing.

William followed Sam's finger to see a woman glancing about in the same bewildered way as they were. Sam ran towards her, and William followed behind briskly.

With the sound of William's and Sam's footsteps, the woman turned to face them. She had short black hair tied into a bun, with curls spilling down her forehead. Her red cheeks and small facial features could only be described as "dainty." She wore a simple white travelling dress flowing to her ankles.

Her eyes widened at Sam's forceful approach, but before she could back away Sam grabbed her by the arm. "Whut's yer name, woman?"

"What is the meaning of this, gentlemen? Are you part of the King's guard?" the woman asked.

"Answer the question!" Sam demanded.

"Sam, release her!" William said.

"But—"

"But what? What if this is the woman your father seeks? What will you do with her? We are stuck in an unknown area, we do not know how to leave, and we may need her if this occurrence is by design. Whatever you plan on doing, it can wait until we find our way to exit this illusion."

"Tch." Sam threw the woman's arm away.

William turned to the woman. "I apologise for the actions of my comrade, miss."

"Thank you, sir," the woman said with a curtsey. "My name is Theodosia Burr Alston. From your speech to your friend, I judge that you too were unfortunate enough to land on an island covered in fog, and now you find yourself here?"

"Yes, and if you were on the ship known as the *Patriot*, you will know us as the crew of the *Freedom*, which you hit a few days prior."

"Yes, yes, I recall that happening. My apologies for not stopping to introduce ourselves, but we were being chased by pirates, and entered the Bermuda Triangle in an attempt to escape. At first I thought the fog that appeared a blessing, but I fear now it is the opposite." Alston paused for a moment. "Are you with the pirates who were chasing us?" Alston asked Sam.

"No, but my father is the captain. Once we get outta here, I'm takin' ye ta him."

Alston turned to William. "You look to be an upstanding gentleman, so I will tell you this in the hopes you will do the right thing: I am on a diplomatic mission of aid to the United States of America. The ship I travel on carries medical supplies for soldiers."

William considered the woman's words for a moment. 'United States of America' was confusing to William, but he quickly gathered that it represented the North American colonies who were at war with Britain in Dominique's explanation. Alston's position from Dominique's account, however, was not the same. "We were told differently," William said eventually.

"I assure you I am telling the truth, but, as they say, actions speak louder than words. Let us find our way out of here, you can judge my actions until then, and we will see if you believe me trustworthy." Sam snorted, but William and Alston ignored him.

"I have one question which may seem odd but will help with another matter. What year do you believe it to be?"

Alston peered at William queerly. "The year is clearly eighteen-thirteen…" Alston glanced from William to Sam, who in turn looked at each other. "Is it not, gentlemen?"

"Before we delve into that subject, we should examine our surroundings. If this is an illusion, we need to find the source."

"And if it be real?" Sam asked.

Then we have far bigger problems than simply finding our way out of here." William allowed his words to sink in. "This way," he commanded.

William guided the others to the side of the long brick building. Though one would think the home to the royal family would be swarming with guards, the grounds of Kensington Palace were surprisingly empty. Coupled with the fog just in the distance, there was a haunted feel to the mansion.

Despite the emptiness, William was no less cautious in walking about the premises. He stepped behind tall decorative bushes and trees as much as possible and peered out behind them to ensure the coast was clear before venturing further. At two-thirds of the way across the side wall, William approached the wall and touched a specific brick, pushing it into the wall.

The brick being depressed caused a portion of the wall to open, creating an entrance. "Inside," William suggested, pointing the way.

After Alston and Sam entered, William followed and flipped a wooden lever to close the opening behind them. After a moment, their eyes adjusted to the dark interior.

They found themselves in a small, plain corridor with a low ceiling and no windows. Lanterns posted every twenty feet provided soft illumination. The only discerning features were the brick walls and wooden floorboards.

"Where are we?" Sam asked.

"We are in a secret tunnel known only to a close few to the royal family. They are meant to be a way to quickly escape in an emergency. These corridors connect to almost every room in the palace." William grabbed a nearby lantern and began walking through the corridor. "Follow me."

William led the group through long corridors and winding staircases for fifteen minutes. Every so often he opened a door a crack to check if there was anyone in the room, but throughout the whole search they could find no one.

The inside of the tunnels felt unused and smelled of rotting wood and stale air. Cracks showed on the brick walls, and cobwebs found their way inside as well as in each available corner. The sound of scurrying tiny feet, animals running away from their approach, could be heard far in front of them.

When they reached the royal apartments, William could hear noise in the King's bedchambers. He opened the door a small amount, as before, but could not see anything due to the poor angle.

Sam moved up beside William, who was just then lowering the lantern, and Sam knocked it with his knee. The lantern swung forward and hit the secret door, causing a clinking noise.

The three looked at the source of the noise, and their eyes widened. Before they could react, the secret door was flung open. A middle-aged man in military dress stood in front of them.

"William, we've been waiting for you. Come on in, son." The handsome middle-aged man was military advisor to William III, and former First Lord of the Admiralty, Edward Russell. He was also known as one of the immortal seven, who helped convince William III to take the throne through a show of force. He had jet-black hair slicked back, and dark eyes. Though he had been nothing short of jovial when speaking to William, William could not help but think the man a snake in disguise. Edward Russell turned his eyes to the other two next to William. "Who are these people, William?"

William was still in shock, but quickly regained his composure. He knew exactly *when* this illusion was taking place now. "These are friends. May they join us?" he asked with a bow.

"Of course, my boy," Russell said, opening the door wider to allow them entrance. "Oh, but before that, it may be prudent to leave your weapons in here. The King's constitution is on the brink currently, and he could not handle the sight of weapons right now, I'm afraid."

William paused for a moment; he recalled having a similar conversation with Edward Russell in the past. The memory of the fateful day when he failed in his charge rushed back to him, haunting his movements.

"Are you well, William?" Russell asked. "You look pale."

"Fine. Perfectly fine," William said, then he took the sword and pistol from his belt and lay them on the floor of the corridor before entering the King's bedchambers.

Sam reluctantly followed suit in removing his weapons, and gave the man a glare as he passed over the threshold. Alston had no worry of weapons, and entered behind Sam, though with reluctance.

The Voyages of Queen Anne's Revenge

The King's bedchambers were lavishly decorated with red and gold touching all furnishings. At the back of the room in the middle was an extravagant bed with oak canopy, and the King sitting up in it.

William walked over to the King and knelt down next to the bed. After a few seconds, he urgently beckoned the others to join him. Sam and Alston played along and knelt down next to the bed.

The King laughed, which sent him into a fit of coughs. "William, you and your friends may rise. You know you do not have to be so formal."

"Yes, Your Majesty... I just..." William shook his head and rose to his feet. "I would like you to meet Mister Samuel Bellamy, and Miss Theodosia Burr Alston. Though Samuel's appearance is ragged, he is a loyal man, and Miss Alston is a visiting dignitary from the New World colonies. Mister Bellamy, Miss Alston, I present to you King William III of England, Scotland, and Ireland in this year of the lord seventeen-oh-two," William said, staring at the two of them.

"Ah, good, good. Thank you for bringing them personally. Gentlemen, and lady, we welcome you to our house. We apologise for the secrecy, but you can appreciate that for a King to have audiences such as this is not normally possible." Sam and Alston nodded woodenly, causing the King to laugh once more. "Oh dear, our grace has rendered you speechless. Rest assured, you may speak freely and your words will be taken with the strictest confidence. William has apprised you of our inquiry, yes?" the King said with arched brow.

"Yes, Your Majesty. I told my friends here how you wished to know the thoughts of the public on the War of Succession," William said, glancing to Sam and Alston.

"So, Mister Bellamy, may we start with you? You are a London native, yes?" the King asked.

Samuel glanced to William and then to the King, and after wiping sweat from his brow he nodded. "Well, sir, the people are... with the war... they..." Sam trailed off, then shook his head and ran his fingers through his black hair. "Sorry, Your Majesty, I'm gonna just talk as I normally does if it pleases you?"

"By all means. We would not have it any other way," the King replied.

"The people don' care 'bout the war. It be a battle over a title that means nothin' ta them. Tha people only care 'bout gettin' food on the table and hopin the war doesn't make it ta their shores. Sir, kids die in tha street every day from not bein able ta eat, and those with a roof o'er head don' fare much better."

William's fist was in a ball, and his jaw was locked. He expected Sam to be Sam, but not to take it in this direction.

The King nodded. "We suspected as much, but we were not aware the poor was as much a problem as you describe. We thank you for your candour. And you, Miss Alston, how do our western brothers feel about the war?"

Alston jumped when her name was called, but quickly collected herself. "The west is currently with you, Sire. The territories siding with Britain are ready to go to war."

"That is reassuring, but your use of the word 'currently' concerns me. Could you elaborate? Also, we must say your accent is interesting. We did not expect such change over such a short period of time."

Alston peered at William and Sam. They had a dire look in their eyes from Alston's 'currently' slip, as they both recalled Dominique mentioning a war between the North American colonies and Britain in his time.

"Well, Sire, to be perfectly frank, the colonies feel similarly to your people here. It is only whispers currently, but over time those whispers could turn into shouts. Shouts for independence. I have seen first-hand what war does to the young, and the old. I do not know if His Highness has participated in war, but I am sure you can imagine the horror, and the grief on the faces of young widows, sons, fathers, and mothers. None deserve that news. None." Alston's lip quivered, and she wiped tears from her eyes. William was watching her intently.

The King was gazing at his bedsheets in a peculiar way, and after a moment he looked up at the three, then to Edward Russell. Russell nodded, silently answering the King's unspoken question.

"Once again, we thank you both for your honesty. We will take your words to heart in the coming months. May we also be candid with you?" Sam and Alston nodded. "We are planning on speaking with Louis XIV to negotiate peace terms. We acted in anger, starting this foolish war."

"Sire!" William spurted, getting lost in the illusion of his memories.

The King held up his hand. "We speak the truth, William, my boy. The people deserve better than a war built on names and titles and lands. The people deserve a better ruler than one quick to anger. The people deserve peace."

The King's words sent chills up William's spine, and he noticed the others had goose flesh. William was reminded that he saw the man in front of him not as a King, but a man who had faults and loved his people. From the looks on Sam and Alston's faces, he thought they felt the same.

"Now, if you will excuse me, Sir William, Mister Bellamy, Miss Alston, I have more matters that need to be discussed with Mister

Russell." The King gestured to a door to the right of William, and after a bow, William, Sam, and Alston left through the door.

After closing the door behind him, William laid his back against it and let out a sigh. Seeing King William III alive and well, regardless of it being an illusion, was almost too much.

Alston spoke up after a moment. "I believe some explanation is in order."

William slowly opened his eyes and stood up straight. "Yes, you deserve as much after that." William stroked his chin. "As I tried to rush in telling you, the man in there is William III, King of England, Scotland, and Ireland up until the year seventeen-oh-two. This... illusion... seems to be drawn from my memory from six years ago, just before his death."

Alston's eyes widened at the mention of the year. William and Sam gave her a moment. "So, that fog took us to the year seventeen-oh-seven?"

William and Sam nodded, but then Sam glanced to the side. "Wait. What if we were taken to the year eighteen-thirteen?" Sam asked William.

William furrowed his brow and stared at Sam. "You do not really think... No, we can worry about this later. For now, we still need to find our way out of this place."

"I still have more questions, gentlemen."

"Yes, of course."

"As you have not asked me a question regarding my words with your King, I will assume you know of how North America is at war with Britain?"

"Yes, we heard as much from the pirate chasing after you," William replied.

"Then why have you pledged to help me if I am technically against Britain?"

"I am not loyal to Britain. I was loyal to that man," William said, pointing to the King's room. "William III raised me as if I were his own son. I owe him a great deal, and I love him. After my conversation with him, an assassin killed him and framed me for the murder. I am loyal to the one whom I think is fit to wear the crown as William III did: with honour and dignity." William turned to Sam. "I feel that if Anne so chose it, she could lay claim to the throne. Her mother is not fit to rule. If we are in the future, or you, Miss Alston, are from the future, perhaps the reason why our brothers to the west want independence is due to mismanagement by Queen Anne."

Sam laughed heartily. "William, yer so cold. I like this side of you." After another laugh petered out, Sam became inquisitive. "Wait, so who killed the King and frame ye?"

"Over the years, I have wracked my brain trying to find the answer, and I believe it was right in front of me this whole time. The man who opened the secret entrance on us, Edward Russell, is the most likely culprit. I recall him taking my weapon from me before I talked with the King, the same as now, and in my haste I forgot to retrieve it when leaving, as I exited via a different route. When I returned to retrieve my weapon, the King was dead, my sword piercing his heart, and several "eye witnesses" were found to corroborate my involvement." William shook his head. "Right in front of me this whole time."

Sam still had a puzzled look on his face. "How long from when you left the room to when the King was killed, would ye say?"

William gazed at the ceiling as he thought. "I returned after thirty minutes, and he was not far gone, so possibly twenty minutes after I left."

"Well, what are we waitin' fer, then? We may 'ave some time left, so let's get back in there and save him!" Sam yelled, reaching for the door.

William grabbed Sam's hand. "I already told you, this is not real. This has already happened. We are simply watching the events unfold as in my memory."

"I ain't dumb, ye ninny. This ain't jus' yer memory. We weren't here in yer memory, and somehow we 'ad a conversation with his kinglyness. Heck, if ye believe me father and this one 'ere," Sam said, pointing to Alston, "then it ain't such a stretch that this could be real, and we could change things. Even if it wus jus' a chance, don' ye want ta take it?" Sam pleaded.

William paused for a moment to consider Sam's words, and appreciate the fact that the man whom he thought cared the least for him, or anything in general, actually cared a great deal.

"No. Even if this is real, I would not change what has happened." Sam was speechless, but it was clear he had a question on the tip of his tongue. "If I save William III, it will drastically change the course of events in history, and in untold ways. We could be delaying a war perhaps, but what if a larger war erupts because of it?

"The greater reason I will not act is for the sake of Anne and Edward. Anne and Edward will never meet, nor will many of the crew onboard the *Freedom*. I have never seen Anne more happy than on *Freedom*. Also, if Anne or myself were not a part of the crew, Edward would not have been able to survive some of the trials he has faced up until now. I have grown to believe in Edward and feel that he will come to do great things.

"You may think that I treat my position as a job, and I need to relax, but I am the way I am because I love the family that we've built on *Freedom*. I would not risk that for anything in the world."

Sam smirked. "Even me?"

William laughed. "Even you, Sam." *If this is real, I am sorry, my King. I love you, but I've found my family, just as you wanted. I hope that is some solace.*

After a moment, William noticed movement in his peripheral vision. The fog was moving closer to the palace, and at an alarming rate.

"The fog is growing. Quickly, hold hands so whatever happens we are not separated."

The two complied and held fast their hands together. As the fog grew thicker and closer, it seeped in through the windows and doors, eventually filling the room. William, Sam, and Alston closed their eyes as the fog, and silence, overtook them.

When William opened his eyes, he was not on the island again as he thought might happen. He, Sam, and Alston, were now on a ship in the middle of the night. They could see a little boy and a middle-aged man dressed just like Dominique You standing on the port side, gazing out to the stars.

12. THEODOSIA BURR ALSTON

Edward opened his eyes and he was free of the fog on his vision and mind. He could see the island in its entirety, an enormous flatland of grass with nothing special, save the mysteriousness. Edward could also see his crew, and others he did not know, scattered about. Some were waking from their trance just as Edward, and others were still in a daze.

Edward noticed Anne, and he ran to her. He wrapped his arms around her tightly, and she pulled him close.

"I was so worried," Edward whispered.

"As was I," Anne replied. Anne parted from Edward, a look of concern in her eyes. "Are you well? What did you see in the fog?"

Edward shook his head. "It doesn't matter. You?"

"I feel the same. I am simply glad to be back. We should help the crew," Anne stated, glancing about, and then she noticed the shore. "Edward, *Le Pandore* and *Patriot* are gone."

"What?" Edward shouted, turning to the shore. He could see it with his own eyes: *Freedom* was still on the beach, but the other ships had vanished at some point. "I will go to *Freedom* and find out what happened. Could you tend the crew, please?"

"Yes, of course," Anne replied, then she went to work.

Edward ran to the *Freedom* and climbed up a rope ladder to the deck. When he boarded, the crew hastily approached him and bombarded him with questions about his and the others' wellbeing, as well as what happened after the fog caused them to disappear.

"Please, please, I will answer your inquiries later. I have more urgent matters to attend to." The crew heard his tone and gave him space. Edward approached Herbert at the helm. "What happened to Dominique?"

Herbert adjusted his glasses. "After the fog overtook us, the *Patriot* suddenly started attacking *Le Pandore*, then left shore. Dominique took his crew in search of it. That was an hour or so ago."

"Damn it, now how are we to find him? He still has the key."

"Not so." Herbert lifted a key in the air. "Dominique exchanged the key for the paper Benjamin left."

Edward cocked his brow. "What does he plan on doing with Benjamin's riddle?"

"Dominique said Alston won't be able to spy on the Americans in our time, so after they took the *Patriot* back they were planning on following Benjamin's instructions to return to their time and strand Alston here." Herbert tossed the key to Edward. "Should I have stopped him?"

Edward regarded the key warily. *Something about this doesn't feel right.* "We'll see, Herbert."

"So Dominique You told you I am a spy? That could not be further from the truth." A voice sounded from behind Edward.

Edward turned to see a woman with black hair tied into a bun, standing next to Sam, William, and Henry. "Glad to see you're safe, men. And you must be Theodosia Burr Alston, I presume?"

"Yes, you presume correctly."

"So, according to you, what am I to believe?"

Alston curiously glanced to William, who nodded to her. "I am on a mission to bring medical supplies to soldiers at war with Britain. Dominique wanted my ship, and the medical supplies aboard, not me."

"Captain," Sam spoke up. "We dunno who this woman is. Ye can't believe what she says."

Alston had a sad look on her face. "Mister Bellamy, we all saw the same thing back there. Dominique pu—"

"Shut it, you bitch. I won't have you lie about my father. Ye don't know whut ye saw." Sam lifted his hand to strike Alston, but William stopped him.

"Captain, I promise you, Alston is telling the truth. She is an honourable person through and through. If what happened to you on that island was anything similar to what we experienced, you will understand why Sam is acting this way." Sam lowered his fist, but appeared angry and dejected.

Edward considered all that was said, and pondered on how he could solve the riddle of whom he could trust. He smacked the key from Dominique in his hand as he thought, and that was when he had an idea. "Sam, don't let your emotions sway your judgement. We have but one way to prove if he was lying or not." Edward lifted the key up for Sam to see. "Dominique supposedly left us the key we were seeking, so all we have to do is test it out. William, Henry, could you help the crew back to the ship?" William and Henry both nodded and left to complete the order.

Edward travelled to the gun deck of the ship and used the key on the bow cabin, with Sam following behind. The key rattled in the lock, but nothing happened.

Sam's anger subsided, but his disappointment was visible on his face. Edward was disappointed as well, as he too wanted to trust the man Sam held faith in.

Edward and Sam went to the stern of the gun deck, passing all the cannons and spare iron balls, heading to the next locked door, the supposed captain's cabin. Edward attempted to unlock the cabin, but he received the same results. Another nail in the coffin.

Sam let out a sigh, but waved Edward away when he tried to comfort him.

The two continued to the berth deck and tried the key once more on the lock at the bow end, but that door would not open either.

"The key is fake," Edward declared solemnly, turning to Sam.

Sam was broken. His eyes flitted back and forth, like he was trying to find the pieces of himself to bring back together. "No, we… we jus' have to try again. Why would he give us a fake key? There be no point, Captain. No point."

Edward shook Sam's shoulders lightly. "Let's ask Dominique why, shall we?"

Edward turned away from Sam. Sam seemed to still be holding onto the delusion surrounding his father figure, but Edward's mind was made up about the man.

I know Dominique has the real key! Now he's trying to abscond with it and his precious medicine.

Edward marched to the main deck and addressed the crew. The ship was now filled with his crew, as well as the unknown men and a few women from the island, presumably from the *Patriot*. "We are setting sail to chase after *Le Pandore*, men. Dominique tricked us and left us a false key, but I mean to take the real one from him." *If he even has a real key. No! I can't think like that. He must have it. He must.*

The crew was confused at first, but didn't question their leader's guidance and prepared the ship to leave port. Feet stamped quickly across the wooden floorboards and hands stretched the rope ladders as men released the rigging and let loose the sails.

Alston approached Edward, calm as could be. "So, you trust in my words?"

"When we catch up to Dominique we will find the truth of the matter. I will reserve judgement until then."

"I have nothing to fear, my words are true." Alston smiled brightly, with an almost angelic serenity despite the insanity of the situation, her white dress swaying in the wind.

Sam shuffled to the quarterdeck in a daze, his hands shaking, the complete opposite to Alston's calm. "What will we do when we catch up to 'em, Captain?"

Edward stared Sam in the eyes. "We will make Dominique tell us the reason for his actions, and his answer will determine what we will do."

"No." Sam shook his head. "No, this isn't right. I won't let you hurt him!" Sam pulled a pistol on Edward Thatch, pointing it straight at his captain's face.

The crew stopped what they were doing and focused on Sam. The crazed eyes, the pistol drawn. This was unlike the Sam they had known for so long. Gone was the laughter, the blithe attitude towards anything and everything. This wasn't Sam.

"Sam," Edward said, his hands raised, "lower your pistol."

"Why the fuck should I?" Sam replied, teeth gritted, pistol shaking. "You 'ad the good life, Thatch. You never been a kid livin' on the streets in England. Starvin' half the time, eatin' rats and stealing the rest. I took my share of beatings. More'n that, I reckon. I was due for fortune or death, either one, n'then Dominique saved us, Captain. Provided a home and a family when none wanted us. What would you know about havin' it bad?"

Edward slowly lifted his shirt, then pointed to a large misshapen scar on the right of his stomach. "Want to know where I got this, Sam?" Sam didn't reply. "I was a year with my uncle-in-law and his family when this happened. Being me, I was always able to push my uncle-in-law's buttons. My uncle's disposition could have been because of the booze too, but I think he simply wasn't fond of me, because he never beat his own kids, nor his wife. Only me.

"Henry lent me a toy the day I got this scar. I was so happy I couldn't wait to return home and play with the wooden knight. Heaven forbid I should be happy once in a while after my father left me. When my uncle saw me playing with the toy, it set him off something fierce. He picked me up by the neck and slammed me against the iron furnace. My uncle held me there while I screamed, and didn't release me until my aunt ran in and yelled for him to stop. He stopped, but not for good.

"The point is, I know more than you think, and I certainly didn't have a good life.

"When my father left, at first I kept wondering why he left, why he didn't return, why, why, why. Then I was angry at him, so angry I *wished* he was dead like everyone thought. But he's still my father and I love him. If and when I see him again, I'll be able to ask him why, and then his answer will dictate what I do afterwards.

"But I'm not a fool, he may be dead and I might never be able to ask him why. You still have a chance, Sam. Don't let this opportunity go because you're afraid of the answer."

Sam still held the pistol with a trembling hand. He was on the brink.

Alston stepped between Edward and Sam. "Everything will be alright." She stepped closer to Sam. Her caring eyes told a story in themselves, and Sam couldn't look away. "Whatever happens, you will never lose your true family. They will be beside you until the end." Alston stepped closer once more, and embraced Sam.

Sam was paralysed. Frozen from this stranger's action. Sam appeared as if he would crack like glass with the slightest movement. Edward took the pistol from him, lifting him from his catatonic state. Sam collapsed into Alston's arms, but she held him up and carried him away to the lower decks.

Edward stood on the quarterdeck, staring at the pistol. The tension was lifted, but the blow to the crew's morale lingered. The men were concerned for Sam's wellbeing, and likely questioned their next move. If *Freedom* set sail, the crew may be forced to face Sam's father figure in battle.

Edward could understand the general mood aboard the ship, as their feelings were being mimicked in himself. "Set sail, men!" he commanded. "Do not worry for Sam; we will find the truth and set him free," Edward recited, channelling the Pirate Priest Bartholomew Roberts.

The crew accepted Edward's words and returned to work, releasing the rigging and pushing the *Freedom* from the beach and away from the Devil's Island once and for all.

"Where are we heading, Captain?" Herbert asked.

"Back to the origin of the fog, where we first shot the cannons into the night sky. Are you able to return us there without Benjamin's paper?"

"Of course. Without the fog wreaking havoc on us, it will be child's play," Herbert replied with confidence.

Edward chuckled. "Sorry I ever doubted you," he said, patting Herbert on the shoulder.

"Edward?" Anne said, stepping up beside Edward. "Are you well?"

"Yes, I'm well. I can appreciate why Sam did what he did," Edward said, gazing off to the horizon.

"But you feel that Dominique is our enemy now?"

"I hope beyond hope I was correct about the man from the start and he is our ally, but I fear I misjudged."

"I fear we all did," Anne replied.

Edward shook his head. "Not all. Henry saw through the lies, but I chose not to listen." Edward pointed to Henry, hard at work with his fellow crewmates in preparing the ship to leave port.

"And I am sure that will not happen again?"

"Not likely. He and I are destined to butt heads until we die, I'm afraid." Edward chuckled.

Anne grinned at Edward's jest. "Here, let me take the pistol back to storage," she offered, hand extended.

Edward was taken aback as he'd nearly forgotten he still carried the pistol. He handed it to Anne and she walked away, but stopped after a few steps. She inspected the pistol and turned around.

"This is empty, Edward."

"I know," he replied. Anne smiled and left.

Alston returned from the bowels of the ship and rejoined Edward on the quarterdeck. At the same time the sails were lowered and the ship was leaving the island.

"The gentleman has much to think about, but he will be right as a trivet soon, I wager."

"You have my thanks. That was a delicate situation, and I don't think I could have handled it as you did."

"I have seen far worse." Alston peered at the horizon as the ship chopped up and down with the waves. "Young men on the battlefield for the first time panic easily. Seeing their friends and family die, losing limbs, shock is common. Your mate has been through a lot himself. In the fog we…"

Edward held up his hand to stop Alston from continuing. "We all seem to have seen something personal and intimate in that fog. If Sam doesn't want to share what happened, I do not wish to know."

Alston was slightly taken aback, but recovered. "Yes, I should not be so insensitive. I am sorry."

"That is quite alright. Now, could you tell me what your job was in the war if not a spy?"

"Nurse, but in the middle of battle the title can mean many jobs. As I stated earlier, the ship I was on carried medicine for American troops, some of which I would have personally delivered to the frontlines. Now, because of Dominique, many could lose their lives from rot and disease." Alston's gaze moved to the waist.

Edward felt hot with anger. This was his mistake, his blunder. Edward would ensure Dominique would be caught and pay for what he did.

"You were told my name, but I never received yours, sir."

Edward laughed. "My name is Edward Thatch, and I am no sir. Truly, you may think no better of us than Dominique. We are also pirates. People have taken to calling me Blackbeard these days, for obvious reasons."

At the last name, Alston's eyes widened.

"What?" Edward asked. "You know me… from the future?"

Alston nodded, her eyes soft again. "Your cognomen is well known. Truth be told, you were known to be an evil man who inspired fear in many."

Edward chuckled. "And what do you think?"

Alston considered Edward for a moment. "I believe your enemies would fear you greatly, but in your eyes I see you care deeply for your men, and they you. William is a testament to your character. You are not evil."

"Thank you."

"Would you enjoy hearing of some of your exploits?"

Edward laughed. "Perhaps it is better I don't. None should know their future. It removes a level of choice to the affair."

"True. And the ability to choose is *Freedom*, after all," Alston said with a smile.

Edward returned the smile, then focused his attention on guiding the ship again. "Ten points to starboard. Close-haul those sails, men, we've a ship to catch!" he yelled.

As the hours passed and approached the fated time of one o'clock, fortune seemed to favour the *Freedom* and its crew. The wind pushed them faster than ever, and from Herbert's approximation it had only started after *Le Pandore* had already arrived at their destination.

Herbert, hands on the ship's wheel, glancing to Edward and across the bow, spoke with confidence. "If Dominique's goal is to return to his time, then *Le Pandore* has been waiting in the same spot for one o'clock. The advantage they had in speed and the headstart are meaningless now."

The Voyages of Queen Anne's Revenge

Just as one o'clock approached, the crew of the *Freedom* could see *Le Pandore* on the horizon. Edward watched through a spyglass as the *Freedom* approached. He could see smoke erupt from the side of the ship, then after a few seconds the sound of cannons rushed to his ears.

Edward watched for fog, but none came. Either by a mistake on the crew of *Le Pandore*'s part, or by providence, Dominique was stuck in this time.

Freedom quickly approached the enemy ship, and *Le Pandore* turned around to let loose its cannons again, this time aiming for *Freedom*.

Edward took a moment to appreciate his mistake. Alston had been telling the truth. Edward eyed Sam, who held a defeated expression on his face.

Edward felt Sam was unable to fight, having grown up with the people they were about to fight against.

Edward approached him. "Sam, go to the crew cabin. You aren't fit to fight."

Sam was ready to object, but Edward's eyes silenced any questions.

"Herbert, bring us next to *Le Pandore*. I don't want her escaping."

"Aye, Captain," Herbert replied.

"Prepare to board, men. It's time to fight!"

As if reading Edward's mind, *Le Pandore* opened her sails in an attempt to leave. Before she was able to move an inch, the *Freedom* caught up and sent grappling lines over. The crew of the *Freedom* tied the lines down, securing the two ships together.

"Attack!" Edward yelled as he jumped the gap between the two ships.

Edward landed on the waist, with his crew joining him after. One of Dominique's men attacked Edward with a knife aimed at his face. Edward swayed to the left and punched the man hard. The man fell to the deck, the back of his head hitting dead-on, knocking him unconscious.

Unequalled rage filled Edward. Edward was back to his old form, his broken arm now healed, muscles taut, and well-fed, he was a force to be reckoned with once more. Edward had placed smoking wick in his beard before the battle, and the light of the moon reflected on the smoke, making him appear otherworldly.

Edward rushed after Dominique, cutting down foes on his way to the Frenchman. A shot here, a stab there. The crew of *Le Pandore* tried to defend their captain, but each fire was a miss, and each cut was deflected.

Dominique, seeing Edward advancing on him, descended into the lower regions of the ship. "Come back here, Dominique!" Edward yelled as he followed the man into the depths.

On the waist of the *Freedom*, William defended against counter-boarders. One man jumped over, standing precariously on top of the railing. William upended his legs. The man fell, hitting his head on the side of the ship before landing in the water. Several others made an attempt to cross, only to be stopped by William.

John showed his normal prowess in battle on the *Freedom*'s poop deck. John noticed an enemy heading towards Anne. He shot his musket at the enemy's back, killing him before he could even get close to Anne. In front of John another man touched down, ready to fire a blunderbuss. John grabbed onto the blunderbuss and the two fought for control of the weapon. John kicked the enemy in the nether regions, causing him to loosen his grip. John took the weapon, and shot point blank into the man's face. The man died instantly, his head a red mess, blood pooling beneath him where he fell.

Pukuh took the fight onto the enemy ship. One man aimed a pistol at him, but Pukuh threw a knife into the barrel. The man fired and the pistol exploded, useless. Pukuh kneed the man in the chest, knocking the wind out of him. A second charged with a sword. Pukuh kicked the man's sword into the air, then stabbed him with his spear.

Henry and Anne, in a rare display of camaraderie, fought back to back. Anne fought with her eastern fighting style, and Henry with his fists. Men attacked the two left and right on the bow of *Le Pandore*.

On the left, a man attacked Henry with a sword while another struck with a kick. Anne grabbed the first man's sword arm, holding him. Henry stopped the second man's kick and punched him in the face. Anne struggled with the first man's sword. Henry turned and punched the man with the sword in the chest causing him to double over. Anne took the loose sword and stabbed the man who'd tried to kick Henry in the chest.

Christina was only suited to use knives at her current level of strength. She stayed on the *Freedom* repelling invaders. Anne had taught Christina several weak points on the human body, and to apply her weight to her strikes. Men jumped over to the *Freedom* and she swiftly cut their Achilles tendons or the backs of their knees while other crew members finished them off. Christina's anger seethed as she fought, allowing her temporary reprieve from the blood and gore around her.

Edward, now in the bowels of *Le Pandore*, couldn't see two inches in front of his face. The darkness of night combined with the dark interior of the ship caught Edward off guard. His eyes were trying to adjust to the dark, with little success.

My only hope is that Dominique is at the same disadvantage.

A flash of moonlight reflected into Edward's eyes. He ducked down as a blade passed over his head and lodged into the wood of the ship. The owner didn't bother retrieving the blade and ran.

Edward advanced slowly, his sword poised in front of him. He could hear the sounds of battle above, and cannons firing nearby. To his right, he could see sparks flying from the gunpowder as the gunners fired their muskets at the *Freedom*. With each musket blast Edward caught a glimpse of the surroundings. Bullets from the *Freedom* broke through *Le Pandore*, letting in some pale light, but not enough to see by.

With each flash of light, Edward thought he could see the shadow of Dominique moving through the ship. Edward's eyes were slowly adjusting and he could see better with each passing second, but not well enough.

Someone attacked him with a sword. Edward deflected the blow and countered, but missed. The enemy blade flashed forward, nicking Edward in the stomach. He swiped his blade across, cutting the person's arms. The blade dropped as the man screamed, but the sound was drowned out by the surrounding din. Edward thrust his blade in the direction of the screams, hitting something solid.

He examined the body. *Not Dominique.*

To starboard Edward could see the faint light of a lantern. It was of little use in this darkness, but Edward picked it up regardless and an idea sparked. He tossed the lantern to the ground and the oil leaked out, starting a blaze which would soon threaten the whole ship. Edward ran forward to another lantern affixed to the main mast in the middle of the gun deck. He once more threw the lantern to the ground, starting another fire. Edward kept doing this until a good portion of the deck was ablaze.

Now able to see clearly, Edward searched for the Captain of *Le Pandore*. He could see men abandoning their stations to stop the fires. The sounds of fighting still filled the area, now mixed with the crackling of the fire. Edward noticed a door at the stern, which, he surmised, led to the captain's cabin.

Edward entered the cabin. The barrel of a pistol was pointed straight at Edward. Dominique pulled the trigger as Edward's instincts made him drop to the floor. The bullet flew over Edward's head. Dominique ran forward, stamped his feet on each of Edward's arms, and pinned him with a sword in his face.

"You couldn't leave well enough alone, could you?" Dominique sneered.

"I need the key, bastard," Edward replied.

"Then consider this all part of the test. You've done well so far, but if you want the key you'll have to kill me first!" Dominique noticed the fires licking at the bow and looked up.

"That can be obliged!" Edward snarled as he kneed Dominique's nether regions. Dominique's power left him, and Edward was able to free his arms. He slashed at the back of Dominique's leg.

Dominique fell. Edward pushed himself back through the doorway and rose from the floor. The fire was filling the area with smoke and crackling sounds as the flames inched closer and closer to the stores of gunpowder.

Dominique stumbled to his feet, and, using his sword like a cane, closed the doors of his cabin. Edward ran and kicked down the door. Dominique had opened a starboard window and was climbing to the outside of the ship. Edward ran and slashed at his feet, but missed by a hair.

Edward sheathed his cutlass and followed the fleeing man through the window. He saw Dominique climbing the stern and quickly followed, using the window edges to prop his feet, and the rigging rope for grip.

When Edward reached the gunwales, a crewman of Dominique's pointed a pistol at Edward. He grabbed the man's arm and pulled him overboard. The man screamed and tried to grab Edward and pull him down, but gripped only air as he plummeted past.

Edward saw Captain Dominique heading down to the waist of his ship, still using his sword as a crutch. The deck was absorbing the fire from below and would soon be ablaze as well.

Edward ran and jumped high in the air, landing both feet on Dominique's back. Dominique fell to the floor with a groan and rolled from the blow. He tried to rise, but he was weak from his injuries.

Edward grabbed Dominique by the coat, dragging him to the port side. Because of the rapidly spreading fire across the ship, many in the crew abandoned fighting, and indeed the ship itself.

"Lay down a gangplank," Edward commanded.

Pukuh covered Edward's back. "Your labour has borne fruit, brother!" he said over his shoulder.

"Aye, this battle is over. Their ship will be lost to fire soon. Make sure our crew are returned safely."

"You may count on me," Pukuh replied with confidence.

A gangplank was dropped across the two ships, allowing Edward to bring Dominique across to the *Freedom*. After finishing their respective fights, *Freedom*'s crew returned to their home by jumping over or traversing the gangplank. The crew of *Le Pandore* were no threat to the *Freedom* anymore.

In short order, the fire started on the gun deck of *Le Pandore* reached the waist, and was burning the ship apart. Bowlines burned, the sails caught fire, and the wooden boards broke as they were turned to ash by the blaze. Explosions boomed from the gunpowder on the gun deck, spreading the fire further and blowing apart the wood. Soon the flames would reach the hold, where the bulk of the gunpowder lay, and would blast the keel apart.

Edward threw Dominique to *Freedom*'s deck, then ordered the crew to cut the lines once everyone was safely over. Herbert eased the *Freedom* over to the *Patriot*. The remainder of *Le Pandore*'s crew surrendered, having seen the battle on their flagship.

The original crew of the *Patriot* boarded to man it once more and *Le Pandore*'s crew were tied up. Edward was able to see the medical supplies in the lower deck of the *Patriot*, once more confirming Alston's story.

Time to finish this.

Edward returned to Dominique, who was on his knees on the waist of the *Freedom*, his hands tied behind his back. "Where is Sam?" Edward asked, but no one answered. "Someone get Sam." One of the crew went below deck to fetch Sam.

"So, what now?" Dominique asked calmly.

"Well, we'll kill you. I thought that rather obvious. But first..." Edward sauntered over to Dominique and rifled through his pockets until he found what he was searching for: The key to the next part of the *Freedom*, and the paper holding the old clue.

Dominique smiled crookedly. "Congratulations. The pawn advances once more. Benjamin always knew how to pick them."

Edward cocked his brow. "What do you mean?"

"You think you're the first? You are just another player in one of Benjamin's games."

Edward's mouth was a line, and his eyes cold. "You're wrong."

Dominique cackled with genuine mirth. "And what makes you think you're not, eh?"

Edward kept a calm face while Dominique continued to laugh. When Dominique stopped due to the stares sent his way, Edward replied, "Because, we're fighting against Benjamin, and..." Edward grabbed Dominique by the neck and held him up in the air. "I'm the King." Edward dropped Dominique and he fell in a heap.

Sam was brought up to the main deck by one of the crew. His hair was dishevelled and his eyes baggy. He ambled over to Edward, in front of Dominique.

"Sam, my son. Let me out of these bonds. Help me. Am I not your father?"

"I saw…" Sam stated softly.

"Saw what?" Dominique asked.

Sam stared into his father's eyes. "I saw the day I wus lost at sea in an illusion on that island. I didn't want ta believe it, but I remember now. Someone pushed me into the Devil's Sea, and only you and I wus on deck tha' night, Dom."

Edward handed Sam a pistol. Sam pointed the pistol with shaking hands at the captain he'd considered a father.

Dominique chuckled. "You think I pushed you? You were a child, you experienced a traumatic event. You aren't remembering correctly."

"I remember perfectly!" Sam yelled. "I jus' want to know why."

Dominique smirked. "A privateer ship is not fit for a kid, but look at you now, you're a strapping young lad. Together, we could rule these seas. What do you sa—"

"Enough!" Sam yelled, and then he pulled the trigger.

The sound of the gun travelled across the ship and out to the ocean, piercing the ears of the three crews present. The wind blew the smoke away as the pistol fell to Sam's side, and the body of Dominique You fell to the deck of the *Freedom*.

Sam walked sullenly back to the crew cabin to rest. The crew watched him as he stepped sluggishly down the stairs and disappeared below deck.

Edward picked up Dominique's body, walked to the edge of *Freedom*, and threw him overboard. It fell with a splash and floated off into the waters of the Triangle.

"Bind the rest of Dominique's crew, and move them to the *Patriot*," Edward commanded, then went to test the new key.

The two doors on the gun deck didn't open, so the key had to open the door in the crew's quarters. The berth deck, the lowest deck before the hold, was lined stem to stern with beds and hammocks for the crew. On the stern, past the crew quarters, was the mess hall and kitchen. On the bow was a locked door, which opened with the key from Dominique.

Fifteen members of the crew gathered to see the mystery room being opened, excited to see the outcome of what the riddle and fighting had brought them. The crew was rather disappointed with the results, however.

The room was a simple brig, a prison aboard the ship for holding prisoners of war or punishing crewmates. The front part of the brig was an open area with some chairs bolted to the floorboards and the remaining two-thirds separated by large iron bars extending the height of the room. The brig itself held a long iron slab for laying or sitting on, but nothing else. All in all a bit disheartening, given the previous treasures left by Benjamin in other rooms.

The crew behind Edward groaned audibly, making Edward laugh. "Come now, we only have two more keys to acquire and we've unlocked the whole ship. Besides, a brig could be useful in the future." Edward's words cheered some of them up.

"Captain, look!" one of the crewmates said, pointing to something on the wall in the brig.

Edward turned and noticed a piece of paper stuck to the wall. *That must be the next clue.* Edward entered the brig and retrieved the square paper. As he grabbed the paper, the door was closed and locked behind him.

The crew laughed and pointed. "In jail again, Captain. Whatever will you do?" one of them jested.

"Har har, very funny. Now please open the door," Edward requested.

The crew stopped laughing and searched for a key, but couldn't find one. "There ain't no key, Captain."

After Edward panicked for a moment, he pulled out the key that opened the door to the brig, then tested it on the ship's prison door. The door opened with a click and Edward was able to leave. The crew let out a sigh of relief and apologised for the jest. "No harm done, mates." Edward tossed the key to one of the crew members. "Take the key to John, he'll want to put it with the others."

"Aye Captain." The crew quickly dispersed as Edward ambled to the main deck while reading the next clue.

In the Gulf the North East Triangles Point the Way.
Four points, four points, three points, three points.
Undo and See.

I didn't think it was possible for these to make less sense. Edward turned the paper over, and found a map on the back. It had no names of countries or landmarks, but even Edward, with his limited knowledge of maps, could see the image of the Gulf of Mexico. *Well, at least we know which Gulf the clue mentions.*

When Edward reached the top once more, Theodosia Burr Alston was waiting for him.

"I am told I cannot return to my time, or perhaps it is you who are not able to return to your time. Is this true?" Alston asked, a distressed expression on her face.

"I do not know. We will try to recreate the events of our meeting tomorrow night. For now I think we should sleep."

Alston nodded. "Yes, you are correct, sir. I hope it works; the soldiers need those supplies, or you may need to return home." Alston studied the crew of the *Freedom*, battle-weary and tending to their injuries. "But, perhaps, the greater need is here," she muttered to herself.

Before Edward could question what Alston was thinking, she rushed across a gangplank to the *Patriot* to talk with the crew. Before long she returned with several women and some of the medicine and bandages from her ship.

"Miss Alston, this is too much. You need these supplies more than we do."

"Nonsense. These men were injured recovering these supplies. A portion belongs to you by rights."

Edward frowned. "I fought Dominique for my own reasons, and we wronged you. If anything, we owe you…"

Alston raised her hand, silencing Edward. "Before entering the fog, Dominique was upon us. The fog, and your ship as distraction, allowed us to escape. Inadvertently, you aided us, so let us say we are even."

Edward paused for a moment, a smile on his face. "Deal."

The following morning, the crews of the *Freedom* and *Patriot* rested, and in the afternoon shared dinner together on the *Freedom*. Edward made a rule that none were to ask anything about the future, and the crew of the *Patriot* would not tell anything of the past. The only one who needed to hold back was Alston, being the most learned of the group, and unfortunately she was not able to keep her promise.

During the night, a few hours before the appointed time in the morning, Alston secretly approached Anne on the waist.

"Miss Bonney, may I bother you for a moment?"

"Yes, of course. What do you need?"

"I must tell you something of dire import. I cannot tell the details, but if you wish your lover to stay alive, you must keep him from Ocracoke Island and Charleston after this."

Anne was shocked, and couldn't help but ask more. "What happens there?"

"As I said, I cannot tell you."

"Why are you telling *me* this?"

"I owe you and your crew my life. And if you tell a man not to do something for fear of his life being in danger, they tend to rush headlong into peril to spite," Alston said with a smirk.

Anne grinned as well, but when Alston started to leave, Anne stopped her. "I must ask you another question, which will seem odd, but I need to know the answer."

"I will do my best to answer," Alston replied.

"What happens to Queen Anne?"

Alston eyed Anne suspiciously. "Why do you wish to know about Queen Anne?" Alston shook her head. "No matter, if you have any connection to her, telling you anything would be dangerous."

"Please, I must know," Anne begged.

Alston frowned. "I will tell you only this. The Queen began acting strangely after her daughter's death by pirates. The Queen later died under suspicious circumstances after an attack on England. George I succeeded her."

Anne was troubled by more than one thing Alston mentioned. "When does all this happen?"

"I am sorry, I will not provide dates. I've told you too much already."

Anne nodded and let Alston leave. Questions swarmed Anne's head, too many to make sense of. Alston could never guess Anne Bonney was actually Anne Sofia Stewart, daughter to the Queen, and the knowledge that her mother would be killed weighed heavily on her heart and mind.

As one o'clock approached, Edward had the crews separate and say their goodbyes in case they were able to recreate the event of a few days prior. Herbert guided the crew once again in lining up the cannons perfectly, and the crew shot precisely when the moon hit the time of one o'clock.

The cannonballs disappeared as they did before, and fog appeared suddenly, filling the night air. In mere moments to fog was so thick they could barely see the *Patriot* a hundred feet from them.

"Alston!" Edward yelled. All Edward received back was a muffled reply. "Alston, can you hear me?" Edward screamed.

Edward heard a thunk beside him on the deck, and noticed a crewmate had fallen unconscious. Edward took a step, but his knees became weak and buckled underneath him. He was kneeling on the deck, and becoming increasingly sleepy. Edward peered across the ship and noticed everyone aboard falling unconscious from the fog. Before long, Edward could not keep his eyes open, and he too fell to the deck with a thud, the world going black.

...

Edward awoke with a pounding headache. With great effort he sat up. Edward regained his senses slowly and remembered what happened.

Edward pulled himself to his feet and searched the horizon, but couldn't see another ship anywhere. The *Patriot* was no longer.

Edward walked to Herbert at the helm, and had to grip the railing to keep himself upright. "Herbert, did you manage to stay awake?"

"No, Captain. I don't think anyone did."

Henry, John, and Anne walked up to the quarterdeck. The crew were waking up one by one and talking amongst themselves, speculating on what had happened.

Edward, Henry, John, and Anne also discussed what might have happened, with no solid theories presenting themselves. Eventually, when the crew became restless and concerned over the event, the four agreed on a course of action, even if it was not the best way to deal with the situation.

Edward addressed the crew. "Men, I know what has just happened must have you questioning a lot of things, but we will not find answers to the questions we seek. Whatever happened, whatever the cause, it is over now. The senior crewmates feel that the best we can do is leave the Triangle as quickly as possible and move on."

Cries from the crew swarmed Edward. "What about what happened on the island?" "Was those crew from the future?" "What caused all the fog?"

Edward soon had enough. "Silence, men!" he bellowed. The crew went quiet, and Edward sighed. "I am sorry, I cannot answer your questions, no one can, and that is why I think it best that we forget about it for now. Whatever caused the fog and made the island appear is still out there, and we are in danger every second we remain in the Devil's Triangle.

"Each of us had an experience like none other on that island. I am not saying we cannot discuss what happened, but for now we have to leave here."

Edward's words calmed the crew, and they seemed to understand what he was saying, but curiosity still stopped them in their tracks.

"It was an illusion," one of the crewmates said. Edward looked to the source and saw Sam there. Sam glanced at the crewmates gathered about. "What 'appened here wasn't real. The time travel, the island, the fog, it wus all in our heads. I wus tricked as a young pup into believin' this fantasy 'bout another time." Sam stared at Edward, and Edward smiled.

One crewmate scratched his head. "But whut 'bout the key?" he asked Sam.

"Shut it!" Sam hollered. "Now back to work."

The crew shrugged their shoulders and went back to their stations, unfurled the sails, and worked to bring the ship out of the Bermuda Triangle.

Sam winked to Edward, and Edward laughed.

"Do you think the crew will accept that?" Anne asked.

"Since it came from Sam, I think it will do for now. At least we are on our way out of here," Edward replied.

"Agreed."

The crew did not speak of the events in the Bermuda Triangle that day, but it became a hotly debated topic in the mess hall. None could really say whether what happened was real or not, and they would never find out. However, all could agree that entering the Bermuda Triangle was not something done lightly, if at all.

13. THE CURE

"So Captain, where are we headed?" Herbert inquired.

A few days had passed since the events in the Bermuda Triangle, and the *Freedom* had just left the area. Focus had been on the shortest distance rather than a solid direction, and so there had not been a discussion on where to go next until now.

"We're short on crew, are we not?" Edward asked, and fortunately John was coming up the stairs to the quarterdeck to be able to answer.

"Y-yes Captain, we are rather short. We have about one hundred and fifty to one hundred and sixty."

"How many should we have?"

"Two hundred and ten should do, Captain," John declared with uncommon confidence. He knew his numbers, and Edward trusted his judgement.

"Any ideas on where we can acquire some crew members, Herbert?"

"The closest would be Bodden Town. Not only would we be able to stock up and receive funds from our benefactors there, but Alexandre is supposed to be there as well."

"Let's head to Bodden Town, then. Can you take a look at this, Herbert?" Edward handed the paper containing the clue to the next key for *Freedom*.

Herbert examined the riddle in detail, along with the map on the back. "I am sure you uncovered that the map shows the Gulf of Mexico?"

"Yes, that part was easy," Edward replied.

"Well, the next location is probably in the north east of the Gulf itself from the paper's meaning, and these triangles must point to a more exact location."

"Good, good. Anything else?"

"That's all I have for now, but I will ponder the riddle. You might want Christina to inspect the paper. She was swift in uncovering the previous riddle."

"Yes, I planned to," Edward said.

The Voyages of Queen Anne's Revenge

After Edward and Herbert's discussion concluded, Sam descended a ratline to the quarterdeck. A week had passed since the fight with Sam's less-than-adequate guardian, and he appeared in better spirits.

"Hello Sam, how are you holding up?"

Sam brushed Edward off immediately. "I be fine, and I don't need yer pity."

Edward glanced at Herbert. "Well, sorry for asking."

Sam was exasperated. "A week ago I killed a man who might have been from over a hundred years in the future who I considered me father. How do ye think any would feel?"

Edward scratched his head. "Well, when you put it that way…"

"Ah, I'll be fine. The bastard had it coming," Sam said, with a spit to the floorboards.

"This event has made me question the nature of your true father."

"Never knew 'im. I think 'e wus from this time."

"How do you know?" Edward asked.

"Jus' a hunch," Sam replied, with no further explanation. His gaze turned to the bow deck. Anne and Christina were sparring. "Lookit them go," he said admiringly.

Edward watched as well. The two women were graceful and deadly in their dance. Christina was a quick learner, but Anne possessed years of experience and training.

Edward remembered Anne's concern over the anger Christina displayed during their training, and Anne was teaching Christina to meditate and keep a calm and level head. Christina had had difficulty at first, and often lost focus when sparring.

Edward, looking at Christina now, thought she was doing much better. *The true test will be when we face marines again. She will have a harder time holding back then.*

But now Edward noticed something off. Anne was slowing down and breathing heavily. She abruptly cut the match short and made her way to the berth deck to rest.

Edward approached Anne to see what was wrong. "Anne, are you well?"

She waved her hand in dismissal, a habit picked up from Henry. "Don't be silly, Edward. I'm fine, I am merely tired from all the recent fighting and the hot sun and I need rest. Now leave me be."

"Alright." Edward stepped aside. Anne continued to walk slowly to the stairs nearby on the starboard side.

Christina wandered to Edward's side. "Is she well?"

"I don't know. What have you observed?" Edward asked, watching Anne.

"She's been progressively slowing and cutting off our sparring more frequently as of late. I didn't pay Anne's condition any heed until recently. She's been sweating more, which isn't normal for the level of exertion she's used to, and today her hands and legs were shaking. See?" Christina pointed to Anne as she was descending the stairs.

Edward noticed Anne's legs were wobbly as she stepped down the stairs to the next deck. Before he could comment, Anne disappeared with a series of thuds.

"Anne!" Edward yelled, drawing the crew's attention

Edward ran down the stairs to the unresponsive Anne. Edward checked her breathing and the pulse on her neck and forearm as Alexandre once showed him. Christina was beside Edward, and the crew were concernedly watching on.

"Is she well?" Christina asked, panic fringing her voice.

"She is breathing and her pulse is normal, albeit elevated." Edward examined Anne. "She has some bruises and scrapes from the fall, but as far as I can tell nothing serious." Edward picked Anne up, took her down to the crew's quarters and lay her on a bed.

With Christina's help, Edward removed Anne's vest and rolled up her shirt sleeves to let cool air reach her body. Christina let out a cry of shock. "What?" Edward asked. Christina pointed to Anne's upper left arm, her bicep, which was red with purple bumps oozing pus.

"Anne must have been shot in the battle against Dominique. The wound must have gotten infected. Oh Anne! Why didn't you tell me? Stubborn woman!"

"You two are perfect for each other," Christina said.

Edward saw Christina's expression change from a frown to a grin. He smiled back. "Yes, we are quite a pair." Edward rose. "I will tell your brother to make haste to Bodden Town. We need our friend the doctor."

...

"Nose: stuffed," Alexandre said aloud, making a mental note. While looking in a mirror, he wiggled his nose, wrinkles drawing creases around his eyes. Alexandre poked and massaged the area around his eyes and face. "Redness and pressure on the eyes and forehead." He then took a deep breath, as best he could. "Difficulty breathing."

He continued to breathe heavily in the silence until there was a knock at his door. "*Entrer.*"

The door opened to reveal Edward Thatch and Henry Morgan. Upon entering, their jaws opened slightly and they frowned.

"What in God's name are you doing?" Edward asked.

Alexandre was hanging from the ceiling of his apartment by a rope tied to his legs. "I am performing a simple experiment." His body dangled slightly back and forth as Alexandre moved and gestured while he talked.

Edward sighed. "We don't have time for this. Henry, cut him down."

Henry nodded and went to find a chair to stand on. After procuring one he went about the task.

"We need you on the ship. Anne is sick."

"Well, it certainly took you long enough, *messieurs*. I was beginning to grow bored," Alexandre said, his stuffed nose mixing with his accent to cause his voice to take on an odd tone.

Henry shook his head as he sliced through the twined fibres. "And we wouldn't want that, now would we?" Henry made one last cut, and Alexandre's legs were free.

Alexandre fell to the floor of his apartment, rose slowly and shook his head. "*Merci.*" He went to the back of the room and grabbed two small bags, and then walked to the door. "Come now, *messieurs*. We have a patient to help."

Alexandre couldn't suppress a small grin at the corner of his lips, which Edward and Henry noticed. The two also grinned, shrugged their shoulders, and took their friend back to the *Freedom*.

...

"Hmm." Alexandre examined the wound on Anne's bicep. After a thorough examination he said, "I believe she has an infection."

Edward rubbed his face in exasperation. "You observations are as astute as always, Alexandre."

"A simple *blague mon Capitaine*. I know how lesser minds sometimes enjoy humour to ease the seriousness of an issue."

"I appreciate the attempt."

"Well, we can cure Anne, this much is certain. She has been fighting the infection too long, and it has spread too much as a result. If we do not cure her soon she may die." Alexandre delivered the news as if he was reading the newspaper.

Edward's eyes bulged and his jaw dropped. Christina gasped and gripped Edward's hand, probably more for her own benefit than his. "You know of a cure, yes? We can save Anne, can we not, Alexandre?" Edward pleaded.

"Bring the Mayan, would you? I need his assistance." Edward asked a crewmate, who then ran off to find Pukuh. Alexandre pointed to John. "John, here." John jumped at the pointed finger, but stepped closer to the surgeon. After Alexandre wrote something on a piece of paper, he handed it to John. "I need you to return to my abode and retrieve a bottle of elixir with this name." John nodded and made his way up the stairs of the swaying ship.

Pukuh stepped into the crew quarters and to the foot of Anne's bed. "Yes, witchdoctor?" Pukuh questioned.

Alexandre sketched a picture of a leaf and seed and showed it to Pukuh. "Are you familiar with this plant?" Alexandre asked.

"Yes, this plant we use in my village for food and medicine."

"We need the plant, Mayan. Tell Herbert to take us to your village." Pukuh nodded, not insulted by Alexandre, and left to tell Herbert the course.

"So the plant will cure Anne?" Edward asked for reassurance.

"Yes, if we procure some soon. Anne is strong, *Capitaine*, she will not succumb to this so easily."

"I know. She's too stubborn for that."

Over the next week, Edward spent the majority of his time with Anne. He was either trying to keep her cool during the day, warm during the night, or still when fever dreams gripped her. In the rare moments when Anne was awake and lucid, Edward talked with her about where the *Freedom* was headed. At first, Anne was able to reply with relative lucidity, but after a few days she was in a constant haze.

The crew visited to check on Anne and on how the Captain was holding up from time to time. Edward didn't eat, and drank only when he was helping Anne to drink. Twice a day Alexandre applied the salve John retrieved from his house in Bodden Town, cleaned the wound, and replaced the bandages. Pukuh prayed daily for Anne. John read the news from Bodden Town from the past weeks. Herbert told of the weather and condition of the *Freedom*, as well as some bad fishing jokes he said Anne always laughed at. "She was probably humouring me more than I her," he told Edward. Henry brought food and drink, and forced Edward to eat as best as he could force Edward to do anything.

The crew took shifts to keep sailing through the night instead of dropping anchor. Christina and Herbert took shifts commanding the helm, with Herbert taking the night and Christina taking the morning. Christina fought Herbert for the night shift, but he insisted on the night due to it being more difficult, and she eventually complied.

The night before *Freedom* arrived at Pukuh's village, Anne was asleep soundly for once, and Edward was ready to join her. He was kneeling down, his hand holding hers, resting his upper body on the bed.

"You can't leave me, Anne, not now. As your captain I order you not to die." Edward closed his eyes, and he could have sworn he heard Anne say, "Aye, aye" before he dozed off, exhausted.

Christina happened upon Edward when he started talking with Anne. Christina watched the scene and delivered the "Aye, aye," posing as Anne. After Edward lay asleep, Christina draped a spare blanket over him.

The next morning, Edward awoke with the blanket lying on the floor of the ship, the cold air hitting him. He took the blanket, trying to remember when he had gotten it, and covered Anne's sleeping body. Edward kissed Anne's forehead, told her he would be back, and walked up the stairs to the top deck where the night crew was still busy, wearily furling the sails.

The ship landed on the familiar shore Edward once descended on to retrieve the gun deck's key. The last time, Edward had met with Pukuh's family and the village he called home, quite possibly one of the last Mayan settlements still in existence. Pukuh had joined Edward to learn about the world and return a better warrior, and a better king, so he could follow in his father's footsteps.

Pukuh was on the waist and had a few bags packed with supplies. Pukuh and Edward had earlier agreed that only the two of them would need to go. Too many would slow them down and they weren't there for pleasure. Alexandre recommended not taking Anne along as stress could agitate her condition.

Edward noticed one more bag than there should have been. "What's in the third bag?" he asked Pukuh.

"That is for the little girl. She claimed you allowed her to join us," Pukuh replied.

Little girl? "Do you mean Christina?" Pukuh nodded his head. "Well, she was lying, I said no such thing."

Pukuh smiled. "Hmm, interesting."

Christina sauntered up to the waist and joined Edward and Pukuh. "Good morning, Captain."

"You can't join us," Edward asserted flatly before Christina could even ask.

"What? Why?"

"You'll slow us down," Edward replied, slinging a pack of supplies over his back.

"I promise I won't. Or at least, I won't slow you down as much as you will."

Edward raised his brow. "What was that?"

"We've been a few months at sea, but you're nowhere near the strength you were before being imprisoned. I know I could keep up with you in your state."

Edward laughed. "I see what you're trying to do. You can't goad me into letting you come to satisfy my pride." Edward threw a rope ladder over the port side.

"I want to help, Edward. I care for Anne too." Christina pleaded softly, all eyes on the pair.

Edward gazed at those sky-blue eyes, then to the crew, then back. He let out a sigh, then turned to Herbert. "Herbert?" he asked.

Herbert shrugged. "If she wants to join you, I don't see the harm. You are just collecting a plant, after all."

Edward folded his arms, internally debating some more while eyeing Christina. "Alright, hurry up," he ordered at last, waving his hand. Christina gathered her pack and joined them at the starboard railing. Edward pointed his finger at Christina sternly. "You had better not slow us down," he warned.

"I won't," she promised.

The three descended to the sandy beach below, moved up an incline, and into a forest of Caribbean pines. Once in the forest, a natural path with little vegetation could be followed most of the way. The tall pines rose around them and created a canopy blocking the sun. The sounds of animals created ambiance for their trip.

"Ready?" Pukuh asked.

After securing their belongings, Pukuh and Edward went into a quick jog, with Christina following closely behind. For the first half of the day, Christina was able to keep up and didn't tire, but come midday she was sweating and slowed down. To her credit, Edward slowed down as well, and despite what he claimed earlier, they were having a competition of pride.

Edward refused to take a breather, and Christina refused to ask for one. By the time the two had slowed to near walking, sweat pouring down their faces, and glaring at each other, Pukuh decided to end the rivalry before one of them collapsed. He suggested taking a break to rehydrate and eat.

Edward stared daggers at Christina, and she at him. "Tired yet?" he asked.

"I could do this all day," she replied.

Pukuh chuckled as he watched them bickering. "You act as siblings."

"Perhaps in another life," Edward postulated with a laugh.

After Edward and Christina were rested as could be, Pukuh started again and set a slow pace. The three travelled at a good pace, despite having to slow down. Normally, the trip to reach Pukuh's village would take a full day and a half, with rest overnight. At the rate they were travelling they would reach the village before nightfall.

The group soon reached a large flat area with a smooth rock and slight hill. On top of the ten-foot-high rock the roots of a tree were snaking down, searching for nourishment which was not present.

"This brings back memories," Edward said between short breaths.

"Yes, this was where you flailed about against the beasts of the forest."

"What happened?" Christina inquired.

"I fought a pack of wolves the first time I arrived."

Pukuh grinned. "Strange, does 'fought' mean 'flailing about' in your language? Ah, the mysteries of you people never end."

"Did you win?"

"Barely. I was heavily injured and fainted."

"I carried Edward to the village because he was too weak. He is still weak, but I will not carry him this time."

After taking another short break, the journey continued. They were not far from the village now, and daylight was dwindling. When they reached the edge of the forest that night, Pukuh stopped suddenly, motioning for the other two to be quiet and duck down.

"Something is not right," Pukuh muttered as he handed his pack to Edward before heading to the village.

Edward and Christina backtracked and hid behind a large pine tree. Edward tried his best to watch Pukuh, but he was like a shadow in the dark. Dressed as he was in his original warrior outfit of eagle feathers and well-fitted leather armour, he was in his element as War Chief.

Pukuh dashed to the closest home, a hut made of mud and clay with a straw roof, similar to most others in the village. He sneaked into the village and sought out the cause of his unusual feeling. In a half hour he was back to where Edward and Christina hid themselves.

"What's wrong?"

"My village has been taken by white men. Before we can retrieve the medicine we will need to free the villagers."

"Where is the plant located?" Edward asked.

"The fields are on the other side of the village, behind the pyramid." Pukuh gestured to the pyramid in the centre of the village, where the Mayans held rituals. The huge structure, along with a few other large stone buildings, marked specific points of religious significance.

"Christina, you should head back to the ship. This is too dangerous.

Christina's mouth made a line. "No, I will not leave. I am not some useless child."

Edward sighed. *We don't have time for this.* "Fine, harvest the plant we need and head back to the ship as fast as you can. Do not stay here, you could be hurt and Anne needs the medicine as soon as possible." Edward took out Alexandre's drawing of the plant from his pack and handed it to Christina.

She nodded as she accepted the drawing, confidence evident on her face. "You can count on me, Edward, I won't let you down."

"Pukuh, I need you to howl like a wolf. I think we'll need some help with this."

Pukuh nodded, knowing full well Edward's stream of thought. Pukuh let out a great howl which sounded like a real wolf. He kept calling until he heard a return call off in the forest.

"Christina, whatever happens, do not be afraid."

The three waited in silence for ten minutes, watching the forest for any movement or sound. Suddenly, without warning, a wolf stepped out from behind a tree. He was a big one, the leader of the pack, with a scar down one of his eyes.

Christina hid behind Edward as Edward stepped forward and knelt down. He glared at the wolf with his fierce eyes as the wolf stepped closer, fangs bared. *You remember me, don't you? I am your master.* The wolf stopped growling and went up to Edward's legs, pushing his head into Edward's hand in deference. *Yes, that's right.*

More wolves, all different sizes and shades of grey or brown, emerged from hiding after the leader's display. Twenty wolves in all joined the three humans.

"Christina, I want you to take one of the wolves and make your way around the village to the field. We will start attacking the guards here, which will draw away anyone guarding the field. Wait until they leave, find the plant, and return to the ship."

As if able to understand Edward, a reddish-grey wolf moved beside Christina and let its fur touch her fingertips. Christina jumped at the sensation.

"Don't be afraid, the wolf won't hurt you." Edward took Christina's hand in his and caressed the wolf beside her. The animal panted, staring up at Christina with grey eyes. "See? Everything will be fine. This one will protect you," Edward reassured Christina while commanding the wolf.

"Whatever you say, Edward." Christina said without much confidence. She set out around the perimeter of the forest with the wolf following beside her.

Edward turned to Pukuh. "Now, let's free your village." Pukuh nodded and the two trekked into the village.

They ran to the nearest hut with the wolf leader sticking beside Edward. Some of the wolves followed or advanced into the village to hide on their own. Edward peered out from around a corner of the hut.

He could see down the main road of the village, a wide swath made between the houses leading all the way to the large pyramid in the centre. He noticed a fire at the base of the pyramid and people gathered around. He also noticed several sources of light moving slowly about the village.

"The white men at the pyramid are guards, they have all my people trapped there. I was not able to see inside, but my fa... the King is probably in the castle. I noticed a flickering light."

"We should free the villagers first so they can fight with us, then help your father," Edward suggested, to which Pukuh nodded in assent.

Edward passed the huts to the closest source of light. He could see a man walking between the huts. A shadow zipped by and then the man fell to the ground with a thud. Another man close to Edward heard the thud and moved closer to inspect. Edward sneaked behind the second man, covered the man's mouth, and sliced his neck. The man squirmed and twitched, releasing a moan, then fell limp in Edward's arms. Edward pulled him back between the huts before moving forward.

The night was dark and the pines surrounding the village afforded no protection from the cool wind blowing through. The scents of the pine, similar to the *Freedom*, along with dust and stone, filtered through to Edward's senses. A faint smell of burnt gunpowder told Edward a battle had happened here a few days past.

Edward and Pukuh made their way silently forward to the centre of the village, quickly approaching a large fire with thirty-plus men guarding all the villagers. The wolves were nowhere to be seen save for the leader at Edward's side.

Edward and Pukuh reached the last hut before the bonfire. The hundred and fifty or so villagers were sitting in front of the pyramid. Some of the white men were napping, others were roasting food on the fire, and still others kept their guns pointed at the prisoners. Two other bonfires were alight along the front of the pyramid. All the men were talking loudly and jovially to let the villagers know they were still awake, and still in charge.

That would soon change.

"So what is the plan, brother?" Pukuh asked in a low voice.

"I don't see any other way than to charge in headfirst."

"I am liking this plan," Pukuh smiled.

"Just… let me…" Edward turned to the wolf, and pointed to the men at the bonfires.

"Are… are you communing with him?"

"Trying to tell him to attack," Edward replied, still gesturing with hand signals he believed the animal might understand. After a moment, the animal turned and strutted away between the huts again.

"What did he say?"

"What?"

"The wolf, what did it say back?"

Edward pinched the bridge of his nose. "Are you daft, man? The wolf isn't psychic."

Pukuh frowned. "I distinctly recall Benjamin stating he could speak with animals."

"I think you were on the receiving end of one of his practical jokes, my friend."

"I do not know. He was very convincing," Pukuh replied, a dubious look on his face and his arms folded.

Edward sighed. "We strike on the count of three."

Edward stepped to the edge of the hut and counted out to three on his fingers. On the third, Edward dashed out with his cutlass forward. The guards only realised what was happening when Edward and Pukuh were upon them.

Edward sliced the chest of a man napping on the ground. Pukuh stabbed another with his spear who was turning around.

The wolves pounced on the guards. One man lifted his musket at Edward. The pack leader jumped over the fire and ripped out the man's throat. The musket fired into the air as the man struggled weakly before dying.

Edward fought with another man for his musket. Ordinarily, Edward would have easily overpowered the small man, but he was fatigued after their day-long trek through the forest. The man twisted and pulled and pushed for supremacy. Edward lifted his foot and stomped hard on the man's toes. The man's grip loosened. Edward jerked the musket forward and the barrel hit the man in the nose. The man released the musket, clutching his broken nose. Edward shot him in the chest.

When the villagers finally gained grip on what was happening, they rushed in to help. The warriors used their fists and legs to subdue the enemy before them. The Mayans once more fought alongside the wolves like their ancestors had before, as the legend goes.

When Edward killed the last guard near him, he found Pukuh. "Let's save your father."

"Onward, to the palace."

The Voyages of Queen Anne's Revenge

Edward and Pukuh ran past the villagers and the warriors killing the guards, and rushed to the steps of the limestone palace.

...

Christina stood at the edge of the forest, and ducked between some pines. She made her way to the back of the village and could see the fields. On the right side, nearest the pyramid, Christina noticed large corn stalks, then to the left of the corn was squash or possibly pumpkin, then tomatoes and other vegetables, and other things Christina didn't recognise at the far end.

The plant didn't appear to be big, but the picture could be deceiving. Christina examined Alexandre's drawing by moonlight. Once she was confident she could spot it, and reasonably sure that the field was clear of enemies, Christina and the wolf entered the farmland.

The smells of the plants, vegetables, and freshly turned soil ignited Christina's senses. Living on a ship had its advantages, but fresh produce was not one. Christina forced herself forward, lest she pick one of the corn stalks or tomatoes. The smell of lantern oil and sweat also helped bring Christina back to her mission.

She scanned the different plants by the subtle and pale light she was afforded, trying to discern which was which. Alexandre's drawing being exceptionally detailed was a boon, as Christina knew nothing of plants, especially the medicinal kind.

I hope none of these are poison.

As Christina was inspecting the plants, she heard footsteps behind her. She turned around to see a fat man with a musket reaching down for her. Before she could react, the wolf struck and suddenly blood spurted from the man's neck. The wolf released the man and backed away. The man gripped his throat with one hand, still alive. Christina lunged at him, pulled out her daggers, and thrust them into the base of his neck. He fell backwards with Christina on top of him. When he hit the ground she fell off him and onto some plants.

Christina quickly rose and pulled her daggers from the corpse. Her face and clothes were spattered with blood. The wolf appeared again in front of the body, and Christina pet it in thanks. The wolf panted, baring its tongue and bloody fangs, in delight. "I think I will name you Shadow. No, wait, too obvious. Tala... yes, I'm fond of that."

Christina went back to the plants and examined them as best she could, taking as much time as she felt she could spare. She narrowed it down to two different plants with the same features in the little amount of light. Even with daylight, She suspected she would still have issues differentiating them.

I don't have time for this. Christina took her pack off her back.

Christina emptied her supplies onto the ground until the pack was empty. She filled the pack with the two types of plants, root and all, taking what she hoped was more than enough to be able to cure Anne.

After Christina had filled the pack to the brim, she strapped it onto her back and ran into the forest, Tala following closely behind. As Christina passed the village she could hear the sounds of battle and war cries still raging.

I hope Edward is well.

Christina ran through the forest, the rush from the previous fight still pushing her on. Once Christina's energy wore off, she slowed down to a jog. She and the wolf pushed themselves the whole night to reach the ship as quickly as possible. Christina took a few short breaks, and shared some dried meat she'd pocketed before.

Christina was long past tired, pure determination driving her legs forward. She herself didn't know how she was still moving, but kept advancing for as long as her body would allow. Anne's life depended on Christina, and she would not let her, nor Edward, down.

When morning approached and Christina was close to the ship, something caused her and the wolf to stop in their tracks. Tala instantly began growling, pulling her front paws down and lifting the hind in an attack stance. Christina was too shocked at first and stood in stunned silence at what she witnessed.

You must be joking.

In front of Christina and Tala was a black bear. Fur dark as jet, beady eyes, large paws with sharp claws, and deadly teeth greeted them. The bear was a medium-sized male, three hundred pounds and much larger than Christina or Tala.

Before Christina could take a safe route around the bear, Tala lunged forward. Being predatory, Tala saw a threat despite there being no cause. Christina flung her hand out at Tala a moment too late. The two animals began fighting.

Damn. Alright then, time to test my skills!

Christina removed the pack, pulled out her daggers, and jumped into the fray.

14. THE KING & BLACKWOOD

Inside the palace's main room, the light of the moon shone on a white man with a grey moustache. The man held a musket and was standing above the King, who was bound and lying on the stone floor. The old man leaned down and gripped the King by the cheeks, pulling his face forward.

"We've been fighting for days, I've taken control of your village, and I am losing my patience. I will ask you one last time, tell me where the gold is, or I will burn this village to the ground," the old man threatened.

The King spat in the old man's face. "There is your gold."

The old man backed up and cleaned his face with a handkerchief as a younger man kicked the King in the chest. "There is simply no reasoning with you, is there?" He turned to one of his subordinates. "Grab one of the villagers. Maybe killing his people one by one in front of him will loosen his tongue."

Before the man could fulfil the order, a gunshot sounded outside. The guards nearest the opening of the palace peered outside to see what the commotion was about.

"The villagers are putting up a fight," the young man reported.

"The men can handle a small uprising," the greying man said.

"I don't think so, the villagers have help." The young man pointed.

The older man walked over to catch a glimpse of what the younger man was talking about. "Well, those savages are making a right old mess of things, aren't they? We've work to do." The old man took his younger companion and the King away, leaving guards to cover them.

...

Outside the palace, Edward and Pukuh were ascending the limestone steps to the top. They could see the light of lanterns or a fire flickering between the stone columns.

Before reaching the top, Pukuh stopped Edward and motioned for him to move off the steps and onto the side. Pukuh went to the right and Edward to the left.

Edward peered over the edge of the stone building blocks. He could see two men facing the stairs with their muskets pointed forward, with another two men behind them. Edward and Pukuh stealthed their way to the top level of the palace, through the columns, and into the large palace room.

Pukuh threw his spear into the chest of the guard on the right. After a blood-curdling thunk, the man fell, dead. All eyes moved to the noise. Edward used his cutlass to impale a man through the chest from behind. When he drew the cutlass out the man fell face down and bled profusely onto the limestone. Pukuh used his knife to slice open a third man. Blood splattered over Pukuh's body as the man lost control over his limbs.

The last man fired his musket at Pukuh. The shot hit the Mayan warrior in the arm. Pukuh clutched the wound with his opposite hand. Edward swung his blade horizontally against the shooter. The power of the blow tore the musket to pieces and sliced open the shooter's stomach.

Edward rushed to Pukuh. "Are you well?"

Pukuh lifted himself off the floor. Blood seeped through his fingers. "I am fine. We must go. The only way out, aside from the steps, is to the roof."

Edward helped his friend walk forward, Pukuh showing the way to the roof of the palace. The two passed through several stone corridors and up a winding staircase until reaching the roof. Upon emerging they could see Pukuh's father and another older white man at the edge.

As Edward and Pukuh crossed the threshold of the stairs, they were greeted by two young men and musket barrels staring them in the face.

"Please, gentlemen, join us," the older man said. "Oh and drop your weapons, if you would be so kind."

Edward and Pukuh dropped their weapons to the ground, and they were prodded forward, closer to the edge of the palace roof. Pukuh's father was at the edge, on his knees, with his hands bound behind his back.

The wind blew coldly on the tall and open viewpoint Edward and Pukuh were perched upon. The two could see the entire village from where they were. From the pyramid, the tip of which reached the palace roof, to the religious stone buildings, and the many huts where the villagers lived.

The old man peered below, to where the fighting was nearing an end. His men were almost all killed and the villagers were freed. "Such a shame, they were good men... Oh well, more gold for me." The older gentleman with the long moustache moved closer to Edward and Pukuh. He lit a pipe and smoked, blowing a pungent yet sweet smell in their faces. "Strange bedfellows you have here, King. Who is this young chap?" he questioned, pointing to Edward.

"My name is Edward Thatch, also known as Blackbeard. I owe this village much, and I could not sit by and watch it be overtaken by anyone."

The old man whistled. "Seems we have a celebrity here, and our fortune doubles. There is a bounty on your head, pirate. We can turn you in after we are done here."

Bounty? No matter, I'd love to see how you will escape here, old man. "Speaking of your business here, what is that exactly?"

"Oh, I am glad you asked." The old man pulled on the rope tied around the King's hands, lifting him up. He then pushed the King out to the edge of the roof, precariously teetering on the brink. "Legend tells of a treasure of gold in this forest. We stumbled upon this village on our search. A Mayan civilisation still standing after all these years, with this much wealth in architecture? It must be where the gold is. If you know where the gold is, tell me now, or your King and benefactor will be taking a trip."

Edward and Pukuh both jerked forward on instinct with the threat. The men with the muskets pushed the barrels into their chests hard. Edward and Pukuh calmed themselves, but didn't give the old man any information. Edward couldn't tell the old man anything because he didn't know of where any gold was, or even if the old man was right.

"I see one of you is injured. So between the three of you, we have two natives who know the location, and one bystander. Can you guess which one of you is expendable?" the old man asked with a sneer. "Johnny, let our bearded friend rest his legs."

One of the younger men nodded, then backed up a few paces. He pointed his musket at Edward's leg and fired.

The bullet seared through Edward's thigh and he fell to the ground with a yell. Edward gripped the wound as it bled onto the stone roof. Johnny pointed a pistol at Edward's head, keeping the threat active.

"Now, the next one goes through his head. Which one of you will tell me where the gold is, hmm?"

Pukuh eyed his father intently. The King nodded to his son. "Alright, I will show you what you seek," Pukuh hissed through gritted teeth.

"Don't, Pukuh," Edward whispered between deep breaths. "Don't let this bastard win."

"We do not have much choice in the matter, Captain." Pukuh eyed Edward intently. "Follow me," Pukuh commanded, walking back to the stairs of the palace.

Edward stood and did his best to stay on his legs. He leaned on Pukuh for support as the two made their way slowly to the stairs.

The old man pulled the King back onto steady ground. "Now, your warrior here is clearly more reasonable than you are."

"You should have tied my legs too," the King scoffed.

The old man's eyes narrowed, and then he looked down at the King's unbound legs. The King reared back and kicked the old man in the chest, shoving him backwards over the edge of the roof. His body hit the stairs and tumbled down to the ground below. Each sickening thud sounded loudly through the whole village and drew all eyes. He was dead on the first step, and by the last his body was a mangled mess.

When the two younger men watched their boss fall off the roof, Edward and Pukuh grabbed their weapons and fired. With those three dead, Pukuh's village was freed from the white men who tried to take their treasure.

Edward, with his arm around Pukuh's shoulder and hopping on one leg, walked to the King. The three peered over the edge of the palace roof to the scene below. They could see the bloody and broken body of the old white man at the bottom of the palace stairs, and all the villagers gathered around.

Edward laughed. "Nice work, Sire. I didn't expect that at all."

"You did not receive my message?" Pukuh asked.

"Is that why you were staring at me? I told you, Pukuh, I don't have such a power. Stop thinking foolishness. Benjamin tricked you."

Pukuh folded his arms. "I don't believe you."

Pukuh's father ignored the exchange and instead overlooked his people who were gathered at the foot of the palace. "My son, and our brother Thatch, returned to save us!" he yelled over the side. "You owe them your thanks."

The villagers cheered and screamed their thanks to Edward and Pukuh. The two of them waved and smiled at the praise. Their timing could not have been more perfect, and they were able to help avert disaster, and hopefully on their own ship as well.

. . .

Their legs were heavy and tired beyond all concepts of fatigue, yet, through willpower alone, the pair continued to move forward, slowly. The one, shaggy fur matted with blood and gaping wounds everywhere, dragged one useless hind leg behind the three others. The other, on two legs, with bloody wounds and deep cuts, inched forward on a broken leg, the bone sticking out the back.

Christina breathed deeply, producing ragged, exhausted sounds. Her vision was doubled, and the world spun. She relegated her sight instead to the ground beneath her, watching as she forced the foot she could use forward.

A bit farther, she told herself.

Christina's animal companion, the wolf she'd named Tala, was beside her, in equally bad shape, or worse. Christina leaned on Tala and on a stick in her other hand.

The bear had done a number on the pair, but it now lay dead along the trail of the woods. Tala and Christina were a good team. They attacked together, with Tala drawing the bear's attention while Christina attacked it from behind. The two managed to kill the bear, but with the state they were left in, the gains scarcely outweighed the losses.

Christina missed her step and tripped over a branch. She fell to the ground, her body heavy and her mind on the verge of shutting down. She forced her face forward, focusing her eyes ahead. She could see bright sunlight in front of her which could mean only one thing: the beach.

Christina pushed with her weak arms, trying desperately to rise, but she could only extend her arms halfway before they wobbled fiercely and collapsed. Nevertheless, Christina would not stop. She knew the crew was depending on her to bring the medicine back, and she would not let them down.

Christina once more pushed on her feeble arms to gain leverage. When she was about to fall again, Tala suddenly appeared underneath her chest and helped to lift her up. Christina was able to stabilise herself on her hands and knees, but she could no longer muster the strength to stand up now that she had fallen this far.

This is all I need. I can do this!

Together, with one arm wrapped around Tala, Christina and her wolf companion were able to keep moving forward. The clear goal in front spurred Christina onwards, and Tala instinctively sensed the mood, picking up the pace to help her ahead.

Christina and Tala passed the threshold as a pair, emerging into the noonday sun and falling forward onto the sandy decline of the beach. They fell and rolled over on their broken bodies twice before stopping and sliding on the sand.

Blackbeard's *Revenge*

The hot sun beat down on them. Christina's vision was on the sun high in the blue sky, and she did not possess the strength to move even her head anymore.

This is far enough, right? Please don't die, Anne.

Tears rolled down the sides of Christina's face as she drifted into unconsciousness. The plant medicine in the pack still on her back was there for the taking; her only hope was the crew would see her and find the plants for Anne.

. . .

"We have to hurry," Edward said as he tried his best to run, the wound on his leg hampering his abilities.

"I know," Pukuh replied. With the bullet wound on his arm, and the constant moving over the past days, even he was beginning to tire and slow down.

"I have a bad feeling about the bear corpse we saw." Edward turned his head, but he could no longer see the body.

"The bear had bite marks and strikes from daggers. Christina and the wolf with her killed it," Pukuh assessed.

Edward stared at the ground. "Yes I know, but there is so much blood on this trail now, I fear we will find Christina's corpse soon."

"Your fears are unfounded. Look, we are at the opening now." Pukuh pointed forward to the entrance of the forest.

The floundering light of the sun was on the horizon, giving a golden glow to the trees and understory. When the pair passed the threshold of the forest they could see the *Freedom*, with much of the crew on the main deck walking and talking and waiting. When one of the crewmen saw their captain and the Mayan warrior on the beach, he informed the crew. The crew yelled and waved at the returning men.

On the way to the ship, Edward noticed two spots of sand dyed red with blood, but whatever caused the blood stains were gone now. *Christina and the wolf?*

The crew threw down a rope ladder for Edward and Pukuh to climb back to the top deck. The two were surrounded by the crew and bombarded by questions about what happened.

"Enough, enough! Where is Christina? How is Anne? I will answer your questions later, but right now mine are more important."

The crew cleared the way to the stairs of the berth deck. Edward entered the crew cabin where Anne was still lying down in bed with Alexandre in a chair next to her. Anne's fever hadn't broken yet, but her bandage was fresh with a green tint underneath, and a cup stood beside her bed.

The Voyages of Queen Anne's Revenge

Alexandre turned to greet Edward. "Welcome back, Captain. I applied the medicine to Anne's bandage and also made her drink some. The rest is up to her now."

"Good, job Alexandre. I'm sure she'll pull through. You are literally a life-saver."

"I try."

"Where is Christina?"

"In a bed over there," Alexandre replied whilst pointing to the stern of the crew cabin. "She and her wolf are resting. Their injuries were severe, but they will recover."

Edward kissed Anne on the cheek and checked on Christina. She was in the middle of the ship on a bed. Sitting next to her was Herbert on one side and the wolf on the other. Herbert was distraught and weary.

"Captain! What happened out there?"

"I'm sorry, Herbert. She was supposed to gather the medicine and then head back to the ship as quickly as possible. Some treasure hunters took over Pukuh's village, but Christina should have been able to escape without harm. On the way back, we saw the corpse of a bear on the trail. Christina could have killed the bear, with help."

"A bear?" Tears welled up in his eyes. "How could this happen? First Nassir's son, and now my sister. When will this end, Edward? At what point will you stop pointlessly endangering others?"

Before Edward could defend himself, Christina's slender fingers touched Herbert's. "Stop," she said softly.

"Christina!" Herbert exclaimed as he pulled her hand close.

"I am glad I went," she stated slowly. "I saved Anne, which was worth all the pain. Don't blame Edward for a decision I made and would make again if I had the choice. Now, let me sleep," Christina commanded before closing her eyes once more and drifting into sleep.

Herbert was silent for a moment. "I'm sorry, Captain. I was upset. My sister is the only family I have left. I can't lose her."

"Christina is strong, probably stronger than you think. She will not die so easily. And don't forget, she is our family too. I will protect her when she needs me just as she will protect us when we need her."

Herbert nodded and continued to watch over his sister.

Edward examined the wolf. She was also very injured, but with bandages covering the wounds and cleaned fur. Edward petted the wolf, but she remained asleep. *You did well to protect Christina. I hope you are alright with being on a ship for a while, as we cannot stay for you to recover.*

Edward left the crew cabin and returned to the main deck. He saw Pukuh telling the tale of what had happened to them at his village, much to the delight of the crew. Jack was providing music for the story, changing the tempo depending on what was happening.

Henry advanced to Edward. "Once again, you somehow turned something simple into an exercise in risking lives."

"Oh, and how did I cause treasure hunters to find Pukuh's village? Do you even care I'm still alive?"

Henry pursed his lips. "I'm glad you're safe, but there was no reason Christina should have been put in danger. She walked an untold length with a broken leg and severe loss of blood. Even Alexandre was shocked at the sight of her."

"I was quite worried for her, I'll have you know. She insisted on gathering the herb while we liberated Pukuh's town. Afterwards, she was to leave immediately. How was I to know a bear would be waiting on the trail?"

Henry rubbed his temples. "You could have *ordered* her to return to the ship, to stay put, any number of things, but you let her out of your sight when she was your responsibility. You talk of wanting to be stronger so you can protect them, then when they're hurt it's not your fault. Do not try and shirk your mistake off on a sixteen-year-old!" Henry stepped close to Edward and whispered with rage in his voice. "If you care so much for your so-called family, take better care of them." Henry left before Edward could formulate a response.

Edward watched as the crew talked and celebrated well into the night, thinking over what Henry said.

15. THE BROTHERS BODDEN

At Edward's behest, the *Freedom* returned to Bodden Town. During the week and few days it took to arrive there, Anne's fever broke and she regained her strength day by day. She was able to talk, eat properly and walk around.

"Christina fought a bear?" Anne questioned skeptically.

"Yes, no jest, she fought a bear and killed it to bring you this medicine," Edward replied as he grabbed one of the dried leaves and began chewing on it. He frowned from the bitterness, but didn't stop chewing.

"I will be sure to thank her. And I owe you thanks as well. I faintly remember you by my side as I dipped in and out of wakefulness."

Edward's cheeks reddened, though the colour was obscured by his beard. "Yes, well, I was worried."

"How are your's and Pukuh's injuries? I notice you have a bandage on your thigh." Anne said, pointing to Edward's leg.

"Just a flesh wound," Edward assured. "I can barely feel it."

Anne looked unconvinced, but didn't press the issue. "Help me up, I wish to see Christina."

Anne extended her hand, which Edward took and pulled as Anne shifted and rose to shaky legs. She used Edward's shoulder as a crutch as she made her way through the crew cabin, past all the swaying hammocks, and to the bed hosting Christina and Tala.

Tala was lying on top of Christina and was roused out of light slumber by the noise of Edward and Anne approaching. The animal panted, wanting to be petted. For a wolf, she became rather docile around Edward and Christina. Tala moving around woke Christina, so she sat up for Anne and Edward.

Christina's wounds were still healing, but the worst was behind her. She had deep gashes on her back, arms, and legs covered by cloth, and her broken leg, set now thanks to Alexandre, would take a long time to fully heal.

"Anne, I'm so glad you are awake and well," Christina said while petting Tala.

Anne laughed. "I have you to thank. I was informed you were through a fairly traumatic experience, and by your appearance you were in as bad a shape as myself."

"I would have fared much worse if you hadn't trained me."

Edward stayed for a bit, watching the two young women talk with beaming smiles, before heading up to the top deck. According to Herbert, they would land at Bodden Town soon, and Edward had business there now that Anne wasn't in danger.

The first time Edward landed in Bodden Town, the town was being run by the Bodden Brothers, Malcolm and Neil, Scottish twins also known as Bodden Town Bandits. Edward muscled his way through taking over the town and became a shareholder in the settlement. He also wanted the brothers to make the town safer for the townsfolk, and turn it into a pirate hub. Edward's direction had seemingly opposed goals, but he knew the brothers were up to task.

Edward hadn't seen the brothers in over a year, and felt he needed to make an impression in case his influence had slipped away over time. He took Sam, John, Henry, and Pukuh with him to see the brothers.

The port of Bodden Town was bustling in the afternoon, with ships constantly docking and weighing anchor. The town had doubled in size since Edward was imprisoned, and the harbour market was teeming with merchants and buyers.

Edward and company entered the overly active market, passed by the people walking to and fro along the harbour, and up the main street. The main street went up a slight incline all the way to the Bodden Brothers' mansion.

The streets were more active than Edward recalled as well. More people were sitting outside the local businesses and engaged in their daily routine. The town had no shortage of regular townsfolk, but Edward also passed taverns and inns occupied by rogues and pirates alike.

Edward also noticed people he assumed were in the Boddens' employ walking about the town, acting as guards. They wore white outfits with black pants to distinguish themselves from the rabble. Edward appreciated seeing the guards.

At the top of the small incline, Edward and company reached an elegant two-storey white mansion with a high wall around the perimeter. An iron gate in the middle faced the main street and two guards stood in front. At Edward and his group's approach, the guards hefted their weapons and stepped up to him.

"No entrance for guests without appointments," one guard asserted.

"The brothers will make an exception for me," Edward declared, not stopping.

The Voyages of Queen Anne's Revenge

The guards planted their hands on Edward's chest, forcing him to stop. He glanced at the hands and then back at the guards. Edward stared daggers at them.

"I am Edward Thatch, the one known as Blackbeard. The brothers work for me, and thus you work for me. Remove your hands, or I will remove them from your body."

The guards' faces turned pale and they immediately moved away. "We are terribly sorry, sir, we did not know. The brothers have been expecting you for some time, ever since word of your escape reached here months ago." The guard opened the gate for Edward. "The brothers are in their study. I trust you know the way?"

"Yes, that will be all, gentlemen." Edward waved them off as he passed the gate.

Edward's friends followed him to the mansion, past two large columns and through the white door to the interior. The expansive mansion was opulent, with a large ballroom at the entrance, chandelier on the ceiling, alcoves in the walls, chairs for reading, and servants at beck and call.

Edward strode up one of the curved staircases in the ballroom and through a set of large wooden double doors into the brothers' study. Along both sides of the walls, more alcoves held different relics, weapons, and books.

The brothers themselves were at a table on the far end of the long room, perusing some documents. When the brothers noticed Edward enter, they dropped what they were doing.

"Mr Thatch." Malcolm, short but stout and muscular due to his Scottish heritage, wore a suit of red silk. He was not attractive, but not ugly in any sort of way, simply average.

"We've been expecting you," Malcolm's brother Neil continued. He had the same appearance as his brother, what with them being twins, but wore a blue suit.

"I heard, and can I expect you understand the reason I am here?"

Malcolm started: "We suspected you would be inclined to claim some of the moneys we accumulated over your year's absence," And Neil continued: "That you need more men on your crew is also within our powers of insight." Malcolm took over once more: "We also believe you are here to make an unnecessary show of power, what with your muscle behind you." Malcolm pointed to Edward's company. "Though, as stated, completely unnecessary." Neil and Malcolm, together since birth, were able to finish each other's thoughts. "We kept the bargain struck many moons ago, and you are free to see and reap the benefits, which are substantial." "Given the untouched accumulation."

Edward approached the table at the brothers' behest. They produced a ledger showing the values of his and their stock over the year. Several pages were filled with notes from various debits and credits, but the brothers skipped to the final page, showing the most recent balance.

Edward glanced at the figure and his eyes widened in shock. He had never seen such a sum before, nor did he know what he could do with all that money. For a simple whaler's son, the amount was too great to think about. Over six thousand pounds filled Edward's reserves over the past year alone. The prospect delighted him, and from past notations, the rate of propagation would only increase in the future.

"John, would you inspect this, please? I want to make sure everything is in order."

"Yes, Captain."

John examined the contents of the large ledger month by month. As he examined the different deposits and adjustments, Edward and the brothers discussed what had happened over the year he was gone. Bodden Town continued expanding with low-cost housing to build the population along with creating and maintaining a local militia. The brothers ensured the men were trained, obedient, and organised so the militia could function autonomously from the brothers or Edward if need be. The militia made sure pirates and thieves understood the townspeople were off limits, and in exchange their goods received fair trade. Bodden Town was slowly turning into a more respectable Tortuga.

John finished his assessment. "The numbers are sound, Captain."

"Good work, John, and you too, brothers."

"Thank you, Edward." "Your praise is much appreciated."

"Our ship needs re-stocking, so, working with John on supplies and new crew members for us would also be appreciated. I would also take five hundred pounds of my stock for personal use, and one to three thousand can be redistributed as you please. Consider it an investment, and with it I want an equal share in this venture. I want thirty-three percent of the shares, to be exact, as opposed to the previous agreement of twenty five."

"Consider it all done," Malcolm confirmed.

"I'll await you back on the ship, John," Edward said, leaving the work to be done by John and the brothers, in many ways better suited to the task than he.

"Brother, you forgot," Neil chided. "Oh, yes I suppose I did. Edward, a moment please?"

Edward turned back around to the Boddens. "Yes?"

Malcolm began. "Two things: Firstly, not long ago, a man dressed in black was here asking about you. He never provided his name, and, so far, our sources have not been able to find any information on who he is, but you should be on alert."

"Why?" Edward asked, his curiosity piqued.

"Something about the man felt off, as if sickness and death followed in his wake. He's dangerous, and you should avoid him. Yes, even you Edward, Blackbeard. We managed to point him to Tortuga, so you should have nothing to fear for the moment."

Normally I would laugh at such a notion, but with the way the brothers are talking, maybe I should heed their advice. "And the other matter?"

Neil picked up for his brother. "We were wondering if you could take care of some local toughs. We would have the militia handle the brigands, but they are attending to other matters at the moment. One of the pirate gangs is growing bolder, and their villainy is affecting the townsfolk. If the famous Blackbeard were to make an example of them, others would be deterred from such actions. Here is their captain's name and where he is staying." Neil scrawled a name on a piece of paper and handed it to Edward.

Edward raised his brow. "I would be glad to help, but didn't you say someone dangerous was searching for me? Isn't throwing my name around asking for trouble?"

"This action is no more than you have already done," Malcolm surmised.

"And besides, you will be doing this to pirates, who themselves don't want their names spread," Neil added.

"And, were you not leaving soon after this? This is not your home, so the town is not in danger. The *Freedom* is your home."

Edward nodded. "True. Alright, we'll take care of those pirates then. John and you two can figure out supplies."

"Re-supplying won't take long, Captain," John reassured him as he and the brothers began working on a list.

Now, down to business.

. . .

"You see, I'm talking about an unwritten rule this town has, one I've helped establish. You aren't understanding the rule, thus why I'm here," Edward said, sitting down in a comfy chair and holding a glass of rum.

Edward and crew were on the second floor in a reserved room for Miles Miller, also known as Miles the Murderer, the murderer-turned-pirate who was causing trouble for the Bodden Brothers. The room was large and long, with a nice bed, hardwood table and chairs, billiards table, and a massive picture window overlooking the street below.

Blackbeard's *Revenge*

Miles was on the ground, blood spilling from his mouth. Sam had taken pleasure in beating him into submission. Miles was known for his murders and ruthlessness, but on his own he was nothing special.

"You broke those rules, and now you must be punished."

Sam kicked Miles in the chest, causing him to flip and fall on his back. Henry and Pukuh had subdued two other crewmates Miles had with him.

Miles coughed up blood, and tears filled his eyes. "What did I do?"

Edward laughed. "Well, your moniker is Miles the Murderer. You tell us."

"They wus whores, why's it matter?"

Sam kicked Miles' chest again, producing a scream of pain and a distinct crack of his ribs breaking. "Who they are or what their profession is doesn't matter, Miles. You broke the agreement each outlaw has when in Bodden Town. Don't make trouble, and trouble won't be brought to you."

"What will you do to me?" Miles asked through ragged breaths.

"Get him up," Edward commanded Sam, who picked up the bloody and weak body of the pirate Captain Miles. Edward took Miles from Sam, lifting him off the ground by the chest. "We will make an example of you, so no one does what you did. Don't worry, you *should* survive." Edward grinned devilishly, causing Miles' eyes to fill with fear.

Edward pulled the ragged body of Miles back and threw him at the large picture window. Miles crashed through the thick glass and fell down the two storeys to the street below. Townsfolk glanced at the body, then up to the broken window of the inn.

Edward returned to the inn's pub area. Edward's crew stood above the many unconscious members of Miles' pirate crew. Broken tables, chairs, bottles and glasses littered the floor of the inn. The innkeeper stood behind the bar, with several of his wait staff hiding in fear. The staff's eyes were on Edward and as he approached they pushed themselves even further against the wall.

"Send the bill for repairs to the Bodden Brothers, would you?" Edward asked with a smile. The innkeeper nodded mutely.

When Edward exited the inn, the citizenry focused on him briefly before moving on about their business. Edward walked over to Miles. His body was broken, but he was breathing.

"You managed to survive. Good, because I have one last thing to tell you." Edward turned over Miles' body to face him. "Pay attention." Edward forced Miles' weary eyes open to gaze at the terror of Blackbeard manifest. "Don't fuck with my town again." Edward left with those parting words, and Miles blacked out.

Miles was no longer called a Murderer after that.

16. MYSTERY IN THE GULF

With the help of the Bodden Brothers and their network, the *Freedom* was restocked with a full crew again in less than a week. The new mates were all people who had been screened before for the militia, but the brothers didn't hire for being too rough. Edward felt they would be a perfect fit for his crew.

Before setting sail, Edward had the new crewmates swear by the pirate commandments made by him and Bartholomew Roberts. If they would not swear, Edward released them from the crew.

Edward also split a generous sum of the money from his shares of the Bodden's stock amongst the crew for their hard work, which was fed back into the town at the local market and taverns and whorehouses before leaving.

Once headed out to sea, Edward had Herbert point *Freedom* towards the Gulf of Mexico, their next destination, although specifically where in the Gulf was a matter of debate.

"So, Herbert, have you had some time to think over the riddle left by Benjamin?" Edward asked.

"Yes, actually. I believe I figured out the answer," Herbert said, obviously irked about something. Before Edward could inquire, Herbert discussed the reason for his ire. "That smug Alexandre claimed to have solved the riddle within a few seconds of hearing the clue, and he had the audacity to give me a clue."

Edward sympathised with Herbert, knowing firsthand how irritating Alexandre's arrogance could be. "What was his clue?"

"What has four points and what has three points?" Herbert questioned before yelling orders to trim the sails.

Four points, three points. Edward decided to read the riddle again.

In the Gulf the North East Triangles Point the Way.
Four points, four points, three points, three points.
Undo and See.

Four points. Four points. Edward pondered. Compass? Cross? X? Those seem too obvious. A square or rectangle? Maybe. What has three points which is related to those? He could only think of the Father, the Son, and the Holy Ghost for the cross, or a triangle relating to the square. What would either have to do with this?

"All I can think of is either a Cross and the Holy Trinity... or a square and a triangle."

Herbert was surprised. "The religious significance is intriguing, but I believe a square and a triangle are the most likely fit."

"How does a square and triangle fit with the riddle?"

"May I?" Herbert asked, his hand extended. Edward handed him the paper and he went to work.

Herbert first folded the paper in half, making a rectangle, four points, then folded the rectangle in half making a square again, four points. Herbert folded the square from one corner to the other, making a triangle, three points, and then repeated the process, three points. After showing Edward the finished product, Herbert unfolded the paper—undo and see.

On the paper now was the outline of four squares, with each square having four triangles pointing to the middle. The triangles in the northeast square pointed to a specific location on the map. The Northeast Triangles Point the Way.

"Incredible," Edward said. "Good work, Herbert. Take us straight there!"

"Aye, aye Captain."

Over the next week, the new crewmates were acquiring their sea legs and familiarising themselves with the veterans. Edward was learning the names and making his presence known as the captain.

Anne fully recovered from her fever and returned to work aboard the ship. The new members were apprehensive having women aboard at first, but after an incident involving a punch from Christina, and some broken fingers from Anne, they realised the two were not to be trifled with, and better sailors than most.

"Already putting the new men in line, I see?" Henry asked Anne one day, soon after she'd returned to active duty.

"Well, one has to teach the young ones manners or they are likely to rebel. Spare the rod..." Anne started.

"Spoil the child," Henry finished and they both chuckled.

After a moment, Anne's expression turned serious. "Is everything well, Henry? You have not been yourself in many days past."

Henry waved his hand in dismissal. "Don't trouble yourself. I'm just tired."

"Henry, from our time spent together before freeing Edward, I can tell when you are lying. Tell me your problems."

Henry opened his mouth, shook his head, and his mouth made a line. "I need to deal with my own problems, Anne. I will not burden another with this. If you'll excuse me?" Henry left, not waiting for a reply.

Henry's mind turned to his friend, Robert Maynard, and what he and Edward did to him. Henry also reflected on other innocents whom the crew of *Freedom* sacrificed to escape Portsmouth. The memory of the houses turning to rubble, and the thought of those caught in the middle, still made Henry sick to his stomach.

Christina's leg was still healing, and probably wouldn't be better for another few weeks, but the wolf, Tala, healed quicker and was often seen exploring the ship. Edward found it a bit disconcerting, but Tala appeared docile and did well with the dried meat normally available.

"So, can I keep her?" Christina asked Edward as they were feeding Tala one day.

"How are we to keep a wolf aboard? We should take her back to Pukuh's village. Wolves aren't meant to live amongst humans, they're dangerous."

"So says the one who used a pack to save a village."

"Hey, don't use logic and wit against me, Missy." Edward sounded upset, but he was grinning. "Alright, I'll allow Tala to stay for now, but any trouble and she's gone. And she's your responsibility."

Christina nearly jumped out of her seat with a hug for Edward. "Thank you, Edward, you're the best captain ever!"

Edward sighed. "I'm the only captain you've had."

Christina stuck her tongue out. "Well, go ahead and ruin the compliment then." Edward ruffled her hair and started to leave, but Christina spoke again, in a more serious tone. "Thank you Edward, for all you've done for me and my brother. Despite what he said earlier, he admires and trusts in you. We've been through some rough times, he and I, and you've given us hope. Despite losing family along the way," Christina turned away from Edward and wiped a tear off her cheek, "you've allowed us the chance to avenge them. Thank you."

Edward smiled. "I will do my best to live up to your expectations."

"I'm certain you will," Christina affirmed in her sweet voice.

As Edward reached the top deck he heard a lively "Land ho!" from the crow's nest. Herbert turned the ship to face the island dead on. Edward went up to the bow for a better view. He pulled out his spyglass and peered to the island beyond.

The island was small and round in shape, with no trees and a large structure in the middle. The structure was made of stone, from what Edward could tell, and rose higher than any building he ever saw. As they approached the island, the crew was truly astonished by the size of the monstrosity. The tower must have been at least four chains in height, or two hundred and sixty-four feet, which was taller than the tallest castles.

The ship landed on the sandy beach and the crew descended onto the island. Edward instructed them to bring weapons and all available supplies for any situation they might encounter. They entered all of these trials unprepared and always paid for it, but hopefully this time would not be the same.

The breeze of salty air flew through the fresh grass and passed over the old stone structure. The beautiful day on a quaint island in the middle of the Gulf of Mexico was not lost on the crew. They took their time to enjoy the sights while they had the chance.

"Here we be again, eh, Cap'n?" Sam questioned, striking up a conversation.

"Yes, there is almost no end to Benjamin's trickery."

"Two keys and you be free of 'im." Sam laughed.

"That is the hope, at least. You never know, Benjamin could show up and demand his ship back once we've opened the final room."

Sam laughed even more at the notion. "Well, the only way ta make *Freedom* yer own ship is ta rename her."

"Rename the *Freedom*? I wasn't aware you can rename a ship."

"Of course ye can. The ship is yers, or at least it will be after we secure all the keys, like ye said. Ye can do whatever ye want," Sam reassured him as he continued to walk up the beach and onto the grassy part of the island.

Hmm, rename the ship? But, *Freedom* fitted so well with what they were trying to accomplish.

"Are ye coming, Cap'n?" Sam inquired, glancing over his shoulder.

Edward shook himself out of his contemplation and joined the crew at the foot of the tower. Edward passed through the stone archway into the dark of the tower and was handed a lantern by Anne.

The room the crew entered was open and spacious, with a note of stale water in the air. The walking area was relegated to a single strip of stone around the perimeter, as the centre of the room was hollowed out, with a hundred-foot drop to water below. Edward could make out the remains of a sunken ship at the bottom.

"Captain, look on the left," a crewmate exclaimed.

Stairs made of stone on the left of the room led up to the next level. Edward decided to move to the steps with caution.

"Let's move to the next level, but be careful, there may be traps," Edward cautioned the men following behind him.

Edward approached the steps on the left side of the room, placing his foot on the first step slowly and deliberately. Nothing happened. He stomped his foot harder across the whole of the step, but nothing bad happened. He did the same thing for the next three steps, first testing and then tempting, but no traps were sprung.

Edward moved to the next level, and soon determined what had happened. On the next level half the floor and ceiling were covered in spikes, except for a walkway in the middle leading to the other side. Dead bodies, now nothing more than skeletons, could be seen impaled on some of the spikes.

Someone had been here.

The room smelled of stale air and decay from the dead bodies. Little air flow caused the smell to permeate the room. Though it was prevalent in the room of the tower, it nonetheless faded over time and did not sting as it did the first time Edward smelled a decaying body. The fact that the bodies had decayed completely meant some time had passed since it was entered.

When Edward realised someone had been here before his eyes widened and he rushed through the walkway between the spikes and up stairs on the left side with little regard for traps. Anne and Henry were worried for his safety and yelled for Edward to slow down, but in the next room they saw more dead bodies and another completed puzzle, and they were able to grasp what Edward saw.

The crew followed Edward through a fourth room, the last one, and up the final set of stairs to the roof of the tower. In the centre of the roof was a pedestal with a chest on the top. Edward opened the chest with shaking hands as the crew flooded the roof to join him. They went up behind Edward, waiting for the final nail in the coffin.

"The key is gone," Edward confirmed, his voice shaking like his hands.

17. THE STRAW

Despite everyone deducing what happened before Edward voiced it, the words produced no less shock upon the crew.

Edward held up a piece of paper, which he had retrieved from the chest.

"What is that, Edward?"

"A letter left from the person who took the key, confirming he took the contents of the chest."

"Is the letter signed?"

"Yes, by a Daniel Richardson, but that could be anyone." Edward nearly threw the paper over the side of the tower in frustration, but Anne stopped him.

"Any clue is better than no clue. We will find him. We must."

Anne read the paper.

I reckon whomever is reading this is either the rightful owner of this key, the snake who set up this trap, or both. By now you shall see that I have taken the key for myself. Its use may be unknown to me at the present, but it is now mine. If you are in need of the key, no need to get torn up about it as I've found it fair and square, and paid a pretty price in slaves to do so. You lost this hunt.

Do not come after the key, or misfortune will surely follow.

Daniel Richardson.

"Might I have a *regarder* at the paper?" Alexandre asked as he made his way through the crowd.

He sauntered over, a small smirk on his face unreflected in his dull eyes. As he strode across the tower roof, his long coat swayed in the wind. He took the paper from Edward and examined it thoroughly: bending, smelling, and eventually licking the paper.

"This is wood from the American Chestnut Tree and the ink is produced in Canada, so Northern America, possibly Maine or New York." Alexandre smacked Edward on the arm. "Not so lost now, *mon ami?*"

Edward's jaw dropped. "How could you possibly know these things?"

"You saw my methods, they should be self-explanatory. The smell of the paper and the taste of the ink are the determining factors."

Anne took over. "Perhaps we will rephrase: How do you know from the taste and the smell they are in fact those types of paper and ink?"

"Over the years I studied many things: ink, papers, soil, plants, along with their defining characteristics. I travelled the world and saw many, so I am able to know with absolute certainty where the paper and ink are made."

"So the man we are searching for is in New York or Maine?"

Alexandre palmed his face. "*Non, non.* Only this note is. The man himself could very well be anywhere now. Judging by the fading of the paper and ink the message is at least two to three years old. You noticed the decayed bodies below? Some time has passed since the key has been *pris* from here. I provided a starting point: America. The rest is up to you."

Edward peered at the paper, smacking it against his hand while he thought. "Thank you, Alexandre. You helped us once more. I believe we should head back to the Bodden Brothers. Their information network could be of great help to us in our search."

"Aye, aye, Captain!" the crew responded favourably.

...

"And so, your surgeon, Alexandre, believes this man to be from New York or Maine?" Malcolm asked whilst holding the paper note Edward found.

"*Non*, I mean, no. The paper itself is from New York or Maine, but the man we are pursuing may not be there any longer. We don't know. He must have had a crew, we could be talking about a sailor, a captain more specifically, or someone rather prolific. In the letter it mentions a number of slaves he sacrificed to get through the trials, and we saw a number of bodies. The whole endeavour would have cost a great deal."

"More from Alexandre?" Neil ventured.

"No, the last part was from my own deductions. Alexandre concurred."

The brothers nodded in contemplation. "We will put our eyes and ears to the task." "We will see what we can find out about this Daniel Richardson."

"Thank you brothers. You know where to find me."

Edward and crew waited for a week in Bodden Town, but the brothers were only able to procure the smallest bit of information on the elusive Richardson. They were able to determine that he was a slaver who may have operated a ship taking slaves from Africa to America.

155

"Unfortunately, our information network only spreads so far on this island." "You may have better luck with a friend of ours: Aaron Cook." "Cook lives in Tortuga. You can take this letter of introduction to him." "We sent a notice ahead of you, so by the time you arrive he should have an answer for you, if any." "But, if he does not, then we are afraid you will not find this man without years more searching."

Edward wasted no time in leaving Bodden Town, and the crew were all for the change in scenery. *Freedom* had travelled back and forth to Bodden Town a few times in the past month, and while relaxing for the crew, they wanted to move forward.

The path to Tortuga led east of the Cayman Islands, where Bodden town was, north over Jamaica, and on the north of Haiti. Along the way, Edward noticed Henry staring longingly to the south, in the direction of Jamaica, and their home island, Badabos.

"Thinking of home?" Edward asked, joining Henry at the starboard railing.

Henry breathed deeply, staring at the clouds along the south. "Yes, it has been too long."

"Not long enough if you ask me." Edward turned around and sat on the railing.

The sun stood high in the sky and wind was in their favour. The sails flapped lightly, as did the rigging lines. The crew was in good spirits now and Edward could see smiles on their faces despite working in the hot sun.

"You don't ever think back on those days? The days before we were forced to start running all the time, before we started killing all the time?"

"Of course I do, I would be lying if I said I didn't. But this life is better. We have family who cares for us, we have *Freedom*. We may have to defend our *Freedom*, but that doesn't make us less free. If anything, we are freer than anyone else. No one can tell us what to do."

Henry chuckled. "Oh, so that's what freedom is? Sounds a bit childish to me, but what do I know?"

"Explain your meaning," Edward commanded, his anger rising.

"I mean exactly what I said. Your notions of freedom are childish, and are becoming tiresome." Henry rubbed his face in frustration as he stood up from the railing. "I'm sorry, I shouldn't have said that. I don't wish to debate with you, so can we stop? I didn't mean what I said."

Edward rose as well, facing Henry while folding his arms. "No, you did mean what you said, and I can't let this go. You think what we're doing is childish?"

"No, but the way you justify your actions by saying you're fighting for freedom, when in reality you're satisfying your own rebellious nature, is childish. Sugar this life how you want, we are outcasts."

"Outcasts?" Edward responded. A crowd of the crew had gathered to watch.

Henry, sometimes as hot-headed as Edward, could not back down now. "Yes, you call this freedom but we've been shunted from society for our reckless behaviour. This is no freedom. *Freedom* cannot be foisted upon someone. We've simply changed prisons."

"How are we imprisoned? We have the whole world to explore! The ocean is ours."

Henry stepped forward to Edward, the two of them didn't even notice the crew watching. "Only the size of the cage has changed. What if we wanted to land in England, or Port Royal, or some other locale owned by the British? Do you think we would have a whole lot of freedom there?"

"Alright, Henry, if you're so smart then how does one actually attain freedom?" Edward spoke with a tone which made it sound like he was calling Henry an idiot.

Henry laughed derisively. He couldn't stop now. "I don't know, Edward, why don't you try ruling the world? That's a good start. Or maybe we can ask your father when we find him? Maybe he found his freedom out here somewhere, what with him not returning and all."

Edward levelled Henry with a thunderous punch to the jaw. Henry held a hand to his jaw, his eyes wide. Edward grabbed Henry by the chest and exacted a pound of flesh from him, blow by hideous blow. The debt Henry took with his words was far too great.

Anne heard the commotion and ran to the top deck to see Edward still punching Henry without end. The crew was trying to tear Edward away but they were like flies before his rage.

"Why don't you keep talking about my father, you bastard? Say something else," Edward yelled, ignoring the men pulling him back.

"I'm sorry, Edward," Henry cried.

Anne ran in front of Edward, pulled back her fist, and punched him. Her fist, whip-like in motion and with pinpoint precision over years of training, landed perfectly on the temple, knocking Edward unconscious in one blow.

"Take him to the crew cabin," she ordered while pointing to the stairs. She then grabbed Henry by the chest and dragged him into the stern war room cabin. She nearly threw Henry onto the oval table in the room. "Start talking. Why was I forced to knock Edward unconscious and why did he assault you?" Her long red curls bounced with rage as she pointed and stared daggers at Henry.

Henry pulled himself together after taking a breather, but was still distraught. "I was arguing with Edward and made a comment about his father, which I shouldn't have."

"Damn." Anne placed one hand on her hip and she bit the thumb of the other. She had seen Edward's anger over his father's disappearance before, but not to that extent. Henry must have truly struck a nerve. "I will speak with Edward and do my best to calm him. Be prepared to apologise if you wish to remain on this ship."

"Thank you, Anne," Henry said as he deflated onto one of the chairs around the table.

Anne went downstairs to the crew cabin. Several crew members watched her as she passed, but none stopped her due to the glare in her eyes. They gathered at a distance from Edward and were waiting and watching to see what he would do, but parted for Anne.

Edward awoke from unconsciousness a while later, his head foggy and his anger below boiling. He sat hunched over on a chair, staring at the floorboards. Edward was chewing on the Mayan leaves, a habit he picked up during thoughtful times.

When Edward noticed Anne he did not rise. "I want him off the ship."

"I am not your cabin boy. If you wish your best friend to leave this ship, you will dismiss him yourself. Although you would be a fool to do so. More fool than when you beat him near to death on the waist."

Edward rose to his full height, causing William, standing nearby, to tense. "What did you say?" He stood a full foot over her, but she did not back down.

Anne pointed her finger threateningly in Edward's face. "You heard me, you big brute. Henry said something he regrets, as all people do, and you cast him out? Only a fool would do such a thing."

"Do you know what he said about my father?"

"Yes, words. Words only have meaning if you let them. Words only make you angry if you let them. Do not let meaningless words anger you."

"But…"

"Quiet! If you cannot find your own fault in all this, and understand how Henry feels, then maybe you were never friends to begin with." Anne turned and walked away. "Meditate on this, and then apologise for your foolish actions, or lose Henry forever," Anne warned over her shoulder before herding the people out of the crew cabin and back to work.

Edward fell back into the chair, defeated. He pressed his thumb and forefinger against his temples to try to dull the pain. He reflected on what he had done as tears fell from his eyes.

...

Edward entered the war room. Henry pulled his head up at the noise, and at the sight of Edward he rose.

"Edward, I'm sor—"

Edward raised his hand. "Don't. Just... don't." Henry sat back down as Edward grabbed a chair and sat in front of his friend. Edward frowned as he sat hunched over in the chair. After a moment, he smiled wistfully. "You remember the first thing you said to me after my father disappeared?"

At first Henry was caught off guard at the question, but a smile formed as he realised where Edward was going with his story. "I said 'He's in a better place now.'"

Edward chuckled and ran his fingers through his wavy black hair. "Robert pulled us apart after I scrapped with you. I still believed my father left me on purpose, not that he could have died. I was so angry because I thought you meant he was with another family, but I understood later, and we made up."

"I remember how you shut yourself in your room for weeks and wouldn't talk to me."

"I was pretty stubborn back then."

"Back then?" Henry asked with a smirk which caused both men to laugh.

"I pushed you, and I shouldn't have hurt you. I'm sorry, Henry."

"I'm sorry too, Edward, I shouldn't have said what I did."

"I know you mean it when you say you're sorry, but I will need some time to forgive you for what you said. So what do you say we act as if a few months have passed, and become friends again? It's been a long time since we were friends." Edward extended his hand to Henry.

Henry shook Edward's hand in agreement, then rose and hugged him. After a moment they left the war room laughing together. When the crew saw Edward and Henry back to normal, smiles abounded, not the least of which was on Anne's face.

None could think their peace would so swiftly and irrevocably be broken in the near future.

18. THE DAY THE DEVIL KNEW FEAR

Edward and crew landed in Tortuga after a few days' travel. The island was ruled by pirates and their ilk. Having no specific ruling class the island was claimed by rogues for their trade. If one journeyed to Tortuga, an unspoken rule was to travel in a group and hold weapons, as thefts and other acts of villainy were commonplace.

Freedom landed on the south end of the small island. Many ships flagrantly displayed Jolly Rogers, and others hid them for fear of a marine raid. The rest were merchant ships not afraid of the treacherous acquaintances surrounding them.

The harbour was a main hub of trade and money flow, with a few businesses thriving on the stolen booty for profit. The area around the docks was a mess of activity, and from the ship Edward could see the mass of bodies moving to and fro in the mercantile apex.

The true town of Tortuga was two miles north of the hub and surrounded by a wooden wall for defence, but security was sorely lacking at times. The merchants who frequented Tortuga were the ones who supplied the men for the militia, but when the pirates became too wild the militia would be taken out until the issue was resolved. Raids, pirate attacks, marines from the British or conquistadors from Spain had all tried their hand at taking over or destroying Tortuga, but the town always managed to return from the brink larger and more festooned with felons.

Jack watched from the sidelines as Edward asked for volunteers to see the man they were after in Tortuga. Ten minutes after Edward left with Anne, William, and John, Jack decided to visit the harbour.

Jack's feet seemed to move under their own accord, and he soon found himself in front of a tavern. He looked at the tavern for a long moment before deciding to head inside.

As Jack was entering, Edward and the others were leaving. Jack overheard them talking about entering the town now that they had a better idea where Aaron Cook was.

Edward noticed Jack entering the tavern, but Jack didn't meet his eyes. Jack wasn't sure what he was doing at the tavern himself, so he didn't wish to be questioned by Edward right now.

The Voyages of Queen Anne's Revenge

Jack examined the tavern. He could see rough men downing rum as if it was water, men in various types of clothing and colour playing a game of cards, and others showing off weapons of various sizes as if they had to compensate for something. The smells of blood, sweat, alcohol and various other things filled his nostrils, and Jack felt at home.

Jack walked to the bar table and sat in an old chair. "Whiskey, if you please, sir."

The bartender nodded and handed him a small glass which he filled generously. Jack paid and thanked the bartender, and the bartender left to tend to his other regular patrons.

Jack stared at the drink in front of him. The liquid had a brown, almost chestnut colour. The smell was strong and brought to mind a warm spice mix of cinnamon and nutmeg, as well as a hint of chocolate and toffee. Jack sniffed the mixture slowly as he turned the drink in his glass, its sweet promise tempting him.

Just a touch, Jack thought, *enough to wet the lips.* Jack tipped the glass up, but stopped just shy of the liquid making contact.

Jack set the glass back down and pushed it away from him before he had a second thought. The bartender asked him if anything was wrong, but Jack reassured him that he was fine. Jack sat and stared at the glass, thinking on the past for a time, and then the future. His thoughts drifted to his love, his wife, Rachel, and his kids, Maximilian and Jessica, and the man who killed them, George Rooke.

I made a promise. A little bit won't hurt. But the Captain saw me, he'll know. No he won't. We'll just have one glass, that's all. No!

Jack went back and forth in his mind, but eventually all the voices drowned out and it was just him and the drink. He pushed the glass back and forth in his hand as the time passed.

Someone came up beside Jack, but he didn't look up from the drink. "Ah, thanks fer the drink, mate," the man said as he grabbed the drink in front of Jack and downed it in one gulp.

Jack's mouth opened and he looked at the person who stole his drink. Sam sat down next to him, smirking in his trickster fashion.

"Samuel. To what do I owe this pleasure?"

"Wanted a drink. No better place, right? Barkeep, another!" Sam shouted.

The barkeep came over and filled Sam's cup again. This time Sam decided to sip and savour the drink instead. Jack and Sam sat in silence for a while.

"So, how have you been coping since… the incident?" Jack asked.

"Fine," Sam said, taking another swig of the drink.

"I heard what happened to some of the crew, some of the things they saw in that mist. I'm glad I didn't have to experience that. I can only imagine what I would see."

"We all have shit we gotta deal wit. It's how ye carry on that matters." Sam lifted the glass and glanced at Jack. "This ain't the way, mate."

Jack hung his head in shame. "I know." Jack ran his fingers through his hair. "Edward sent you, didn't he?"

"Ran back to the ship a'soon as he saw ye enter," Sam confirmed. "Wanted someone ta watch ye. I volunteered."

Jack laughed. "Maybe we both could learn something from Edward. He chooses to deal with his problems head on, always moving forward."

Sam knocked back the last of his drink. "He 'asn't hit the wall yet. All us broken souls git there, you know better'n most." Sam stood up from the chair. "When he's drownin' we'll need ta be there ta help him surface."

"Right," Jack agreed, then joined Sam. The two left the tavern and headed back to *Freedom* to await their captain's return. As they walked, Jack patted Sam on the back. "Thanks, Sam."

...

Edward, Anne, John, and Henry passed through the open gates of Tortuga, and were met with a glimpse of how Bodden Town might have been under different rule. Townsfolk gallivanted about, talking and drinking and singing together without a care in the world. Others fought without anyone to stop them, and some made wagers on the outcome.

"I suppose this is to be expected in this locale?" Anne asked, gaping.

"Business as usual, perhaps?" William added.

"They are rather, e-enthusiastic," John nervously stuttered.

Edward eyed the various villains warily. "Stay close."

They moved in a tight-knit group to the nearest tavern, a seedy building made of rotting wood full of bullet holes. The tavern was occupied by gentlemen of questionable repute—and one man also full of bullets, dead on the floor. When Edward asked the bartender, he directed them to a green house on the west side of town.

"I don' know how Aaron comes by his intelligence as he never leaves his home, but his information is true as can be. He's the man you're huntin' for," the bartender confirmed.

The Voyages of Queen Anne's Revenge

Edward thanked him, and they left to find the green house. Edward and company passed by other taverns and businesses selling weapons and stolen merchandise as well as people walking the streets of the town. The filth was evident with garbage and dirt covering the pathways and the residents. Quite the contrast to Bodden Town where the streets were regularly patrolled and kept relatively clean.

Edward found the green house after wading through the throngs of debauchery and unwanted solicitations. The small house had faded green paint falling off in chips from decay and neglect. Aside from the pale green colour the house was rather plain.

Edward unconsciously eyed the road they were on before knocking on the door to the house. He heard no sound of movement at first, but after knocking a second time he could hear someone bustling about. After much noise and curses an iron peep hole opened up in the door.

The pair of eyes showing had a furrowed brow above them and moved about to scrutinise each of the people there. "What business do you have with me?"

"The Bodden Brothers sent us. I have a letter of introduction here, and you should have received correspondence recently regarding our arrival." Edward presented the letter to the slot.

The man eyed the letter, and then Edward, carefully before snatching it. Edward could hear the sound of the paper being ripped into and then silence as the letter was read. After a moment the door was unlocked and opened for the visitors.

In front of Edward stood an older man, hunched over with a cane in one hand. He did not have grey hair or wrinkles, and appeared to be in good health, save for the cane and a limp from injury, not old age.

"Well, get in here. I don't have all day," Aaron said.

Edward entered first, with his group in a line behind him. The inside of the house was unexpected, but understandable, given Aaron's reclusive habits. The first room was plain with very little furniture and almost every inch covered with books and papers. Shelves filled with books lined the walls and spilled into piles on the floor. Papers from different locations across the globe were strewn about in no discernible pattern, some dating back many years. The house smelled of stale air and old paper.

Aaron walked to a door at the far end of the room as Edward and his friends ogled the many texts surrounding them.

"Come on, then." Aaron beckoned.

Edward focused and walked into the other room to sit down in one of the chairs after Aaron did the same, and his company followed suit. "I trust you know why we are here?"

"Yes, and in another week you shall have your answer. The best I could do on such short notice is find out your man, Daniel Richardson, is a slaver. Richardson's last raid took him to Calabar, in NiTalaa, in the past few months."

Edward's mouth went agape in shock over the name of the village. He shared knowing, and equally troubled, glances with his crew.

"If you are upset with the progress you can show yourself to the door. I only had two days' notice to find you this much..." Cook began, but Anne stopped him.

"No, we are pleased with your results. The location is what is troubling."

Edward picked up where Anne left off. "One of our crewmates has been there for some time. He is coloured."

Cook scratched his chin. "That is troubling. He took many slaves from Calabar. I do not know Daniel's role, but he supplied the ship and men."

"We have more reason to meet with this man than before."

Before they could continue the discussion a knock at the door pulled the group's attention. Cook excused himself with a grumble about not expecting anyone and returned to the other room, closing the door behind him.

"So N-Nassir's village was attacked by slavers?" John questioned.

"That appears to be the case," Anne answered.

"There's a high probability he was taken." Edward stroked his beard. The crew left their carpenter after the death of his child so long ago, long enough that Nassir had to have been there at the same time as Daniel Richardson. *Where are you now, Nassir?*

The noise of a punch came from the front room. William glanced to the door. His brow was low, which brought to mind the perked ears of a hound.

William rose silently, motioning for silence. He went to the door and used another slit like the one on the main entrance to see through. What William saw made his eyes widen and he immediately shut the slit.

"We must leave, now," William whispered.

Edward followed suit by lowering his voice. "Why, what is happening?"

The Voyages of Queen Anne's Revenge

"There is no time to explain. The man who arrived is dangerous and we must leave immediately." William pulled Anne silently from her chair and herded her to the back door.

Edward could not let go of his curiosity, and disbelief over the danger, so he peered through the opening in the door. He could see Cook being held up by the neck by another man dressed in black with slick, jet-black hair, and dark eyes. Edward felt something from those eyes. On the surface they lacked emotion, similar to William most of the time, but Edward could see something in them, deep and endless, like a bottomless well.

A brutal, ruthless corruption filled those eyes. Edward felt that he had seen those same eyes before, but couldn't recall where. Edward was gripped with fear, and he could not turn away.

"I will ask you once more. Tell me where the Blackbeard is and I will spare you pain," the man in black said.

"I told you, he's in Mexico. My sources never lie," Cook replied.

"No, your sources may be free of fraud, but your words are not free of contamination." The man in black pulled out a small needle, like a pin, from his belt. "You will clearly not provide assistance, and only death awaits." He flicked the pin into Cook's neck.

Cook pulled his cane up, pointed it against the man in black's chest, and pulled on a hidden trigger. The man in black pushed the cane to the side, but not swiftly enough. The cane shot a bullet through his shoulder. Blood spurted from the wound, and the man in black dropped Cook to the floor.

Cook tried to flee, but the strength left his legs before he could rise. He crawled on his hands and knees, but in a matter of seconds he fell to the ground. Cook futilely tried to pull himself forward, but then rolled over. Cook's eyes rolled up in his head, he foamed at the mouth, and convulsed in muscle spasms. The seizure gradually lessened until stopping completely. Within moments Cook had died from whatever poison was on the needle.

The man in black watched until the end, after which his eyes moved up to the slit where Edward was still watching.

John pulled Edward away by force. Together, Anne and William, Edward and John, left post haste. John and William agreed to split up and meet back at the ship. John pulled Edward to the right of the home.

The man in black emerged from the back door soon after they started running, and noticed Edward and John turning a corner. Edward glanced back, slowing them down, so John pulled him into a nearby abandoned house.

John took Edward up the decaying stairs to the second floor and then forced Edward to climb a ladder to the attic. John entered the attic, then pulled the ladder up so none could follow and covered the hole with a nearby wooden box.

John slapped Edward across the face. "This is no time to be afraid!" he reprimanded forcefully.

Edward returned from his stupor. "What? I'm not afraid of anything."

"Edward, I've been in enough battles during the war to know when a man is afraid. Whoever that man is, he caused you to feel fear, but fear is not something to be ashamed of."

Edward reflected on what he felt moments ago, and asked himself why he froze. He came to the conclusion that John was correct, and Edward was afraid of the man.

"Something about him screamed danger," Edward admitted.

"Good, good. Use your memory to help condition yourself to the feeling."

Edward closed his eyes and recalled the man in black's eyes, and what he'd said. *He was after me, but who could he be? He was too... dark... to be a marine. An assassin? But who would have hired him?* Even in the shadow of Edward's mind, those eyes held no less power.

John strained his ears to try to hear any noises in the old house. After a few seconds, John and Edward could both hear the sound of slow methodical footsteps marching up the stairs. The man in black had followed them, which neither John nor Edward doubted, and he wanted them to hear those footsteps. They became louder and louder with each step up the stairs.

When the assassin was at the top of the stairs, he searched the different rooms one by one. The sound of the footsteps as well as the not so subtle creaking of the old wood allowed Edward and John to know exactly where he was.

Suddenly, a sword thrust up from below with a thunk a few feet from where Edward and John were sitting. Edward was about to rise and move, but John stopped him.

The sword was removed slowly and Edward once more could hear the movement of the man in black. The sword was thrust into the attic through the floorboards once more, closer to Edward and John, then removed quickly. The footsteps moved into the room directly below them. The sword shot up with more frequency, closer and closer to hitting Edward and John.

The Voyages of Queen Anne's Revenge

The hideous sound of the metal scraping through the old wood sent shivers down Edward's spine. He could not release the image of those eyes from his haunted mind. Edward recalled others recoiling at his own glare. *Are my eyes the same?*

Edward wasn't able to dwell on the question for too long, as the man in black was still approaching. He thrust his sword into the box over the attic entrance and pushed it forward, opening the way.

Edward and John had nowhere left to run, so John rose silently with Edward doing the same. The sound of scraping furniture was heard below as the man in black moved something around for him to step on. He climbed up and jumped to the hole, pushing the box aside as he climbed into the attic.

When the man was halfway up, John rushed over and kicked the wooden box into his face. The box busted with the force and caused the man in black to lose his precarious grip on the opening to the attic. The man fell with a crash.

"Run!" John yelled as he jumped down the hole.

John landed on the lower floor and immediately began running. Edward did the same, landing right next to the man in black. The man grabbed Edward's leg with an iron grip, and he struggled to free himself as the fallen man rose to his feet.

John took a knife from his belt and stabbed the man in black on his forearm above the elbow. The iron grip released. The man himself seemed oblivious to the pain, like his body was deadened to it.

John grabbed Edward's arm and pulled him. "I said run, soldier!" John screamed.

Edward and John ran to the closest window and ploughed through. Glass shattered in their wake, the shards dancing in the light. John and Edward both rolled onto the dirt alleyway between the houses to break the fall and ran to the south, to the ship.

"We will not escape this man by simply running," John asserted.

"What do we do?" Edward asked, glancing behind him. Though he could not see the man in black, he could feel his presence. Edward knew he was still chasing them.

"Stay focused," John commanded.

"Right."

"We'll need a distraction. We need to start a riot," John suggested.

"How do we do that?"

"Start hitting people," John answered as he levelled a large man with a haymaker as he ran.

Blackbeard's *Revenge*

Edward and John both began punching and kicking the townspeople as they ran. John led Edward to the town square full of people. The townspeople who were hit ran after the two, pushing and forcing more people aside in their wake, causing fights to start in the streets.

In the square, Edward and John indiscriminately hit people standing about. Edward threw one man into a group of other people, and John used some people as shields, causing scraps not even involving him to start.

Before long, the whole square erupted in an all-out brawl of pirates, thugs, and drunken revellers. Edward and John didn't check for the man in black, and continued to run through the streets to the gates of the city.

"John, look!" Edward pointed to the gates.

The merchant guards were closing the gates, and Edward could see Anne and William behind the gates with four horses. Anne was arguing with the gatekeepers, trying to get them to stop closing the gates, but they wouldn't listen. The wooden gates were closed and locked before Edward and John reached the wall.

"This way," John ordered, not stopping.

John went to the side of the wooden wall close to the gate and ran up a set of stairs to a walkway around the perimeter of the city wall.

Guards rushed after them and one man threw a punch at John. John blocked the punch, took a musket from behind the guard's back, and smashed the butt against the guard's face. The guard fell over the side of the walkway to the ground below.

Edward scanned for a way they could jump over the wall safely. "There!" He pointed to a large haystack on the east side. "We can climb the watchtower and jump into the hay."

"Lead the way, Captain," John offered as he fired the musket at a guard.

Edward ran along the walkway. Guards attacked him as he ran and he used his broad shoulder to plough through the men blocking his way. Near the base of the watchtower, one guard gripped him by the shoulders from behind while another attacked with a sword from the front. Edward flipped the guard holding him over his back. The man flew through the air and knocked down the one with the sword.

Edward entered the open watchtower. The inside had four wooden pillars with crossbeams on the ends and a perch at the top for the guards. The walkway was completely open and one had to climb up a ladder to reach the top.

The Voyages of Queen Anne's Revenge

Edward climbed the ladder as John followed behind. Edward switched to the other side of the ladder and stepped onto the crossbeams. He jumped, dropping twenty feet and into the middle of the haystack, softening his fall.

Anne and William had noticed the skirmish and Edward jumping down from the watchtower. They rushed over with the horses and shot at the guards outside the walls of Tortuga with pistols.

John reached the crossbeams and was readying himself to jump when a guard shot at him. He started to jump and was shot through his side. The bullet caused John's jump to turn into a fall.

"John!" Edward yelled as he ran forward. John fell onto Edward, and the two dropped to the ground together. "Are you well, John?"

"S-sorry, Captain. I didn't quite make the jump."

Edward helped John rise. "Will you still be able to ride?"

"I believe so. We don't have time to waste anyway, that man is surely on our tail."

Edward, John, Anne and William all mounted their horses and travelled south. The sounds of fighting slowly diminished as they got closer to the harbour.

"William, you saw the man. Who was he?" Edward asked while they were riding.

"Edward Russell. I believe he is the man who killed William III— your uncle, Anne—and framed me for the murder. If I were to speculate, he was sent by Queen Anne."

"Well, I am the target this time. Anne, I know you were not able to see his face, but do you think what William said is true?"

"I was never involved in my mother's affairs, nor did I wish to be, so I cannot say if she has used an assassin." Anne turned away in disgust. "However, sending an assassin after you is consistent with something she would do. You took her heir away from her and humiliated her, twice. First she sent over a hundred naval ships, and now a covert assassin. She won't stop there, I'm afraid."

"It will take more than one man to stop us," Edward declared, full of bravado, but the feeling the man in black gave him was still affecting him.

Anne smiled at his reassurance, but Edward could tell that she didn't believe him by the look in her eyes.

The four riders reached the harbour in no time, and they rushed to the ship immediately. The crew were conducting menial tasks aboard *Freedom* until they saw Edward and company come in with all urgency. The crew dropped what they were doing to see what the commotion was, but Edward stopped them.

"Prepare to set sail, we must leave now!" he yelled for all to hear.

Edward ran up to the quarterdeck where Herbert was at the helm with Christina at his side. Christina had crutches to help her move around as her leg was still healing. Her wolf Tala was lying at her feet.

"What's wrong, Edward?" Christina asked.

Herbert turned his wheelchair around to face Edward. "Did something happen in town?"

"We met with an assassin. He killed our source of information before he was able to find out where Daniel Richardson is," Edward answered.

Herbert adjusted his glasses. "What do we do now?"

William took over explaining. "We were able to find out where Richardson has been: Calabar, NiTalaa."

Herbert and Christina glanced at each other, eyes wide. "But, that's where…" Christina didn't finish her sentence.

"We know," Edward confirmed. "All the more reason why we need to return there as soon as possible. And, did we mention the assassin? Is the whole crew here, or did some men go ashore?"

"Some did, but all crew members have returned," Herbert reported.

"Good, then get us out of here, helmsman!"

19. CALABAR REVISITED

After a brief stop in Port-de-Paix south of Tortuga, to send a letter to the Bodden Brothers about what happened to their friend Aaron Cook, the crew of the *Freedom* set off for Calabar. The journey would take at least seven weeks, so they stocked up before leaving.

Along the journey, the daily routine of maintaining the ship and training kept everyone busy. Without a fully-fledged carpenter, the *Freedom* needed more time for maintenance, so the long trips served her well.

After a few weeks, Christina was up and about without her crutches and back into training. One day Anne proposed a team fight to promote group dynamics. To demonstrate, she and William showed what they were capable of doing together.

Specific manoeuvres, when performed as one, not only helped cover each other's backs, but also increased their effectiveness. Anne would jump off William's back as he was kneeling down to fire a musket. In the air she would land with a double kick using the downward momentum for additional power. William helped Anne jump higher using his hands to vault her up, and then she would latch onto something and pull him up. They worked beautifully together because of their experience.

"Why can't we train together?" Edward asked Anne after one of the demonstrations. There was a twinge of anger in his voice.

"I wish we could, but the difference in our skill levels is too great. If you wish to train with someone, maybe Christina would be better. Your power and her speed would make a good combination."

"I don't think we should team up, Edward would slow me down." Christina spoke loudly enough for Edward and Anne to hear. Anne could see Christina, and at Anne's questioning expression, Christina winked, to which Anne smiled back.

"Slow you down?" Edward questioned as he turned around.

"Maybe she's right, Edward, you are quite a bit taller, and slow. Christina learns very quickly, so I'm not sure you can keep up," Anne asserted, folding her arms and inspecting Edward up and down.

Edward gritted his teeth. "I can run circles around you, little one."

"Oh yeah, see what happens when you try," Christina challenged.

"We will train together then, and we'll see who is better."

"Yay! Thanks, Captain." Christina smiled with genuine mirth, to Edward's confusion. She thanked Anne and talked with her a bit.

"Why do I feel as if I was tricked?" Edward asked to no one in particular.

Sam was passing by on his way to spar with William. "Cause you wus, mate. Cause you wus." He sauntered off with a laugh.

Anne clapped to grab everyone's attention. "Alright, how about we start a duel then? What about Henry and Pukuh against Edward and Christina?"

Henry and Pukuh walked over at hearing their names. After explaining, the four combatants were more than eager to have a good scrap. They stood on the forecastle deck with the crew watching on the railings or on ratlines.

"Watch out, Ed, I'm going to get payback for before," Henry said. He was in a fighting stance, his massive arms flexed.

"We'll see about that," Edward replied.

"I do not wish to hurt you, girl, so I will ease my blows," Pukuh teased Christina.

"Don't mock me."

The groups fought with everything they had, each working together to defeat the other group. Being the first time working with each other, Edward and Christina were less than graceful, and tempers flared, but they were able to turn things around.

Together Edward and Christina managed to throw Henry overboard and forced Pukuh into the corner of the bow. The crew moved away when the three drew close. Christina whispered something in Edward's ear and he nodded. Edward and Christina backed up a few steps and locked hands. Edward pulled her and swung her towards Pukuh. She kicked Pukuh in the chest and he was pushed to the edge of the deck. Edward put Christina down, ran to Pukuh, lifted his legs, and tossed him over the side. The Mayan fell over into the sea like Henry.

Rope ladders were lowered for Henry and Pukuh while Christina and Edward celebrated. Henry and Pukuh climbed up, and dried off.

"How does being beaten feel?" Christina boasted.

Henry and Pukuh eyed each other and laughed. "We went easy on you two," Henry claimed.

"Oh yea? Round two, right now. We'll show you who the best team is," Edward said.

"We are ready to battle when you are," Pukuh confirmed.

The four fought again, laughing as they bonded. Anne watched from the poop deck, joyful over the smiles on their faces.

"Dangerous, leavin them two together," Sam warned, walking over to Anne.

"What do you mean?" Anne said curtly with arms folded.

"Christina an' the capt'n. She admires him, could turn ta infatuation."

"I see what you are trying to do, but it won't work. Jealousy is not part of my vocabulary. I trust Edward and Christina both."

Sam laughed. "I wusn't trying ta make you jealous, jus' a warning. Love is blind, they say." Sam laughed again and strolled away.

Anne watched Edward, Christina, Henry, and Pukuh all laughing. *I trust Edward.*

. . .

The *Freedom* landed on the almost non-existent harbour of Calabar at dusk. The harbour was deserted, save for a few small fishing boats, and the only sounds were the subtle knocking of the boats against the pier and the lapping of the waves.

Edward stepped onto the harbour and scanned the horizon. He was joined by other crew members as the sails were furled and the *Freedom* moored.

"What happened here?" Henry thought out loud.

"Daniel Richardson happened," Edward answered.

Edward and the crew left the harbour and rushed up a small hill to the village of Calabar. What they saw as they topped the rise stopped them in their tracks. Edward's mouth opened wide from the sight of the devastation.

Calabar used to be a thriving African community full of life and promise, but now the village appeared like the remains of a war zone. The ashes of homes made of wood and straw were burnt to the ground. The dwindling populace moved about in a trance, many of them children, women, or the elderly. The grave site was clearly visible from the hill Edward and his crew were on, and larger since last time they visited.

At the sight of Edward and his crew, the few villagers shuffling around shouted something and ran into their homes. "No, wait! We're not here to hurt you!" he yelled, but none listened.

Soon after the villagers ran to their homes, men ran out with spears and muskets. Twenty men ran to Edward and his crew, threatening them back to the ship.

"Return to your ship and leave," one of the men in front warned. He wore a set of tattered and worn trousers made by English hands. He didn't wear a shirt, and his raw and powerful chest muscles were exposed. He was tall and his face looked familiar to Edward.

"Please listen to me. We are not here to harm you." Edward stepped forward.

The man in the lead shot his musket at Edward's feet. "Not another step, unless it is back where you came. We have had enough of the white man taking our people."

Edward motioned for his crew to stay back and not draw their weapons. "We are searching for a friend of ours, Nassir. If you can tell us what has happened to him we will leave with no further discussion."

The leader of the aggressors glanced briefly at his men. "What is your name?"

"Edward Thatch."

The leader lowered his weapon "Nassir has told me of you. You can rest assured, as far as I know he is alive." He turned to his men, speaking in their native tongue, and the men lowered their weapons.

"Thank you. Might I have your name?" Edward asked.

"My name is Dumaka. I am Nassir's brother."

"His brother? Well, you do look similar, but he never mentioned anything about you."

"Well, considering he believed me dead, that is unsurprising. Let us talk by a fire, you must be cold and tired."

"Yes, some rest would be nice."

Dumaka took Edward, Henry, Anne, and William to an open area behind one of the remaining homes. While the fire was started, Christina brought blankets for the crew to help ward off the cold air. She laid one over Anne's back and sat down beside her.

"The ship appeared out of nowhere at dawn about four months ago."

"Four months? That couldn't have been very long after we landed," Anne surmised. She held hands with Edward and sat close to him for more warmth.

"No, only about a month. I did not have much of a chance to reunite with him before he was taken. He was still grieving for his son, but he had fond things to say about you all."

The crew's eyes turned downwards as they thought of their friend and what was happening to him now. "So what happened?" Christina asked. Her eyes held anger hidden deep within them, and she gripped the wooden rose at her neck.

"They took over one hundred villagers as slaves. Nassir and some of the men fought, but were not able stand against their numbers. The fighting enabled us to help the less able villagers to escape into the woods. We are all that remains of our warriors. When I returned, Nassir was gone and his body was nowhere to be found. I assumed he was captured."

"Do you have any idea where they were taking the slaves?" Edward asked.

"One of the villagers who escaped overheard the white men say they were travelling to Boston."

Anne turned to Edward. "That lines up with the location of the American Chestnut tree Alexandre mentioned."

Edward nodded. "Your brother took his possessions with him when he left the crew, and I know his papers of freedom were amongst them. If you have his bag, those papers will help us at least free him."

Dumaka shook his head, his eyes betraying his disappointment. "No, his belongings were in the house over there." Dumaka pointed to the remains of a house burned to the ground in the attack.

Edward nodded. "No matter, we will still head for Boston in the morning. Not having those papers makes things more difficult, but we've been in worse situations. We'll get your brother back."

"I thank you for your concern over my brother, and I have no doubts you will succeed in saving him, but I have another request. I wish for you to save the villagers too."

Edward took a drink of some water as he considered what Dumaka requested. "I hope you realise the difficulty of what you are asking?"

"Yes, but I want you to understand what is happening to our people in America. Nassir, and others who were able to make their way home, have told us the horrors. We have dealt with slavery throughout all of history, but at least here we had some chance of reward for our families. In America, death is preferable to how our people are being treated. My brother helped you to be free, and according to him this is something close to your heart. If you truly are a vessel for freedom, then you cannot stand by as my people die for nothing."

"All I can say is I will try. If the risk is too great for my men…"

"I understand. That you will try is enough for me."

Edward turned to his crewmen gathered around the fire, all the senior officers of the *Freedom*, and Christina. "So we are all in agreement then? We leave for Boston tomorrow, and try to save Nassir and the villagers?"

"Agreed," the crew replied.

Their course was set, and soon the fox-hunt for the elusive Daniel Richardson would end.

20. BONDS IN BOSTON

The trip to Boston would take over two months, so the crew stocked up as much as possible in Calabar before leaving. The people in Calabar were generous in their patronage and provided all they could in the hopes Edward and his crew would be able to bring back their family.

Along the way the crew continued training with Anne and William. The new members *Freedom* had gained from Bodden Town were becoming better at working as a team in battle and out. The crew functioned more as a team, making up for each other's weaknesses and aiding in their strengths.

Jack also participated in the training, having an adeptness in fist fighting and fencing. Anne practiced her eastern fighting art with him to hone his hand-to-hand combat, and, as Alexandre was the best fencer, he helped Jack fence. At first Alexandre lamented Jack's lack of skill, but Jack learned quickly and impressed the Frenchman.

Christina and her pet wolf were nigh on inseparable since their fight in the woods of Mexico. Christina trained Tala some commands in French to assist aboard the ship and in fights as well. The only two who could issue Tala orders were Christina and Edward. If anyone else commanded Tala, she merely gawked at them.

Edward and Christina grew closer as well. They continued their training and created some impressive moves. With Edward's strength he was able to swing Christina around by the hands, allowing them to attack while being surrounded, and at the end Edward vaulted her feet-first at the enemy.

"You two are quite the pair," Anne said as she walked up to the poop deck where Edward was.

Edward scratched his chin through the beard. "You mean Christina?" Anne nodded. "Yes, she and I work well together," Edward pulled Anne in close, gazing deep into her green eyes, "but I think we work better." Edward kissed Anne passionately, and she gladly accepted.

Anne patted Edward on the chest. "I want to talk to you about something."

Edward leaned on the railing of the poop deck, allowing him to overlook the whole of the ship. "I am listening."

"What do you plan to do in Boston?" Anne asked, joining him on the railing.

"I haven't decided. I haven't been to Boston, so I don't know how best to secure Nassir and the villagers, let alone the key."

"Well, doing nothing and letting someone else assess the situation would be a prudent first step."

Edward cocked his brow. "Why would I do that?"

"As I am sure you are aware, England is at war, my mother's war, and the American colonies are at the forefront of the conflict. Boston is an English territory." Anne paused for a moment.

Edward picked up on what Anne was saying, grasping where she was headed. "And so, information on our escape would be popular news. What about the ship itself, wouldn't the *Freedom* be well known as well?"

"There are many ships, and *Freedom* is a common name, I don't believe we have to worry about us being ousted," Anne speculated while she patted the railing.

Edward ran his fingers through Anne's curly red hair. "So I won't be able to leave the ship, but what about you?"

Anne sighed and leaned on Edward's chest. "I resemble my mother, so I too will be confined to the ship."

"We'll have each other to keep company, so I'm not complaining." Edward kissed the back of Anne's head. "But I suppose William will be here too."

Anne turned around and stretched out along the railing, laying her head in Edward's lap. She played with his beard. "I could always send William on some errand so we can be alone." Anne smirked.

Edward laughed. "You're so devious, I love it." He leaned down and kissed her once more. Edward noticed Henry on the quarterdeck, talking with Herbert. "Oh, Henry! We need to discuss something."

Henry strolled up the stairs to the poop deck. "Yes?" he inquired.

"I'll need you to act as my proxy in Boston. Apparently, Boston is British territory, which doesn't allow Anne or me to step ashore for fear of being noticed. Isn't it nice to have people in the crew that know about these things?" Edward asked with a smile.

Henry ignored the question. "So you'll need me to find Daniel Richardson for you?"

"Yes, when you find Richardson we'll need to do an assessment of the best course of action to retrieve the key and free Nassir and the villagers. If you present the letter he left, you'll no doubt be let into his home, and while inside you can see what kind of security he has."

"Sounds simple enough. I can pose as someone who wishes to buy the key."

"Something tells me he won't part with the key easily, judging from the trouble he went through, but that's the best option at the moment."

"Might I interject?" a voice asked from behind.

Edward noticed Alexandre listening to the conversation. Alexandre sauntered forward to the three of them. Back hunched, eyes dark, and appearance dishevelled as usual, he presented the air of one too busy for sleep or personal hygiene, but the glint in his eyes bespoke his greater faculties of the mind. "I wish to join this *expédition*."

"Not that I'm saying no, but why?"

Alexandre shrugged his shoulders while shaking his head like the answer was obvious. "You need someone who is capable of seeing things the ordinary cannot. I am the only one *compétent*."

"Are you saying Henry isn't qualified for this?"

"*Non*, I am saying lesser minds will miss the big picture. Anne and William are not fit to leave, so I am forced to step in."

Henry glared at Alexandre. "I can understand you being smarter, but your arrogance is groundless. I'm up to the task."

"*Mon ami*, arrogance has nothing to do with this. I possess a dexterity of mind greater than others, this is fact. If you are still in doubt of this even after my *pouvoirs de déduction* have been tested thus far, then we will play a game: we will see who is able to extrapolate the most useful information from Richardson."

"You're on!" Henry said, extending his hand to shake on the deal, which Alexandre accepted.

"This will be interesting," Edward whispered to Anne.

"Mmm, but I have a funny feeling Alexandre might have been trying to bait Henry for some reason."

Edward stroked his beard. "Seeing how this plays out will be fun."

...

When the *Freedom* sailed into the port of Boston, the crew expected to see a few ships, but the harbour was filled with fifty or more ships of all shapes and sizes. More than a few of those ships were outfitted for battle and some were even the same size as the *Freedom*.

The Voyages of Queen Anne's Revenge

As the *Freedom* navigated the few small islands in the crescent-shaped port, they passed by many ships docking and leaving Boston. The noise from the travellers rose in the spaces between the land and sea. Colourful sailors and merchants travelled to and fro across the decks of the full-sailed ships.

The noonday sun, the sea air, and the smell of nature from the land could not calm Edward's mind from this sight. He believed a raid could be a fall-back plan if they had issues rescuing the villagers from Richardson's grasp, but the amount of military ships was insurmountable for the *Freedom*. Edward held little hope they would be able to achieve the goal of even saving Nassir.

We must play our cards right if we are to secure the key and Nassir.

Edward and Anne descended below deck before the ship was docked. Edward told the crew to act as if Henry were the captain for the duration of their stay.

Henry and Alexandre, dressed in more elegant clothes than usual, left the ship immediately after docking. Henry paid the harbour master and set out to find Daniel Richardson. Richardson was a famous Bostonian, so he wasn't hard to find.

"Old Richardson lives on the west end of town. Head west and ye can't miss 'is cotton fields," a local businessman suggested.

Henry and Alexandre took a ride in a coach to Richardson's residence. The dirt road was bumpy, but straightforward. "So, Henry, have you pondered on our game? How will you compete with my genius?"

"Worry about yourself," Henry barked, pulling at the decorative silk bow tying his fine brown hair in a ponytail.

"I am not worried," Alexandre said with a hollow smile, slapping Henry's hands away from the bow.

Henry glowered at Alexandre. "You should be. One of our crewmates' lives is at stake."

Alexandre feigned shock and placed his hand over his chest. "*Mon dieu!* You do not think I care?"

"Hard to tell with you, sometimes."

"I very much care. You are all of you so… interesting. Without you for amusement whatever would I do?"

Henry rolled his eyes and folded his arms. "Of course. Wouldn't want the good doctor to die of boredom."

Alexandre grinned. "I also recall you did not approve of a *négre* aboard the ship, so are you trying to act holier than thou, or have you had a change of heart?"

Henry's mouth opened in shock by Alexandre's clairvoyance at knowing exactly how to rattle someone. Henry knew he couldn't lie to Alexandre to save face. "I was raised differently from Edward. Negros aren't my favourite company, but Nassir is part of the family. He's different."

"And the villagers?"

"They aren't my concern. Edward can try to figure out how to save them if he wants, but that already appears impossible."

Alexandre laughed. "Yes, well, *le Capitaine* delights in making the impossible possible."

"You have a point," Henry agreed.

"So, while on the subject of making the impossible possible, how do you plan on convincing our *marque* to part with the key?"

Henry cocked his brow. "You're letting me do the talking?" Alexandre answered with a smile and a nod, and Henry sighed. "I suppose I'll play it straight. Tell him it's needed for our ship and see what he's willing to take for it."

Alexandre appeared bored. "Are you sure it is wise to tell him the truth?"

"I don't see any other way of going about it. He knows the key has some story behind it. Whatever we tell him, there's no way we can downplay its importance. The only thing we can do is remove the key's importance for him."

Henry's last comment seemed to pique Alexandre's interest. "And how does telling him the truth remove the importance of the key?"

Henry couldn't help but grin a bit at evoking more than a passing interest from Alexandre. "Assuming he still has the key, he's no doubt been wondering for years what the key was for. In the letter he left he mentioned something about a hunt, and you said he might be of southern descent. So, he's a hunter. Not that much of a stretch." Alexandre nodded. "So, he's been hunting passively, or actively, for the lock that the key belongs to. After so many years, it's not about the key anymore, it's about the door, about the hunt. If we tell him exactly what the key is for, then the hunt is over, and in the most disappointing way possible. I'm also not the best liar, so we'll be more convincing if he can't tell we're lying."

"Remove the prey, and the hunter is left with no more use for the gun," Alexandre posed.

"Exactly. At least, that's the hope. If we can't get the key or Nassir back from Richardson then we'll have to rely on Edward to get everything."

Alexandre chuckled. "You know, perhaps you are not as dull as I first thought."

"Thank you, I think."

Alexandre and Henry finished their exchange a moment before the coach lurched to a stop in front of a white mansion.

The coachman jumped down and opened the door to help Henry and Alexandre down. Henry paid the man as Alexandre surveyed the property.

To the left and right of the mansion a large field of cotton was primed for harvest. In the field, black slaves by the dozens picked cotton from the small plants in the hot sun. The back-breaking work was made worse by the many guards with whips to punish slackers, or to flex muscle. For every five slaves one guard walked up and down the field.

The mansion itself was two storeys, but, while impressive, rather plain. Each window was either shuttered with black wood panels or covered with lace drapes, making it difficult to see inside.

Some of the slaves were entering and leaving an annex building on the right side of the mansion.

More muscle were stationed at the double doors at the front entrance. When Henry and Alexandre approached, the guards stepped forward. "What business do you have here?" one of them asked, then he spat chewing tobacco onto the ground.

"Is this the residence of Daniel Richardson?" Henry asked.

"Yes, and what brings you to Mr Richardson's residence?"

Henry took out the letter Richardson left. "If you take this to your boss, he will understand."

One of the guards took the letter, and the two glanced at each other and shrugged. "Wait here," the first said, then he entered the building.

Henry scanned the field, taking a rough count of the people there. "There are about twenty guards here," Henry whispered.

"Sixteen, to be exact."

"The fields are low, which would make it hard to sneak in or out without being seen even at night."

"One small group would be best. Leaving with so many *esclaves* is a problem. We also have the problem of taking the villagers through town."

"This doesn't appear good."

"*Non*, it does not."

"Mr Richardson will see you now." The guard who went inside had reappeared without the letter. "I will take you to him."

Henry and Alexandre followed the man into the house. Inside, several guards and more slaves worked. In the centre of the main room, a large set of stairs went up and off to the left and right to the second floor. One of the servants passed through a door to the side of the stairs allowing Alexandre to see into the kitchen where slaves were working at preparing food. In the kitchen, he could see a door leading to the slaves' quarters.

The guard led them up the stairs to the second floor. On the far end, a lavish love seat and chairs were set in front of a fireplace. Along the sides, more closed doors led to various rooms.

The guard opened the first door to the right of the fireplace and beckoned Henry and Alexandre to enter. After the two entered, the guard closed the door.

The room they entered was a large and spacious study with tall bookshelves and ornamental relics, possibly from some ancient tomb. A mediaeval set of plate mail, swords, an Egyptian urn, a stone bird, and several animal heads plastered the walls like trophies. The fireplace from the previous room was mirrored into the study, with a small table holding expensive drinks between two high-backed chairs. At the back was a desk with several chairs in front and one behind. Large windows on the back wall allowed light in and provided a stunning view of the road leading up to the mansion. In the centre of the wall, above the desk and chairs, a key hung in a picture frame.

"Come on in and sit down, gentlemen. We have much to discuss," Daniel Richardson said, standing at the desk. His accent was a southern drawl, not native to Boston.

Henry and Alexandre sat down in the chairs offered. Richardson was still eyeing the letter as he sat down in his seat, a soft metallic click sounding under the desk when he moved his feet.

Richardson was an older man with salt-and-pepper hair slicked back. He had a greying beard on his full face, and the plump aspect of a man used to wealth and having others do the hard work for him. He was wearing a black and red suit with his coat draped over the back of the chair because of the heat.

Henry could smell cigar and wood ash in the air, as well as warm alcohol. The smell of fur and raw poultry also came from the many animal heads adorning the walls.

"Would any of you fine gents care for a drink. Ah have some fine whiskey if ya'll 'er interested." Henry and Alexandre both declined. Richardson peered at the letter once more with a smile. "Ah never thought ah would see this again, boy. Been a few years since ah stumbled across that island. Took some doin' to reach the top, and what do ah get for the trouble? A key." Richardson laughed. "Boy, at first ah was mighty angry, but curiosity has a way of increasin' over time. Ah never was able to find out what the key was fer, nor who left it there. Ah am sure interested if you fellers have any information you can provide."

Henry took the lead. "I believe our story may be rather disappointing to you. I was sold a ship by a magnanimous trickster who left clues as to where to find the keys for specific sections of the ship. The island you found was built specifically for his game, and the key is the next one in the line. Without the key, I have a fraction of a ship."

Richardson laughed heartily. "How positively fascinating, to find intrepid adventurers such as myself. My boy, you remind me of myself in my youth."

Henry glanced at Alexandre awkwardly. "Yes, well, as you can see we need the key so we can continue with our journey. We are willing to pay you for your troubles."

Richardson raised his hand. "I am sorry, my boy, but I simply cannot part with the key. The years have made me attached inexplicably and inexorably to the key. I will, however, purchase your ship from you for a more than generous price and you can be assured she will be in good hands."

Henry's mouth hung open. "I'm sorry, but we are in similar sorts. I cannot part with the ship. We have been at this for years now, and the ship means so much more to the whole crew, not just myself."

Richardson stopped smiling. He didn't seem the type used to being denied something. "Then, no amount of money will change your mind?"

"No. I ask you the same."

"No," Richardson replied with a sigh. "Such a disappointment. Well, gentlemen, if you'll excuse me, I have other business I must attend to."

Alexandre finally took the helm. "There is another *afaire* which you may be more amicable towards. A slave named Nassir may be in your possession, or previously has been, who is actually a free man and our crewmate. We are searching for him to bring him back into our fold."

Richardson laughed. "Your French friend is rather funny. I do have a slave with a savage name of Nassir, but all my slaves are slaves, and as such they cannot be free men. You realise the flaw in your logic?"

"We are not lying," Henry replied, growing more frustrated.

"Produce his papers of freedom and I will have no choice but to comply. No papers, no nigger."

"How much to part with him?"

Richardson smirked, knowing he held all the cards. "I refuse. My slaves are all so precious to me. I cannot spare a single one."

Alexandre stood. "Expect a summons to a court of law soon. We will have our crewmate back one way or another."

"I shall await with anticipation."

Alexandre left the mansion with Henry following closely behind, albeit with a misstep due to confusion. Henry and Alexandre entered the coach and headed back to the ship.

"What was that?" Henry asked.

"That will buy us time to steal the key and formulate a proper plan to save Nassir and the *villageois*."

"How do you expect to prove Nassir's freedom without papers?"

"Depending on certain factors, we may be able to win, but it is a ploy. The rest is up to *le Capitaine* and what he wants to do."

Henry sighed. "I hope you know what you're doing."

"Always," Alexandre replied.

21. BAIT & TRAP

"So he lives on the outskirts of town in the middle of a field, and has over twenty guards?" Edward asked. Henry and Alexandre nodded. "How will we free them?" Edward questioned, frustrated.

"You're giving up?" Anne asked, anger seeping through.

"I don't see any way we can save Nassir and all those villagers. If we cause any trouble, there are a multitude of warships here which can best us. We can't kill the guards without a protracted battle, and before the crew arrives we'll be found out by locals because of the numbers."

"But there must be a way," Christina pleaded. "What if we spread out, small groups of people all heading to the mansion, then we strike at once?"

Edward shook his head, running his hand through his wavy black hair. "No, Boston has a local garrison, not an unorganised militia. We would be outed well before we reached the edge of the city. Barring that, we wouldn't be able to escape for the same reason."

"Then what do you suggest?" Anne asked.

Edward considered all the eyes on him. The senior officers were staring at him, expecting an epiphany of a brilliant plan from Edward like in the past. Edward sighed. "I'm sorry, I don't know what we can do. For now, I will sneak into Richardson's mansion and spirit the key away. Then we can confer with Nassir if he has any ideas on how to escape with his people. Sam, can I count on your help with this?"

Sam nodded. "Aye Capt'n."

"Henry, you mentioned the best way to enter was through the slave quarters, and the key was in a room on the second floor."

Henry nodded. "Yes, the key is inside a picture frame on the wall. He keeps a lot of trophies in the room, and the key is one of his accomplishments."

Alexandre laughed, drawing all eyes to him. "Something to share Alexandre?" Edward asked.

"Oh, nothing of importance. Just, if you steal that key you will be taking a *faux*."

A foe...? Ah, Fake. "The key is a fake?"

"He has a lockbox under his desk with the real key inside."

Henry's jaw dropped once more. "How do you know?"

"He shuffled in his seat and tapped his foot against something metal. The sound was faint, but easy to hear if you were paying attention."

Henry folded his arms. "So what makes you think the key is in the lockbox? You weren't able to see inside."

"You said yourself, the man has *trophées* of his accomplishments. Do you think finding the key was an accomplishment? He was never able to find what lock the key was for. *Non*, the picture frame is not a *trophée*, it is a reminder."

Edward shrugged. "A nice theory, but I don't think the game is won yet. We'll test your theory later. We take both. Alexandre, please draw us a floor plan of the mansion so we can work out a plan to sneak inside. When is the court battle to start?"

"Tomorrow. Richardson is a prominent businessman, so the magistrate is speeding things along for him," Henry responded.

Edward rubbed his face in equal parts frustration and exhaustion. "Well, I guess we also have to deal with preferential treatment. Excellent."

Anne held Edward's hand in support. "But what about the villagers?"

"I don't know, I can only focus on one thing at a time. We need to trick Richardson somehow, but I don't know how. I will think of something in time."

The crew left Edward alone, but he wasn't able to formulate a plan. Alexandre was cryptic as usual, and more interested in seeing what Edward could create rather than suggesting a plan. *Damn Frenchman probably doesn't know any way we can save everyone anyway.*

The next day, Alexandre and Henry both went to the office of the local magistrate who was to see them and Richardson together. Richardson brought Nassir along with him. The office itself was a medium-sized room with small bookshelves and a desk. The four sat in chairs in front of the magistrate's desk.

The portly magistrate wore an expensive coat and a powdered wig atop his head in the English style. "Make your claim, gentlemen," he demanded coldly. The smell of alcohol wafted from his breath.

"This man, Nassir, has been wrongfully taken into slavery. He has already served once before and was freed," Alexandre stated.

"Produce his papers of freedom and let this be done then."

Alexandre glanced at Henry and then Nassir. "We can produce them, but we have not had occasion to discuss their whereabouts with Nassir."

The Voyages of Queen Anne's Revenge

The magistrate sighed. "Then go into the next room and discuss. And be quick about it."

Alexandre, Henry, and Nassir rose and entered the room to the right of the magistrate's office.

"I must say, friends, I did not expect to see you today. Thank you for trying to help me," Nassir said in his thick accent.

"You're our family, there's no way we wouldn't come for you. Edward wishes he could be here, but it's safer for us all if he's not."

"I understand."

"Focus, *messieurs*. Nassir, your brother believes your proof of freedom was burned in the attack on your village. Please tell us this is not so."

"My papers were on my person... until Richardson destroyed them."

"Excellent. Now what?" Henry lamented.

"This is simple, we make a forgery. Do you remember the name of the man who freed you?" Alexandre asked.

"David Cooper was the issuer of the papers."

Alexandre pulled out a piece of paper and pencil. "Do you remember the papers enough to provide his signature?"

Nassir took the paper and pencil in hand. "I stared at those papers every night for five years after I was freed. I can provide the entire wording."

Richardson and the magistrate were laughing and hitting it off. Henry and Alexandre eyed each other with worried expressions.

"We do not have the time, the signature will do. Alexandre will finish the rest," Henry said.

Once Nassir finished the signature, Alexandre pocketed the paper. "What about my people?" Nassir asked.

"We are focusing on trying to free you, and Edward is working on a plan to free the villagers, but you must understand the difficulty," Henry replied.

"I will trust in him then."

Henry and Alexandre both nodded to Nassir and they returned to the other room. "We know where the papers are and will retrieve them for you post haste," Henry told the magistrate.

"Yes, yes. We will reconvene tomorrow." The magistrate and Richardson each poured a glass of brandy and continued talking with each other as if they were the only ones in the room.

Henry and Alexandre glanced at Nassir one last time, as he had to stay with his master. Despair was written on his face, but his eyes held a glint of hope.

187

"Do you think the forgery will work?" Henry asked in a whisper outside the magistrate's office.

"It is not a question of whether it will or will not, but whether the magistrate will let it work. I fear the man may be *corrompu*. Daniel and the magistrate seem to be *amis*. Perhaps his rise to his current position was not done entirely honestly."

"So, what we do will not help?"

"*Non*, I did not say that. This is merely to serve as a distraction from the real plan. *Le Capitaine* will provide the means for all to escape."

"Assuming he's up to the task."

"You have *doutes*?"

"Let's just say my faith in Edward has been shaky of late."

Alexandre nodded. "Yes, I have noticed. He will come through in the end. He always does."

"What makes you so sure?"

Henry saw something rare: a light deep in Alexandre's normally dull eyes. "I'm not."

...

In the dead silence of night, two figures stalked through the town of Boston and the forest of chestnut trees on the outskirts. They moved silently, but with purpose. Their destination was a cotton plantation owned by a certain Daniel Richardson.

Edward and Sam ran through the woods and travelled light, carrying no weapons aside from knives and a blow gun with darts provided by Alexandre. The moon was full and shining brightly through the slender leaves above them. The wind was cool and breezy so close to the coast, and brought the smell of fresh chestnuts and grass to their nostrils.

As the two reached the western edge of the forest they slowed down to catch their breath and move with more stealth. Edward and Sam both hid behind the trees as they moved forward, seeing if the coast was clear and then motioning to the other to move forward. When they finally reached the edge they ducked down and hid behind a large tree together.

In front of them they could see the large mansion with adjoining quarters for the slaves along with the large cotton field surrounding the building.

Edward examined the location. "This is the mansion, exactly as described."

Edward could see guards with lanterns walking around the property, though none were close to the forest. The guards appeared more vigilant than they normally would be, which did not bode well in Edward's mind. *Henry and Alexandre must have spooked him.*

"So are we gonna kill these wankers or what?" Sam whispered.

"No, we'll use these darts Alexandre provided. According to him they will knock someone out and leave them with particularly bad aches in the morning."

"Blimey. How does the Frenchman create these things?"

"Alexandre said he had an epiphany when thinking about the gas the surgeon in Winchester used. The gas reminded him of a plant some natives used to help them sleep on one of his treks around the world. He kept some with him and dried the leaves. Somehow he made this from the leaves."

Sam shook his head. "What about when they fall? And what about the other guards?" Sam asked as he motioned to the three on patrol.

"Sneak up and catch them as they fall. I'll attack the two on the left, you attack the one on the right."

Edward and Sam went their separate ways after dividing the darts. Edward moved to the left to a row of the cotton which led behind one of the guards. The guard was standing still and scanning the field with a lantern to aid him. Edward dropped to the ground and crawled into the field of cotton.

Edward crawled between bushes of cotton shrubs, trying to make as little noise as possible. The guard was staring in Sam's direction. Edward crawled forward slowly, inching closer and closer. The guard turned around and walked towards Edward who moved closer to the shrubs and lay motionless.

The smell of the cotton mixed with alcohol as the guard approached. Edward turned his head to watch the approach of the patrolling man. His nose passed over a cotton bulb. Edward's nose itched and he felt an urge to sneeze. The guard was nearly on top of Edward. He took out his blowdart and shot the man with a dart in the neck. Before the guard recognised what was happening, he fell. Edward caught him and let him fall gently to the ground as he let out a sneeze.

The other guards turned to the noise. Edward picked up the lantern and waved. The guards returned to their lookout. Edward allowed himself to breathe again as he wiped his nose.

He moved forward, lantern in hand. The two guards didn't notice anything wrong. Edward moved towards his second target closest to the slaves' quarters. The slightest noise came from the right. Edward and the guard's eyes flashed over, and the man waved back.

Sam must have made his move.

Edward stalked over to finish the trifecta so they could move on. When Edward advanced, the guard waved to him. Edward lowered his lantern so his face was not illuminated.

"See anything, Gary? I don't see nothin' over here. I think the boss is jus' spooked."

Edward shot a dart at the man's neck. The man grunted and his hand moved to the dart. He pulled out the dart and had enough time to focus on the needle before he fell. Edward ran over and caught him so he could let him fall gently to the ground without another sound.

Sam rushed to Edward. Edward had another dart ready just in case. "Sam?"

"It be me Capt'n," Sam whispered back. "Ready to head in?"

"Yeah, let's move."

Before the two could move any closer to the slave quarters, the door opened and another guard emerged with a lantern in hand. Edward and Sam blew out their lanterns and ducked to the ground. The guard peered left and right, and he noticed something was off.

In the darkness, the guard could see the third lantern, but not Edward and Sam. Edward shot a dart, but missed and hit the building. Sam tried his shot, but the guard bent over and the dart flew over his head. The guard picked up the dart Edward shot.

"Damn it, I'm out of darts," Edward said softly.

"I be out too. I used two on the first bloke."

"What do we do?" Edward asked, watching the guard examine the dart.

"I don't know, we wouldn't be havin' this discussion if ye were a better shot."

"Me, a better shot? You're the one who missed twice, I only missed this one."

Thump.

Edward and Sam turned in the direction of the noise and noticed the guard passed out. Upon examination, they noticed that the guard had pricked his finger on the tip of the dart, thus injecting himself with the concoction and knocking himself out.

"What a fool," Edward laughed.

The guards at the front entrance of the mansion heard the noise. "Is everything alright?" one of them questioned.

Edward and Sam both jumped at the voices. "Uhh, Gary's been drinking again," Edward replied.

The guard at the front entrance sighed. "Put him inside, we'll tell the boss in the morning."

"Right," Edward replied.

The guards at the front went back to watching the road. Edward picked up the two unused darts, then he and Sam picked up the man who just fell. They carried the body inside the slave quarters.

The inside was a horrid sight to behold. The annex building next to the mansion was a quarter of the size and no inch of the space was wasted on comfort. Wooden cots lined the walls, with a thin strip down the middle for walking. The cots were stacked on top of each other with barely any space to breathe between them.

Some of the slaves' eyes were on them, but they didn't move for fear they would be punished. The slaves probably didn't know the ones before them were not guards.

Edward scanned the annex building, but he could see no guards. "Nassir?" Edward whispered. "Nassir?" he asked a little louder as he moved further into the room.

"Edward?" a voice replied.

A man descended from a cot near the middle of the room. Others paid more attention at the odd display.

"Edward, what are you doing here?" Nassir questioned as he walked over to Edward and Sam.

"We have several reasons, but firstly: I am glad to see you are alright. I cannot imagine how Richardson is treating you."

"I have been through this before, but some of my villagers are children, and they are not coping as well."

"Do you have any ideas for how to reach the shore without raising alarm?"

Nassir shook his head. "I know not of any way without alerting anyone. Trust me, I have been thinking, but I am a simple carpenter, not a trickster."

Edward leaned in close to Nassir and whispered, "Then join us and we can at least save you, then we can think of a way to save your villagers after."

Nassir shook his head. "No, I will not leave without my villagers. I leave with them, or not at all."

Edward placed his hand on Nassir's shoulder. "I had a feeling you would say that. I promise you, I will find a way."

"Capt'n, we'd best be leavin'," Sam said.

"Right." Edward glanced over his shoulder. "The other reason we arrived was to retrieve the key for the ship."

"The slaver has a key to the *Freedom*?" Nassir asked.

"Yes, we travelled to the location the clue pointed us to, but the puzzles were solved and we found a note instead of a key. The note was signed Daniel Richardson. Once we procure the key, we will return to the ship and invent a plan to save you." Edward glanced at the near hundred watching him. "All of you."

Nassir hugged Edward. "I believe in your words."

Edward nodded and held Nassir's gaze for a moment before he passed through the door joining the annex building to the mansion. Nassir and the villagers watched as Edward and Sam crept into the mansion. Their hope was leaving, but Nassir knew they would return, and they would all leave as one.

Edward walked through the empty kitchen and pulled out the mock blueprint Alexandre provided. The picture showed a rough detail of where Edward was and where they should go. The kitchen had one exit to the left leading to the dining hall, and another to the right leading to the entrance room. Edward opened the swinging door on the right to peer inside.

Two guards were conversing on the side Edward would walk into, but no others from what he could see. He slowly pulled the swinging door back to a point of rest.

"Take one dart, head through the dining hall, and we'll hit both of the guards at the same time."

Sam nodded and took one of the darts. He went through the door to the dining hall after checking for guards. Edward peered through the swinging door. When he saw Sam at the other door, they both nodded and pulled out their blowguns. They fired the darts at the same time, hitting both of the guards.

The guard Sam shot fell to the ground after a few seconds, but the other was still standing. First, he pulled out the dart, inspected it, and then tried to wake his friend.

Edward's and Sam's shock was written on their faces, and each rushed out to correct the mistake. The guard noticed Sam approaching him, then opened his mouth to yell. Edward ran and clapped a hand over the guard's mouth. The guard struggled and writhed against Edward, but couldn't free himself. Sam punched the man hard in the stomach, then again in the temple, knocking him out.

Edward lowered the guard to the ground. Sam carried a grim expression. "We only have a few minutes before he wakes up," Edward whispered.

"What happened to the dart?" Sam asked.

"I must have picked up the one the other man pricked himself on."

"No use cryin' now. We 'ave to move."

Edward and Sam moved quickly and quietly up the stairs to the second floor. They kept an eye on the corners for any movements in the dark of the upper part of the mansion, but the hallway was quiet and empty.

Edward went to the fireplace and opened the door to the right. He peered through the slit, and saw an empty room. Edward and Sam entered, shut the door, and rushed straight to the desk at the back.

Moonlight from the windows, and the eyes of dead animal heads following their movement, lent an eerie atmosphere to the empty room.

Edward's eyes moved across the trophies, and settled on the key above the desk. He moved a chair behind the desk to stand on top of, and took the key down.

"Isn't that the fake?" Sam asked.

"We don't know yet. We shouldn't make assumptions. Alexandre could easily be wrong about the whole thing." Edward opened the picture frame and pocketed the key. "Take the lockbox," Edward said as he set the picture frame back on the wall.

Sam bent under the table and on the left side, hidden under the legs, was a small iron box with a slot on the front meant for a key. Sam set the iron box on the top of the table.

"Can you pick the lock?"

Sam laughed. "Can you pick a lock, he says? Who do ye think I am mate?" Sam pulled out some tools from his pockets and showed them to Edward.

"Well, get to it. I'd rather not have to take the whole box with us if we don't have to."

Sam went to work on the lock with Edward watching intently over his shoulder. Edward was on edge, and he was sweating from the pressure. The tiny sounds of the clinking metal on metal sounded like gunshots. Sam perspired in concentration, the stress of the situation hitting him as well.

After a tense few minutes, Sam turned the metal pick and the lock clicked. The top of the lock box popped ajar. Edward and Sam both smiled at the sight.

"I'm afraid you won't find what you gentlemen are searching for in that trinket."

At the entrance stood Daniel Richardson, portly with salt-and-pepper hair, just as described by Henry. He held a musket in his hands as steadily as any trained soldier.

Twelve guards filed into the room and pointed muskets and pistols at Edward and Sam.

"The key in the picture frame is a forgery, and there is nothing in the lockbox aside from money and deeds to several foreign estates." Daniel pulled out a slender key on a chain around his neck. "This is the real key. I'm in the habit of trying to open any strange locks I find. Who would believe the owners of the lock would fall into my lap as a gazelle into the lion's maw? One way or another, your ship is mine."

"Over my dead body."

"That can be arranged." Daniel raised the musket once more.

Edward grabbed the lockbox and threw it at the window. Richardson and the guards let loose their guns on Edward and Sam as the lockbox crashed through the pane, shattering the glass. Bullets flew past them as Edward and Sam jumped out the window and fell to the ground below. The two rolled as they hit the ground, and jumped up to run, but were stopped in their tracks.

In front of them were the magistrate's men with weapons ready to fire.

Edward and Sam surrendered. They were shackled and thrown into a carriage to be taken to the local jail.

22. TRICK & SWITCH

Edward and Sam sat on the floor of a small cell, thick wooden walls and iron bars keeping them caged. On the back side of the cell a window with iron bars let air inside. Inside with them were a few local toughs and a drunken old man.

Edward and Sam were both incarcerated until they could have a meeting with the local magistrate about sentencing. Luckily the locals didn't know who Edward was so he was only being tried for attempted theft, but even theft could carry the death sentence depending on the magistrate and the load on the jails.

Overcrowding isn't a problem here, but the magistrate is. If I could get word to the crew...

"So, how's it feel ta be back in prison, Capt'n?" Sam asked with his trademark smirk.

"Terrible," Edward replied. He leaned over to Sam. "We need to find a way out of here."

"Way I sees it, a jail such as this has one weakness: the guard. When they open the door to let someone out, we rush the guard and escape."

"Sounds simple enough. I overheard those two will be let out today, so we can ask them for help." Edward pointed to the two local ruffians.

"Work yer magic, Capt'n," Sam said with a laugh.

Edward sat down beside the two thugs. "We want to escape, what say you help us out?"

The two men laughed. "And why should we help you?"

"Money. If you help us we will reward you with money and take you wherever you wish."

The other man spoke up. "How much money are we talking about?"

"One hundred pounds split between the both of you," Edward replied confidently.

The two men smiled and one offered his hand. "Give each of us one hundred and you have a deal."

Edward sealed the deal with a shake, then told the short version of the plan. They would wait until the two men were let out, then the four of them would jump the guard and run. After sealing the deal, Edward went back over to Sam. The co-conspirators whispered afterwards, laughing and deciding what they would do with the money.

"I suppose that went well?" Sam asked.

"Yes, money is an easy motivator," Edward replied.

After another half hour, the sound of clinking keys could be heard down the hallway between the cells. Two guards, one with the keys and the other with a musket, approached the cell Edward and Sam were in.

"Alright Greg, Jim, time ta go, you worthless sacks of bullshit." The guard set the key in the lock and turned.

Edward, Sam, Greg, and Jim all tensed. The guard swung the door open. "Now!" Edward yelled as he ran to the open gate. The guard's eyes widened and he grabbed the iron bars to close the gate.

Edward balled his fist and was about to punch the first guard when he was sent to the floor suddenly and violently. Greg and Jim attacked Edward and Sam, allowing the guard enough time to close and lock the gate. Once Edward and Sam were subdued, more guards were brought in.

"Why?" Edward asked Greg as the man pinned him down.

"You think we're stupid? You were using us. There ain't no money, and you ain't no captain. Besides, this'll put us in good with the magistrate. No hard feelings?"

Edward and Sam tried to struggle against the men, but neither was able to escape.

The extra guards entered the cell and aimed muskets at Edward and Sam. "Don't you move unless you want to be shot!" the guard with the keys shouted. Greg and Jim moved away from Edward and Sam and then left with the guards through the gate. The gate was locked and the guards left through the hallway.

Sam stood and rubbed his neck where Jim had pinned him. "Well, wonderful."

Edward rose up and moved his arm around to bring the feeling back. "Now what?"

"Don' look at me. I'm not the one with the plans."

Neither am I, apparently.

Edward and Sam sat in silence as the day passed by. Eventually the drunken old man was also let out, this time with five guards pointing muskets at Edward and Sam while they took him out. Edward didn't try anything, and Sam wouldn't if Edward didn't. A guard told them the magistrate would see them tomorrow, and they were given mouldy bread with thin soup to eat.

Later that night, Edward and Sam were trying to sleep on the hard wooden floor when Edward heard a curious noise outside. He rose and peered out the gated window, but he couldn't see anything. He rested his ear to the edge and listened intently.

"Edward," a voice softly sounded in the dark.

"Henry?" Edward asked into the darkness.

Henry appeared from the shadows. He was wearing a cloak and kept searching to and fro to make sure no one was around.

"What are you doing here?" Edward asked.

"We bought some time by giving fake *Freedom* papers to the magistrate. He's having them inspected for authenticity as we speak. We were also able to talk with Nassir, he's the one who told us you were captured."

"I'm sorry, Henry. Everything was going smoothly. Richardson is sharp, and I think we underestimated him. I don't know how we're going to get out of this one." Edward's eyes hit the floor, his disappointment in himself evident.

"Don't worry yourself. After seeing you captured, Nassir came up with a plan to save you and his villagers."

"Will his plan work?"

"Trust me, if we play our cards right, this one can't fail."

...

The next day, the *Freedom* was no longer in the harbour. The ship had left in the early hours of the morning. The crew were in a rush to leave, and headed south to an unknown destination.

Henry and Alexandre, however, remained. They entered the magistrate's office and stepped into pure chaos. People were running around, talking with locals and the authorities about something. Daniel Richardson was there, with Nassir at his side, talking with one of the officials about what happened.

Henry and Alexandre walked up to them. "What is this madness?" Alexandre asked.

One of the officials spoke up to answer. "The magistrate was kidnapped in the night, and, the Devil smiles, so was the mayor and the sheriff and some other officials."

Blackbeard's *Revenge*

Henry and Alexandre grinned. "Perhaps we can shed some *lumière*," Alexandre said as he handed a piece of paper to Daniel Richardson. Richardson opened and read the paper.

Richardson, if you are reading this, my crew of the Freedom have taken Boston officials as hostages. If you want to see them again, you will meet these demands: Myself, Edward Thatch, and Samuel Bellamy, will be released from prison and surrendered to the crew of the Freedom. Along with us, our crewmate Nassir, his villagers, and the key, you know which one, will be brought to exchange for the lives of these officials. Take all these to Gloucester in four days and the exchange will be made.

After Daniel was finished reading, he pulled the paper away with a flash of rage. "What is the meaning of this?" he asked, shaking the paper at Henry and Alexandre

"Was the paper not self-explanatory? Follow the instructions and your people will return safely," Henry said, then he and Alexandre turned to leave.

"What do you think you are doing, sirs?" one of the officials yelled.

"We are leaving. We will be watching from afar to make sure you follow through with our *demandes*." Alexandre waved goodbye to Nassir as they left. Daniel and the official were not armed and thus powerless to stop Henry and Alexandre. After leaving, they disappeared and were not found again.

Later that evening, a meeting was held with the remaining authorities over how to handle the situation.

"These pirates have our leaders in the palm of their hands. There should be no question we must give in to their demands," one man declared, with some in the meeting agreeing.

"Where is the justice? Doing this will let other criminals know they can make a mockery of our city," another refuted, with an equal amount of people siding with him.

"What of it? All pirates are caught eventually. This Edward Thatch is the infamous Blackbeard we've been hearing about. All we need to do is let our motherland know he is here and the Queen will send naval reinforcements. We can use this situation to our advantage."

Daniel Richardson was also a part of the meeting, being central to the demands. He slammed his fist on a desk. "Is no one taking a mind to my loss in this? They have a snare around my property alone and it is unacceptable any of you think I should transfer my slaves to this pirate!"

The Voyages of Queen Anne's Revenge

"You have an overabundance of plantations in many cities, Richardson. Your duty in this situation is to sacrifice for the greater good," the first man said. "And, might I remind you that several people whom helped you acquire said plantations are amongst those missing?"

The argument continued for over another hour with the participants in the meeting clearly split down the middle. Some were swayed back and forth, but they couldn't reach a consensus on what to do.

The doors to the meeting hall were opened and a newcomer barged in. "I believe I may be of some assistance."

"Who are you? This is a private meeting!" Richardson yelled.

"I am Captain William Wilkinson of Her Majesty's ship, the *Diamond*. I have been tracking the Captain of the *Freedom*, Blackbeard, to here." William stood in full captain's attire, clean-shaven, black of hair, chiselled body and straight posture.

"You are late, Captain. We have captured your man, Blackbeard, but his crew has taken the mayor, along with several other prominent Bostonites, hostage."

"Such a shame. What are their demands?"

"They want their captain and crewmates back, along with the slaves of Daniel Richardson." One of the men motioned to Richardson.

"Then the answer is simple: we will give in to their demands," William confirmed, his hands folded behind his back.

"What?" Richardson yelled. "Those are my slaves we're talking about. You can't order me to surrender my slaves."

One of the Boston officials spoke up. "We've been over this, Richardson. We are willing to compensate you for the slaves."

"And let those pirates just get away with this? That is base cowardice and I will not be a part of it."

William raised his hand before the argument could continue. "I did not say we would be relinquishing them. My plan is thus: We will act the part of cooperating with their demands, then at their desired meeting spot, my crew will attack in the *Diamond*. You will gain your slaves back, and we will capture Blackbeard and his crew to execute."

Richardson was more amicable, but still wary. "But how do you know you will be able to stop him?"

"I know because it is my job to know. Ensure everything is in order when the crew of the *Freedom* arrive for their spoils. If anything is out of place, they will know. I imagine some of their crew are watching to confirm your compliance?" William asked.

"Yes, they are," Richardson answered.

"This is a common tactic of theirs. If the pirates are spooked, then this will be all for naught. As such, I will pose as one of the crewmates aboard the slave ship along with half of my crew. We can buy some time to allow the *Diamond* to sail over by fighting Blackbeard's crew on the slave ship."

Richardson sighed. "Hold a moment now. Who are you truly? You arrive as if from thin air, claiming to be a Captain of a Royal Navy ship, and you are telling us to comply with these pirates demands. How do we know you are not part of the pirate crew as well? Where are your credentials?"

"Hmph," William scoffed. "I assumed, judging from your character, you would be able to measure who you were dealing with on sight. I guess I was wrong. Tomorrow night, join me on the *Diamond*, and I will show you my credentials." Captain William turned to leave, but turned back after a moment. "Please do keep yourself hidden. We do not want these scoundrels finding out I am here."

Richardson gritted his teeth in anger over the gall of this William. *He may be a Captain of the Royal Navy, but he has no right to issue orders in my town.*

Richardson used his skills as a hunter to stalk through the town the next night, making his way to the pier. He had noticed marines in their uniforms manning and cleaning the ship in the afternoon, but something felt fishy.

Richardson sneaked silently through the alleys of the buildings in Boston, doubling back often to ensure he wasn't being followed. The cold night brought the noise of animals, vagrants, and late night drunkards to his ears, but none followed him.

When Richardson reached the pier, he still maintained his vigilance as he passed by the sleeping ships with dropped anchors and solitary guards. When he approached the *Diamond*, the name painted in white on the side, the crew pointed muskets at him.

"Who goes there?" one of them asked.

"I am Daniel Richardson. I was asked to appear by your captain, William Wilkinson."

"At ease, men," William ordered, appearing behind them. The crew lowered their weapons at his behest. "Come aboard, sir. You are welcome, and our credentials await your presence."

Richardson raised his brow, but he didn't ask any questions. He walked up the gangplank to the deck of the ship and followed William to the stern cabin.

"You will have to forgive me for the secrecy, but what you see next must be kept with the utmost confidence. I must have your word."

The Voyages of Queen Anne's Revenge

"And you have my word. On with it, man."

"Please, remain courteous as well."

William opened the door and entered first. Richardson followed closely behind. A woman sat in a high-backed chair behind an oval table. She had red hair falling in curls and beautiful green eyes. She appeared young, but at the same time very mature.

"Your... Your Majesty?" Richardson exclaimed.

Richardson had seen Queen Anne once many years ago in England, before she was Queen, and this woman in front of him looked exactly as he remembered.

William knelt down, and after Richardson recovered from his shock he knelt as well. "Your Majesty, Daniel Richardson is here as I explained."

"You may rise, both of you."

Daniel Richardson rose and his gaze met the Queen's. Her eyes held a force deep within them which hit him deeper than any lion's fangs. Richardson had heard rumours that the Queen could cut with a glance, and now he believed them.

Anne rose from her chair, assisted by a guard at her side, and strode to the front of the table where Richardson stood. She placed her hand in front of Richardson, and he knelt down again to kiss it. "We are sorry for our appearance, but practicality often trumps fashion, especially in battle."

"You look magnificent, my Queen, and, I must say, quite youthful."

Anne laughed daintily, placing her hand over her mouth. "We see the hunter strikes swiftly and charmingly."

Richardson noticed a ring on the Queen's finger, not altogether an abnormality, but the ring itself was what caught his attention. That ring was meant for the heir apparent or presumptive of Britain.

"I must express my deepest apologies for your loss, my Queen. You must be grieving and yet have to deal with such trivialities after such tragedy. It is inspiring to see you in such good health despite the rumours."

There was a slight pause before the Queen spoke again. "Yes, well, we must always set personal matters behind us in times of war. Though difficult, we are recovering. As for those nasty rumours, you should know better than to listen to everything you hear. Now to business. You have doubts about our Captain Commander William, yes?"

Richardson flushed. "I must admit, my doubts feel a bit foolish now, but when posing a venture one must make all certainties when one's livelihood is at stake."

"The necessity is not lost on us. We trust this meeting has proven evident truths about our sincerity in the capture of this villain, Blackbeard?"

"I have no more doubts, but there is one small matter..." Richardson said hesitantly.

"And what might that be? Speak."

"The reward for Blackbeard's capture. As your men are capturing him with my assistance, will I be claiming some of the fortune?"

Anne laughed. "That trifle? Why of course, your collaboration will be met with compensation in full."

"May I keep his ship as well?" Richardson asked.

Anne's demeanour changed. "That is a bit too much. The ship is a frigate as we understand, and could be used for the war effort."

"Then what if I do not take the reward? The ship is important to me, as it relates to the key the pirates want from me."

Anne considered the proposition. "You may keep the ship in exchange for none of the bounty from Blackbeard's head."

"Most excellent. In two days' time I will load a ship with my slaves and your men can be the crew. Together we will capture this villain."

Captain William stepped forward. "Forgive me, your majesty." William bowed and faced Richardson. "As our business is concluded, I wish to remind you, Richardson, to bring the real key with you, as the attack will only begin when this ship catches up to yours. We may need to buy time by letting the pirates test the key on their ship, including the slaves and their crewmates. All must appear in order so we do not scare them away."

Richardson's eyes narrowed suspiciously. "How did you know the key I mentioned worked on Blackbeard's ship?"

William paused for a half-second. "Not a few moments ago you mentioned your desire to take the ship, and how the ship related to the key Blackbeard wants. Assuming the key works on the ship is not a stretch. Do you disagree?" William raised his brow.

"No, you are correct, I did say as much, didn't I? You are most astute, William. I will bring the real key. A true hunter knows that to catch an animal the trap must be well disguised."

Anne went back around to the other side of the table and sat down in the ornate chair. "Now, our business is concluded, and you must excuse us, sir. We must discuss more details with our Captain William."

"Yes, of course. Thank you for this audience, your majesty." Richardson bowed low and then left the room and the ship.

After confirming Richardson had left the ship, William and Anne both let out a breath they seemed to have been holding in the whole time.

Anne looked to William. "Do you think he believed us?"

...

The next day, Richardson prepared his ship, a large cargo ship without cannons, with supplies and had his own men inspecting the rigging and making it seaworthy. The lowest deck was similar to the slaves' quarters at his mansion: row after row of stacked wooden planks meant to hold as many bodies as possible with no regard for comfort. Many had died during the trip due to those conditions, but it didn't matter to slavers and was a common design choice.

The day after Richardson loaded the ship with his slaves, William and half the crew from the *Diamond* functioned as the crew.

"You have everything prepared?" William asked. This time he was dressed in civilian clothes, akin to what a sailor might wear.

"Yes, the slaves are loaded, I have the key, and the ship was inspected yesterday. She is in fine shape. Is your crew ready?"

"Always," William stated. "Where is Blackbeard?"

"He and the other prisoner are arriving as we speak." Richardson pointed to a coach with barred windows pulling up to the harbour.

The Boston jailers brought Edward and Sam from the coach and aboard the slaver's ship in shackles. Richardson grinned when he saw Edward being brought aboard.

Edward and Sam had been told of the exchange before being brought to the ship, but not that marines were involved. The *Diamond* was in plain view next to the slave ship, and a marine captain, William, was standing next to Richardson. "So my crew is heading into a trap?"

Richardson laughed. "Yes, my boy. And after this is done, your ship will be mine, as I foretold."

Edward struggled, but couldn't do anything in his condition. "I'll make you pay for this, Richardson. Mark my words!"

"Yes, yes. Said the fly to the spider," Richardson replied as Edward was taken below with the slaves.

After the ship was double checked, the sails were unfurled and the ship left the harbour. The *Diamond* followed behind as they left Boston and headed east.

Richardson pointed at the marine ship. "Isn't your ship supposed to be farther behind us for the ambush?"

"The destination is a day away. My people will slow when we are closer," William replied.

The two ships kept moving east, however, and not north to the supposed destination. After a few hours Boston was completely out of sight, and they still hadn't changed course. William gave instructions to one of the crewmen, who ran below deck to carry them out.

Richardson was growing impatient. "Are we not to head north to Gloucester?" he asked.

William was about to answer, but Edward and Sam both appeared from the lower deck. The two were no longer wearing shackles and the crew were welcoming him as a friend. Edward smirked as he approached William and Richardson.

"What is the meaning of this? Why is he not in chains?"

"The same reason why we aren't heading to Gloucester," Edward said with a grin, "and why these men are not actually marines: we tricked you. William here is one of my crew members, as is the woman you spoke with posing as Queen Anne."

Richardson glanced left and right to the many crew members advancing on him. What once were sheep turned out to be wolves. The hunter was now caught in a snare, tightening like a noose. He began sweating with all the eyes on him.

"And what of the mayor and the magistrate?"

"They are currently at an inn in Boston, probably still unconscious thanks to Henry and Alexandre. Once they wake, I'm sure someone will help them. As for you, well, there are a few people who would enjoy seeing you dead, and I don't plan to disappoint."

Edward stepped closer to Richardson. The man kept backing up to the edge of the ship. When he bumped into the railing, he peered over the edge to the water below. Richardson gritted his teeth and reached into his pocket. He pulled out the key to the *Freedom*.

"You forget I still hold the ultimate bait," Richardson hissed as he dangled the key over the side of the ship. "Take me back to Boston or you can say goodbye to the key."

Edward's face turned grim, but he didn't move. "Think about the situation you are in. You cannot win here."

"Oh, I don't think so. You and I, we're birds of a feather. I saw the drive in your eyes that night. You won't let anything stand in your way to retrieving this key, and I won't let anything stand in my way to getting what I want. You would sacrifice everything for this, even your precious crewmate Nassir and his filthy, savage family."

"You're wrong," Edward said.

Richardson laughed with sincere joy. "We're alike, Blackbeard! We both know I'm right. This is the only way to achieve your goals. Turn the ship around, return my slaves, and the key is yours."

Edward couldn't see a way out of the situation without giving Richardson what he wanted. The entire crew watched the deadlock between the two, and no one dared move with the key poised to be lost to Davey Jones' Locker.

"This is all a big game of cat and mouse. Even if we did turn the ship around, you would throw the key into the ocean when we let you free."

Richardson sneered. "That is the game you must play."

William, noticing Richardson's attention focused solely on Edward, saw his chance. He moved in a flash and kicked Richardson in the temple. Richardson fell to the deck with a crack. The key flew up in the air. Edward ran, leaped off of the ship, and thrust out his hand to grab it. The key was inches away, twisting and turning in the air. Edward's fingers touched the tip of the metal but he could not grasp it. The key fell, Edward falling parallel to it, but still he could not reach.

The key fell into the water with a small plop. Edward made a splash as he followed into the drink. The murky water was impossible to see through. Edward scanned the waters, trying to see where the key went, but darkness invaded his vision. Edward swam deeper, searching harder for the dark metal through the murky water.

Edward had lost all hope and started to return to the surface when a splash came a few metres from him as another swimmer jumped into the drink. The crewman swam with ferocity and purpose, deeper and deeper until Edward couldn't even see him.

That's the fastest swimmer I've ever seen. Edward peered at the point where the person had disappeared. After another moment, Edward had to surface for air.

When Edward emerged, several of the crew members were at the side of the ship, including Nassir and some of the villagers, watching the water. When the crew noticed Edward they were relieved.

"Does anyone know who dove into the water?" Edward asked. The crew replied negatively.

Edward swam in the water waiting for the crew member who dove in. The slave ship furled their sails and stopped movement as best as possible, allowing the *Freedom* to sail up beside them. The crew was able to explain the situation to the crew of the *Freedom* in full, and the crewmate hadn't yet surfaced.

Something is wrong.

No sooner had Edward's thought passed than the surface broke and the body of the crewmate float on top. "Bring him aboard the *Freedom*!" Alexandre yelled over the side.

Edward swam over to the crewmate and carried him back to the *Freedom* where a rope ladder awaited him. He climbed to the top post haste, with the crewmate slung over his shoulder.

When Edward rose to the edge of the ship, the crew helped the crewman off Edward's shoulder. The crewman's hand was clenched over something, but his hand opened when he was set onto the deck. The key fell out. The crewmate wasn't moving.

Alexandre leaned over and listened. "He isn't breathing."

23. THE THIRD

Alexandre grabbed the key, then picked up the crewman, to the confusion of others.

"Alexandre, what are you doing?"

"Saving this one's life," he yelled as he carried the crewman to the gun deck. On the gun deck he set the key in the door at the bow end and it opened with a click. Alexandre kicked the door open and rushed inside. Those who followed caught a glimpse of a surgeon's room, with various medical devices and bottled liquids, but once Alexandre was inside, he closed the door and locked it behind him.

Edward knocked on the door. "Alexandre, let us in!"

"*Non*! I am performing surgery. Now leave me be!"

Edward turned to the crew behind him and shrugged. There was no dealing with the Frenchman when he was in one of his moods.

The crew, including Edward, Anne, and Henry, waited in silence in front of the room while listening intently for sounds beyond the door. For an hour, all that could be heard was a random click here or a metallic scraping there.

Edward pulled out a Mayan medicinal herb from his pocket and began chewing on it. The bitter taste hit his tongue and he became lost in thought as he chewed. "Wait a moment," Edward said after a few moments, his brow raised. "How did Alexandre know that this was a medical room?"

Anne, Henry, and the other crewmates peered at each other, as if asking the other people if they knew the answer.

"I noticed him pass a whole day once just sitting with his ear pressed against the door of each locked room," Anne stated. "Perhaps he was able to hear the rattling of the instruments and bottles?"

"Now that you mention it… I saw him with some apparatus up his nose and a tube through the bottom of the door. He was sniffing about with the device. Maybe he… smelled what was inside?" Henry postulated, unsure of himself.

The other crewmates delivered similar strange tales of Alexandre occupying himself by prodding each room to no end. Separately, the stories show how odd the Frenchman is, but together the action painted a picture of a man deducing what each locked room contained inside via process of elimination.

"Alright, so how did Alexandre know the key we received was meant for this door?" Henry asked this time.

"I can tell you that one," Edward replied. "The last two rooms are on this floor at opposite ends. It's a safe bet to think the room at the stern is the captain's cabin, as that is similar to other ships of this rate. The architect of this game would no doubt keep the purpose of each room in mind when thinking about which key we should get next. Benjamin wanted us to survive without cannons for a time, as a test, so they were unlocked second, and after we recover the last key the ship is officially mine. Technically I'm not captain until then, so the captain's cabin should be unlocked with the final key. Alexandre knew that, thus his confidence in knowing the key would unlock this door."

Alexandre emerged from the room, his clothes dyed red in spots. "Excellent deduction, *mon Capitaine*." Everyone stood and stared at Alexandre expectantly. "Victor will live."

Instead of a sigh of relief, the name was met with confusion. "Who's Victor?" Edward asked, curiosity written on his face.

Alexandre rubbed his eyes. "Victor has been with us from the *début*. Since Port Royal."

Edward shrugged, still not recollecting. Alexandre sighed.

Anne's face lit with recognition. "Oh! I remember I had a rather short conversation with Victor once, long ago."

Edward turned to Anne. "Only once?"

"Yes, as I recall he was shy and not very talkative. Perhaps that's why you're unable to recall Victor?"

"I assumed I talked with every crewman aboard at least a few times. Can we see him? I may be able to remember if I see his face." Edward attempted to enter the surgeon's room.

Alexandre blocked the way. "*Non!*" he commanded. "The patient is resting." Alexandre handed a piece of paper to Edward. "Here, play with this. You will need time for this one."

Edward took the paper, the next clue from Benjamin Hornigold. The last clue, leading to the last key for the *Freedom*. Edward was about to open and read it when he stopped himself.

"Wait, you're saying you figured out the clue already?"

"Yes, I read the riddle quickly before performing surgery and discovered the solution during. It was all very fascinating. Now leave," Alexandre ordered, pointing to the stairs.

Edward pocketed the paper and headed up to the main deck. "You won't read the clue?" Anne asked.

"I think we should wait until we finish what we set out to do first. Once we return the villagers to NiTalaa and find out if Nassir will rejoin us, then we can worry about the next key."

"These riddles take some time to solve. Are you sure we shouldn't start work on it sooner?" Anne asked.

Edward glanced back and forth to make sure no one was listening. "The crew needs a little rest after all the running around we've been doing. This is for the final key, and it will no doubt be the hardest trial we've faced. That means that there's potential some could lose their lives. If we have an excuse to stave that off for the time being, I'll take it."

Anne nodded, but wondered to herself if it was for the crew's sake or his own that he wanted to put off the riddle.

When Edward and Anne returned to the main deck, the crew brought Richardson over to the *Freedom* via a gangplank. "What do you want us to do with 'im?" Sam asked.

"Take him to the brig. We'll deal with him later," Edward replied.

Anne and Edward watched as the crew took Richardson below deck. "I cannot believe I had to act as my mother for Richardson to go along with the plan. I never want to do that again," Anne lamented with folded arms.

"The crux of the plan was convincing Richardson he had a chance to take the *Freedom* for himself," Edward said as he pulled Anne close and rubbed her arm. "Besides, I heard your acting was impeccable. That he was fooled is all that matters."

"Yes, I am happy this worked well." Anne carried a troubled air about her, despite the success of their plan.

"What's wrong?"

"I was thinking about something Richardson mentioned. My mother suffered a loss recently, but he didn't mention what kind. I worry one of my family members might have died."

"We've been travelling much, so news of the world is scarce. There's also a bounty on my head we didn't know about."

"A bounty changes nothing."

"Yes, we're still pirates so there's always people after us." Edward faced Anne and held her by the arms. "Don't worry about what Richardson said. You have us now, remember?"

Anne gazed deep into Edward's dark eyes. "I know, Edward. I'll be fine." Edward pulled Anne close and hugged her. Despite what Anne claimed, Edward could tell she was still holding back her true feelings.

...

Back in the locked surgeon's cabin, Alexandre was sitting in a chair in the corner of the room. He was meditating as he waited for the patient he'd operated on to regain consciousness.

The reason Alexandre was so adamant that none see his patient, the shy and reserved Victor, was because Victor was not who he appeared to be. The "he" was actually a "she." Victor was the third woman who had hidden her appearance aboard the *Freedom* from Port Royal, and she was the best at hiding her true nature by far. Alexandre had had a hard time discovering the secret as she possessed an uncanny ability to be transparent in a crowd.

'Victor' awoke with a start, sitting up straight on the raised operating table. She wore a thin white tunic stained in blood. She had short-cropped black hair and black eyes with a thin face and small nose. Her lithe body bespoke her agility and natural fitness. Her eyes flitted left and right quickly like a bird with purpose.

Alexandre noticed the change and slowly opened his eyes. "So you have finally awoken. You should rest more, *ma chére*. You are in no shape to be moving."

"What happened?" the patient asked. Her voice carried a hint of a Greek accent.

"After you dove for the key, you fell unconscious. I revived you, then forced you to sleep again so I could perform *chirurgie* on you."

Victor looked daggers at Alexandre, but he was unfazed. "What kind of surgery?"

"A bullet was lodged in your stomach. I noticed weeks ago in our last battle, and you were hiding the pain ever since. If the bullet was left, you could have died. I was planning on knocking you unconscious, but this provided ample opportunity."

Victor examined the remnants of the operation on her stomach. A blood-soaked bandage covered her abdomen.

"I need to change the bandages once more." Alexandre pushed her down to the table gently. Victor grabbed his arm in a vice grip, but after peering into his eyes she let go and lay down. Alexandre grabbed cotton gauze from one of the many cabinets and prepared it. "So, would you have me call you Victor, or will you tell me your true name?"

"Victoria Theriault. You may call me Tori if we are being so intimate."

Alexandre smirked as he removed the old bandages. "You should know by now you cannot lie to me. Victoria is not your *prénom*."

Tori winced as the bandage was taken off. "My given name is not a name I wish to be called. Victoria is the name I chose for myself, and what I will be called."

"Victoria, then." Alexandre dabbed the gauze over the stitching, soaking up the remaining blood first. "Are you not going to ask how I knew you were a woman, or how I knew about the bullet?"

"Why bother? Five times you stopped others from discovering I was a woman. Noticing my pain would be simple."

Alexandre grinned as he wrapped the new gauze around Victoria's stomach. "Six times now. And if you are observant enough to notice, then you must know I will eventually uncover where you are from and why you insist on staying aboard this ship. Tell me now and save us the *difficulté*."

This time, Victoria smiled deviously. "Perhaps you are getting ahead of yourself, surgeon. Only one who doesn't believe they can win would try to force another's hand with sly words."

Alexandre felt an excitement welling inside him like never before. "To finally meet another whose intellect *may* match my own is… nice. I will enjoy playing this game."

Victoria stood, dressed and adopted the mannerisms of a man again. Soon she was indistinguishable from the 'Victor' she claimed to be. "You will lose." Victoria said, a glint in her eyes.

It would take two months to return to Nassir's homeland. During that time Nassir and the other shipmates remodelled the cargo ship and until it was a remnant of its former self. The interior was opened like a proper ship, and could transport real cargo. With the addition of cannons, the villagers could also turn the it into a decent-sized warship.

The crew of the *Freedom* did the best they could to teach the villagers how to sail a ship during that time.

Nassir reunited with the *Freedom*'s crew and heard about all the adventures since he left. He was particularly interested and concerned for Christina. The story of how Christina acquired her 'pet' was particularly disturbing to Nassir, but Christina assuaged him by telling of how Tala was instrumental in saving Anne's life.

The Calabarians also discussed what would be done with Daniel Richardson. Edward expected Richardson would be sentenced to death, but they decided to judge him upon returning to the village. The return to their families would be celebrated with the death of a slaver.

Christina pushed for Richardson to die immediately, but after talking with Nassir she backed down. Her anger towards the slaver festered and grew during the travel, but she stayed her hand for Nassir's sake.

Anne, however, had questions that needed to be answered before his death. Late one night she left the bed she and Edward shared and entered the brig not two feet away. Richardson was sleeping, but Anne prodded his feet with a sword to wake him.

"Oh, the Queen Anne impersonator is here. Come to gloat?" Richardson spat.

"No, you have information I need."

"And what would you want to know from me?" Richardson asked, still lying down with a face of utter indifference.

Anne toyed with the heir apparent ring now on a chain between her breasts. "During our conversation, you mentioned some loss the Queen suffered. A personal tragedy?"

"What of it?"

"What was the loss she had?"

Richardson cocked his brow and considered Anne more closely than before. His eyes moved to the ring Anne was touching, then to her face. Anne's remarkable face, so similar in appearance, and the ring, so perfect a forgery if there could be one.

"Who are...?" Richardson's eyes widened with shock and then he began laughing. "Oh, this is rich. Why, you're the Queen's daughter. But that would mean..." Richardson laughed again.

"What's so funny?" Anne seethed through gritted teeth.

"Ho-ho, I'll never tell, this is too precious, my dear. I know I am heading to my grave, so there is nothing you can do to pry the information from my lips. I must say, though, your family is certainly a piece of work." Richardson laughed all the harder.

Anne, her anger swelling with nowhere to go, left the brig and closed the door hard. The laugh could still be heard through the wooden wall between her and Richardson.

...

The hot sun was high in the sky as the crew of the *Freedom* landed at the shores of Calabar along with the former slave ship. The *Freedom* once more bore its name on the side, and no longer the name *Diamond*. The two ships were met with unprecedented joy upon landing.

The villagers of Calabar stood at the harbour and cheered as the ships docked. The men helped bring the ships in and tied them to the dock as the crews set gangplanks down.

Wives and husbands, mothers and sons were reunited with joyful tears and embraces.

Nassir and Edward descended together, with Nassir's brother, Dumaka, rushing forward to embrace his kin. After he had a moment with his brother, Dumaka embraced Edward as well.

"Thank you, you saved my brother and my people. I will forever be in your debt."

"I do not deserve your gratitude. Your brother came up with the plan when I was caught by Richardson."

"As I understand, you and your crew were instrumental in putting forth that plan. Without you this could not have happened."

"Saving Nassir and recovering the key for my ship was part of the reason for helping. I was being selfish."

Dumaka sighed. "And through your selfishness you brought joy to all these faces. A good deed is a good deed, regardless of why or how the act was initiated. Be humble elsewhere and accept our gratitude." Dumaka took Edward's hand and raised it in the air. "People of Calabar, this is the man who gave our people freedom again: Edward Thatch!"

The villagers of Calabar cheered for EdwarYd and the crew of the *Freedom*. As Dumaka pulled Edward through the throng, the villagers embraced him, shook his hand and kissed him in thanks for his actions. The same gratitude was showered upon the crew of the *Freedom* as they disembarked and walked to the centre of the village.

The people held a feast in honour of their heroes, and their loved ones' return. After the feast, and after a few hours of song and dance, Richardson was brought from the brig and to the centre of the village. As he was pushed forward, the villagers shouted insults and spat on him, but he did not flinch once.

Richardson was brought in front a fire pit with Edward, Nassir, and Dumaka standing before him. "You are brought before us so we may have justice for the pain you caused our brothers and sisters. For your crimes, we sentence you to death."

"What a crock of shit. You sentence me to death? You niggers don't have rights," Richardson yelled. Edward took out his golden cutlass and handed it to Dumaka. "You were meant to serve our superior race from the beginning of time!" Dumaka tested the heft of the blade, nodding in admiration. "I was affording you greater purpose than your former, miserable lives. You are merely dogs, and dogs are nothing without masters!"

Dumaka fixed the blade at Richardson's neck. "You are no one's master." Dumaka pulled the blade back and cleaved Richardson's head from his body in one stroke. The head and body fell to the ground with a thump, the blood spurting from the stumps left behind.

Dumaka turned his back on the body and lifted his arms in the air, the golden blade in one hand. The people of the village and the crew of the *Freedom* cheered as one. The people of Calabar would never let another take their freedom away.

24. THE ISLAND OF HEAVEN & HELL

"Take care of my brother," Dumaka said.

"I will," Edward assured him as he held out his hand.

Dumaka shook Edward's hand and embraced him before saying a few words to and then embracing his brother.

Nassir walked over to Edward. "Ready?" Edward asked.

"Yes, it is time we leave," Nassir said.

Together, Nassir and Edward boarded the *Freedom*. The crew waved to the villagers as they shoved off and let loose the sails. They continued to wave and holler until the villagers were completely out of sight. Two months' travel had created a strong bond between the crew and the Calabarians, one which would not be broken.

As *Freedom* sailed across the ocean, Edward focused on the paper left in the surgeon's room, the final clue to the location of the last key. That piece of paper meant the journey was almost at an end. Edward sat at of a table at the quarterdeck with Herbert nearby at the helm.

"Are you simply going to stare at the paper, or will you read it?"

Edward returned to reality to see Jack sitting beside him at the small table. Edward chuckled at the comment. "I was thinking on how far we've come because of these little clues. Hard to believe this will soon be over."

Jack pulled out his violin, set his feet on the table, and played a light tune. "This has been quite the adventure. I've been on the sidelines, but I believe it has afforded me perspective."

Edward joined Jack in his relaxation, placing his feet on the table as well. "And what has your perspective allowed you to see?"

Jack closed his eyes as he pondered the question. "I've seen brave men and women die in battle and against deathly traps. I've relived tragedy through the eyes of a father. I witnessed a journey across the world, and a boy accused of being a pirate become a man in a short time." Edward smiled. "But, most importantly, I think, I saw a group of wayward vagabonds and lost souls brought together by that man and made into a family."

Edward was moved by Jack's words and his violin. "You have quite the way with words, Jack. You've almost made a song out of our adventure."

"I considered writing one, and I may after we are done. The journey may be more important than the ending, but there is no song which never ends."

"Then let us move towards that end." Edward opened the paper up to read the clue.

> At the point between Heaven and Hell
> In the palm of God's left and right hands.
> An island of duality sits.
> Two crews follow two paths.
> At the centre lies the final trial of man.

Edward pondered about the clue for a few moments while Jack read. "The clue seems very simple to me."

Jack handed the paper back after reading. "What do you propose?"

Edward folded his arms. "Well, Heaven and Hell are often depicted as being above and below, and since we are seeking an island this would mean north and south. The point between north and south is the equator."

"Yes, that makes sense. What of the left and right hands? East and west?"

"That would only be logical given the first part. The right hand of God often symbolises a position of honour and distinction. The holy land, Jerusalem, lies to the east, and the New World to the west. I believe the island lies between the New World and the Old."

Jack smiled as he switched the tune to a faster tempo. "You know a lot about the Bible for one who claims to not know anything about God."

"My father taught me a few things when I was younger, but after he disappeared I stopped studying. I have a hard time believing in God."

Jack sighed. "I must admit, with everything that has happened, I find it hard to believe in God as well at times. Then I think on all the blessings He has provided me now, and it is easier to believe."

Edward contemplated Jack's words for a moment, but his mind was not swayed. Edward turned in his seat. "Herbert, you've been listening, yes? Can you tell us what you think?"

Herbert locked the helm and turned his wheelchair. He adjusted his glasses as he wheeled himself over to the table. "You mean about God or about the clue to the key?"

"The key. I think I've had enough theology for one day. No offence, Jack." Edward handed the paper to Herbert.

"None taken," Jack replied while tuning his violin.

Herbert examined the paper. After he read through, he folded the paper and gave it back to Edward. "Your assessment is sound. There is a book in the cabin below called *Atlas Cosmographicae*, would you mind grabbing it for me, Edward?"

"Certainly. I'll be back in but a moment." Edward went below and into the stern cabin, the war room, and after a few moments' search he found the *Atlas* and brought it back up to Herbert.

Herbert read through the dusty old tome, scanning different maps until he found a map of the known world. The map was separated into two half-circles with a line horizontally down the middle. The two circles were separated directly between the New and the Old world.

Edward laughed. "This is perfect. This map shows exactly where the island should be."

"Yes, and we should arrive in about two to three weeks," Herbert estimated.

"But, Captain, what about the last part about needing two crews?" Jack asked, pointing in the general direction of the paper.

"We'll need to return, but there's no harm investigating."

"Fair enough."

Edward gathered the crew and let them know the plan. After the crew realised this was for the last key, they cheered and wanted to feast and break out the strong stuff, but Edward dispelled all hope of merriment.

"You may celebrate and feast after we retrieve the key. Currently, there is nothing to celebrate, but I can assure you once we are done we will have a party to end all parties!" Edward exclaimed.

Much to Edward's dismay, but simultaneous delight, his comment elicited more cheering than before. He was eventually able to calm the crew and focus them on work so they could head to the next island.

When the *Freedom* reached the estimated spot of the equator, Herbert travelled from east to west, moving north and south in a zigzag along the equator to maximise sight for the crew.

Edward peered through a spyglass onto the open sea. The air filled Edward's lungs with the feeling of the sea and invigorated him despite the monotony of their task. Days passed with his and others' eyes behind spectacled vision.

"What I don't understand is how this island was not found before," Edward said to no one in particular.

"Is that really so odd, brother?" Pukuh asked as he joined Edward at the starboard railing on the waist.

"Pukuh, I haven't seen you in ages."

"All this trickery and deception is not my strength. I am a warrior. The only deception I use is when I resemble the tiger stalking my prey."

"Yes, well I'm rather glad we didn't have to resort to a battle to save Nassir. I don't think we would have been as lucky as our previous battles. So you think this island not being found is normal?"

Pukuh leaned against the railing. "Well, yes. Benjamin created this for you, so it is natural you should be the first to find the island."

"What about the last island that Daniel Richardson found?"

"He was meant to find that island, as you are meant to find this one."

Edward stroked his beard. "You say it so elegantly, but perhaps I should ask how, then. How would no one find this island?"

Pukuh shrugged his shoulders. "How would none be able to open the locks on this ship? How does a man have a golden arm? How were any of the islands we travelled to created? How does one travel from the future? These are things men are not able to explain. Over what we have seen, is a lost island so hard to believe?"

"Well, when you put it that way," Edward said, turning around and leaning on the railing with Pukuh.

"My father, after regaling me with amazing stories about his adventures with Benjamin Hornigold, said to me: 'My son, I tell you truthfully, if Benjamin wanted to stop the sun in the sky, he could do so. That man makes the impossible possible.'"

Edward, still sceptical despite all evidence to the contrary, folded his arms. "He must have been some man."

"You two are alike, but perhaps you are a bit more."

"A bit more what?"

"You have done impossible things, and you are being moulded by Benjamin. Soon, I think you can surpass him. If I stay with you, maybe I will see you stop the sun in the sky. Then I will tell my father: this man made the day stand still."

Edward laughed and slapped Pukuh on the back. "You truly do have a vivid imagination, Pukuh."

"Captain!" a man in the crow's nest yelled. "I see land off the port bow."

"Good work, Richard." Edward turned to the stern. "Herbert, did you catch that?"

"Aye, Captain. Changing course now." Herbert spun the helm to port, turning the ship southwest.

As the *Freedom* drew closer to the island, many of the crew crowded around the bow of the ship to watch. Some were on the waist, others hanging off the rigging, and some standing on top of the railing or on the shoulders of others.

The island itself was large and covered in foliage. Palm trees surrounded the island without end, and was too thick to see through. Edward had Herbert do a circle around the whole island, which took several hours, but eventually Edward found what he was searching for on the expansive beachfront.

There. A path between the palms. "Land us here, Herbert!" Edward yelled.

Herbert turned the ship to the island and commanded the crew to trim and furl the sails, then drop anchor. The ship slowed until gently gliding to a stop just off the shore.

Edward and nearly the whole crew departed in longboats to the island below. Edward led them through the path. The path so cleanly led through the multitude of palm trees, it had to be man-made.

The canopy of palms swayed with the wind from the ocean, rustling and crinkling as if they were trying to say something to each other or the visitors to their island. The grass too sang its own song for the crew of the *Freedom* as they passed by.

The crew was taken in by the beauty of the island so greatly that when Edward happened upon a set of stone steps he nearly stubbed his toe. His jaw dropped with what he saw.

In front of Edward, two massive stone platforms stood side by side up a set of steps. Beyond the stone platforms was an impossibly tall wooden carving of an angel with a spear standing atop a devil, ready to strike. On the left and right of the carving were two giant stone double doors. The doors were covered by a spiked wooden wall which extended as far as Edward could see, and by his guess around the whole island.

Edward climbed the steps to the top. He noticed a moss-covered stone tablet between the two platforms. He pulled off the slimy and slick moss to reveal a carved tablet depicting people climbing onto the platforms and opening the stone doors.

Edward turned around to the crowd. "Alright, I want half of you to step onto the left platform, and the other half onto the right platform," he yelled.

The crew followed their captain's direction and separated as best they could into halves. Once everyone stepped onto the platforms, nothing happened. The stone doors didn't move an inch.

Edward addressed the crew once more. "Everyone on the left platform, I want you to move to the right platform."

Edward ascended the right platform once more as the crew on the left joined him. As more and more of the crew stepped onto the right platform it slowly descended with the weight until the platform became completely flush with the top of the steps.

Rumbling started underneath their feet. The stone double doors left of the angel and demon opened. When the door was fully open, the rumbling stopped.

The crew stepped off of the right platform to investigate, but as soon as a few left the stone doors closed. Edward called them back, and the door opened again.

"Anne, see what's beyond the door, would you please?" Edward asked.

"Certainly," she replied.

Anne went to the left stone door and peered inside. "There's not much to tell, really. There is a path leading to the left with high walls, and a platform fifty feet ahead. Do you want me to head inside?"

"No. Come back." Anne followed Edward's direction. "Now, to the left platform."

The crew moved to the left platform, and this time the right stone door opened. Anne passed through the right door and examined what lay beyond.

"This side is the same as the other, but mirrored. A path leading to the right and a platform down a ways," Anne yelled.

"Alright, come back. I have an idea of what we need to do." Anne did as requested and returned to the platform as the crew descended the steps and sat down. The only ones left up the small set of steps were Edward, Anne, and Henry.

Edward folded his arms and sat on the edge of the left platform. "We'll need help to proceed through this trial, and not the help Captain Smith provided last time." Edward alluded to the marine captain who chased them halfway around the world before Edward was finally captured and sent to prison. "We need a pirate crew who will cooperate with us on this."

"Do you have one in mind?" Henry asked.

"Well, I think the choice is obvious. We need to find Bartholomew Roberts and the *Fortune*."

"How do you expect to find Mister Roberts?"

"How did you find him to help us escape Portsmouth?" Edward asked the two of them.

Anne leaned against the right platform. "Well, we found Roberts rather by accident, or we had the good *Fortune*, if you would," Anne said with a smirk, "to be found by him. He heard, as the world had, about your capture, and the Bodden Brothers pointed him in our direction."

"Perhaps Roberts left a way to find him with the Boddens, or with the Boddens' information network they may be able to find them anyway."

Henry stepped down from the platform he was on. "So, back to Bodden Town then?"

Edward stood up. "Yes. Back to the ship, men."

Anne stepped ahead, and Edward followed down the steps, but Henry's hand on his shoulder stopped him. "Edward, can we talk for a bit?"

Anne stopped halfway down the steps, waiting for the two of them. "Go on ahead Anne, I'll catch up," Edward said. Anne nodded and headed back to the ship with the crew. Edward sat down, and Henry sat opposite him. "So what did you want to talk about, Henry?"

"I'll make this brief. I want us to make a stop in Badabos."

Edward's brow shot up. "Our hometown? Why?"

"I haven't seen my family in two years. I want to see my mother. I want to see if she's doing well."

"How to say this delicately… No."

"Why not?" Henry asked, anger seeping into his tone.

"Going back is too dangerous, Henry. The people of Badabos know us, and they've seen the ship before. I'm not subjecting the crew to danger because you're homesick."

Henry stood up from the platform. "We can land the ship on the north beach, away from the harbour, only a five-minute walk through the woods to town. None would know we arrived, and I can disguise myself."

"A disguise, really? That's your plan?" Edward scoffed. "You and your father are well known in Badabos, you're bound to be recognised."

Henry motioned towards Edward. "All I need to do is don as big a beard as you and no one will recognise me. Hell, the way you are you would never be spotted either."

Edward was going to object immediately, but shut his mouth for a moment. "You know, that is true. My appearance has changed in these two years. This could work."

"See? Trust me. Everything will be fine. I'll see how my parents are, and then leave. We'll stay a day at most."

Edward folded his arms and stared at Henry. "I don't enjoy our hometown, but I don't want my personal distaste to affect my judgement, so we'll visit for one day."

Henry embraced Edward tightly. "Thank you, Edward."

"Don't make me regret my decision."

"I promise, you won't."

25. THE BLACK DEATH

The *Freedom* landed on the north side of the island of Badabos. Some Badabos natives had joined Edward and Henry before they were labelled pirates, but few were left. John was one of them, but he, along with most, decided to stay on the *Freedom* and opted to send a representative with letters and money.

"John, why don't you join us? If you don a disguise I'm sure no one would recognise you either."

"N-no, Captain, I think I should stay on the ship. The more people we send in the more risk we take. Besides, I don't have any family to see."

Edward frowned. "Well, as long as you're sure."

"I am sure. Please be careful."

"I will."

Edward and Henry travelled into town with a few of the crew. Pukuh insisted on helping gather supplies so he could stretch his legs. He wore civilian clothes, but he somehow managed to carry a concealed spear.

While walking through the forest, Edward and Henry recounted childhood misadventures together in those very woods. The crew smiled at the light-hearted nostalgia amongst the friends.

When they reached town the crew left Edward and Henry, heading off to do their business. "Are you joining me, Edward?" Henry asked. "I'm sure my mother would love to see you as well."

"No, I don't wish to intrude. I will walk around town for a bit then head back to the ship. You can tell your mother I said hello."

Henry nodded and left to see his home for the first time in two years. Edward watched as Henry jogged away between the houses.

Well, now what? Edward scratched his head.

As he glanced about, the town brought back memories for Edward, both joyous and melancholic. The hate he held in his heart was vaporous, like trying to grab smoke. Edward could see the bad memories, but all he caught in his net was nostalgia.

Memories of Henry, Robert, and Edward playing in the streets, going to school, working in the fields. A face long since forgotten filtered into Edward's consciousness as well: Lucy, his former flame. *I wonder if she is still here.*

"So where are we headed, Captain?" a woman's voice asked behind Edward.

Edward turned with a start. Behind him stood Christina in a leather vest and a loose tunic underneath. She also wore comfortable trousers and boots.

"What are you doing here?"

Christina placed her hands on her hips. "Am I not allowed on shore?"

"Well, you are, but…"

"As I understood, anyone was allowed ashore as long as they wore a disguise if they were from here. I'm not from here, so there's no risk, correct?" Edward pursed his lips. "I'll take that as a no. Now, I want the full tour. I want to see where the great Blackbeard grew up." Christina grabbed Edward's arm and led him through the streets and into the town.

The two walked along a small market street curving up from the harbour. Christina was more fascinated by the market in Badabos than any island she had been to before. She was laughing and pulling Edward along the whole time, eliciting chuckles from passersby.

When Christina bent down to admire some wares from a local merchant, her wooden rose necklace dangled out in front of her.

"What a pretty necklace," the merchant commented.

Christina glanced at her necklace and smiled. "Thank you." She leaned closer and held the pendant out so the merchant could see better.

"Impressive quality. Would you be willing to part with it?"

"No!" Christina snapped, anger flashing forward in an instant. She pulled the necklace close in a protective stance and eyed the merchant like she would a lecherous vagrant. Others in the market stared at Christina and whispered to each other.

Edward placed his hand on Christina's shoulder, making her jump. She became aware of the eyes on her, and the way she'd acted to the merchant. Christina sincerely apologised to the merchant and explained how the necklace was sentimental. The merchant accepted her apology, and the mournful empathy in his eyes told her he understood what the pendant meant to her.

Edward and Christina traversed the market street for a few more minutes. Christina stared at the ground, melancholy painted on her face, while her fingers unconsciously caressed the rose.

Edward grabbed her hand and pulled her to the northern side of the town. He took her through the different whitewashed and brown houses and stores until they reached the edge of Badabos.

"Where are we going, Edward?" Christina asked.

"To the only spot which matters to me in this stinking town," Edward replied.

Edward took Christina to a small grassy hill which went higher and higher until the whole town was visible at the peak. At the edge there was a straight drop of about two hundred feet to the ocean below. Edward sat at the edge, overlooking the ocean. *Freedom* had arrived in Badabos at about noon, and now the sun was halfway to setting on the horizon. Christina sat down beside Edward, their feet dangling in the air.

"Before we set out on our journey, I, Henry, and our friend Robert Maynard used to come here nearly every day. We used to play games, tell stories, and talk about the ports we would visit when we were older." Edward smiled as he recalled those halcyon days.

"Who is Robert Maynard?" Christina asked.

"Do you remember before we stole the *Freedom* back from Portsmouth, when we bound a marine before departing?" Christina nodded. "That marine was Robert Maynard."

"Oh." Christina laid her hand on Edward's. "That must have been difficult."

Edward gave her a hollow smile before staring at the ocean and the bright sun. The wind breezed gently through his black and her strawberry-blond hair.

"Can I tell you a secret?"

"Of course."

"Betraying Robert wasn't difficult for me at all. I acted without hesitation, and I don't feel ill over what I did. The one thing I feel is confusion over how I don't feel anything."

"Why should you? He would have stabbed you in the back if he had the chance."

Edward whipped his head over and leaned back. He hadn't expected an answer so quickly and succinctly. After Edward took a moment to process what she said, he nodded.

"I guess you're right. Robert was always on the side of the law, which is why he joined the marines. Well, I feel foolish. I'm receiving life lessons from a young pup."

Christina laughed. "I'm not a young pup." She playfully pushed Edward.

Edward grabbed her arm for support. "Don't, that's dangerous." But he grinned.

The two gazed at the ocean, not saying anything. They listened to the people in the town below, their muffled voices filtering to the top of the hill, the breeze travelling across the ocean, and the calls of the birds as they flew over the island.

Christina leaned over on Edward's shoulder. "Thank you, Edward."
"For what?"

"For helping me forget, even if but for a moment." Christina touched the wooden rose hanging around her neck.

Edward wrapped his arm around Christina's shoulder, pulling her close. Christina wrapped her arms around Edward's waist and held onto him. Warm tears soaked through Edward's shirt, but he did not say a word. Soon, Christina lay on his lap, breathing softly from slumber.

Edward lay back, closed his eyes, and slipped to sleep as well.

...

Edward opened his eyes and the cliff was gone, replaced by a drab house with a fireplace. A boy was playing with a wooden knight. He wore a smile on his face as he made the knight jump.

Edward remembered the toy Henry lent him so long ago. Edward also knew what happened next.

Edward's uncle-in-law flashed in and grabbed the toy in one hand, an open bottle in the other. His uncle-in-law cast the toy into the fire.

"No!" both the young and old Edward yelled.

"Think ye can bring trash into my house, can ye?" Edward's uncle-in-law yelled. The man picked the boy up by the neck and pressed his body against the fireplace, the flames licking the boy's stomach. Little Edward screamed and thrashed in pain, but the man held him still.

The fireplace disappeared, and the boy Edward lay in front of the door. Edward's aunt stood in front of Edward, protecting him. His aunt and uncle began arguing, but he couldn't hear the words. His uncle back-handed his Aunt, ending the argument, but she refused to move.

Boy Edward rose up. "When my father comes back, he'll kill all of you!" the boy yelled, rushing out the door after.

The house turned to smoke and transformed into the cliff again. Little Edward sat, his head on his knees, bawling. Another boy was consoling him.

"Why did he leave, Rob?" Edward pleaded. "Why did Dad leave me?" He cried between his legs.

"Your dad didn't leave you."

"Then where is he?" Edward yelled, angry.

The young Robert Maynard pulled Edward's arm away from his tear-filled face. "He's waiting for you." Robert pointed to the sea. "He's waiting for you on the sea."

"You think so?" Edward asked, wiping his eyes.

"You always told me he said 'A man knows no greater freedom than the sea.' He wants you to become a man and find freedom, to find him, out there."

"You promise?"

"Promise," Robert replied immediately, his youth-like assuredness in full force.

This was the day Edward decided to go to sea. It didn't matter how, he would make it happen.

The smoke returned, shifting and transforming where Edward was.

"Come back to me," Edward heard whispered in his ear.

Edward was now on the port of Badabos. Beside him was the ship he'd bought, his *Freedom*. Before him was Lucy, the woman he loved, the woman who loved him. The old him. The whaler, Edward.

"Wait for me," Edward replied. The old Edward.

Edward was suddenly staring down at his old self and Lucy as they kissed for the first and last time. Edward was on the port and in the air at the same time. His old self, and yet also his new, simultaneously.

Lucy turned to Edward in the air. Edward peered at Lucy from above, and she aged before his eyes. A scar grew across Lucy's eye, blinding one eye and marring her dainty prettiness. Her eyes changed in the same way as Edward, darkening from the sorrows of life. The eyes carried an edge like a knife, different from Edward's hate-filled eyes; Lucy's filled with what could only be called righteous fury.

Edward could not bear to stare at those eyes any longer and turned away. Edward noticed Lucy's right hand fall away, and was replaced with the claws of an animal. Suddenly, Lucy was no more, and Christina was there instead.

Christina took her right arm, the hand still an animal claw, and removed it from her body. Christina knelt down, offering the arm to Edward on the port, and Edward accepted.

Edward then stared at his counterpart on the port. Edward's beard grew on his face, becoming long, filling with smoke from lit wick. Edward's eyes grew dark as he grew older, until the eyes resembled another's. Foreign and filled with malice, Edward didn't recognise them. Those demonic eyes filled the dream with a darkness Edward couldn't escape. The eyes were dragging him into shadows, whether he liked it or not.

. . .

Edward shot awake and a chill crawled up his spine. Within seconds his dream was a forgotten memory, but the feeling he felt at the end remained. "Something's amiss."

Christina rose up, wiping sleep and tears from her eyes. "I'm sorry, Edward."

Edward shook his head. "No, no, not you. Something doesn't feel right."

Edward scanned the ocean, the harbour, the town itself and back, but he couldn't see what was causing his unease. He rose from the edge of the cliff and Christina joined him. Christina was focused on Edward and his mania. Edward peered at the town again, and like a bloodhound his head moved this way and that. He stood on the tips of his toes as if tracking a scent.

Edward ran back down the hill and into the market street. Many shops were closing despite a few hours of daylight being left. Edward glanced left and right up and down the market until settling on the right, down the market street.

"What do you see?"

"You can't feel that?"

"No," Christina said with confusion evident in her voice.

Edward kept staring down the street trying to see something through the throng of people milling about. His eyes were furrowed and focused like an eagle. Christina also focused her senses in the same direction, imitating Edward. Edward's eyes soon widened with recognition.

Edward quickly grabbed Christina's arm and pulled her into a side street and ran. "What's wrong Edward? What did you see?" Christina asked through laboured breaths.

"Not right now. Keep running." After Edward rushed Christina up and down different streets at random, their legs tired, and they ran out of breath, so he stopped. "I think we'll be safe here, for now."

"Safe from what? What are we running from?" Christina asked while holding onto her knees.

"You recall me mentioning the man in black?" Edward said through ragged breaths.

"The assassin? How could I forget? Your tale of his countenance was riveting. He's here? How did he know to come here?"

"I imagine Captain Smith, our previous pursuant, was forthcoming about our hometown to help this one's investigation. His timing is impeccable."

"I recall you saying he was injured several times when you met with him, but he didn't feel the pain and kept chasing you."

"Well, then you know how dangerous the man in black is. We need to find Henry and leave before he finds us." Edward took a few deep breaths and began walking again, albeit slower.

Christina followed Edward closely. "Why run away? We should fight."

"We are far too outclassed. I'm not sure any of our fighters could match him, even fighting together." Edward weaved through the houses, making his way to Henry's parents.

"But we've been practicing together. We can take him."

Edward stopped and turned around, facing Christina head-on, and gave her a glare so fearsome she was frozen still.

"If we fight him, at the least we will be horribly injured, at the worst we will die. The latter is more likely." Edward turned back around. "We must keep moving."

Christina didn't say another word as they made their way between the houses of the town to where Henry's parents lived. Edward sprinted up to a small whitewashed house of simple design for a poor farming family, and knocked on the door loudly and swiftly. No answer came, so Edward knocked again.

A shuffling noise preceded the door slowly opening. An older woman peeked out behind the door and eyed Edward up and down with confusion and fear. Until she peered into his eyes.

"Edward? Is that you?" the woman asked.

"Yes, it is me, Mrs Morgan. Henry is here, is he not?" Edward asked politely.

"Ed?" Henry's voice sounded behind the door, before it was opened wide. "What are you doing here? What's wrong? Don't we still have a few hours left?"

"We must cut the visit short. The man in black is here."

Henry's eyes widened. He turned to his mother and embraced her. "I am sorry, but I must leave."

"Is something the matter?" she asked.

"No, no, all is well. We are simply being cautious."

"Well, please be careful. I love you."

"I love you too, Mother."

"How touching," an unknown voice said behind them.

Edward, Christina, Henry, and Mrs Morgan turned their heads swiftly. In front of the house was the man in black, the Royal Assassin. His cold eyes filled the group with fear and the image of death flashed before their eyes.

Edward raised his fists, Christina pulled a dagger from her belt, and Henry joined Edward in a defensive stance.

"Hmm, I did not see your ship in the harbour. It must be hidden somewhere. I suppose I can have a little fun for a bit." The man, dressed in a black leather longcoat, flashed a knife from his sleeve and held it lightly in his fingers with the least amount of effort.

He's toying with us. Edward's anger replaced his fear.

The jet-eyed man threw one of his poison needles at Edward. Christina, reacting faster than Edward, pulled him aside. The needle slipped past Edward's forearm. At the same time, the man with the hair slick like crow's feathers ran and slashed with his knife. Christina blocked the strike with her own knife.

Normally, the needle missing Edward would be a fortunate occurrence, but someone was standing behind him.

Henry's mother.

The needle hit her in the neck and pierced the skin. She pulled out the needle, peering at it through unfocused eyes before fainting.

Edward turned his gaze to Henry's mother. Henry had bent down and was crying her name. He examined his mother as Alexandre taught those aboard the *Freedom* to do. "She's alive, but I don't know for how long."

The clang and flash of blades brought Edward's attention back to the street. Christina was fiercely attacking the man in black, her anger driving her blade faster and stronger than ever. The assassin deftly blocked and parried the blows with ease.

"You have ten minutes, more likely eight, judging from her size and frailty," the assassin said, still blocking Christina despite looking the other way.

"Edward, my mother needs help." Henry lifted her off the ground.

Edward gritted his teeth and turned back to the assassin. "Take her to the ship, Alexandre will be able to help her. We'll hold him." He pulled out his golden cutlass and began a charge.

Edward slashed down. The assassin jumped back, out of the way. Edward stood beside Christina and lowered his stance. Christina set her foot on Edward's bent knee and flashed another knife into her other hand. The two were ready to battle as one.

The assassin watched as Henry headed north with his mother in his arms, and grinned maliciously. "Interesting."

Edward stared down the man in front of him. A crowd of spectators had gathered behind the man. "So, what is your name, so I may stop thinking of you as 'The Assassin'?"

"My name is Edward Russell, but as we both share a name you may call me by the name I have amongst those who fear me: The Plague."

Edward wasted no more time talking. He ran over, leaping into the air and descending with his blade. Plague stepped to the left. Christina jumped off of Edward's back and into the air with a flip to move behind Plague, then sprang forward to slash at his back. Plague spun, blocked the strike with his dagger, and kicked Christina in the stomach.

She let out a muted cry and doubled over in pain. Edward slashed at Plague. The man in black, surrounded by the air of death, ducked and dodged each oncoming swipe from Edward's golden blade.

After a momentary exchange, Plague jumped away from Edward and Christina once more. "Christina, are you hurt?" Edward asked.

She rose as she clutched her aching stomach. "I'll be fine. I can keep going."

"Eagle and the Bear," Edward said while holding out his golden blade to Christina.

Christina nodded, taking the cutlass and handing Edward her dagger.

Edward threw the dagger at Plague. Plague ducked down. Edward turned and bent down, cupping his hands. Christina ran at Edward, jumped, and landed in his cupped hands. Edward launched her into the air, then ran to the Plague. He grabbed the man in a bear hug while he was distracted by Christina, and turned around. Christina fell with the blade aimed at Plague's back.

"Foolish!" Plague said.

The assassin flexed his muscles. Edward's grip broke. Christina was still falling. Plague stepped forward, pulling Edward with him, and thrust his dagger into the air. Christina was impaled on the short blade. Edward was sliced in the shoulder with his own cutlass. Christina dropped the cutlass as her strength left her. It fell to the ground with a clang.

Plague threw Christina to the ground and she lay in a heap. "Christina!" Edward yelled, holding his shoulder. His eyes were drawn back to Plague. "Damn you!" Edward yelled furiously. "You'll pay for that."

"Doubtful."

Plague flicked his wrist and sent a dagger flying towards Edward's throat. Edward pulled up his hand in a pathetic attempt to guard himself.

From above, a spear swiped the air. The dagger flew away with a metallic ring.

Pukuh landed in front of the kneeling Edward. He didn't have on his usual warrior clothes, but that did not detract from his countenance. His strong back and arms stood stalwart in front of his brother. He had one hand on his hip and the other held his spear at his side.

"Pukuh!" Edward exclaimed.

"Take the little warrior back to the ship, brother. I will take care of this one."

Edward glanced from Christina to Pukuh to Plague. "But..." Edward shook his head and stood up. "Right. We'll wait for your return."

Pukuh and Plague watched as Edward grabbed his cutlass, then picked up Christina. She was bleeding out rapidly. Edward wished Pukuh luck, then headed north to the ship.

"So you share the name of the Mayan God of Death. We are similar. I'm called Plague."

"I do not know what this 'Plague' is, but it is not your true name, no?" Plague shook his head no. "Then we are not similar. You merely adopted a name of death. I *am* the God of Death."

"Let us hope you live up to the name. I have become rather bored."

Pukuh grinned at Plague's gall, and because he too was bored with those he'd fought aboard the *Freedom*.

Against this man, Pukuh could go wild, and he was excited.

...

Edward ran through the town, following paths memorised as a child. *Pukuh will win. If anyone can, it's him.*

Edward emerged on the market street where the people of Badabos were walking back to their homes after a long day. They turned to watch the tall man with long black beard carrying a young woman and leaving a trail of blood behind them. Edward kept running through the people and once more into the alley between the houses and businesses.

The blood didn't let up, and kept falling at a steady pace. Christina had fallen unconscious not long after Edward began running, and she was turning pale.

"Hang in there, Christina!" Edward yelled, unsure if his words were reaching her.

Edward picked up the pace as he ran deftly through the trees of the small forest along the path created over the years. Animals turned to watch their passing and cried out at Edward's urgency.

Edward emerged from the trees to a small sandy beach hosting the *Freedom*. The crew aboard were readying to set sail, no doubt apprised of the situation by Henry. When the crew noticed Edward with another body in his arms, they lowered a small dingy into the water for him.

Edward laid Christina down in the small boat, then gave a thumbs-up to raise it. As the crew gently pulled the ropes, Edward climbed up a ladder.

"Someone call for Alexandre!" Edward yelled as he jumped over the railing. "Tell him to bring the needle and thread."

Edward helped the other crewmates on the pulley bring the dinghy and Christina in. After the dinghy was lowered onto the waist, Edward scooped Christina into his arms and laid her down on the deck.

Blood poured onto the ship, soaking into the pine planks. Edward pulled up her shirt and lowered her breeches. The wound was lower and the cut deeper than Edward anticipated

Alexandre ran up the stairs to the top deck as Herbert crawled over to his sister's body.

"What happened?" Herbert yelled at Edward.

"Did you not hear the story from Henry?" Edward screamed back. "The Plague is upon us. The man in black. The assassin. He did this when we were trying to fight him. If Pukuh hadn't shown up when he did…"

"How could you let her fight that monster?" Herbert asked, his eyes shooting daggers at Edward.

Before Edward could defend himself, Alexandre pushed between the two of them. "Argue later, fools. I need to work quickly. Hold her down."

Edward and Herbert held down Christina's arms and legs with all their weight, just in case. Alexandre used a needle and thread to pinch closed the wound on Christina's lower abdomen. His thread-work was better than anything Edward had seen, and the wound was closed in a matter of minutes. The wound still bled, but not as badly as before. After Alexandre finished, he washed and cleaned the wound once more with his bottled water and cloth.

Alexandre set another clean cloth over the wound, and made Herbert lay his hands over it lightly. "Press gently. Clean any blood, but do not disturb the thread." Herbert nodded in affirmation, and Alexandre headed back downstairs.

"Capt'n! Lookit over there," one of the crewmen exclaimed, pointing to the island of Badabos.

Edward peered in the direction the man was pointing. He was viewing the small cliff he and Christina were on earlier, and he could see two figures moving towards it. *Are they fighting?* "Somebody bring me a spyglass," Edward commanded, and one of the men obliged. Edward gazed through the spyglass and was able to see the scene on the cliff. Pukuh and Plague were still fighting. Edward's heart sank. *Pukuh is losing.* The thought shocked Edward. The assassin was more skilled than Edward's best.

"Is everyone back from the shore?" Edward asked, to which one of the crewmen answered yes. "Set sail! Head to that cliff," Edward commanded as he ran to Christina and knelt down next to Herbert. "Herbert, I need you at the helm. I can take care of Christina."

"Just as how you took care of her before?" Herbert snapped, tears in his eyes.

"Christina will survive, but Pukuh may not! I need you on the helm, no one else can navigate the shoals." Edward stared Herbert in the eyes.

After a moment the ship was pushed off of the beach and the sails were lowered. Herbert nodded and headed back to the quarterdeck. Nassir helped Herbert to the helm. Edward dabbed at Christina's wound. Despite the pain of the needle, Christina hadn't been roused.

Could the blade have been poisoned as well? Edward shook his head. *Alexandre would have noticed. It must be blood loss.*

Anne and William ran up to the main deck and over to Edward and Christina. "Did the assassin do this?" Anne asked.

"Yes, but Christina's wound is stitched, it's up to her will now," Edward said, holding the cloth tight.

Anne knelt down next to Edward, examining Christina's body. "She is strong, she will be fine."

Edward gazed into those green eyes, the ones which filled him with strength when he felt all was lost, and nodded. "Can you take over? There's one more person we need to save."

Anne took the cloth from Edward as she rose to her feet. "Whom?" Anne asked.

"Pukuh," Edward replied, glancing at the two-hundred-foot cliff approaching. "Someone grab a spare sail from the hold, quickly!" he shouted, slashing his hand through the air to emphasise the urgency.

Several of the crew went below deck to follow the order. Herbert was shouting orders to trim and furl several sails to slow the ship in the shoal.

Edward watched the fight between the man known as Plague and Pukuh as it progressed further and further towards the small cliff. The Mayan didn't glance to the side, but Edward could tell he saw the ship.

"Don't slow down!" Edward yelled to Herbert.

Herbert leaned over. "What?" he asked, confused.

"If we slow down, the assassin will jump aboard. We need to speed up so only Pukuh has enough time to jump on."

"How will he know what to do?" Herbert shouted back.

"He'll know."

Herbert shook his head. "Lower the sails. Close-haul to the wind as best you can, men!"

The men who went below returned with a spare sail rolled up and held under their arms. "Up to the poop deck. Pull the sail taut so Pukuh can jump onto it," Edward commanded.

Edward and the crewmen unfurled the sail and pulled it tight in a circle on the poop deck. The crew watched the cliff side as the ship passed under, picking up speed. *This is your chance, Pukuh, jump.* The waist of the ship was passing under the cliff. *Jump, Pukuh, jump!* The stern approached, and the men with the sail were staring straight up. *Now Pukuh!*

Suddenly, a body flew off the edge of the cliff. Nearly two hundred feet the man fell and landed neatly onto the cloth sail, which broke his fall.

Plague! "Crew, attack!" Edward commanded.

Some of the crew drew knives and swords while others ran to grab weapons as quickly as possible. None were prepared for a fight so suddenly.

Edward saw another man jump off the edge of the cliff from the corner of his eye. *Pukuh!*

Pukuh fell towards the ship. He had a dagger in his left hand, and he was holding it outstretched. Pukuh thrust the dagger into the aft sail as he fell into it. The sail broke his fall, and the dagger cutting through the thick canvas slowed him until he was halfway down. Pukuh's grip was lost and he fell to the deck in a heap.

The crew attacked the assassin known as Plague with full intent to kill, but Plague was holding his own. Whether it was shots from pistols and muskets, or slashes from swords and daggers, even simultaneous attacks, he seemed to avoid them even if by the skin of his teeth.

Plague was adept at using each opportunity to his advantage. When he was about to be shot, he pulled a crewman trying to attack him with a sword in close to use as a shield. When he was being attacked by multiple people in close quarters he manoeuvred them around so their own attacks threatened each other.

Edward ran over and knelt down next to the Mayan. "Pukuh, are you well? Can you stand?"

Pukuh was breathing heavily, and one eye was closed in pain. His right arm was limp at his side, and at first Edward thought the arm broken, but the reality was far worse. The Mayan's arm was turning black. Pukuh's hand and half his forearm was overtaken by the devil creeping up it.

Pukuh kept his eyes on Plague. "That man is a demon. One lapse in concentration invites misery."

Edward stared at the man called a demon by the God of Death. The crew was cautious in attacking now that they knew how capable their target was. Plague used the break to search the ship for something, or someone, but his search seemed to be fruitless.

Who is he searching for? I'm sure he heard me say his name. Am I not his target?

Before Edward's question could be answered, Plague was hit with a kick to the chest, sending him back a few steps. William appeared out of nowhere in front of Plague on the cloth sail.

Plague smiled genuinely. "Why, if it isn't William, the Arcing Light himself. I haven't seen you in ages. Not since your disgraceful failure to protect your King. Oh, wait, I mean to say when you betrayed the Crown and killed him. Yes, that was the story… Perhaps I said too much." Plague shrugged.

William's normal facade of calm indifference faded and was replaced with fury. "Edward! Your sword, if you please."

Edward glanced from Plague back to William. Plague wouldn't let his eyes leave William for a second. Edward took out his cutlass and tossed the shining gold sword to William, who caught the blade in the air, not letting his gaze leave the assassin.

"I have been waiting for this day for seven years. No one interfere! This is my fight!" William said.

"Best make it count then, my boy."

The two warriors circled each other, with all eyes on them. William's knees were bent and he held the cutlass close with one arm braced behind the blunt edge. Plague held two knives, one high and one low, while he stalked the small battleground like a lion out for prey.

William moved first, and Plague joined him. The two warriors danced on the *Freedom*'s deck. The two men were evenly matched, and the only sound was the occasional stamp of a foot on the wooden deck or a scraping of metal as they dodged, ducked, and deflected the other's strikes. To those watching, the fight was like a choreographed play.

Edward and Pukuh observed the battle with wide eyes. Edward, at the close angle he was, had difficulty keeping track of the two men. "William will not last. We must remove this man from the *Freedom* or he will destroy us all," Pukuh whispered.

Edward glanced over to Pukuh. The man was holding his right arm, the Black Death still crawling steadily up to his elbow. Edward carefully concentrated on the two fighters in front of him and waited for an opportunity.

William's and Plague's blades flashed as they swung them through the air. William took a wide swing horizontally. Plague ducked down, then jumped up and slashed at William horizontally. William leaned back to avoid the blade then thrust the golden blade forward. Plague jumped back, almost to the edge of the ship.

Edward saw movement in his peripheral vision on the waist of the ship. Christina was still lying there, and beside her stood Tala. Edward knew what he needed to do.

"Tala!" Edward called. "*Épaule!*" he yelled, pointing to Plague.

Tala rushed up the steps and leapt at the assassin. Plague was so focused on William, the wolf caught him completely off guard. Tala bit down on Plague's shoulder, stopping him in his tracks.

"Tala, *courir!*" Edward commanded as he rushed towards Plague. Tala released her prey and ran away. Edward slammed into Plague's chest with his shoulder. The assassin was sent flying backwards. He hit the aft railing and flipped overboard into the water, hitting with a splash and sinking below the surface. Bubbles rose from where he fell in.

"Men, fire at will!" Edward shouted.

The crew ran to the aft railing and fired into the water. The dozen cracks and snaps from the pistols and muskets sounded out, and the bullets popped into the sea where Plague had fallen.

The ship was still moving forward, but the crew continued to fire where they thought Plague landed until they were out of range.

Edward searched the sea, then the aft of the ship in case Plague was hanging onto the back, but he couldn't see him anywhere.

"Captain, look!" A crewman yelled, pointing to the water a couple of hundred feet away.

Plague was treading water, seemingly unharmed. He had swum out of harm's way as soon as he fell into the water. Plague stared at the *Freedom* as she left the island of Badabos far behind.

26. THE BREAK

"William, you must cut off my arm!" Pukuh yelled.

Pukuh was kneeling and holding his right arm extended. The black disease was still silently creeping past his elbow and up his bicep. The progression of the poison Plague had hit him with was rapid, to say the least. Pukuh had trouble keeping his arm steady in the air.

"Someone bring Alexandre!" Edward commanded. Edward knelt down beside Pukuh. "Pukuh, there's no need to go to such lengths. Alexandre will cure you."

"He will not. The poison is spreading too quickly. Do it, William," Pukuh said forcefully; sweat coated his tan face, dripped off his brow, and fell to the wood deck.

William bent his knees and held the cutlass in two hands. Edward stood and approached William. "You cannot seriously be considering this. What are we to do after we cut off his arm, hmm? Let him bleed to death?"

"The man has chosen his path. We will find a way. Step aside," William said.

Edward ignored the order. "If we can find a way to stop Pukuh from bleeding out then we can find a way to stop the poison." Alexandre ran up to the poop deck. "Alexandre! There you are. Can you please talk some sense into these two? You can cure the poison, no?"

Alexandre stared at Pukuh's outstretched arm. Alexandre, his eyes tired and defeated, shook his head. "This poison is beyond me. Dismembering is the only way, and that we have the chance to amputate is a *merveille*."

William and Pukuh both tensed for what was to happen. Edward jumped in between them. "Hold, hold! What will we do afterwards? In case you are not aware, it is rather difficult to start a fire on a blasted ship! How will we heat the oil to stop the bleeding?"

Alexandre folded his arms. "We can produce the same effect with a chemical burn. Continue on, *messieurs*, I shall return presently." Alexandre ran and disappeared to the deck below.

Edward refused to move. "There must be another way."

William inspected Pukuh's arm. The poison had spread halfway up his bicep by now, and was no doubt further along internally. "This is no time to argue. If you will not move I will show you why I am called the Arcing Light."

William stood straight and closed his eyes while holding the sword at his side. After a moment, William opened his eyes. With speed unparalleled, William ran past Edward in the blink of an eye. When Edward turned around, William was standing behind Pukuh, his back turned and the blade at his side. Pukuh's right arm fell with a thud.

Alexandre ran up to the poop deck with a bottle of clear liquid in hand. He took charge of the situation. "Hold him down!" Alexandre commanded.

Edward, William, and several of the crewmates laid Pukuh down and piled on top of him so he couldn't move. Blood was gushing out of the stump on his shoulder, but Pukuh didn't scream once. His teeth were bared, his eyes were wide, and he breathed heavily like an animal.

Alexandre didn't wait or slow down to warn Pukuh, he pulled the cork stopper out of the bottle and poured the clear liquid over the wound. The perfectly sliced cut boiled and bubbled as the acidic chemical burned Pukuh's flesh. The remainder splashed to the deck and ate through the wood.

Pukuh thrashed and screamed in pain. The sound was like the low rumble of a wolf and then turned to a high-pitched cry of an eagle as Pukuh lost his breath. He continued to howl and writhe in pain against the crewmates holding him down.

"*Mon Dieu!*" Alexandre yelled over the screams. "He should have passed out from the pain by now. Quickly, make him unconscious before he goes mad!"

"Sorry Pukuh." Edward raised his fist and punched Pukuh in the jaw, causing the Mayan's head to strike the floorboards, knocking him out. His eyes closed and his body went limp. The crew fell off of him and let out deeply held breaths. Pukuh's wound was closing like Alexandre had said, but the skin was still boiling from the burns.

"Move him downstairs so he may rest," Edward commanded.

The crew lifted the Mayan and carefully carried him down to the waist with Alexandre in tow, hanging onto the blackened arm.

Edward rushed to Christina's still body on the waist of the ship. Anne was at Christina's side, stroking her strawberry-blond hair. "How is she faring?" Edward asked.

"Still pale as a ghost, but her breathing is normal. I think she'll be fine," Anne replied with a smile.

"Let's take her below deck and place her in a bed."

Edward picked up Christina's body with Anne's help and they carefully took her to the crew cabin. On the way, Edward noticed Alexandre and Henry in the surgeon's room next to an obscured body.

Edward and Anne continued down another flight of stairs to the crew's quarters and laid Christina onto one of the beds. Anne filled a bowl with water, then dipped a cloth into it and wiped Christina's forehead.

"I'll be fine here. Henry needs you."

"Thank you, Anne." Edward kissed Anne on the forehead and then ran swiftly back up the stairs to the gun deck and into the surgeon's room.

The shelves were lined with bottles in protected cabinets so they wouldn't sway and crash with the movement of the ship. A broad operating table stood in the centre of the room, and at the sides were small cots and chairs. A body lay on the table, covered by a large cloth sheet, and in one of the cots Pukuh was resting.

Edward stopped at the sight of the covered body, then slowly lifted the covering, and saw his fears made true. Henry's mother lay there, dead. A different poison from Plague had reached her heart and killed her before she could be saved. For one last sign of hope, Edward looked to Alexandre, who shook his head and dashed Edward's tiny hope to pieces.

The smell of death already hit the small room and mixed with the scent of unfamiliar chemicals that prickled Edward nose. Edward's eyes also watered, but not from the smell.

Edward wiped his eyes and moved to Henry, who was sitting down in one of the chairs, tears in his eyes. "Henry…"

Henry raised his hand weakly. "Don't, just… don't. I can't take this anymore, Edward."

Edward was taken aback. He didn't know what to say to comfort his friend.

Henry ran his fingers through his straight brown hair. "I can't take the fighting, the killing, and death any longer. I'm tired, Edward. I want out."

Edward's mouth went agape. "W-what?"

"I want off this ship. I have the money according to the commandments, so I want you to take me to the next port and we'll go our separate ways."

"Y-you must be joking. After all we've been through? After what the assassin did to your mother?"

"The assassin is not the real reason my mother died. He may have poisoned her, but we put her into harm's way."

"What? Us? If we're to blame anyone for this it should be the assassin, not you or I. Listen to what you're saying, Henry."

"I know what I'm saying. The fact of the matter is that we broke the law and these are the consequences. This all stems back to the day you decided to hold the pistol to Captain Smith's head. I'm not saying I'm without blame. I could have left you, but I didn't. I've paid the price of ignoring the truth, but I will not pay any more. I'm done."

"What about all we've been through? What about our friendship?" Edward pleaded.

"I've seen what happens to a friend who disagrees with you. I've made my decision, Edward, and it is final. I won't be your accomplice anymore. I won't be another victim in your never-ending game for freedom."

Upon seeing Henry's unwavering expression, Edward lowered his hands. After the initial shock subsided, anger crept in, and Edward wanted nothing more than to hurt Henry. But Edward saw the covered body of Henry's mother once more, and realised Henry had already been hurt enough.

Edward quickly left the room and closed the door behind him. He was exhausted and it all hit him at once. He shuffled downstairs and sat on the edge of his bed. On the opposite end Anne was still sitting next to Christina, and upon noticing Edward she came over and sat next to him.

"So Henry has told you his decision, has he?"

Edward opened his mouth to respond, but the words didn't come. He ended up nodding slightly before he sank to his knees.

After a moment Anne stroked Edward's back. "I won't leave you," she whispered.

Edward shot up. "Promise me," he said grabbing Anne's hand and gripping it like a lifeline.

"I promise you, Edward, I will never leave you."

Edward peered into Anne's steely gaze, the strength of her words reflected in the window of her soul. The oath Anne swore was etched in the deepest parts of her.

Edward fell into Anne's shoulder and she stroked his wavy hair; he took the strength she wanted to impart, until night was upon them.

27. PUSHING HIM INTO DARKNESS

Christina bolted upright, taking a deep breath and waking from the stupor she had been in for so long. She let out a scream of pain as her movement shifted the wound in her stomach. Christina clutched her chest as Anne pushed her back onto the bed.

"Easy, easy, you're still healing. Lay back down, gently now." Anne's voice was soothing but firm.

Tala, sitting at the side of the bed with Anne, had jumped up when Christina awoke and now gazed at her expectantly, panting. Christina petted Tala's luscious fur, calming the wolf down.

Anne lifted Christina's shirt and, sure enough, her stomach was bleeding from the movement. Anne took a dab of water and cleaned the wound before applying a green paste which made Christina wince.

"What's that?" Christina asked.

"This is the plant you recovered from Pukuh's homeland. It will help heal you faster." After Anne applied the paste she covered the wound in cloth to seal it.

Christina's eyes opened wide as she recalled the circumstances of her receiving the wound. "What happened? Was Edward hurt?" Christina asked, nearly bolting up again.

"Edward is unharmed. Pukuh assisted in the fight, affording Edward the necessary time to bring you back here. You lost much blood and were unconscious for several days."

"Days? How did we escape Plague? Did Pukuh kill him?"

"Unfortunately, no. Pukuh was injured with poison and we were forced to amputate his right arm. We only managed to flee because of William and Edward."

"Even Pukuh was no match for him? I never believed it possible." Christina winced and lightly touched the wound on her stomach. "The man's eyes were terrible. It was as if I was struck by a knife… Well, I was," Christina said with a chuckle, "but you know what I mean." Anne nodded. "I don't think I was fighting as well as I could have before I was hit. I imagine that's how people feel when they behold Edward's eyes."

Anne faltered for a moment when she realised what Christina meant. "If Plague has eyes similar to Edward's, he is fearsome indeed. I haven't yet seen the man for myself, but the waves he has caused are clearly visible."

"Can no one stand against him?"

"I fear we may be wholly outclassed." Anne let out a sigh. "We must intensify our training if we are to stand a chance."

"I am with you, sister." Christina raised her hand.

Anne smiled widely and grasped Christina's hand. "I don't have a sister, but I will be glad to call you mine."

"So, sister, what would you say to helping me take a walk? I wish to feel the salt air on my face and see my brother again."

Anne frowned. "Alright, but we must be careful. We don't want the stitches to come undone."

Anne helped Christina up from the bed and then lent Christina her arm. Christina held firm to the offer, with her other hand on Tala's back as she moved on her wobbly legs to the stairs.

After slowly making their way to the gun deck, the two took a break at Anne's insistence. "So what about Tala, has she been cared for?" Christina asked Anne.

"She has not left your side since you were injured, and growled at anyone who approached. Alexandre could not get close, so I have been taking care of you and feeding her. She is very loyal."

Christina scratched Tala's chin. "I wish she was with us when we fought Plague. Things might have turned out different."

Anne nodded. "She actually helped in removing Plague from the ship. She's quite the fighter, as are you… Oh, one detail I neglected to mention: Edward wishes for us to use aliases when in town to help avoid another run-in with the Plague."

"I'll be sure to create one."

"Well, one more flight and we are done."

Christina and Anne resumed their trek up the stairs. After some time, the two women reached the top deck and the open air.

Christina took a deep breath in through her nose and let out a joyful sigh as she smiled. She scanned the horizon, taking in the ocean and the crew moving about on the *Freedom*. Her smile soon faded as she noticed the melancholic faces on those passing by.

"Is it because of Pukuh's arm?" Christina asked Anne.

Anne shook her head. "No." Anne opened her mouth, but needed a moment to speak the words. "Henry has chosen to leave the crew," she whispered.

Christina would have reared back in shock had she not been tied to Anne for support. "Why?" Christina's shock blurted out the question, then she added, "No, don't tell me? His mother?" almost directly after.

Anne nodded solemnly.

"Poor Henry. I would not blame him for his decision."

"Nor would any, but Edward seems fit to blame himself," Anne said, her oft-withheld emotions showing for the first time in her eyes and face. "Enough of this bitter melancholy. The crew has yet to notice us here, so let's show them you are well that their spirits may yet be raised."

Anne and Christina roamed the ship and talked with the crew, who, upon noticing her up and about, turned from frowns to smiles immediately. Many gathered around, causing Christina to say a few words to calm a growling Tala, and wanted a recounting of the battle against the Plague. As Christina told her story to those gathered the crew became more animate with each blow and manoeuvre. When the story was over, the men shouted curses to Plague and promised he would be killed for what he did to Christina.

Christina smirked. "You'll need to get in line, boys. The next time I see him I plan on returning his gift to me a thousandfold." As she said the words, she stood a little taller.

The crew laughed jovially while wishing her a swift recovery. After a few more moments of talking, Anne pushed everyone away.

"Back to work, men. Christina needs to see her brother." Anne helped Christina past the men and up to the quarterdeck where Herbert was at the helm.

Herbert was speaking with a crewmate when Christina approached. The crewmate's eyes wandered, which caused Herbert to turn himself around. The sight of Christina up and about nearly brought tears to his eyes.

Christina moved away from Anne and gave her brother a hug. "Don't worry, I'm not going anywhere."

"This is all my fault. I should never have brought you with me to this ship," Herbert whispered, his eyes cast downward as he gripped her hands like a vice. "I never wanted my quest for vengeance to hurt you."

Christina hushed him. "I'm the one to blame because I wasn't strong enough," she whispered. She pulled back, caressed Herbert's cheek, and touched the carved rose on her chest. "You're not the only one on a quest."

Edward stepped down from the poop deck and Christina's gaze was drawn to him.

"Edward!" Christina yelled.

Edward's smile to Christina was accented by cold eyes from a deep depression, but the young girl paid it no heed.

"You have recovered nicely," Edward commented.

"If not for you and Pukuh I would probably not be here."

"We both owe Pukuh a debt. I would have suffered the same fate if he hadn't arrived."

"Henry's mother wasn't so lucky, I hear."

Edward's mouth opened as he was caught off-guard by the comment. "No, she wasn't. If you'll excuse me, Christina."

Christina carried a sad expression on her face as she nodded slightly. Edward descended to the main deck and further into the bowels of the *Freedom*.

Anne approached Christina as she stared at the descending figure of their captain. "He just need a bit more time. The wounds are still fresh."

Christina turned to Anne, concern on her face. "The world seems to be conspiring to thrust Edward into darkness."

Anne's eyes reflected the sadness in Christina's. "The world is full of darkness. Some who live too long in the dark can lose themselves. We can only hope our Edward is strong enough not to let himself be lost."

"Or hope becoming darkness itself is what makes him strong," Christina added.

Anne couldn't be sure, but she noticed a slight grin twitching on the young girl's lips.

...

The *Freedom* landed at Port Royal a few hours before nightfall. The sun had disappeared behind the heavy dark clouds covering the sky. Garish lightning and screaming thunder loomed in the distance.

The mood aboard the *Freedom* was reflected by the dull and depressing weather. The crew knew why they were there, and none liked it. One of their family was leaving, and they couldn't do anything about it despite varied attempts during the travel from Badabos to Port Royal.

The crew were gathered on the main deck, and after a gangplank was placed over the port side they watched the stairs leading to the lower decks expectantly. Edward stood on the quarterdeck with Anne, Christina, and Herbert. Anne held Edward's hand as they silently watched with the crew.

After a moment of waiting and a clap of thunder, Henry emerged from the gun deck. In his arms he carried a wrapped body, his mother, and over his shoulder he held a sack with his meagre belongings.

When Henry reached the gangplank, he turned around, making eye contact with many in the crew, but not talking to any. His eyes eventually met Edward's. Edward gripped Anne's hand tighter as Henry stared at him coldly.

Henry turned, adjusted the weight on his shoulder, and slowly disembarked. The wind gusted strongly in his direction, urging him forward to Port Royal and further from *Freedom*, from his now former family, from his surrogate brother.

Henry's brother, Edward, also felt the push of that wind. The same sea winds which had guided Edward's father away from him were seeing fit to take his brother from him now. The wind pushed Edward to the sea years ago, and now pushed him to land.

Edward's feet moved of their own volition. He released his grip of Anne and quickly found himself on the gangplank to the harbour of Port Royal. Edward chased after Henry to the main street and out of sight of *Freedom*.

"Henry!" Edward yelled. Passersby stared at the tall bearded figure, short of breath and with desperation in his eyes, and then hurried about their business. Henry stopped, but didn't turn around. "Please don't leave. I need you."

Henry stood stock still, eventually raising his head to the heavens before he glanced over his shoulder. "No you don't," Henry said, and started walking again.

Edward gripped his hand tightly, so tight it shook. He remembered all the times they'd laughed, fought, and cried together, and how those times would never happen again. The feeling hit him like a bullet and, before Edward knew what he was doing, he was pointing a pistol at Henry in a shaking hand. "I won't let you leave, Henry."

Henry sighed and turned around. When he saw the pistol he took a step back. "What are you doing, Edward? Are you out of your bleeding mind?"

The townsfolk who saw Edward pull out the gun either ran away or hid in their houses for fear of what was about to happen. The sky grew darker and the wind shifted, blowing against Edward's face and pulling back his longcoat, but he took no notice.

"I can't lose more of my family!" Edward yelled over the din of the wind.

Henry shook his head. "You don't have a choice in the matter, Edward. You lost me a long time ago." Henry turned and walked away.

"Stop!" Edward shouted.

Henry half-turned. "What are you going to do, shoot me? That won't make me stay."

Edward held the pistol trained on Henry, his hands still shaking, as his friend moved farther away. Edward began lowering the gun when a soldier tackled him from the side.

The gun went off. The bullet hit Henry in the back. Henry took two more steps and fell to his knees. He dropped his bag and his mother's body, then felt at his back. Henry beheld his hand full of blood before falling to the ground.

"Henry!" Edward screamed.

Edward fought the soldier off and ran to Henry, but more soldiers showed up with muskets pointed at him. With clenched teeth and eyes staring at his friend bleeding out on the street, Edward turned and ran. He ran as bullets followed his shadow. He ran as the rain finally set in and the winds urged him back to the sea harder than ever.

The officers chased Edward all the way back to the *Freedom*, now with swords out as the rain made their gunpowder useless. When the crew saw Edward being chased they quickly made the ship sea-ready. When Edward ran up the gangplank and onto the main deck, Anne yelled, "Cut and run!" causing the crew to cut the anchor line and dropping it into the sea. Without the anchor, or the hours needed to raise it, the *Freedom* was able to leave shore immediately.

The *Freedom* sailed back into open water and lost all pursuers in the storm. Amidst the rain, the lighting, and the thunder, none could hear the roars of their captain as he was haunted by his actions.

He truly had lost his brother now.

28. THE HOUNDS OF PORTUGAL

During the weeks of travel to Bodden Town, Edward didn't speak a word of what happened with Henry. Instead, he silently suffered with his shame and sadness. Not even Anne could pry the secret from his lips.

Edward kept his distance, and by the end of the trip his face was cold and like stone. The emotion was drained from his eyes and replaced with detached purpose.

Once arrived in Bodden Town, the gangplank was settled and Edward stalked across with leaden feet. Each foot fell with all his weight, and Edward looked as if he could collapse at a moment's notice.

Edward kept himself up and moving, and headed straight to the Bodden Brothers' home with Anne and John following behind him. When Edward arrived, the gates were opened for him and he was led up to the business room on the second floor he was so used to.

"The brothers with be with you shortly," One of the attendants said before closing the doors to the room behind him.

"Edward, can we talk about what happened? Naturally you would be upset with Henry gone"—at the word gone, Edward winced and closed his eyes—"but this feels different. You can talk to us." Anne reached for Edward's hand, but he pulled away.

Edward stared at the ground, then ran his fingers through his hair. "I fear if I say what happened it will make it become all the more real." Edward searched for an exit, but he had nowhere to escape the interrogation.

Anne glanced at John, concern in her eyes. John pulled Edward close. "It's alright, son, we're here for you."

Edward's eyes flashed open and he pushed John away. "I'm not your son, and you're not my father! Don't you dare pretend to be him."

John looked hurt by Edward's lashing out. Anne pushed forward. "Peace Edward, John meant nothing by it."

"And nothing's all he'll have. I don't need your sympathy, so leave me be. I don't need you two to talk with the Boddens." Edward stared daggers at the both of them.

Anne stared back at Edward with equal fury. "By your leave, Captain." She stalked out of the room.

John glanced at Anne and then back to Edward. "Your father wouldn't approve of how you're acting, Edward." He didn't meet John's disapproving gaze, and John left the room.

Soon after, the Bodden Brothers Neil and Malcolm entered, peering behind them with confusion. "What has happened with the young lass and your accountant?" Neil asked.

Neil and Malcolm were wearing white satin ruffled shirts and loose blue vests with gold trim. The brothers matched, as always.

Edward shook his head and retracted to his current cold and distant demeanour. "Nothing. I need you to find me someone."

"Name them," Malcolm started, "and we shall find them," Neil finished with a flourish.

"Bartholomew Roberts. I believe you helped him find my crew before my escape, and now we are in need of his help again."

The brothers held disappointed expressions on their faces. "Such a shame you had not arrived sooner," Malcolm lamented.

"Roberts was here not two weeks ago," Neil clarified.

"Two weeks ago? Why?"

"He was searching for a man as well," Neil explained. "He was hunting a Walter Kennedy, and lost the trail months ago. He turned to us for help," Malcolm continued. "Our information network is simultaneously the most well-known and secret of the New World." Neil said, which made Malcolm laugh. "Aaron Cook has died, and we have acquired all his contacts with none of the subterfuge."

Edward chuckled; the Boddens having more power meant he had more power. "I recall the name, Walter Kennedy. Roberts said the man stole some of his treasure and left him for dead. Where did you send him?"

"Portugal. Specifically Lisbon."

"Portugal? Why there?"

"The Pirate Priest didn't elaborate, but he claimed Portugal was the last location he would have looked for Kennedy." "Perhaps the treasure you mentioned was in fact stolen from Portugal, and thus the last country Kennedy would think Roberts would head to."

"Your assessment, as always, is sound. I'll need the *Freedom* restocked for the trip, and a new anchor, as we cut ours to escape Port Royal."

"We will send word to our suppliers to gather a list." "And then take the cost from your shares, of course."

Edward nodded and said his goodbyes to the brothers, then headed back to the ship. Over the rest of the day and the whole of the next, the ship was resupplied with ammunition and food for the trip to Portugal and then some.

Anne, angry with Edward, ignored the captain until the night of the second day. While Anne and Edward slept on their bed in the crew cabin, the sounds of sleeping neighbours in the swaying hammocks nearby, and the slight lapping of the waves against the side, filled the ship.

"I forgive you," Anne said, her back against Edward's.

Edward turned around slowly. "Forgive me? For my outburst?"

"Yes. I know what you are experiencing is trying, and the wounds were still healing. You will talk with us when you are ready, so I will not press the issue."

Edward kissed Anne on the cheek and returned to his slumber. Edward didn't know when he would be able to talk about what he did. Talking about what he did made it more real, and the reality was what scared Edward most.

...

Freedom landed on the shores of Lisbon, Portugal, after a month and some weeks of travel. What met the crew was a venerable paradise unlike any they'd had the pleasure of visiting before.

The long stone bow-shaped harbour stretched from the sea and into a large inlet. Along the coast the harbour was broken up by sandy beach. The harbour, inlet, and beach were filled with ships of all sizes and styles and people of several nationalities. A number of warships were docked, as Portugal was involved in Queen Anne's War, siding with the Queen and fighting their neighbour Spain.

The harbour and beach quickly changed to stone houses hundreds of years old. As the *Freedom* approached the harbour, Edward noticed each house had different designs and additions setting them apart, aside from the broad strokes like the common red-tiled roofs. The tiles of stone on the sides of the houses were painted with floral patterns and murals attracting attention with bright colours and unique decorations. The houses and tall buildings were built on rolling hills covering the horizon.

For the first time in a long while, Edward noticed Pukuh coming out from the lower decks. Pukuh was recovering, or as much as one could call recuperating when half the time he was doing push ups with his one arm, and very rarely was let out of Alexandre's sight. Pukuh raised his left hand in front of his eyes, blocking out the harsh rays of the sun. He bid good-day to those wishing him well, and moved to the forecastle deck to gaze at the beautiful scenery.

Edward joined the warrior at the railing. "Breathtaking, don't you think?"

"Yes, this shall be a treasured memory, alongside many I have on this journey," Pukuh replied.

Edward peered at Pukuh's bandaged right shoulder. Alexandre said the wound had long since stopped bleeding, but the bandages were for the sores, which would take longer to heal.

"How's the arm?" Edward asked indelicately.

"Gone, brother, but not forgotten." Pukuh flashed the stump. He took a long breath in as he stared at the railing, and Edward could see tears welling in the warrior's eyes. "I still feel my hand as a demon haunting me, and my fingers yearn to be moved."

"I cannot imagine the pain you feel."

"No, you cannot," Pukuh said with bite. "If not for the princess's dog, that beast would have torn this ship apart."

"Aye, Plague was a tough bastard. You did well, brother." Edward placed his hand on Pukuh's shoulder.

Pukuh shoved the hand away. "Do not pity me! I am weak, and I paid the price." He turned his gaze to the ever-closer town, turning his back to Edward.

Edward's mouth was agape, trying to find the words, but none came. He felt like he was losing another brother.

"Captain!" Herbert yelled, waving for Edward.

"Leave me be," Pukuh said coldly.

Edward stood for a moment, then granted Pukuh's wish and joined Herbert on the quarterdeck. "What is it, Herbert?"

"I see the *Fortune*, she's docked to the northwest," Herbert replied, pointing off the port bow. Providence saw fit to swiftly bring the two together.

"Excellent, bring us around and drop anchor next to her," Edward commanded.

"Aye Captain!" Herbert replied before commanding the crew to furl the sails.

The *Freedom* floated beside the smaller *Fortune* and the anchor was dropped, causing them to draw to a halt just shy of being parallel to one another. The crew of the *Fortune*, upon seeing the *Freedom*, were waving and hollering to their friends.

Edward, Anne, Sam, and John entered a skiff and paddled over to the *Fortune*. A rope ladder was lowered, and the four boarded. When Edward pulled himself over the side of the *Fortune* and stepped onto the waist, he was met with a multitude of grins, albeit with some missing or discoloured teeth.

"The prodigal son has returned," a voice boomed from the stern.

Edward shifted his gaze to see none other than Bartholomew Roberts, the Pirate Priest, in the flesh. At seven feet tall, he stood well above most, even taller than Edward, and his loose white cotton shirt was rolled up to expose his massive hairy arms. He was at all times impressive, intimidating, but, with his smile, welcoming.

"Don't I need money to be prodigal?" Edward asked with raised brow.

Roberts laughed heartily. "Too true, too true. Let us say you are returned and have us a feast, shall we?" Roberts yelled, pulling Edward in close and raising his fist. The crew yelled in agreement to the festivities. "How have you been, young one? Let us head to my chambers so we may speak in private."

"Please, lead the way," Edward said.

Roberts took Edward and company into a cabin at the stern. Inside was a small room with a table, chairs, and a cabinet. Roberts bade the others to take a seat while he took some choice brandy from the cabinet, poured it into glasses and offered some to his guests. After brandy was distributed and Roberts had sat down, he restarted the conversation.

"So, my dear Edward, what brings you all the way to Portugal, and how, pray tell, did you happen upon me?"

"Yes, well, we were searching for you, and the Bodden Brothers helped point us in your direction. We need your help with something. I don't believe I told you the story of our ship and what we've been after this whole time, have I?" Edward asked while sipping his brandy. It had a scent of cherries and the taste was sublime on Edward's palate.

"*You* have not, but I was apprised of the situation by your red-haired beauty before we assisted in your escape," Roberts replied with a nod in Anne's direction. "Otherwise I would not have tested God's will that day and advised you to buy a new ship."

"That makes things easier, but that reminds me: when you met Anne, did you not think I broke the Pirate Commandments?" Edward asked, referring to the code he and Bartholomew Roberts created for how pirates are to act aboard the ship.

"I believe the rule is you had to seduce the woman aboard, yes?" Bartholomew asked rhetorically with a raised brow. "If you can find me any woman you could seduce aboard your ship, I will owe you a gold coin." Bartholomew grin as the others in the room laughed at his jest.

"Fair enough," Edward said with a smile. "Now, to the business of the *Freedom*'s keys. The final trial to reach the last key is upon us, but it's a dual trial." Edward passed the piece of paper with the clue to Roberts. "The trial requires a massive crew of possibly five hundred, or two crews working together. And, since we don't have the former, I was hoping you could help with the latter."

Roberts read over the paper as Edward finished his proposal. "Mmm, this does sound intriguing, but I'm afraid I cannot help you right now. We have problems of our own we must attend to."

Edward glanced to his comrades then back to Roberts. "Well, our business isn't pressing, so if you need assistance then our crew would be more than happy to oblige. You've helped us much in the past, it is only fair we should aid you in your time of need."

Roberts smirked. "A quid pro quo, as it were? You help us and then we help you?" Edward nodded. "The Devil is ever present, but the Lord provides to his faithful." Roberts rose and extended his hand. Edward stood and returned the hand to complete the arrangement.

"Now, tell us what you need."

"We are hunting for Walter Kennedy to pass the Lord's judgement upon him for his betrayal, but we have run into some problems. The Hounds of Portugal are protecting Kennedy, and, furthermore, kidnapped one of my crewmen as hostage."

"Kidnapped? Whom did they spirit away?" Anne asked.

"My first mate, Hank Abbot."

Edward's eyes shot wide open. "How could that happen?"

"Do not mistake these Hounds for some common group of bandits, they are well organised and have been the bane of the populace for some time. The Hounds came in a group upon Hank and a handful of my men in an alley. The Hounds killed everyone but Hank, perhaps to set an example, but they clearly do not know with whom they are dealing."

"And with us here the Hounds don't stand a chance." Edward raised his glass. Roberts shouted a 'Hear, hear!' in agreement before downing the remainder of his brandy. "Do you know who their leader is?"

"Unfortunately there is scant information about them. Rumours state the Hounds are led by a pirate who gathered ruffians and put them to task. Others say the Hounds are a front for a noble, or the Spanish, who are trying to dethrone the King of Portugal. No one knows what the truth is, but whoever their leader is, he is powerful and ruthless."

"Well, as always, we'd best proceed with caution. We'll split into groups and take a few different approaches. Anne, I want you and

Roberts to take Alexandre and see if he can glean anything from where Hank was kidnapped." Anne nodded in consent. "Sam, I want you to see if you can be recruited by the Hounds."

"I'm yer man. I'll loosen some purses and try ta make friends in all the wrong places. I'm good wit that sorta thing." Sam laughed with glee.

"John, you and I will see what information we can gather. Maybe we'll have more luck asking around."

"Y-yes, Captain," John replied.

"And don't forget not to use your given names. This is a territory loyal to Britain, so there may be British navy here. Agreed?"

"Aye, Captain!" Edward's company replied at once.

Roberts bellowed a laugh. "So decisive, and no objections from anyone. I always knew you were special, Edward. I can tell great things are yet to come for you. I do have one question before we move forward: Where is your Welsh friend, Henry?"

Edward pursed his lips for a moment, then produced a hollow smile. "We… had a disagreement, and he's… no longer with us."

Roberts had a genuine expression of mourning on his face. "Such a shame. Perhaps someday he will return to the fold."

Edward showed another false smile, and after a moment to compose himself he responded with a simple, "Perhaps." Then with a deep breath he continued. "Let's find these Hounds shall we?"

"Agreed. Whoever their leader is, he must be trembling in his boots now."

…

In the bowels of a ship, Hank Abbot hung by his arms from the rafters. His body swung with the rocking of the waves. His eyes were swollen and blood dripped slowly from gashes on his cheek. His nose stung from multiple fractures and the horrible stench of rotten wood, vomit, and unwashed bodies. His lips were dry despite his damp surroundings. He had four broken fingers, three broken ribs, and a shattered knee.

Cold water was thrown in Hank's face, causing him to wake from his first moment of sleep in a week. "Wake up, wake up!" a man in front of Hank yelled.

The man was unkempt from head to toe, with long greasy hair, rotted teeth, and beggar's clothes. His eyes were wide and he didn't appear sane. The most striking feature on the man was a medium-sized chest stuck to his right hand. As the man moved around, a clinking sound could be heard in the chest, possibly of gold. Gold forever within his grasp but beyond reach.

The man moved close to Hank's face, staring at him with demented eyes. "This ain't tha time ta be sleepin' Hank, I told ya."

Hank lifted his weary head and spat blood in the man's face.

The man reared back his right arm, the coins clinking in the treasure chest, and punched Hank in the face, breaking his jaw against the solid wood and metal. Afterwards, the man wiped his face off. "That weren't smart, Hank."

Hank gave a weary laugh, and with much difficulty sputtered out, "Worth it."

The two were in a hold in the lower decks of the ship, a hold for prisoners. Hank was in a cage with iron bars surrounding him. Other people were in cages like Hank, but none hanging as he was, and none so bloodied.

Someone from the crew ran down from the higher decks to the cell with Hank and the other man. "Captain, we received news about the *Fortune*."

The captain of the ship laughed maniacally. "Did they cast off?"

"No, not yet," the crewman replied.

"Well…" The captain paused, gripping Hank's cheeks. "Maybe we need ta teach 'em another lesson." He threw Hank's face away.

"There's more. Another ship showed up, seems to be in league with the *Fortune*'s crew. A fifth-rate frigate, could be trouble if they find us."

The class of ship piqued the captain's interest. "What wus tha name of tha ship?"

"*Freedom*. Isn't that the name of the ship what that famous bloke Blackbeard is on?"

The captain squeezed his fists tight. "I want the captain of dat ship," he seethed through gritted teeth.

"Kenneth?" the crewman asked.

The captain, Kenneth Locke, pulled the crewman in close. "I said, I want tha captain of that ship, and I want 'im now."

"Aye, aye, Captain." The man saluted before running back to the upper decks.

Kenneth turned back to Hank. "Now, where wus we? Ah yea, we wus gonna have some fun before the party starts. I hope ya last 'til then."

29. CACHE-HAND

"What do you see, Alexandre?" Anne asked the Frenchman.

Alexandre, eccentric as always in a silk robe and grey pantaloons, examined the scene of the attack and kidnapping. The bodies of Roberts' deceased crewmen were gone, but blood stained the stone alleyway. The doctor squatted down to peruse the dirt and mud, sometimes dabbing his finger into the wet dirt then smelling or tasting it.

"Assistant, my tools *s'il vous plaît*," Alexandre commanded with outstretched arm.

Victor, better known to Alexandre as Victoria, brought Alexandre's bag and dropped it on the ground beside him. Alexandre glanced back to Victoria as she re-joined the others with arms folded.

Alexandre reached into the bag, produced a magnifying glass, and further investigated the scene. He moved around in a squatted position, waddling back and forth as he studied the ground.

"So, anything?" Anne probed, becoming impatient.

Alexandre placed the magnifying glass into his bag and stood up again. "*Non*, nothing. The only thing left is the blood and the *boue*... the dirt, and too much time has passed to glean anything. The soil is local, but I have no way to tell if this area has been contaminated or not."

Anne sighed, and Roberts prayed. Victoria's finger was pointed towards her feet, away from the area Alexandre was focused on. Beside Victoria's feet was something small and white which was barely noticeable.

Alexandre picked up the object in front of Victoria, not commenting on how she had been blocking his view beforehand on purpose. What Alexandre picked up was the petal of a flower. The petal had small purple dots and a yellow hue at what would be the throat of the flower.

"What is that?" Roberts asked.

"This, *mon prêtre de pirate*, is a step in the right direction," Alexandre replied.

. . .

Sam drank his glass full of ale to the end without stopping, then slammed the glass on the table loudly. "I win again!"

The Voyages of Queen Anne's Revenge

The man in front of Sam, a large burly brute, finished his ale after another second of drinking. He reluctantly pulled out his coin purse and paid Sam a few coins for their wager.

"Much obliged," Sam said before the man left the table. Sam then nodded to a crewmate who bumped into the man, deftly stealing the purse. "Another round on me!" Sam yelled, to much applause.

Another man approached Sam's table and sat down. "You're good," he commented.

"Not good 'nuff. That last one drowned me. I'll settle for an arm wrestle. What say the winner takes two quid?" Sam offered, placing his arm up to start the match.

"Sorry, I'm not here to lose money. I'm here to offer you an opportunity."

The words piqued Sam's interest, and for the first time he measured the man in front of him. By all appearances he was out of place amongst the rabble in the tavern. He wore a cavalier hat with a feather out the back, and long blond hair flowing past his shoulders. His face was handsome, as if untouched by fists or knives, or even the weathering of the sun. He wore a long-sleeved blue doublet with wide white collar up to his chin. His breeches ended past the knee and he wore long leather boots and white socks in between.

No way this nancy is with the Hounds. "I'm not interested in small time." Sam slapped the barmaid on the behind and winked to her after she delivered his ale.

"Trust me, this is not small time. Now, before I play my hand I want to congratulate you on your boy's cut-pursing. I must admit, I missed quite a few of the exchanges." The man leaned in close and whispered. "Now that that is out of the way, have you heard of the Hounds of Portugal?"

Sam's brow raised. "Who are you?"

The man smiled. "I'll take that as a yes. My name is Philip Culverson, and I am the second in command of the Hounds. We're always seeking promising young men such as yourself, and the rewards are much greater than the pittance you gained here today. Now, I've given you my name, may I have yours?"

"The name's James Bellamy." Sam leaned back and set his feet on the table. "Well, ye answered the 'why me?' and the 'what's in it for me?' Now how about the 'how can I trust ye?' and 'where do I sign up?'" Sam said with his usual hyena's smile.

Philip smirked. "I'm fond of you, James. I'll answer your latter question first: I need to be sure of two things before we take you in. One: You're good on a ship, and two: You're good in a fight."

"I've been sailing since I was a wee mate, and no one's better in a scrap than me," Sam said confidently.

"I'll take the sailing on faith, but the fighting I'll need to see for myself." Philip rose from his chair, picked it up, and smashed it into the back of one of the larger patrons. The other patrons in the dank tavern went silent and watched intently. When the man rose up and turned around he immediately saw Philip and started after him. "Sir, sir, I was not the one who hit you, this man over here did." Philip pointed at Sam.

To Sam's surprise, others in the tavern corroborated the story Philip told. *More Hounds?* Sam tilted his head to the man, rose from his chair, and drank the last of his ale.

The man reared back and swung at Sam. Sam pulled back, letting the man hit air. The man tried to hit him again and Sam smashed his glass into the man's face. The glass broke into a dozen pieces and lodged in the large man's eyes. Sam kicked the man in the chest and he was sent flying back to the bar counter. Sam pulled back his fist, and punched the man's face. The man fell to the ground with a thud, unconscious.

"Another round, if you please!" Sam yelled as he returned to his table.

The crowd in the tavern erupted into cheers and hollering. The barmaid quickly brought him another drink with a kiss on the cheek and a wink.

Philip grinned and bent over to whisper in Sam's ear. "One-Fifteen Rue Passadico, midnight. Come alone and tell them the *Caballero de las Flores* sent you." Before Philip left he dropped a flower into Sam's hand. A white flower with small purple spots and a yellow throat.

. . .

Edward leaned against the stone building. The rich floral design on the building contrasted heavily with his black leather longcoat and tricorn hat. Edward examined the hat, remembering the circumstances behind his first receiving a captain's outfit.

John had bought the outfit for him the first time they visited Port Royal. Edward was so happy because it felt like the first step in him becoming a real captain. Immediately after Edward received the outfit, however, he found out Henry was about to be hung at the gallows for his mistake.

Anger seeped in when Edward recalled what he did to Henry, and he crumpled the hat. Moments later, John emerged from the building. "Anything?" Edward asked as he reshaped and donned the hat.

"N-no, Captain. Still nothing. Either no one really knows, or they aren't telling us, I c-couldn't tell."

Edward scoffed and started walking down the street with John at his side. "Probably the former, the same as the others. They know nothing about the Hounds save from the rumours we've already heard. None have been captured and the Hounds ransom out high-ranking individuals for coin."

John wrung his hands with his usual trepidation. "P-perhaps the others will have more luck."

"Perhaps. Let's take a break. The day is hot and we've been walking much too much."

John pointed down the road. "There was a pub back a ways. Mayhap we can nourish ourselves as well?"

Edward led the way. "Now that you mention food, I also feel a bit peckish." Edward and John trekked along the cobblestone street, past the colourful houses and into the pub John mentioned.

The pub was a well-to-do establishment with clean stone walls and a well-lit interior adorned with chandeliers. The expertly crafted tables and floors were made of polished hardwood and filled with proper ladies and gentlemen.

When Edward and John entered, sweaty and ragged, the patrons and servers immediately stared at them. Many whispered about the new customers, no doubt appalled by their presence.

Edward paid them no heed and sat down at one of the lavish tables. After a moment a server arrived to take their order.

"Some rum and whatever you're serving today, miss."

"That will be two reals, sir."

"John, do we have any Portuguese currency?" Edward asked.

"N-no Captain," John replied.

"Do you take British currency?"

"Yes, two crowns will do."

Edward reached into his pocket and pulled out and handed three crowns to the server. The gentlemen and ladies were shocked to see such a man give such an exorbitant amount as if it was nothing.

The server smiled, thanked Edward, and went back to fetch the food for them.

"C-Captain, that was worth several bottles of rum and a week's worth of food," John whispered.

"The look on their faces was worth the price," Edward replied as he smirked and waved to the other patrons.

The server brought back their rum first, then in mere moments brought a plate full of steaming vegetables and thick cuts of herb-roasted meat. Edward received more share due to his generosity. Edward and John slowly enjoyed every bit of their exquisite meal.

"John, I wanted to apologise for before," Edward said out of the blue after downing some rum. "What I said was uncalled for. You've always been there for me, and you deserve better."

John was taken aback. "D-don't trouble yourself, Captain. I know how sensitive the subjects were, and I acted inappropriately."

"Nonsense, I know you wanted to help. I couldn't talk about…" Edward paused, the words hard to find. "The truth is… when I tried to bring Henry back I…"

Before Edward was able to continue, a smooth-faced gent in a feathered cap, long blond hair, and a blue doublet sat down loudly at their table.

"Oh, pay me no heed, please continue with your conversation. My business can wait," the man said, absentmindedly smelling a flower in his chest pocket and gazing at everything but the people he rudely interrupted.

Edward gritted his teeth. "You stepped into a private conversation, so you'd best state your business quickly or I'll force you to leave."

The man raised his hands. "I apologise, I meant no offence. I hoped you men were searching for the Hounds of Portugal, but I must be mistaken." The man rose from his seat. "I will leave you to your conversation."

"Hold! Hold, sir," Edward said urgently. "How did you know our business here?"

The man turned back around, took his cap off and bowed. "Philip Culverson, at your service. Knowledge is my game, and my birds told me where I could find you." Philip sat back down in the seat. "I trade information for money, and wherever I stand to profit you can be sure I am there."

"So you know where the Hounds are? How did you acquire such information?" Edward asked, dubious of the stranger in front of them.

"I do know where they can be found, and procured this information by having friends in the right places. Often it is not the questions you ask, but who you know to ask. I know who to ask," Philip said with a smirk.

"How much is your price?"

"This information is a bargain: free."

"Free? Why would you give away this information for free? What profit do you stand to gain?" Edward asked with raised brow.

Philip leaned closer and whispered, "Profit comes in many ways, my friend, and when the one and only Blackbeard is hunting for someone, he can't mean to conduct a pleasant conversation."

Edward frowned at John. They hadn't used their true names all day, yet Philip knew who Edward was. *Perhaps this beard really is a problem.*

"How did you find us out?"

"The name of your ship is famous, and, I mean no offence, but Edward Teach isn't the best *nom de plume* for Edward Thatch, if you ask me."

"Before you take us to the Hounds I have a few more questions. You say our ship is famous. Is my crew in any danger?"

"Do not worry, I've made the necessary arrangements to stall the marines. Your crew is safe, for now. Any other questions before we leave?"

"You said profit comes in many ways. How will you profit from our destruction of the Hounds?"

The smile left Philip's face. "The Hounds took my brother from me. I vowed to make them pay, but, alas, I am only one man. If I can point you in their direction, then my brother will be avenged. Whoever pulls the trigger matters not to me."

Edward peered into Philip's eyes. His story was believable enough, and the man himself appeared to be trustworthy. "Alright, we will avenge your brother after we conclude our business with the Hounds, I assure you. Lead the way and we'll formulate a plan to take them down."

Philip closed his eyes. "Truly I thank you." Philip rose from his seat. "I will show you the way to their hideout."

Edward and John followed Philip out of the pub and into the streets. They ran north through the side streets and alleys. Edward tired and needed to slow down after a few minutes.

"Hold, Philip. I think I ate too much, my head feels light." Edward leaned against a building. John, too, was leaning against a building on the opposite side of the street, until he fell to the ground with a thud. "John!" Edward yelled, stepping closer, but he fell to his knees abruptly. His body was shaking and he was having trouble staying upright. *What's happening to me?*

Philip knelt down in front of Edward. "Did you know the extract of certain flowers cause you to fall asleep when ingested?"

"You did this?" Edward's vision began blurring.

"Yes. Oh, and Blackbeard? Kenneth Locke says hello," Philip said with a laugh.

Edward grabbed Philip's collar, mustered the last of his strength, and punched the man in the face. After delivering the punch Edward fell unconscious.

Philip rose up and spat on Edward's motionless body. He took a handkerchief from his pocket and wiped off his bloody lip. "Let us bring these two back to the ship. Mustn't keep the captain waiting."

As Philip walked away, the Hounds of Portugal took Edward and John in their jaws and away from the safety of their friends.

...

Edward awoke slowly, his head pounding, and the effects of whatever he was drugged with still coursing through his veins. He couldn't lift his head, and his eyes only slightly opened. His feet and hands were bound in chains, and he was hanging from the ceiling of a ship in a barred cell.

Edward moved his eyes around, noticing John hanging beside him in the same dulled state. In the dark ship he could see other barred cells, similar to the one he occupied, with other prisoners. The wooden floor was wet and rotting from too much water exposure. Rats slinked by Edwards' feet on the search for whatever food they could steal.

To Edward's right was the bow of the ship, and to the left, the aft. The aft had a set of wooden stairs leading upwards. Edward and John were near the middle of the ship on the starboard side.

"John? John, can you hear me?" Edward asked.

John did his best to swing himself around to face Edward. His eyes were open and he appeared unharmed. "I can h-hear you, Captain."

"You're not hurt, are you?"

"No, not that I'm aware. Where are we?"

Edward recalled the words Philip had said to him before he passed out. "We're on Kenneth Locke's ship."

John's eyes bolted open. "Kenneth Locke? B-but you left him on a deserted island."

"Yes, well, he must have escaped somehow. Doing well for himself apparently. He must be out for vengeance."

"Finally awake, ye bastard?" Kenneth Locke said, striding into the hold.

"Look who the rat dragged in." Edward planted his feet as he regained some of his strength. "I thought you were dead."

Kenneth smiled, showing his foul teeth as he entered the cell. "Oh I bet ya would'a enjoyed that real good, ya? I almost did die, a bunch o' times almost, but fortune favours me." Kenneth grabbed Edward by the cheeks. "Don't favour ye much, now does it?" Kenneth threw Edward's face back.

"How did you escape the island?" Edward asked while adjusting his jaw.

"Yer Captain Smith found me, locked me up. When I wus about ta lose me arm," Kenneth lifted his right arm, causing the coins in the chest to rattle, "I escaped. Been huntin' fer ya off and on ever since, and now fortune favoured me once again."

"So now what? You want to kill me? Get on with it. You're boring me."

Kenneth moved so close to Edward his rancid breath invaded Edward's nostrils. "Ye'd fancy that wouldn't ye? I love ta break this to ya: I'm gonna take things real slow with ye. Make ye bleed, make ye hurt, make ye beg for the end before I send ye ta Davy Jones."

Edward grinned. "There's just one problem with your plan Kenneth."

"Oh, whut's that?"

"I'm not very good at begging."

Edward smashed his head into Kenneth's face. Kenneth was sent back to the bars of the cell. Edward jumped from the ground and pushed his feet forward, pressing the chain binding them against Kenneth's neck. Kenneth was being choked against the iron bars of the cell.

Kenneth pulled his right hand back and struck Edward on his side with the heavy chest of gold. The force of the blow was so great Edward couldn't help but loosen his legs, releasing Kenneth. Edward fell back to the ground, his strength gone out of him.

After a moment's breather, Edward spat blood out of his mouth. The blow from the chest hurt more than any other punch he'd received before. "You have quite the right hook, Kenneth."

Kenneth lifted the chest on his right hand with ease, showing it to Edward. "They're callin' me Cache-Hand now. Your face is gonna be best friends with this hand o' mine by the time we reach our destination." Kenneth swung his arm back and uppercut Edward's jaw.

Edward's world went black once more.

30. JOHN THE FEARLESS

Edward shook himself awake. Kenneth was gone, and had been replaced by two men with muskets outside the cell. The ship was now swaying up and down with the waves.

Are we sailing now? "How long was I out for?" Edward asked John.

"An hour. Kenneth released the other p-prisoners, or killed them, perhaps. Either way, we're on our own now."

"I wonder if Hank was with them."

"I couldn't tell, all of the prisoners had rags on their heads."

"Well, if Hank was among them I hope to God he wasn't killed."

"Shut yer holes in there!" one of the guards yelled to Edward.

Edward decided to comply and bide his time. There would be a proper time to fight later, and now, when he was bound in every way imaginable, was not the time.

"Oi," the second guard said to the first, "grab us some eats and chairs, mate. This guard business is a bore, so at least let's be comfortable about it."

"And why do I 'ave to git 'em? Yer new, you do it," the first guard said.

"Precisely why I can't, mate. I don' know where nothin' is."

The first guard glared and pointed at the second. "Alright, but next time yer on yer own."

As soon as the first guard was up the stairs, the second turned around to reveal his face to Edward and John.

"Sam! What are you doing here?" Edward asked in surprise.

"Shhh, ye bleedin' idiot! They'll hear. I did jus' whut ye asked and got recruited by the Hounds. I didn't know whut happened to ye until I walked down 'ere not a half hour ago."

"Well, you'll need to play your role a bit longer than expected now that we've left Portugal."

"Aye. Wus sudden too. Luckily I managed ta scrawl out a letter before we left. *Freedom* should know what happened soon."

"D-do you know where we're headed?" John asked.

"Somewhere in Ireland. I found out after we set sail, so the *Freedom* only knows you've been captured and I'm with you."

"T-that is truly unfortunate."

"Did Kenneth not recognise you?"

Sam laughed nervously. "Not yet, at least. He don' seem to remember me. Got right up close too. Ye seem ta be the focus of his rage, and the year an' some made him forget everyone else."

"Well, at least we can be thankful for that." Edward noticed movement from the ship's stairs. Edward motioned his head to the stairs, causing Sam to turn and see the other guard returning. The three stopped talking.

Over the next week, Edward and John did not see hide nor tail of Kenneth Locke. Various guards came and left during the days and nights, and each time Sam was able to he brought them extra rations to keep up their strength. If he hadn't they would have starved.

The ship docked at an unknown port, and, after Edward and John were blindfolded, they were let out of their cage and led away from the ship. The two were pushed along a sandy beach to a grassy plain, and then to a rocky road for a few hours, until finally being led into a building made of stone.

Edward could hear the crackling of a fire and the sound of wind through small openings high above him. He also heard a snapping noise like a carpet flapping against a wall in the wind. *Are we inside a castle?*

Edward and John were taken down a long winding stone staircase, then through a hallway and into a room. Their blindfolds were removed. The room they stood in was an old cellar. On the right side of the room two thin beds were provided, but were more fit for holding rocks than men. On the left side of the room a wooden table had been pushed against the wall with two chairs. The back wall was covered by a wooden wine rack which probably used to hold much more wine.

The guards who led Edward and John down to the cellar took the chairs from the table and moved them in front of the door. The two sat watching Edward and John intently, pistols at the ready.

"Where are we?" Edward asked after taking in his surroundings.

"We're at shut yer shit-hole, that's where."

The other guard laughed. "Nice one, Markus," he said, then the two slapped their hands together.

Edward moved to the corner of the room where the beds where, and John followed. "We could easily kill those two and escape if they didn't have those guns," Edward whispered.

"We have to w-wait for an opportunity, but it must be tonight. We cannot allow Kenneth to start whatever it is he wants to do."

Edward nodded and lay down on one of the beds. After three hours, a knock came from the cellar door. Edward rose from his bed and tensed.

Sam entered after a few words with the guards. He had a loaf of bread and two cups of wine on a tray. Sam handed Edward the tray.

Sam had his usual hyena smile. "Enjoy the bread, ye bastards."

Edward inspected the bread and noticed a long cut across the middle. Sam winked at Edward, then left the cellar. Edward sat on the bed next to John, his back facing the guards and blocking their view. Edward reached into the bread and pulled out a knife.

He glanced at John; both knew what to do. John moved to the wall of wine and began rummaging through the remaining bottles. Edward hid the knife in his pocket, and walked over to one of the guards.

"I need to take a piss," Edward told one guard.

"There be a bucket over there. Piss in that," the guard said, motioning to the bucket with his pistol while still sitting in his seat.

"Oi, don't touch the wine, old man," the second guard yelled to John, standing up.

"I don't enjoy the wine you provided, so I'm taking another." John's voice was steeled with purpose.

The second guard walked over to John, leaving the first alone with Edward. "That wine's not fer you, old man. Hands off, I said."

John peered over his shoulder and nodded to Edward, which nod Edward returned.

Edward pulled the knife from his pocket and thrust it into the first guard's throat. First came a loud thunk, then blood splashed onto Edward's face and clothes.

The second guard turned when he heard the noise. John pulled a bottle of wine from the rack and smashed it over the guard's head. The guard fell from the blow. John caught the man by the hair and stabbed him in the throat with the broken bottle. He died without being able to make a sound. John lowered the man to the floor silently.

After the two relieved the dead men of their weapons, Edward started to leave, but John stopped him. He motioned to his feet and then removed his boots. Edward followed suit. Barefoot might be difficult after escaping, but they could move stealthily.

Edward went to the door and opened it slowly. No one was waiting outside in the hallway. Edward motioned for John to follow him as he left the room.

Edward and John passed through the short hallway, passing by several wooden doors and up the winding staircase. Edward held the knife in one hand, and the pistol from a dead guard in the other.

When Edward and John neared the top of the staircase they could see two guards at the top standing at the entrance. Sam was one of them. The way the staircase winded Edward was able to stay well out of view from the other guard.

Edward knelt down and tapped the knife against the stone. Sam turned his head to the noise and saw Edward.

"Did you hear something?" another voice said.

"Nah, wus jus' me boot." Sam tapped his foot.

Sam motioned for Edward to back up. Edward and John headed back down the stairs and waited. Sweat beaded on Edward's forehead as the silence and tension turned oppressive.

After a moment Edward could hear Sam say, "Did you hear that?"

"Hear whut?" the other guard said.

Sam didn't reply, and started walking down the stairs.

The sound of footsteps neared Edward and John. Edward backed down the steps slowly. *Whatever you're planning on doing, Sam, do it now please.*

As if hearing Edward's thoughts, a loud cracking noise preceded the footsteps stopping. They started again a moment later. Edward lifted his pistol in the air. Sam turned around the corner.

"Blimey, watch where you point that thing."

"I wasn't going to shoot you, trust me." Sam cocked his brow. "Alright, I almost shot you. I'm sorry, it's been a rough week."

"Well, best stay on yer toes, this is where things git dicey. We have to cross the great hall, up the stairs to one of the corner towers. I snuck some rope up there earlier so as we can climb down." Sam motioned his thumb in the direction of the tower.

"Why not head out the front?"

Sam raised his brow. "The front's too heavily guarded, mate. We'd not make it past one man. Our best chance is ta climb down silent and then make a run through the forest. I 'eard from some boys there be a town not ten miles south of 'ere."

"Lead the way," Edward said.

Sam moved swiftly and silently up the stone stairs, his feet lightly touching each step before moving to the next. The musty air of the castle was oppressive as they walked up, coupled with the smell of blood, sweat, and charred wood from torches on the walls.

When Sam reached the top, he stopped Edward and John, then casually walked through the opening, examining the room before him. After a moment he motioned for Edward and John to join him.

The great hall was an expansive rectangular room with a high ceiling and balcony walkways on the left and right sides. At three points in the middle of the hall were large stone fire pits, permeating the room with heat and an orange-yellow glow. Along the side walls were tapestries depicting battles Edward didn't recognise, and one depicting the crucifixion. All were weathered and worn and contributed to the room's musty smell.

Sam guided John and Edward to the tapestries and pushed them behind the dusty fabrics. As Sam sauntered along in plain sight, John and Edward followed slowly whilst trying not to expose their movement. When John and Edward reached the edge of the first tapestry Edward peeked out from behind and when Sam gave the signal they moved to the next covering.

The castle was quiet. Too quiet. The only noise beyond the crackling of the fire and the billowing and snap of the swaying tapestries was Sam's footsteps. Edward and John did their best to minimise the sound of their feet against the cold floor and muffle their deep breaths.

Where is Kenneth's crew? Or Kenneth, for that matter? Sweat dripped from Edward's brow despite the cold.

Sam whispered, "Stop," and Edward froze with John behind him. The two pressed up against the wall, motionless.

One of Kenneth's crew descended the stairs, an effeminate man with a feathered cap, the same man who had captured Edward and John in Portugal, Philip Culverson.

"James, yes?" Philip asked, brow raised in question.

"You should know, pretty boy, you brought me 'ere," Sam replied, trying to maintain his smooth, cocky, composure.

"Yes, I suppose I did. I haven't had much chance to talk with you since then." Philip leaned against the wall of the castle, in the middle of the tapestry between Edward and John. Philip was centimetres from touching Edward's shoulder with his own. "Tell me: what do you think?" Philip asked, gesturing about.

Sam glanced at where Philip was leaning, then back to Philip's eyes. "This castle be nice an' all, but we be pirates, eh? When do we be pirates? I don' understand why we're torturin' those blokes in the basement if we ain't getting' us no gold."

Philip gazed into one of the fire pits. "In truth I do not know much either. Kenneth refuses to tell me any details on why he has a problem with the Blackbeard pirates. All I was able to squeeze out of him is that it relates to his hand. Anything involving his hand is a sore subject with my dear captain." Philip lifted himself from his leaning position and started walking away from Sam.

Sam, Edward and John all let out silent sighs at their narrowly avoiding catastrophe. Sam turned around. "So why do you follow him so blindly?"

Philip turned around, walking backwards as he talked. "Despite his eccentricities, he always brings the gold eventually. And, I owe him a life debt."

Sam nodded, and Philip turned back around, heading to the front door of the castle. Sam turned and began walking slowly toward the stairs, listening for the door to open.

"James?" Philip yelled suddenly, making Sam jump.

Sam peered over his shoulder. Philip was standing in front of the spiral stairs leading to the cellar. "Yea?"

"Why is no one guarding the stairs?" Philip asked, pointing to the empty opening.

"Oh, that'd be me, boss. Jus' takin' a walk round the hall ta stretch me legs," Sam replied coolly.

Philip eyed Sam curiously. "Yes... well don't go too far."

After Philip started walking again, Sam did as well. Sam made his way to the foot of the stairs as he watched Philip exit the castle.

"C'mon boys! Let's move," Sam whispered.

Edward and John peered out from behind the tapestry, then ran to Sam. He gestured for them to move up the stairs and to the left side of the second floor. Slow and steady wasn't cutting it, and the three knew that. They bounded up the stairs, Sam trailing behind to not make noise with his heavy boots.

"Head for the stairs at the end of the hall," Sam commanded, pointing to the other end of the balcony walkway.

Halfway past the hallway, the doors of the castle opened and three of Kenneth's crew entered. Sam, Edward, and John all jumped behind one of the tapestries covering the walkway.

"So then the bloke said, 'Oi, she didn't say mittens!'" The three laughed at the punchline Edward, John, and Sam would never know the setup for.

One man stopped and pointed to the cellar stairs. "Ain't people suppose'ta be blockin' the cellar?"

"Yea, two blokes: The greenhorn and Gregory."

"Somethin' don' feel right," the first man surmised, and all three pulled out weapons and descended the stairs.

"Go, go!" Sam whispered urgently.

The three ran up the stairs as fast as they could. Noise was not an issue now, speed was the only advantage that remained. The sound of

Sam's boots reverberated off the stone walls loudly as he rushed to the top of the tower.

When the three reached the top, the wooden door to the tower was being opened by one of Kenneth's crew. Edward pulled out the bloody knife. The fat man had a split second to realise his doom. Edward jumped and thrust the knife deep into the man's eye and they both fell to the floor.

John leapt over Edward and cocked his fist, blitzing towards a sitting man on the left side of the circular tower room. The man got to his feet. John delivered an intense blow between the man's eyes. The man fell, unconscious. John knelt down and snapped the man's neck, killing him.

To the right, a third man stood and pulled out a pistol. John flashed demonic eyes at him and the man flinched. Sam kicked the pistol out of his hands, and then delivered another blow to his unguarded centre. The man fell backwards and out the window of the tower. He plummeted to his death in front of more of Kenneth's crew.

Edward ran to the window, and saw the reaction of the crewmen at the bottom of the tower. They saw Edward and ran to the front of the castle.

"We need to get out of here, quickly," Edward said.

"Jus' need ta find the rope I left 'ere," Sam replied, frantically combing the room. He overturned boxes and barrels and other odds and ends, but couldn't find what he was searching for. "Where is that blasted rope?"

Edward and John both were scouring the room, but their lifeline was nowhere to be found. "It's not here," Edward said, nailing the coffin shut. He could see no alternate escape route, save jumping out the window to their deaths. The three could hear the voices of shouting people from below. "I won't have *all* of us dying here. There's only one thing we can do." Edward tossed the knife to John. "John, you know what to do." Edward closed his eyes and spread his arms.

John adjusted his glasses, flashed forward, and sliced Edward's chest. With John's precision, the wound was superficial at best, but it looked bad to the naked eye. Edward let out a groan.

"What in blazes are ye doin'?" Sam yelled.

"You're the only one who can make it out of this alive, Sam. Punch John to make it more believable."

Sam paused, the pain over what was to come evident on his face. "I can't."

"You must, son," John said, unwavering.

"This is my last command as your captain, Sam. I command you to live." Edward's eyes bored into Sam.

Sam took one last glance from John to Edward, then he reared back and punched John hard in the jaw. Philip and a dozen crewmen burst through the open tower door. John fell backwards, his head hitting the stone wall.

"What happened here?" Philip shouted.

Sam took in a heavy breath and smirked. "Jus' after ye left these jokers busted out and ran fer the tower. I chased 'em and took 'em out."

Philip beheld the scene. Edward lay on the floor, still clutching his stomach and breathing heavily. John spat blood and struggled to rise to his feet, making a show of it.

"Good work, James. I knew you were a good choice for this crew. Shame we lost so many in the process." Philip planted his boot on Edward's stomach, beside the wound. "I guess the Devil lives up to his reputation. You're quite the troublemaker, Blackbeard." Philip pulled the blade out of Edward's stomach. "Take them back to the cellar. I will talk with Kenneth." Philip shoved the bloody knife into Sam's hands, then pulled out a handkerchief and wiped the blood off his palm. "This ends now."

Sam joined Kenneth's crew and took Edward and John back to the cellar. Edward's and John's hands were bound in front of them and they were forced to kneel on the wet stone. Two people stood behind Edward and John with pistols aimed at their heads. Two more aimed muskets from the front, and several more sat in the room, watching them like hawks.

Dad damn these bloody bastards! There be no way out of this now. I'm sorry, Captain. Sam's apology was written in his eyes as he stared at Edward, hoping his words would reach.

After a few moments, Kenneth and Philip entered the cellar together. Kenneth was furious, but no moreso than he had previously been around Edward. His left arm balled into a fist, and no doubt his right hand, inside the chest, was clenched as well.

"Oh, so glad you could join us, Chest-Hand. Thanks for gracing us with your presence. Wait, was it Chest-Hand? No, no, Fortune-Fingers? Money-Mitten? Oh! I remember: Prize-Paw!" Edward jested.

Kenneth shook with rage. He pulled back his right arm and slammed Edward's face with a blow so hard it broke his nose and sent him to the stone.

"Six men! Six men of mine you killed!" Kenneth yelled as he kicked Edward in the ribs. Kenneth kept kicking and kicking until Edward's rib broke with a loud snap, then he stopped to catch his breath. "I demand compensation, and I will collect," Kenneth seethed.

One of Kenneth's men pulled John to one end of the room, and another propped Edward up to watch. Kenneth pulled out a knife and stepped behind John. He set the blade underneath John's neck.

No! Not John! "Kenneth, stop!"

"Oh? What will you do if I don't? Hmm?" Kenneth asked, not removing the blade.

Edward looked daggers at Kenneth. "I will kill you."

Kenneth was not fazed. "You can't kill me when you're dead."

John raised his bound hands. "It's alright Edward, I'm ready to die. The only regret I have is I couldn't keep the promise I made your father. Tell him I'm sorry, will you?" John said, stoic and unflappable even with the blade against his neck. Despite John's strength, he was so old, so tired. Edward had never seen John this way before, and only now realised how much he'd pushed John over these years.

"How can I?" Edward asked, tears streaming into his black beard.

John smirked even in the face of death. "Your father is in the Caribbean, Edward."

Kenneth's blade sliced through flesh, leaving a red streak across John's neck. Blood fell like tiny drops of red rain, joining its clear brethren on the damp stone. John followed the blood, his eyes slowly losing their lustre, and fell to the floor with a thud.

Edward reached out to John, his mouth agape. His mind splintered like shattered glass. He could neither feel, nor speak. As Edward's mind recovered, the shards played the scene of John's death again and again in his mind, coupled with Henry falling to the ground, a bullet in his back. Edward was responsible for both. Edward's heart filled with anger. Anger at himself for Henry, for allowing this to happen to John, and letting his crew down.

Edward peered up at the face of Kenneth Locke. The smug grin on his repulsive face was salt on the wounds.

Edward lunged at Kenneth, jumping over John's body and gripping the man's throat with his bound hands. Edward pressed hard on Kenneth's Adam's apple, choking the life out of him.

"I'll kill you, you fucking bastard!" Edward yelled as he slammed Kenneth's head against the stone. Kenneth's men tried to pull Edward off their captain, but he was too powerful. "Is this what you wanted, huh? You wanted to die? Let me fulfil your wish!" Edward continued slamming Kenneth's head into the stone, blood seeping into the crevices.

The Voyages of Queen Anne's Revenge

Kenneth's men punched and kicked Edward relentlessly. Edward's strength faded from him with each blow and his grip eventually loosened. Kenneth's crew pulled Edward to the other side of the room and kept beating him until they were satisfied. When they were finished, Edward was numb from the pain. Kenneth recovered and dispensed a few swift kicks as well.

"That all ya got?" Edward sputtered.

"Save your strength, you'll need it to beg for your life," Kenneth said.

Edward used his remaining strength to pull himself up to his feet. He stood tall, towering above everyone else in the room. "I will never beg you for my life, nor will I beg to die. I will live, and I will make sure the last thing you see is my hands around your neck as I choke the life out of you."

Kenneth stepped on John's lifeless body, staring up into Edward's eyes. "Let's see how long your declaration lasts."

31. ESCAPE FROM LISBON BAY

"Where is Edward? He should have returned by now," Anne said to no one in particular. She stood in the stern cabin of the *Fortune*, gazing out a large window to the port of Lisbon, watching the boats and ships and people passing by as night fell.

"Shall I find him for you, your—?" William asked, nearly slipping out what Anne thought was a "your majesty," in front of everyone.

Anne contemplated her answer for a moment. "No, not yet. It's better to stay in one group. If something happens and we must find you too it will waste time."

William nodded in assent. Roberts bellowed a laugh. "He is probably boozing and brawling at this hour."

Anne stared blankly at Roberts as he continued laughing, then turned back to the window. "That's not something Edward would do. He's not a heavy drinker of wine, nor a gluttonous eater, and he is slow to wrath for silly reasons." Her arms were folded, trying to hold in the worry in her heart. *Something is wrong.*

Roberts laid his hand on Anne's shoulder, turning her away from the window. "Edward will be alright. Do not worry, child. As you say he is no fool. He would not run headlong into danger."

Anne turned away from Roberts. "Danger has an uncanny way of finding us, and that is what I am afraid of."

Alexandre and Victor were sitting at the table in the cabin examining the petal they found and talking in hushed tones.

"Are you discussing anything we should be privy to, *chirurgien*?" Anne asked.

Alexandre gazed lazily at Anne with his dark eyes. "Victor and I were merely *débattre* over whether this flower is from Northern or Southern Ireland." Alexandre was content to continue his argument, but Anne pressed for more.

"And what are your assessments?"

"I, correctly, say the flower is from Southern Ireland, as I visited there not a few years prior to moving to Port Royal. Victor has not been there in some time through his own admission, and things have… *évolué* since then."

Anne eyed Victor for an objection so a decision could be made. Victor simply sat staring daggers at Alexandre and then Anne.

Anne took it as Alexandre being correct. "Now we know the flower is from Southern Ireland. That could mean the Hounds' base is there, or it could mean nothing. Until we hear from Edward and John, or Sam, the only fact is the Hounds may have been to Ireland and one of their crewmates fancies flowers, yes?" Anne stared a cold, Queen's stare at Alexandre.

"*Oui.*" Alexandre lost his smug smile and turned away from Anne's glare of disappointment.

"Useless," Anne said with frustration, turning back to the cabin window.

The room was thick with tension. William approached Anne and whispered in her ear. "Perhaps you should sleep, my lady. Waiting is of no use. I will search for him, so you may rest easy."

Anne turned around and patted her hand on William's chest. "Perhaps you are right. Thank you, William."

William bowed slightly, then led Anne to the cabin exit, but halfway there someone knocked on the door. William and Anne both glanced at Bartholomew, as they were guests of his ship and cabin.

"Enter," Bartholomew commanded.

One of *Freedom*'s crewmates entered with a letter. "Uh, Miss Bonney?" the crewmate asked sheepishly, unsure of whom to address. "The harbourmaster had this letter for us. It's addressed to you." The man held the letter in front of him.

Anne took the letter. William peered over Anne's shoulder as she read, and soon Bartholomew joined them.

"It's from Sam," Anne said aloud with excitement. She read the letter quickly and with each line her visage turned a new shade of pale. "Edward and John were kidnapped by the Hounds. Their leader is a man named Kenneth Locke. Sam says they dropped all their previous victims at the west harbour and left Portugal."

"Does the letter mention where they travelled?" Alexandre asked.

"No, Sam was not privy to that information, just that they were headed north," Anne replied.

"Who is this Kenneth Locke?" Roberts asked.

"He was an old crewmate whom we banished and left to die on an abandoned island. Somehow he survived and must be out for revenge. More importantly, Sam wrote that all other people they kidnapped were left at the west harbour. Mister Abbot may be among them."

Roberts glanced at Anne, then to the other members of the *Freedom* in his cabin. "But what of Edward? Time is not to be wasted here, child. The longer you wait the more danger your captain is in. Leave our problems to us, we'll join you later."

"We made an oath. We help you find Mister Abbot, then you help us. We have an obligation to help you in your time of need, and we would help you regardless."

Roberts glanced at the crew again, and they all nodded in consent with Anne's declaration. "You are, all of you, more honourable than any others I have met in my travels. Let us quickly see if Hank is alive, and then we'll save Edward from the clutches of evil!"

Bartholomew left the cabin with the others following behind him. Roberts commanded his crew to take them into the harbour, and the *Fortune* was manoeuvred to the closest opening. Despite the unusual amount of ships and people moving about for this time of night, the crew of the *Fortune* worked like a well-oiled machine. The helmsman swayed *Fortune* in between the myriad of ships and slowly eased the ship into the harbour.

After the gangplanks were set, Bartholomew wasted no time moving ashore to the city of Lisbon, heading straight west. Anne and William followed, but Alexandre and Victor headed back to the *Freedom* to notify the crew of their impending departure.

The three ran quickly through the streets, dodging the occasional passersby on their way west. The hulking figure of Bartholomew attracted attention as he stormed by, a stark contrast to the average William and the slender Anne following behind him.

"Mister Roberts, if we find Abbot, and he is…" Anne couldn't complete the sentence.

"I am prepared," Roberts replied, slowing his pace. "If God's will is to take Hank from me, then who am I to argue?"

Anne felt the resolve in Bartholomew's words; he did not have even a hint of doubt in his heart. *He is a true man of God, through and through.*

"It is not to say He and I will not have some words later if that is the case," Roberts continued with a hearty laugh, causing Anne to smile. "Rest assured, I have faith Hank and Edward are safe. And even those with faith the size of a mustard seed can move mountains!" Roberts said with aplomb before he started running again.

As the three ran, they noticed a crowd gathered in the direction they were headed. At this time of night, it could only mean something of import was happening, and the release of kidnapped nobles would fit. The three made their way to the centre of the disturbance.

The Voyages of Queen Anne's Revenge

A dozen people lay on the ground, wounds covering their thin, malnourished bodies. Surgeons were treating the wounded as best they could, but were focusing on the nobles first and foremost.

"Hank!" Roberts yelled, running to his friend. Anne and William were a step behind.

Hank was lying on the stone ground, a shadow of his former self. His right eye was gouged out, blood staining his ear and hair from the wound, and his left arm and leg were broken, the bone like shattered glass sticking out of the skin. Beneath the surface, his wounds were probably much worse, but he was alive.

"Didn't reckon I'd see ya again, Capt'n. Prayed my damndest." Hank's body convulsed as he coughed up blood.

"We're here now, so save your strength and don't talk."

"No, you need to listen," Hank gripped Roberts' coat. "They sent word to the military. They're gonna attack. Ye gotta run, Capt'n." Hank's last words fizzled out and he fell unconscious.

"Hank? Hank!" Roberts yelled, trying to wake him.

"He's still alive," Anne reassured him. "But he needs help, and if what he said is true we need to return to our ships. Alexandre has the skill to save Hank."

"Yes." Roberts pulled himself together and picked Hank up gently.

Roberts—with Hank in his arms—Anne, and William returned to where the *Fortune* was resting. They couldn't rush for fear of worsening Hank's condition.

When Anne reached the harbour, she could tell something was off. The small boats and ships were docked, and a few large warships in the distance were preparing to set sail.

"We must be off. Those warships will soon be upon us," William said as they boarded.

When Roberts entered the ship with Hank's fragile body in his arms, a crowd of crewmen gathered. "Listen men, our enemies will soon be upon us, so there are two things needing done: Firstly, we need to return to the *Freedom* to warn them, and have their surgeon heal Hank. Secondly, we must escape Lisbon with all haste. Understood?"

The crew responded with a firm "Yes," then set about removing the *Fortune* from the harbour. Once the mooring lines and gangplank were pulled back, Roberts' crew moved the *Fortune* to where the *Freedom* awaited. The *Fortune*'s crew fixed a gangplank across the two ships, and Anne and William crossed.

The crew were busy at work, but stopped when Anne and William came aboard. Alexandre and Victor were there waiting, Herbert and Christina were at the helm directing the crew, and Nassir was preparing the sails with help from the crew.

"Alexandre, Hank is at death's door and he needs your skills." Alexandre nodded and crossed the gangplank with Victor. After they were across, the gangplank was drawn. "All hands, release the sails! Herbert, head for the throat of the bay," Anne commanded.

Herbert nodded and when the sails were unfurled he threw the wheel hard to port, turning the ship parallel to the harbour. As the *Freedom* approached the throat, three ships moved in, blocking the exit.

"Three ships dead ahead!" Herbert yelled.

Anne ran up the steps to the quarterdeck, took the spyglass offered by Christina and examined the ships blocking their path. Two sloops of war on the left and middle, and one sixth-class frigate on the right. All three smaller, but faster, than the *Freedom*.

"We can turn broadside and fire a full volley," Herbert suggested.

"That won't help. Ships are behind us too. By the time we turn full circle we'll be attacked on both sides," William said.

Anne focused on the bay. William was correct: two battleships the same size as the *Freedom* were on a pursuit course. There was no possible way the *Freedom* and *Fortune* would make it out alive in an offensive battle.

"We have one chance," Anne said, closing the spyglass with a snap. "We ram between the sloop and frigate, fire our cannons, and escape. The *Fortune* can escape between the two sloops or follow us."

"What? That's insane!" Christina exclaimed. "Even if we break through they'll attack us on the way. We'll never make it."

Herbert studied the ships ahead of them, then peered over his shoulder at the larger ones behind. "No, Anne's right, this is the only way. The *Fortune* is a sloop, and won't be able to handle a battle head on." Herbert turned the wheel starboard into the wind. "Achieving ramming speed," he said.

Christina didn't appear happy, but she didn't object further. Anne moved to the edge of the quarterdeck to issue orders.

"We need men in the bow deck. Fire those cannons at will! Gunners below deck, ready for broadside volleys. Close-haul the sails. We are pushing through the blockade, men!" Anne yelled.

The crew hesitated only a moment before rushing to work. Alexandre had explained the situation already, but the crew felt odd taking orders from someone other than Edward, Henry, or John.

The enemy ships closed the gap between each other as the *Freedom* picked up speed. The crew on the sloops and frigate fired their cannons. The iron balls hit the ocean, splashing water across the deck. *Freedom* retaliated with the bow cannons, easily hitting the broadside of the frigate. More cannonballs were fired. The iron hit the *Freedom* on the railing and bowsprit, sending splinters of wood flying.

When the ships were close enough, the marines fired muskets and rifles. Anne grabbed a rifle and shot back, with the crew of the *Freedom* following suit.

Night was upon them, and the ships continued to fire upon each other in the moonlight. The large flashes of the cannons and the smaller guns, each with their own puff of smoke, reflected on the water in the pale luminescence.

In the battle, ear-splitting shots from more than six dozen cannons, loud pops from the guns, and never knowing where the next bullet would appear from, made even the hardest of men shake. The crews pressed, either through fear, anger, courage, or blind ignorance, to save theirs and their comrades' lives.

"Brace for impact!" Anne yelled as she gripped the railing.

The *Freedom* smashed into the bow and stern of the other ships. Wood scraped on wood as the sloop and frigate were pushed to the sides.

"Fire port and starboard!" Anne commanded.

The sound of fifty cannons pierced the crew's ears. The cannonballs left their iron prisons and ripped the enemy ships to shreds. The sloop's hull was instantly honeycombed with a dozen different holes, and it began sinking into the bay waters. The frigate survived, for the moment.

The crew of the two enemy ships jumped over to the *Freedom* in droves to escape the sloop, and to attack from the frigate.

A crewmate of the *Freedom* ran up from below deck. "We're takin' on water in the berth," he yelled to Anne.

Anne fired her rifle at one of the marines' legs, then kicked another in the chest, sending the man overboard. She scanned the ship until she found who she was searching for. "Nassir, take men below deck and seal those holes."

Nassir, towering above the marine in front of him, delivered a fierce punch which sent the man violently to the deck of the waist. "Yes ma'am." Nassir immediately went to work, helping free some of his mates from fighting to assist him in the belly of the ship.

Suddenly, the *Freedom* lurched to the port side. Anne peered up and noticed the problem. The sloop sank on its starboard side, and the sails had tangled in the *Freedom*'s main sail. If the sloop sank enough, it could take the *Freedom* with it.

"William, I need you on the sail with me." William nodded and began climbing the ratline to the main top. "Christina, will you be able to protect your brother on your own?"

Christina pulled out a pistol from her belt and fired it on a marine climbing the stairs to the quarterdeck. Out of nowhere, Tala appeared and ripped out another man's jugular before landing beside her companion. "Of course." She grinned, petting the wolf.

Anne nodded and followed William up the ratline to the main top. Some of the marines were crossing over from their mast to the *Freedom*'s main yard.

One man sliced across at William. William ducked down and kicked the man in the legs. The marine fell sideways, cracking his ribs on the spar before tumbling and snapping his neck on the waist below. Another man advanced and attacked. William grabbed the marine's hands and kicked him in the chest. The second man was sent back against a third and they both lost their balance and fell.

Anne gazed solemnly at the dead marines. "So much for trying not to kill them."

William didn't turn around. "After your mother sent the Plague, I realised there is no use saving those trying to kill you. I vowed to protect you, and I will live up to my vow this time, no matter the cost."

William moved forward to the edge of the spar before Anne could reply. He pulled out a knife from his belt and began cutting the rope binding the spars of the two ships together.

Another marine ran across the sloop's mast, about to jump over to the *Freedom*. Anne pulled out a pistol and shot him in the chest. The man clutched his chest and fell backwards.

"I too will not risk the lives of our family on the one I left behind," Anne said. William nodded and returned to cutting the cable.

Anne glanced down from her vantage point. The crew fought tooth and nail against the multitude of men boarding the ship. Christina protected her brother, with Tala's help, from forces boarding the aft. Herbert yelled orders to the crew, despite having been shot in the arm, and occasionally fired a musket as he managed the wheel. Pukuh was there too, trying his best to fight with his left arm.

Cannons were being fired at close range from the frigate, and the sloop was nearly submerged. The *Fortune* was fighting the other sloop ahead of the *Freedom*, and was almost out of the bay. *Freedom* was moving forward, but was severely slowed by the sinking sloop. Behind them the warships were closing in and would soon be within firing distance.

William sliced through the cords several times before throwing them away. "Help me lift the mast, Princess," he said, crouching under the spar.

Anne knelt down and lifted with all her might. William used his shoulder and pushed hard with his legs. The sloop's spar inched up slowly, but not enough to separate the two ships. After a moment's futile struggle William and Anne resigned and caught their breath.

"How are we to move a whole ship?" Anne asked, not expecting an answer.

William was breathing heavily while viewing to the scene below. "We don't need to move the ship, just the mast." William stood staring at the chaos below. "Charles!" He yelled to one of the gunners. The man named Charles ducked down to avoid the rain of bullets and peered up to the sound of his name being called. "Chain shot on the sloop mast!" Charles studied the mast stuck to the *Freedom*, and then to the sloop. He smirked and nodded to William.

William moved back under the sloop's spar, and Anne prepared herself. Charles ran to the bow cabin, dodging bullets and slashes, and returned with a specialty ammo. He held two cannonballs attached by a thick iron chain. Charles loaded the ammo into a cannon, aimed for the sloop mast, and fired.

The cannonballs spun in the air, and the chain hit the mast, rending the hardwood and separating the mast from the ship.

"Can we leave the mast?" Anne asked William.

William assessed the situation. "No, if we leave it and it falls the wrong way as we move forward it could damage *Freedom* or fall on one of the crew. If possible, we need to remove it."

William and Anne pushed and lifted the spar away from the *Freedom*. The sail swayed and pitched in the wind. William dug his back into the heavy wood. Anne lifted the mast like she was tossing a caber, her legs and arms straining with the effort. The two threw the mast to the port side of the sloop and it lurched forward and fell into the water with a giant splash.

Freed from the shackles of the smaller ship, *Freedom* moved quicker towards the mouth of the bay. The frigate was sinking, but the majority of the crew had jumped ship to continue the battle atop the *Freedom*.

Anne noticed several enemies heading to the *Freedom*'s lower decks. "Help rout the enemy on the waist, I'm heading below to ensure we are not sunk." William nodded, then climbed down the ratline. Anne jumped off the spar, grabbed a rope and swung down to the waist.

Pukuh was a few paces in front of Anne, fighting with a spear in his one arm. Pukuh's striking was efficient for not having his right arm, but he had difficulty parrying and blocking blows without the power of two hands.

The man Pukuh was fighting sliced his sword down. Pukuh blocked with his spear. The powerful blow broke the spear in half, leaving the Mayan defenceless. The man lifted the sword high in the air again. Pukuh was on his knees, his teeth gritted.

Before the man could attack, Anne stabbed him in the throat with a long dagger. The man fell to the ground, blood gushing from the wound.

Anne handed Pukuh a dagger. "Use this, Pukuh."

Pukuh accepted the dagger grudgingly. "Thank you, Princess."

Anne ran past those fighting and to the stairs to the lower decks. She jumped down several steps at a time, on the heels of the men heading below. She caught one on the arm, twisted him around, and punched him in the temple. The man fell to the ground unconscious and Anne ran to the next set of steps.

When Anne reached the crew cabin, she could feel a small layer of water on deck, seeping into the bilge. If enough trickled through the cracks, the bilge would fill and the ship would sink.

Anne could see the marines attacking the crew trying to patch holes. As Anne was about to run over and dispatch the attackers, a glint of light caught her eye in the darkness. On the bed Anne and Edward shared lay the golden cutlass Edward used. Anne grabbed the eagle-hilted blade, then rushed to the crew in need of help.

Anne slashed the back of one marine and slit the throat of another. The others were quickly dispatched by the crew. "Patch those holes now!" she commanded. Anne didn't wait to see the order followed through and instead jumped down a hatch located at the centre mast to the bilge.

The lowest part of the ship, below the waterline and the worst spot for a cannonball to hit, was rapidly filling with water. Anne landed feet-first and the water reached her chest even as she stood on the keel.

In the pitch darkness of the bilge, Anne saw five of the *Freedom*'s crew fighting three marines, the latter gaining the upper hand due to having weapons. Nassir and his helpers used timber meant to patch the holes for protection against the swords.

Nassir blocked a slash from one man, the cutlass embedding itself in the wood. The man tried to remove the weapon, but couldn't get enough leverage. Nassir twisted the timber to the side and the man released the cutlass to save his fingers. Nassir smashed the wood into the man's face, breaking his nose. The man fell backwards, clutching his bleeding nose.

The Voyages of Queen Anne's Revenge

Anne stabbed the man through the back as he floated towards her. Hearing his mate die, one of the marines turned and attacked Anne. He slashed at her. The water slowed Anne's reactions and she was barely able to bring the golden cutlass up to block. The man pushed down and his blade dug into Anne's shoulder. She used both hands to push back, only managing to stop the blade from going any deeper.

Nassir attacked from behind and cracked a hammer upside the marine's head, embedding it in his skull. Anger flashed in Nassir's eyes as he swung around, a cutlass in his other hand. The last marine fell, his neck cut half off. Nassir let out a yell, swinging the blade again and again at the dead marine. Great splashes erupted from Nassir's fury as he kept pounding the water.

Anne gripped Nassir's hands from behind. "Now is not the time for you to lose yourself, Nassir."

Nassir took a deep breath and stopped struggling. Anne released him, and he reached into the water to pick up his hammer from the dead marine's head, then went back to work.

The crew helped Nassir, quickly covering the holes with spare planks. Anne helped by holding the planks while the others secured the timber with nails.

"The job is not yet complete, men. This only slowed the flow. We need to clear the bilge of water to bring our full speed back. Then we can cover the beams with tar." Nassir moved to the aft of the ship.

The small space held little, aside from a few spare parts and extra cargo, but one piece of equipment was constant: a chain pump at the aft. Each pump was a chain and a winch, which, when turned, pulled water up and out of the ship.

Anne ran aft, grabbed the winch handle underneath the water along with Nassir and the two began the laborious process of hand-pumping water from the dirty bilge. The other men went to steps at the fore, and opened an entrance to the bilge. They grabbed buckets and helped drain the bilge by running upstairs to dump the water into the ocean.

Over the course of two hours the fighting finished on the top deck, the bilge water was drained, the holes fixed and covered in fresh tar, and the *Freedom* and *Fortune* escaped Lisbon and their pursuers.

Wiping the sweat from their brows, Anne and Nassir took leave of their posts. Anne returned to the top deck. The crew were cleaning the ship of debris, dumping the bodies of marines into the sea, and readying their dead comrades for a funeral pyre.

The disheartened and tired faces said more to Anne than any words could. Lost and leaderless, the crew of the *Freedom* had no energy or morale left. Their captain and quartermaster kidnapped, the first mate gone, a dozen crewmates dead, many more injured, the past weeks and months being hounded by an assassin who took the arm of one of their greatest fighters, all culminated into stress mounting on the shoulders of everyone.

Right now, Edward would deliver a rousing speech, turning the mood and focusing the men. I guess it is my turn.

Anne pulled herself up straight and walked to the quarterdeck. Christina was applying a bandage to her brother's forearm as he sat in his wheelchair. Anne could tell Christina too was in low spirits. Christina afforded Anne a cursory nod before returning to work.

Anne leaned forward on the quarterdeck railing, staring at the crew as they milled about. "Attention, crew!" she yelled. The crew of the *Freedom* stopped all they were doing and moved closer to the quarterdeck to hear Anne. "These past weeks and months have been difficult. We have had our share of battles, and losses, but we must not let this bring us down. We must press onward to save our captain."

Anne's speech seemed less than inspiring to those listening. She pressed on. "Our captain has been taken by an enemy we all know: Kenneth Locke. Unless we find Edward, Locke will more than likely kill him."

"What more do ye want of us? We be workin' ain't we?" another crewmate said, hunched shoulders of defeat hanging on him like a shroud.

"I am asking you to fight," Anne boomed. "I am asking you to fight for your captain, and for this ship's namesake." Anne pat the railing of the *Freedom* before gazing into the eyes of the crew. "This ship is our home, but it is also a symbol. A symbol of what we all strive for, what we would fight for, what we would sacrifice our lives for." Anne pointed to the bodies of the dead crewmates lying in a line beneath her on the waist. "Those men sacrificed their lives for that cause, for you. We all owe Edward our lives and our *Freedom*, and if you are not willing to yell from the bottom of your hearts that you will fight for his *Freedom*, for our family's *Freedom*, then perhaps this is the wrong ship for you." Anne turned her back to the crew and sat on the railing, closing her eyes.

She rubbed her eyes; the stress was wearing on her. She felt defeated. *I failed these people. I am no leader, only a shadow of someone greater.* The image of her mother entered Anne's mind, and bitter tears welled in her eyes.

But Anne's words sank in, and after a long silence, one crewman stood tall and said: "I will fight." Anne turned and focused on the crewman, smiling at his declaration. "I will fight," another repeated, stepping forward. "I will fight," a third chanted. Soon the whole crew repeated the sentiment, their fatigued eyes changing.

"I will fight," Christina joined in proudly, raising her fist in the air.

"I will fight," Herbert resounded with his sister.

The crew all focused on Anne. "For *Freedom*!" she yelled, pumping her fist in the air. The crew yelled the words back to her. "For *Freedom*," she yelled again, louder than before, the strength of the crew boosting her as they shouted the mantra back all the louder. "For *Freedom*," Anne yelled one last time.

"For *Freedom*!" She heard back, even louder than before. Anne observed the crew of the *Fortune* yelling the same declaration to their brothers. They were all waving, hooting and hollering with large smiles on their faces.

The crew of the *Freedom* were back to their old selves, Anne included.

"Where to, Captain?" Herbert asked Anne.

Anne gazed at the fore, the faintest bit of dawn's light on the starboard horizon and wind blowing her long red curls back. "North, to Ireland." She declared.

"Aye, Captain," Herbert said, turning the ship north.

We are coming for you Edward. Do not die on me.

32. DEAD & ALIVE, LOST & FOUND

"I need your help," Pukuh declared solemnly. After Anne's rousing speech, he'd asked to speak with her. He wore a serious expression on his face, like none Anne had seen before.

"Anything you need, Pukuh," she replied.

Pukuh fell to his knees and prostrated himself before Anne. "I want you to train me to fight."

Anne was taken aback at the Mayan's plea. "You are stronger than this. You have trained yourself your whole life, and in time your arm will not be a hindrance to you. Why ask for training now?"

"I wish to fight for *Freedom*, for my brothers and sisters, but I am weak. A weak man thinks he can learn everything on his own." Pukuh raised his head and stared Anne in the eyes. "If I am to fight for Edward, for *Freedom*, for my village, and face Plague again, I must learn how to be the best, from the best."

Anne smiled. "Well said. However, I am not the best. William?" Anne beckoned.

William stepped up to the quarterdeck. "Yes, my lady?" he asked.

"Would you be willing to train Pukuh to fight?"

William peered over to Pukuh, who once more bowed low before William. "Stand," he commanded. Pukuh followed William's orders and even displayed his best attempt at a salute out of respect. "I will train you, but this won't be a master-pupil relationship. We can both learn from each other, so we train as equals, and I will have it no other way. Agreed, Prince?" William extended his left hand to shake on the agreement.

Pukuh lowered his salute and smiled. "Agreed," he replied, shaking William's hand with a firm grip.

The two then left to start training immediately. Pukuh was eager to learn from William, and Anne couldn't be sure, but she thought she could see the inkling of a smile on William's face too.

The recognition of the sun being out finally hit Anne, and she realised she was exhausted. The crews of *Freedom* and *Fortune* had fought through the night without sleeping.

"Herbert, when we can, tell the *Fortune* to drop anchor and we'll allow the crews to rest. It has been a long night."

"Aye, Captain. I will begin now," Herbert said, yawning as he spoke.

Anne descended to the crew cabin, and lay down on the bed she and Edward had shared not a few days before. She could still smell his scent, and when she closed her eyes she could swear he was next to her. Anne drifted off into slumber, Edward forefront in her mind.

...

"How are you faring, Mister Abbot?" Anne asked, sitting beside Hank in the crew cabin of the *Fortune*.

"Doin' a mite better, Miss Bonney, thanks ta yer surgeon's skills," Hank replied softly.

Hank was still the worse for wear. His body, bruised and battered, was healing, but slowly.

"Stay rested, and when you're better we'll have a drink in your honour. It would be remiss for you to be late for your own party," Anne said with a grin.

"I reckon the Lord himself couldn't keep me from bein' there."

Anne patted Hank on the leg, then advanced to the steps of *Fortune*'s crew cabin where Roberts stood watch. "He claims to be better, but he appears worse. What did Alexandre say?"

"He said to pray and wait. Alexandre has done all he could for Hank, it is up to God now. Two weeks have passed and Hank is able to stay awake long enough to talk, but he can barely keep even the least bit of food down. I fear God may have left us." Roberts gazed at his comrade, struggling to breathe, then his eyes fell.

"Do not say that. The *Freedom* has not given up hope, nor should you." Anne placed her hand over Roberts' and squeezed.

Roberts squeezed Anne's hand back and shook his head. "Aye, I shouldn't give up so easily. Our plight is nothing at the moment, we should be focusing on finding your captain."

"I fear God may have left us there as well," Anne said.

"My dear, Hank is one thing, but Edward is another entirely. He would not die so easily. We will arrive in Ireland soon and before you know it you two will be reunited."

"I hope you're right."

"I know I am. Besides, one should follow their own advice, lest they be a hypocrite." Bartholomew winked, and Anne smiled.

A crew member came down the steps to speak with Roberts. "We can see land, Captain. We'll be arriving in Cloankilty soon."

Roberts nodded to the crewman, then turned back to Anne. "Let's renew ourselves with some fresh air."

The two walked up the stairs to the top deck of the *Fortune*. The sun was approaching noon, but the cool air made it feel earlier in the day. Anne could see the *Freedom* off the port stern, the crew hard at work under William's direction to keep speed with the smaller *Fortune*. Anne moved to the bow of the *Fortune* and gazed at their destination.

The town was a few hours away and only a small dot on the horizon. As the ships drew nearer, Anne could see the outline of small wooden and stone homes and a small harbour. When *Fortune* was close to landing, Anne was able to see the whole village in front of her. She could tell from her vantage point that the small village had been built with care.

The small wooden harbour led directly to cobblestone streets with various businesses scattered about. One tavern, a blacksmith, bakery, a fishmonger, a butcher, an inn, a church closer to the centre of town, and the rest were homes. A quaint village, but Anne could tell something was off.

"There is no one outside," Roberts commented as he stood beside Anne.

Anne inspected the flags the *Fortune* was running. Plain and white as could be; Roberts ensured the pirate flag they traditionally used for battle was taken off before they were even close to port.

"I wonder why?" Anne contemplated aloud, not expecting a response.

"I guess we'll find out when we land," Roberts replied.

The *Fortune* was brought as close as could be to the small port, then the anchor was dropped into the sea and the sails furled. Anne and Roberts, along with a few of his crew, entered a rowboat to go ashore.

Even as the small rowboat was docking, Anne could see none walking about the town, but she did notice movement in curtains covering the windows. *So there are people.* Anne trekked along the cobblestone street of the town. She went to the closest shop, the butcher, and knocked loudly on the door. No answer. Anne rapped once more. Still nothing.

"Hello? We mean you no harm, we are only here for information," Anne yelled loudly, then tried again in Gaelic.

Roberts joined her. "Nothing?"

"No, the town refuses to answer." Anne turned around, her hands on her hips. She could see another rowboat approaching, this one carrying some of the *Freedom*'s crew. "The curtains move and bend, and I can feel eyes upon me."

"What must we do to coax them out of their homes?" Roberts asked, glancing about.

Anne strolled down the road. "I think the better question is what has caused the townspeople to act this way." She ambled around a bend onto another long street lined with houses. At the end of the street she could see a fountain spraying water in the middle of a large open area, possibly the town square.

Anne moved towards the town square with Roberts following behind. "Do you know where you are headed?"

"No," Anne replied, not turning around. "Eventually, someone has to leave their home, and we won't depart until they do."

Anne kept walking with Roberts on her tail, unequivocally caught in her pace, as most were when next to the headstrong red-haired woman. Anne slowed down when they reached the small fountain.

She searched the square, and she could see an old man sitting on a bench at the foot of the fountain. He was wrinkled, with long grey hair and a lengthy beard of the same hue, and a cane in his hands. He didn't notice Anne and Roberts, so Anne began walking in his direction, but she was stopped by a voice from behind.

"Anne," Roberts called softly, provoking her to gaze in his direction.

Fourteen men had weapons pointed at Roberts. Bartholomew's hands were in the air. Some of the locals held swords and pikes, while others had more modern pistols and muskets. They approached Anne with caution, and she also raised her hands in the air.

"What do you want with our town?" one of the men yelled in Gaelic.

"We mean you no harm," Anne replied, also in Gaelic.

"What are they saying?" Roberts asked.

"I will handle this, Roberts," Anne replied.

Before Anne could follow through with her promise, things turned from bad to worse. Christina and ten crewmen from the *Freedom* and *Fortune* ran up behind the locals.

"Drop your weapons!" Christina yelled to the crowd.

The locals turned around, moving behind Anne and Roberts, using them as shields and leverage at the same time. What followed was a tense shouting match between Christina, Anne, Roberts, their respective crews, and the locals.

Anne tried her best to yell in English and in Gaelic for everyone to cease talking and lower their weapons, but her voice was a mere drop of noise in the bucket. Roberts also tried to command his men to lower their weapons, but fear drove them to keep the muskets up, if not steady. Christina, in her usual hot-headedness, was determined to shout louder until she was the victor, and the more shouting did not work the closer she was to pulling the trigger on her musket.

"Silence!" a booming voice cut through the din, and all eyes focused on the person it originated from. The old man who was at the bench stepped in between the two crowds and faced the locals with a steely gaze. He talked with one man specifically, the leader of the young men. The young man heatedly argued with the older man until the old man whacked the young one on the head with his cane.

After a flash of contempt, the younger man walked to the edge of the town square, motioning for his crew to follow. The threat was gone as quickly as had come, but the hostility remained. The young men still held their muskets close, disdain evident in their eyes.

The old man passed Anne and entered the street leading to the harbour. "Come now lass, let us talk. The quicker we know what you want the quicker you will leave," he said.

"Thank you, we feel the same," Anne replied with a smile. She turned to Christina, instantly losing the smile. "Take the men back to the harbour and wait there. Don't make more trouble than you already have."

Christina was about to object, but Anne raised her hand, silencing her. She scoffed and stormed off down the street to the harbour, her cherry-blond hair whipping in the wind.

Anne caught up to the old man who was entering a nearby inn, and followed him inside. He sat at a bar stool at the back and ordered something from the barkeep. Anne sat next to him, and Bartholomew joined a moment later.

"So, lass, what do you want with my town?" the old man asked, not wasting time with introductions. He downed his drink in one gulp.

"My companion does not understand Gaelic, can you speak English?" Anne asked. The old man nodded and Anne continued talking in English. "We require information. We are hunting for a group of pirates who took our captain and two crewmates hostage. We have reason to believe they are somewhere here in Ireland."

"There's many pirates these days, too many. That's why the boys you met were hostile. Pirates have been terrorising our coasts for the past year. They've soured our outlook on visitors."

Anne sent Roberts a knowing glance. "These pirates, would you be able to describe their leader?"

The Voyages of Queen Anne's Revenge

"Aye lass, none would forget such a man. His eyes were dark and devoid of any compassion, teeth rotted, hair matted with grease and face covered in dirt. His most striking feature had to be the chest on his hand, clanging with the sound of treasure and doom approaching. Any who mentioned the chest was killed immediately. Called himself Cache-Hand, he did. That the man you be searching for?"

Anne nodded. "Yes, the same. Do you know where he is hiding himself?"

"I see by your manner you are educated. You already know the answer. I wish I could help you. The best information I can provide is that the ship always approaches from the east whenever they attack, and they've attacked other towns all along the coast. Follow the coast and you may be able to find where they call home."

"Thank you, you have been most helpful." Anne rose from the bar stool.

"One more thing," the old man said, stopping Anne and Roberts before they left. "Gut Cache-Hand and avenge my son, will ya?"

"I planned on it," Anne replied, not missing a beat.

The old man lifted his cup to Anne before downing another large gulp. Anne turned without another word, and left the inn. Christina was waiting at the harbour with arms folded and a sour expression on her face. When Christina noticed Anne, she stalked over to her.

"What did the old man say?" Christina asked.

Anne dismissed the other crewmates crowding around her and Christina, and stared at Christina with cold authority. "Firstly, use your head and be more responsible. Your rashness could have turned this whole town against us. You are not to act without orders again. Am I clear?"

"You and Roberts would have been shot if—"

"Silence!" Anne cut in severely, causing the crew to peer in her direction. "Am I clear?" she repeated.

Christina bit her lip and gave a sideways glance to everyone staring before saying, "Yes, Ma'am."

"Good, now let's leave. We have a clue as to Kenneth's whereabouts." Anne stepped into the small boat, assisted by Roberts.

"Where are we headed?"

Anne moved her red curls behind her ear as she stared at the moving seas and the rolling coast. "We're headed east."

Shortly after, the two ships set sail east of Cloankilty in search of more information on their lost captain and Kenneth Locke. They stopped at each town and port, and every small village in between, asking for information.

Similar to Cloankilty, the townsfolk displayed open hostility because of *Freedom*'s and *Fortune*'s size, and the cannons aboard. Some towns fired upon them before the ships could reach port and forced the crew to turn around and keep heading east.

After weeks of searching and slow sailing, the crews of the *Freedom* and *Fortune* met with a strange sight. They found towns untouched by any pirates. The towns and villages welcomed them, and recounted hearing of attacks on other villages, but were blessed not to be among them.

Anne wondered what made the villages special, and arrived at one conclusion: they were getting close. Kenneth was smart enough not to attack too close to home, but not smart enough to cover his tracks.

Instead of asking about attacks, Anne and the crew started asking the villagers if they had received any warships in port over the last months. They didn't find any more information until landing in Youghal about midday.

The town of Youghal was a quiet, small town of about a thousand residents, with a large port for fishermen and tall ships alike. A port of that size was uncommon in a small town like Youghal, which Anne felt required further inquiry.

Anne, Christina, William, and Roberts all went to the local tavern to see what information could be gathered there first, before trying the local officials.

Inside the tavern, scarcely anyone was present. At midday most would be working in some fashion, and the place only held men who were permanent fixtures. They were the type who had nothing else to do but listen, and had loose lips with the proper motivation.

Anne noticed a few men sitting around the various tables. She motioned for William and Roberts to talk with different people, then she and Christina approached the barkeep.

"Hello sir. I would enjoy some wine to wet my lips, and," Anne plopped a gold piece on the table, not interested in wasting time, "information if the favour suits you."

The tall, thinly bearded man went wide-eyed at the gold and pocketed it quickly before any could see the glint, then turned to a shelf at his back hosting his precious stock. He poured a good wine into two clean glasses and handed one to Anne and the other to Christina.

"English?" the man asked softly. Anne nodded. "Good, the fellows here don't know the tongue, so I suppose your friends are wasting their time."

Anne glanced back to see Roberts joining William, having no success in talking to the locals, but William knew the language.

"What did you want to know? I suppose it's of import if you part with gold."

"Indeed. We are searching for a band of pirates who frequent Southern Ireland. Would you know anything about pirates in the area?" Anne asked, slowly sipping her wine.

At the mention of pirates, the barkeep's eyes widened, then quickly became devoid of expression. "What would a lovely lass such as yourself be interested in pirates for?"

"We have some business with them," Anne replied vaguely.

The barkeep's mouth made a line. "Not heard anything about pirates in these parts. Sorry, maybe they're further east."

"So you have not heard any word about pirates attacking the shores near here at all? What about the harbour, it looks recently expanded to allow tall ships to dock. Care to explain why?" Anne pressed.

The barkeep was sweating. "Nothing wrong with that. Merchantmen frequent here. If that is all, I would appreciate it if you would kindly leave."

Christina slammed a knife into the counter. "He's lying," she said through gritted teeth.

The barkeep backed up at Christina's threat. Anne held Christina's hand at bay. "Now, now, let us not be hasty. May I have your name, sir?" Anne's voice was sweet and inviting, meant to offset Christina's threatening tone.

"Lucas."

"Lucas, we're not here to harm you. We simply wish to find these pirates, and then we will be on our way. Any information you could provide would be of immense help to us. Please."

Lucas peered back and forth between the two women, then leaned in, beckoning them closer. Anne and Christina glanced at each other, then leaned forward, closer to Lucas.

"The pirates own this town. They live in an abandoned castle a ways up the Blackwater River, to the north, but you'll not find them there now. They only return once every six months and left not a week and a half ago. Sorry, that's all the information I can give you. I'll be in trouble if they ever find out. Now, please, leave."

"Thank you," Anne said hollowly, then she turned and left the tavern quickly.

Anne's mind reeled with the knowledge. If the pirates left, there could be only two reasons: Either Edward and John had been killed and they left, or they left with the Hounds. If the latter happened,

Anne had no way of finding them. She left the tavern, stepped into the nearest alley, and leaned against the wall of one of the buildings.

"My lady, are you alright?" William asked, pulling her up.

Anne shook herself and separated from William. "I am well, sorry for worrying you. Kenneth's hideout is a castle north of here. We must head there, now." Anne pushed past William.

She stalked ahead as William gazed at her back. William thought if Anne were to stop moving forward for one second she would break. Her hope was all keeping her feet moving. *What will happen if that fragile hope is shattered?*

Roberts and Christina approached William after watching the scene from a distance. "What happened?" Roberts asked.

"Is Anne well?" Christina asked, concern in her eyes.

William's eyes never left Anne's striding figure. "She will be fine for now. Later, however…" William turned to Roberts; the tall brute had a subdued worry in his eyes. "We are heading on foot to the enemy stronghold. They have a castle north of here. Tell your men to prepare for battle, and ready cannons for transport."

"There's no need for the weapons. The barkeep claimed Kenneth and his men left weeks ago," Christina said.

"A small force could have been left behind to guard the castle, or the barkeep could be lying. We would do well to be prepared rather than caught unawares."

"The men have been itching for a fight. I hope the pirates are there. It would be a stain on my honour if the Lord's wrath were to be denied by something so trivial as chance." Roberts punched his fist into his palm, then headed to the harbour.

William then turned to Christina. "Head back to the ship and instruct our men to prepare also. Keep watch over Anne," William said before walking away.

"What are you doing?"

"I will buy supplies for the trek. Cannons will be difficult to carry, we need wagons."

"What? Cannons?"

"Yes, they may be necessary. And if they are not, we will be all the better for it."

Christina grinned and nodded, then returned to the harbour with the others. William purchased supplies, buying several wagons and horses, bullets, and food. He took the supplies to the harbour with some of the locals' help. The residents were astonished at what they saw on the harbour.

Almost three hundred people from the combined crews of *Freedom* and *Fortune* were descending from their ships armed to the teeth. Each man, regardless of stature, was muscular and intimidating. Those itching for a fight wore fiendish grins, and some tossed around daggers and sliced at imaginary foes with their swords. The sight was fearsome, and the villagers who helped William quickly ran away when they realised what was happening.

When the crews noticed the wagons, they worked together to quickly load them with cannons, cannonballs, and spare weapons.

After preparations were complete Anne addressed the crews. "Move out!" she yelled.

The crew slowly made their way through the small town of Youghal as the citizens watched half in wonder and half in horror. When they reached the edge of town they were met with a large crowd of citizens with one standing out in front.

Anne ordered the crew to stop, and she approached the man in front. "Step aside," she commanded, the Gaelic tongue making the words sound all the more cutting.

The man was sweating, but he stood his ground. "I am the mayor of this town and I beg of you, please do not do this. When the pirates return they will kill us."

Anne grabbed the mayor's chest with both hands, shaking him as her eyes bored into his with fury. "Hundreds of your brothers died because of these pirates! Have you not seen the towns ravaged, the eyes of the victims who lost loved ones due to their savagery? The lot of you are without spine, the same as dogs bending to the will of their master." Anne pushed the mayor away. "You deserve whatever fate brings you. Now move, before we do their job for them."

The mayor appeared as if he would object further, but instead stepped aside with his head hung in shame. When he made way, the townspeople followed and allowed the crews room to leave.

The war procession moved out of town, leaving the passive citizens behind as they headed for battle. Soon, all that remained was the marks of footsteps and treads from the wagons.

"She's right, we deserve what's coming to us," one of the citizens said solemnly.

The mayor took a moment's pause, then shook his head. "No!" he yelled as he turned to his people. "We don't deserve a pirate's justice! Nevertheless, we do need to take responsibility. For too long we have stood aside and let those men have their way, but I say no more! We have the advantage here: They think we are too afraid to strike back. So when the pirates come back, we will be ready to ambush them and exact our revenge for what they've done to our brothers and clansmen. Who's with me?" the mayor yelled.

The townsfolk roared in agreement. Anne's scolding had put fire in their bellies once more, and the townsfolk set about making defences for when Kenneth returned, and informing the neighbouring villages to do the same.

...

Anne and William scouted ahead and found the fortress Kenneth and his men called home.

William scanned for movement along the curtain wall walkways, but found none. "It appears empty."

Anne peered through her rifle sights at the keeps on the corners, taking special note of the arrow slits. "I concur. How long until our men arrive?" she asked, double checking the castle walls.

William glanced at the forest behind him. "Five minutes, give or take."

"We should invade the castle first. The cannons could endanger Edward, John, and Sam's lives." Anne stood up and slung her rifle over her shoulder, but before she could make her way to the castle William stopped her.

William placed his hands on Anne's shoulders and stared deep into her eyes. "My lady, are you truly prepared for what we may see when we enter?"

Anne shoved his hands away. "What a thing to say to one you claim to serve."

William immediately bowed. "Forgive me, My lady. I only meant to help."

Anne sighed. "I am no queen and you are not my subject. Rise," she commanded, and William obeyed. "Tell me truthfully, William, you loved my uncle, yes?"

"Yes, My lady, I did. My hope is to one day make amends for my failing His Majesty."

"So what would you do if you faced his murderer, Plague, again?"

"I would kill him without mercy." William's face was devoid of emotion, but his eyes filled with promise.

"Exactly. I will fill myself with hate until I see Kenneth beneath my heel begging for mercy. Then, I will laugh as his body burns and his bones crack." Anne smiled in a way which made William sweat.

She glanced over William's shoulder to see their small army drawing near. She made a gesture for them to halt their advance. Roberts, Hank Abbot, and Christina all approached William and Anne to see what the plan was.

"William and I will see if the castle is safe, then we'll send you a sign to bring in the troops," Anne said.

"What will this sign be?" Roberts asked.

"We will open the doors," Anne replied before walking to the clearing's edge with William.

Anne and William crouched down behind some bushes and trees. "We'll need to scale the walls so I brought a few grappling hooks." William reached into a small bag behind his back and pulled out two large grappling hooks. "The hardest part will be the castle approach. There is no cover."

Anne took her rifle out. "I will cover you." Anne lay down flat on her stomach and positioned the rifle in front of her between the bushes to allow full view of the castle.

William moved a few paces away for Anne to be able to see through the rifle, then, on the count of three, he ran at top speed to the castle. When he reached the halfway mark the sound of gunfire hailed from the castle. William turned to his side instinctively. The bullet grazed his arm, drawing blood.

Through the rifles sights, Anne noticed a man with a musket. Before Anne could fire a shot, he ducked down beneath the castle wall to reload.

"Stop hiding so I can shoot you," she chanted under her breath, but her prayer was not answered. Anne peered at the castle wall, searching for her mark.

The man who shot William suddenly reappeared halfway across the castle wall. Anne cursed under her breath as she re-aimed a full second behind the attacker. The man took another shot. The bullet hit the ground in front of William and forced dirt into the air. Anne shot. The man ducked. The bullet took a chunk out of the stone behind him.

William removed the grappling hook from behind him and swung it, gathering momentum. He threw the hook at peak speed and it swooped over the top of the wall. William tugged on the grappling hook to secure it, and started climbing.

Anne noticed another man with a musket running across the castle wall. He pulled himself partially over the wall to aim his musket at William. Anne shot him in the shoulder. He dropped his gun and fell off the side of the wall.

William pulled out a pistol from his belt and aimed it above him. The first man popped out from the castle wall and aimed at William. William shot the man in the chest and he slumped down on the castle wall, dead.

William continued his climb unhindered. At the top, he jumped over the edge of the wall and onto the castle walkway. Anne watched

William as he stalked about, reloading his pistol as he walked. After a moment he was out of sight.

Anne tensed at the silence. Sweat dripped from her brow as she stared through the sights of the rifle. Every ambient sound from the forest caused her heart to skip. On the outside her body was calm, but inside the minutes passed like hours as she gazed intently on the castle of their enemy.

The large double doors of the castle opened slowly without warning. Anne called over some of the crew with muskets to stem the possible tide. A figure emerged from the opened door.

"Hold your fire!" Anne yelled.

William was leaving the castle. Anne stood, put her rifle on her back, and then ran to the castle doors where William waited. The crew followed behind her.

"Was there anyone else?" Anne asked.

"None aside from the two we shot. The castle appears to be empty, though I have not had time to search everywhere," William replied.

Anne turned to those who followed her. "Search every inch of this castle. If you find anything, return here," she commanded.

The men dispersed in groups throughout the castle, doing as commanded and searching the castle's every nook and cranny.

"Now, you have a wound which needs to be tended." Anne pushed William to the ground.

She examined his arm, and found his bicep still bleeding. Anne pulled gauze out of her pocket, and wrapped it around William's arm. After she finished, a group of crewmates returned from a room below the castle.

The crewmates had grave expressions on their faces. "You need to see this," one of them said, motioning with his thumb to the stairs leading down.

Anne pushed past and practically ran down the stairs, her hair and cloak swaying with the motion. William and the two crewmates kept in step with Anne all the way down the spiral staircase. At the bottom, they were met with a corridor, doors to other rooms ajar, and light spilling from the room at the end.

Anne stepped forward slowly, taking breaths as she did. She reached for the door, closing her eyes, holding the air in her lungs tightly like a fist clenched. She pushed on the door with one hand. The light from a candle illuminated the room.

Dried blood stained the middle of the floor where pools had previously been. The room stank of gunpowder, vomit, and death.

There was no body to account for the blood, just a cot, a table, and an empty wine rack.

Most men and women might retch at the scene and the smell, but Anne was not most people. She stared at the blood intently for a time as William searched the room for clues.

"Anne." William held a letter out in front of him.

Anne glanced at the letter, then to William. "Where did you find this?" she asked, opening it.

"Under the bed," William said.

Anne read the letter, and William could tell something was wrong. He motioned for the two crewmen to leave the room and the three slipped out. William closed the door behind them and they went back up the spiral stairs.

"What was that about? What did the letter say?" One crewman asked.

"Nothing good, that much is assured. We shall find out soon enough. For now, gather the crew and tell them to stop searching, we are done here." William instructed.

The crewmen did as instructed and soon the crews of both *Freedom* and *Fortune*, save those watching the cannons and wagons, were in the main hall of Kenneth Locke's castle.

Christina, Tala, and Pukuh approached William, who was guarding the staircase. "Where's Anne? Why are we still here?"

"Anne is below." William motioned behind him. "We found a letter, Anne is reading it now."

"What did this letter say?" Pukuh asked.

"I don't know," William replied.

"Then why are we standing here? Let's find out what it said." Christina tried to walk down the stairs, but William stopped her, causing Tala to growl at him.

William glared at Tala, and the wolf hung her head in submission. "She is not to be disturbed."

"We are wasting time here, brother. Was not our goal to find the captain? Our captain is not here, thus we must be elsewhere."

"I think what Pukuh means is move, William." Christina once again tried to push her way past, more aggressively this time.

William pushed her back. Soon after, an argument erupted amongst the crew who were anxious to leave. William tried his best to calm the crew, but the noise rose louder by the minute, and all communication was breaking down.

Because of the noise, none noticed Anne walking up the steps. When she returned to the main hall, the arguments stopped and all eyes were on her. She gazed at all the hopeful eyes of the people inspired and loved by Edward.

Anne's eyes were red, and she looked tired. "John and..." Anne placed her hand on her mouth, then shook her head and continued. "John and Edward are dead," she stated solemnly, listlessly lifting the letter.

The room quieted. The cold wind from the Irish hills filled the castle, howling hauntingly and sending chills down everyone's backs.

"No!" Christina yelled. "There's no way they could die." She screamed, her eyes closed tightly to shut away the forming tears. Her hand was balled into a fist around the rose hanging from her neck, Ochi's memento.

Anne's mouth made a straight line as she stared at Christina with pity in her eyes. "Read for yourself." Anne shoved the letter into Christina's hands then left, wading through the throngs of crewmen gathered as Christina read the letter out loud.

"This is Sam," Christina started, glancing up to the onlookers. "I hope you find this before that bastard comes back. I tried to help John and the captain escape, but I failed. John and Edward saved my life, and sacrificed their own for me. Kenneth killed them. I'm sorry, I've failed you all, but I'll make it right. I swear I'll kill the ugly sod if it's the last thing I do. If I don't see you again, tell Anne I'm sorry." Christina's hands fell, the letter dropping from her fingers.

The faces of hundreds were filled with melancholy. As the reality of what had happened dawned on those gathered, they realised exactly what the words from Sam meant. Edward, their captain, their brother, was no more. They would not hear him laugh again, they would not be inspired by his words and deeds again, and they would no longer take comfort in his presence. And John, the father some never had, would never express uplifting words to his sons, nor make people laugh with his timid nature, nor watch their backs in battle. And Sam was lost in a den of wolves on a suicide mission, blaming himself for what happened.

Christina shook her head like she was awaking from a dream. Her eyes focused and she ran outside to where Anne stood, the crew following slowly after. "There may still be hope, Anne. There are no bodies here, how do we know they truly died?"

Anne shook her head, pulled the girl closer, and hugged her tightly. They embraced for a moment before Anne spoke. "Sam would not lie to us. He saw John and Edward die," Anne whispered bluntly into Christina's ear.

Christina pushed away from Anne, the tears she tried to hold back rushing down her face. "Then what do we do now? What are we to do without Edward?"

"Simple: We kill Kenneth Locke and make him pay for what he did. I won't let Sam take my revenge from me." Anne's words piqued the interest of the crew, and took them away from their depression as they focused on her. "For too long over this past year we've been on the run. Too long we've been on the receiving end of extortion, slavery, lies, secret assassins..." Anne gazed through the crowd, pointing to Nassir and Pukuh, and Christina, as she spoke. "And death." Anne paused, noticing the crowd hanging on her every word.

"This is the time for revenge." The crew chanted their agreement to her resolve. "Our revenge!" she continued. More of the crew joined in the resonating chant of agreement. "Our comrades' revenge!"

"This is no longer about *Freedom*, as when we first left Portugal. We have our *Freedom*. This is about those whose *Freedom* was stripped from them long before it should have been." Anne paused before gazing at Nassir. "Ochi." Anne turned to Christina. "John," she continued, peering at other crewmates as she listed off names of those who had died on board the *Freedom*. "And our captain, Edward. They had their *Freedom* and lives taken, and, though we cannot restore their lives, we can free their spirits so they may rest in peace. Revenge will be our new charge. Revenge." Anne finished with reverent emphasis on the word.

Christina lifted her hand in the air. "Revenge!" she yelled for all to hear.

"Revenge," Pukuh echoed.

"Revenge," the crews chanted one after the other and then in unison until the whole room was filled with the sound of their voices. The mantra renewed the crew's hope, and bestowed new purpose to drive them forward.

"Our first order of business," Anne stated when it quieted. "Destroy this castle."

The crew yelled their agreement in furious abandon, rushing out of the castle and to the armaments they brought. The cannons were lined up and aimed at the fortress.

"Fire!" Anne yelled, followed soon after by William down their long line of men. Bartholomew and Hank continued the command soon after their counterparts, and the cannons fired in succession.

The sound of each cannon blared like a volcano erupting in sequence. The thunder was ear-splitting and terrified the creatures of the wood, as well as the humans from the town.

The cannonballs smashed into the hewn rock and cut stone, sending pieces flying in all directions. Wave after wave of cannon fire broke into the walls, demolishing the castle bit by bit.

Before long the job was done, and the remnants of the castle were nothing more than a pile of rubble. The first part of their revenge was complete, and the crew returned to Youghal.

The townspeople were waiting. From their faces, Anne could tell they knew what had happened, but some townsfolk decided to see the wreckage for themselves. None talked to the crew as they passed through the streets to the harbour.

Anne held her head high and didn't glance at the mayor or the nearby gawkers. Her focus was on moving forward.

First we will need to resupply, then wait for Kenneth Locke to return. However, one of the townsfolk could send word. Threats of violence should suffice. I may not have Edward's eyes, but I have something close. The mayor was easily dominated, so the others should fall in line.

Anne processed their next steps like a game of chess, keeping a hundred moves ahead of the enemy. So great was her concentration, she did not notice when she arrived back on the ship and accidentally bumped into one of the crewmen on the *Freedom*.

"I'm sorry, I was not watching myself," Anne said absent-mindedly and with her head down. She continued walking without waiting for a reply.

"Anne," the crewman called in a familiar voice.

Anne spun her head back in the direction of the voice. *It cannot be!* She gaped with disbelief at the figure in front of her.

"Don't worry. It's really me," he reassured her, as if reading Anne's mind.

Anne burst into tears and leapt into the man's arms. "Edward!" she cried.

Edward wrapped his arms around Anne tightly and ran his fingers through her long red curls in that familiar way. Edward, too, wept as he took in the full presence of the woman he loved more than anything in the world.

"I'm finally home."

33. BENJAMIN'S GAME

The entire town of Youghal was not able to sleep that night due to the raucous partying of the crew of the *Freedom* and *Fortune*. The town's reserve of alcohol was drained during the hours between dusk and dawn, and the butcher made a fortune selling his entire stock off to the hungry pirates. Much singing and laughter and rejoicing was had on and off the harbour. Even some of the townsfolk joined in and made friends with the rebels visiting their home.

On the *Freedom*, Edward was surrounded by a crowd of people from the two crews. Throughout the night, Edward's cup was continuously refilled and food was never far from his reach thanks to attentive friends.

Edward was telling the sad story of his capture to all listening, but to them the tale was of their captain, or friend, surviving against all odds. "For three days Kenneth's crew took turns beating me throughout the day and night. I resisted as best I could, all things considered. People were switched out when I broke their arms, legs, or noses. After that frustrated Kenneth enough, I was poisoned from what I could tell. I don't know what the poison was but my insides burned for a whole day."

"How do you reckon you survived?" Hank Abbot asked, brow raised.

"Well, the only thing I can think of would be either the poison wasn't meant to kill, or because of the special weed from Pukuh's village," Edward surmised, motioning to the one-armed Mayan.

"Did the gods appear with some in their hands for you, brother?" Pukuh jested.

Edward chuckled. "No, over the past months I've been chewing on the leaves. I happen to enjoy the bitter taste, and we had more than enough to go around. Perhaps I gained a defence against poison from eating so much." The company nodded at the explanation. "So after the poison, they decided to up the ante. One night, I was taken to a river a short distance from the castle, Blackwater River. Kenneth and several others shot and stabbed me a dozen times, then Kenneth kicked me into the river and left me for dead. The next thing I remember was the coldness of the water rushing me to the ocean. Somehow, I was seen by a small whaling ship in the early hours of the morning and brought back to Youghal to heal. As you can see, I'm still not quite my old self, but I'm walking again, which I couldn't say a week ago."

Edward's body was bandaged from head to toe beneath his clothes, and where he wasn't bandaged he was bruised in varying colours and stages of healing. Hank had looked as if he'd crawled from hell when he was recovered, and Edward had suffered worse, so one could only imagine how he looked when the whalers saved him.

"Those devils will pay for their injustice on you, I so swear," Bartholomew said with his fist clenched.

The crew joined in with their own curses and promises for revenge against the man who'd killed John and nearly killed their captain.

"No," Edward said. The crew went silent and confused expressions abounded on their faces. "I'm not saying we won't avenge John, God knows I want to, but we can't wait six months. We have a job to do, and that's acquiring the final key to the *Freedom*."

"Edward, we know you've been waiting a long time, and we're so close to the end of the journey we started three years ago, but can't it wait?" Christina asked.

"No, our priority now and always has been finishing Benjamin's game and restoring full functionality to the ship."

"The Hounds need to pay for what they've done, partner, it's not solely your crew who've been wronged, but ours as well," Hank said.

"If you want to break our oath and leave to take out revenge, then you certainly may," Edward replied, slowly standing up from his seat. "But my crew will find another to help us finish this."

Jack Christian, who would normally be entertaining the crews, stood up and tried to calm Edward. "Edward, let's not say something we may regret now, alright?" The wise older man had a calming nature, but Edward was not swayed.

"My orders are final. We will be heading to the Island of Heaven and Hell." Edward turned his gaze to Bartholomew. "If your crew still wishes to maintain an alliance with mine then you may join us." Edward stormed off to the upper deck.

As Edward left, Bartholomew spoke to his crew and calmed them after Edward's harsh words. He was far more understanding and slow to anger than his stature suggested, and he stopped his less patient men from blowing things out of proportion.

Anne told the crewmates not to worry, and left the crew cabin to follow Edward. He had gone to Alexandre's medical cabin. Before Anne opened the door, Jack stopped her.

"May I?" he whispered.

Perhaps Jack is better suited for this. Anne nodded, pulled herself back, and allowed Jack the room. She returned to the lower deck with the crew as Jack entered the cabin.

When Jack opened and closed the door silently behind him, he could see Edward reaching with a shaky hand into the bag of the Mayan crop. Edward chewed on one of the leaves as he sat on the floor in front of the island table in the middle of the room.

Jack joined Edward, took a leaf from his hand and chewed. "Not bad."

The two sat silently as the noises of the party, though muffled, persisted through the walls of the ship from all sides.

"I keep having this dream," Edward chuckled nervously. "I'm standing in a white room, and uh... John's there. Except it's not John, it's my father." Edward fidgeted and tore at the small leaves absentmindedly as he talked. "My father talks to me, but I can't understand what he's saying. Then suddenly a red streak appears across his neck, and... I'm holding a knife in my hand." Edward laughed again. "I know what the dream means, it's so painfully obvious, and I know I did not kill John, but that doesn't change the fact that I've had the same dream almost every night for the past month." Edward rubbed his eyes and let out a long sigh.

Jack took some of the broken leaves from Edward's hand and chewed on them. "Sometimes when I'm walking through the towns we've been to, I see the image of my wife passing by. I've even stopped a few ladies, but once I take a second glance I see the mirage made plain. Kids too. I see my kids, Maximilian and Jessica, running about here and there, playing with a hoop and stick, alive and well.

"When someone you love is taken from you, it feels as if a piece of yourself is replaced with something... rotten. A sickness of hate which never seems to fade. Sometimes the rot can be healed, one way or the other: over time, talking about what happened, forgiveness and sometimes revenge. The problem is finding out what to do next."

"What do you think I should do?" Edward asked the older man.

"I feel only you can know what's best for you, Edward. If you think we should finish the game then that's the best thing to do. Whether that decision is good or bad, your family will help you through."

Edward turned away from Jack's gaze. After a moment Edward held up his hand in front of him and stared as it shook from the slight bit of strain.

"Whenever I think of facing Kenneth my body tenses and my heart feels as if it's being held tightly, as if a snake coiled itself around and won't release me."

"Fear?" Jack asked.

"Not exactly. I've felt terror before, under the gaze of the man in black I'm sure you've heard about. This is different. I feel powerless to dangers ahead. I feel as if Locke is around the corner, waiting for me to lose concentration, then everyone I love will be dead, or he'll torture me until I no longer have the will to live. Like I'm trying to push down a brick wall, it feels as if I can't stop it from happening." Edward clenched his fist and turned away from Jack. "This is foolish. You lost your wife and kids. My troubles pale in comparison."

Jack squeezed Edward's hand tightly. "Don't ever think that. Your burdens are our burdens, your worry is our worry. It is real and we are here for you. A wise man once told me the worst thing you can do is think you are alone and have no family. You are not alone, and we are your family, remember that."

"Thank you, Jack," Edward said, wiping away tears before they could fall from his eyes.

The two men sat, silent at times, listening to the sounds of the crew outside. And, for the first time in the months since his abduction, Edward relaxed.

When all thoughts of celebration were gone, and the sombre reality finally set in, Edward held a funeral for John. There was no body, so the crew gathered John's belongings and set them in a rowboat.

John was a man of simple means and simple needs. All his belongings amounted to a few gold pieces, two sets of plain clothes and a spare set of leather boots, a journal, and spectacles.

Bartholomew delivered a eulogy as the crews watched the boat float away from the Irish shores. A single arrow was set ablaze and fired into the boat to create a funeral pyre.

Edward stared at the tall fire, the last remnant of a man Edward wished he'd known better. *I promise I will find my father, and I will tell him of your bravery*. Edward breathed deeply the sea air. *Thank you, John. Rest peacefully, you earned it.*

34. TSUNAMI VS. PLAGUE

Thousands of miniscule parts of leaves burned as air was drawn through a pipe. The resulting smoke entered the mouth and lungs of an old man. The old man held the smoke in his lungs for a moment, letting it do its work, before blowing it away to the ether.

"So, ye see, I simply must do somethin'," the older gentlemen said.

Across from the old man, a younger one with slick black hair sat on the deck of a ship. He held his hand to his chin and appeared to be deep in thought.

"Yes, yes, I do see the dilemma. So, let us consider you the ferry captain, and I the passenger. I require passage to a destination, and you require payment to allow passage. What payment would you think suffices to allow me crossing?" The younger man gestured off the bow towards an island that was currently only a dot on the horizon.

"Hmm..." The old man sounded thoughtful as he sucked on his pipe again.

The wind howled across the ocean. The sound of the ocean breeze passed unabated across two gargantuan ships. The crews were deathly silent as they watched the two captains negotiate. The elder was a feared pirate known as William Kidd, the Tsunami, and the younger was a powerful Earl, Edward Russell, but was known in some circles as Plague, a master of poisons.

"Eyes," Kidd offered.

Plague mockingly considered the offer and mulled it over for a moment. "No, I rather enjoy the ability to see."

Kidd took another drag and puff of the weed. "Arms."

Plague was quick in his answer. "I'm rather fond of my arms, so, sorry, but no."

"Legs."

"Again, I have to decline. Though we would have much more in common if this was done," Plague said, gesturing to Kidd's wooden leg, "I find that wood chafes, and I do not wish to have splinters."

"We seem ta be at an impasse, then."

"Well, speaking honestly," Plague held his hand up, "if we are being honest, there is not much of a negotiation occurring here. Generally, when one is haggling a price, there is a back and forth where the price is fluctuating in a downwards direction. If anything, the price has gone up. If I may make a suggestion in your tactics to make the proposition more appealing, perhaps moving from pairs to singles would continue this little transaction we are having."

Kidd sighed. "One eye."

"No."

"One arm."

"Sorry."

"One leg."

"I refuse."

Kidd's face was like stone. He said nothing further, but instead stared down Plague and waited for him to make the next move.

"Wait," Plague said, holding up his finger. "There is another option in our scenario which I neglected to mention. I could threaten to kill the ferry captain unless he allows me free passage," Plague said with a savage grin.

Kidd lowered his pipe and stood up. "Now ye've gone and done it."

The wind howled again moments later, but, unlike before, the din of a battle overshadowed its cry.

35. OF HEAVEN

The *Freedom* and *Fortune* landed on the final island hosting Benjamin's game. The crew of the *Freedom* were familiar with the island, but the *Fortune*'s crew were not used to the strangeness awaiting them.

Edward stepped onto the waist of the ship. "Secure those lines, there could be a storm at our backs and I don't want anything to happen to the ship should the winds change," he commanded. The ship had felt hard waves over the last few hours and Edward didn't want to take any chances.

"Do you think it safer to wait before trekking onto the island?" Anne asked.

Edward mulled the question over for a bit while stroking his long black beard. "There is something strange about these waves. I think they were meant for someone else." Edward kept eyeing the waves crashing against the hull before shaking his head. "I'm talking foolishness, let's ask the expert." Edward turned his head to Herbert, who was preparing to leave the ship as well. "Herbert, what would you say about these waves? Will the ship be in any danger while we are on the island?"

Herbert wheeled himself over to the starboard side and gave the waves he had been watching throughout the voyage a final perfunctory glance, then eyed the horizon. "We don't have to worry, if I'm not mistaken the waves are beginning to subside."

"Perfect." Edward turned back to Anne. "Nothing to worry about."

Anne nodded, but took note of Edward's odd choice of wording earlier. *Meant for someone else? What is your intuition telling you, Edward?*

Edward and Anne gathered gear they felt necessary for the job ahead: Guns, muskets, swords, food, water, rope, lanterns, and various other survival items. The rest of the crew followed suit under William's supervision.

Only a few members of the crew were left to guard the ship, eager volunteers who knew what could await them and opted out in favour of the easy job. Edward warned the men to stay on alert and not to drink any alcohol while on duty. Edward also told Christina to leave Tala on the ship as he knew it would be dangerous. She protested only slightly.

After preparations were made, the crew descended to the sandy beach below, joining the crew of the *Fortune*. Altogether, near to four hundred souls walked on the beach.

Edward walked over to Bartholomew, who, at Anne's instruction, was loaded with supplies like his crew. "How are you feeling, Roberts? Ready for the unknown?"

"I have no need to fear. Your tales of previous trials, while nothing to snub the nose at, were good preparation. My men know we are moving into dangerous territory. Their hearts and minds are prepared."

Edward laughed. "Whatever you think you may expect when we enter the forest, I can assure you, you will be shocked."

Edward led the crews along the path between the swaying palms. Anne ran to catch up to Edward, and William followed closely behind with Roberts. All the senior officers were dispersed amongst the crew. Jack, Pukuh, Christina, Herbert, Alexandre, Victor, and Nassir were peppered throughout the crowd, sharing stories with the crew of the *Fortune* as they trekked through the path.

After a short walk, Edward and Bartholomew emerged upon the small hill in front of the two stone pressure plates. Bartholomew ran up the steps and the sight of the angel fighting the demon and the double doors caused his jaw to drop open.

Roberts turned around to Edward with a big grin on his face, unbecoming of the man's oft intimidating figure. "I see why you wanted to call upon our assistance, my boy! This trial of yours is dipped in Biblical symbolism."

"If anyone can solve deadly puzzles about the Bible, it would be you, Pirate Priest."

Roberts noticed the stone tablet between the pressure plates. "Ah, I understand now. One crew stands on one of these altars and it opens the door for the other to enter."

"Yes, and during our previous visit we found that beyond the doors is a similar slab, which will most likely allow the second crew to enter." Edward observed the two crews crowding around the field near the pressure plates. "So, Roberts, which side do you wish to take your crew through?" Edward asked.

Bartholomew stroked his clean-shaven chin. "Well, I will allow you to be on the right hand of God. Our crew will take the left path."

"Alright, men, onto the right platform," Edward commanded.

The crew of the *Freedom* did as commanded. As more stepped on, the stone slab slowly descended, and before the last few crewmen were able to crowd onto the pressure plate it became flush with the rest of the altar.

A loud grinding could be heard beneath the earth and soon above ground by the stone doors on the left of the angel. After the sound and movement of the earth settled, Bartholomew and crew entered the open doorway.

Before Bartholomew joined his crew, he talked with Edward. "Well, my boy, if I believed in luck I would take this time to wish you good fortune, but instead I will say this: Let us meet on the other side." Bartholomew stretched out his hand.

Edward smiled and gripped his friend's hand, then pulled him close and embraced him. "Whatever happens, don't die."

Roberts laughed. "Aye, aye, comrade." Roberts then embraced Anne and kissed her cheek before leaving to join his crew.

"When you hear the sound of gunfire, it will mean we are safely inside," Edward yelled when Roberts and crew were halfway through the door.

Roberts waved his hand, and after a few seconds he was beyond sight. Another minute more and the stone doors on the right opened.

Edward left the platform and the crew followed. He entered the door and stood near the entrance, waiting for his crew to enter the path leading to the right. After everyone was inside, Edward took out a pistol and shot at the ground. A few seconds later the ground rumbled once more and the stone doors closed behind the crew of the *Freedom*.

Edward joined his crew and they trekked the path guarded by impossibly high wooden stakes, and past the second stone pressure plate a third of the way down the path. Pukuh waited to talk with Edward.

"So, brother, what do you think awaits us around the corner?" Pukuh asked, pointing with his spear in his left hand to the end of the path which opened up on the left.

"I hate to mimic Roberts, but after all we've seen on our travels I'm not sure I can be surprised from Benjamin's trials anymore."

Pukuh mimicked Edward's response to Bartholomew with a laugh. "If only you knew the stories my father told me of his travels. I used to think they were fanciful tales for young warriors to be inspired by, but never held them to heart as truths. After time with you, I became doubtful. Impossible stories of islands floating in the sky, an invisible city of gold in the middle of a desert, and beasts taller than the tallest ships are sounding not so childish now."

"Maybe we should ask him the truth of the matter once this is over. Speaking of which, do you plan to return home after we are done here?"

"Do you wish me to leave?" Pukuh asked, brow raised in question.

"No, of course not. You never told me how long you planned to journey with us, simply that you wanted to gain experience."

"I still have a ways to go. I believed I was strong, but the man called Plague, he showed me I still have much to learn." Pukuh motioned to his missing right arm. "The princess's do... I mean... William has been helping me turn my weakness into a strength." Pukuh stopped, causing Edward to stop as well. "I am with you until you no longer find a use for me."

"Then I am afraid you will be with me a long time yet, brother." Edward smiled.

Pukuh returned the smile. "I would not have it any other way, brother."

"Edward! You must see this," Anne yelled from the front of the crowd. Half of the crew already passed the bend in the path.

Edward and Pukuh both ran forward through the crowd to see what the commotion was about. When the two turned the corner, their jaws dropped at what they saw.

In front of them was a large field five hundred feet across, lined by more sharpened wooden stakes, and in the middle of the field a massive one-hundred-foot-tall ship stood. The ship was bevelled at the bottom like a normal ship, but from what Edward could see the top was completely flat. On the far right side of the ship a large slanted gangplank allowed entrance to the ship.

"This may be a reference to Noah's ark," Anne surmised.

"Yes, and if we are to follow the rules, we must enter, I suppose," Edward replied. "But let us see if we can bypass that, shall we?" Edward walked over to the side of the ark.

The sides and top were so smooth that from afar it appeared to be carved from a single piece of wood, but upon closer examination the ship was made of planks.

Edward removed a long line of rope from his sac of supplies and tied a grappling hook to one end. The rope wasn't long enough on its own, so Edward took rope from Anne's supplies as well as some other crewmates and tied the ends together until he felt he had enough.

The crew were dispersed about, some examining the outside and inside of the ark and others the wooden stakes, and some talking amongst themselves or watching Edward.

Edward swung the grappling hook around and around, building speed. When the hook reached the apex he threw it into the air at an angle over the top of the ark. Edward tugged on the rope, but the hook slid back down to the ground in front of him. He tried this again and again and again, but received the same result.

"The ark is too smooth." Anne ran her hand along the side of the ship. "We have no choice then, we must enter."

Edward sighed in frustration. "It never gets easier, does it?" Anne shrugged her shoulders and grinned.

Edward jogged to the entrance at the far end of the ark and entered, followed by Anne, Pukuh, and an excited Christina. On the inside, a wall blocked them from the bulk of the ship, the roof went only halfway up the height of the ark, and a pedestal stood in the middle of the hundred-by-fifty-foot room.

Edward examined the pedestal. On the top of the elbow-high wooden pedestal was a carving in the shape of a book with an inscription.

"Come thou, and all thine house, into the ark. Only when the door to sins of the past is closed may thou be granted entry to salvation," Edward read aloud.

"Edward, look." Christina pointed to the inside walls. Wooden pulleys were set on either side with rope attached to the gangplank. "Those must be to close the doors."

Edward nodded in agreement. He noticed William standing at the bottom of the gangplank. "William," Edward yelled. "Gather the crew in here."

William circled around the field and issued Edward's command to enter the ark. The people slowly lumbered their way into the gigantic structure as they examined the surroundings.

"I want two teams on the pulleys to raise the gangplank," Edward yelled over the din of the talking crew while pointing to said pulleys.

Volunteers went to task and in teams of two began pulling on the wheel spokes, gradually raising the monstrous gangplank. As it closed, the light of the day left, and was replaced with a deep darkness. When the light was completely gone, and the gangplank could be raised no more, a loud clicking and clanking noise could be heard behind the walls.

As alluded to on the carved pedestal, the wall blocking them was lifted by whatever mechanism lay behind the walls of the ark. As the wall rose, light was reintroduced to the crew, and they were able to see the vast interior of the ark in full.

The first fifty feet of the room was open space all the way to the roof. Two massive structural beams supported the left and right sides, with glass panels on the ceiling between the beams to provide light. On the floor between the beams, a carved pedestal similar to the one at the entrance stood. Behind the pedestal were twelve unique statues, six men and six women, and behind those were another twelve statues of animals in a row. Behind the statues, and taking up the rest of the nearly four hundred feet left of the ark, was a wall of wood separated into square cubes about ten by ten feet in size. In the corner of the wall, one of the cubes was open to allow passage, which Edward assumed was the way to exit the ark.

Edward started to walk over to the statues, but was stopped when the sound of gunfire startled him. He turned to see Anne holding a rifle.

"Anne, what are you doing?"

Anne pulled out a spyglass, and peered at the ceiling. "Not even a crack," she murmured. "If we could but break the glass then we may have been able to use a grappling hook, but the glass must be too thick. The bullet lodged into the pane, but did not pierce the glass." Anne handed her spyglass to Edward, and he confirmed what Anne said.

Edward handed the spyglass back. "Well, let's see what we're dealing with." Edward approached the pedestal. Alexandre and Victor were reading the inscription and talking in hushes voices when Edward approached. "May I?" Edward asked.

"By all means, *mon Capitaine*." Alexandre backed away and motioned to the pedestal.

As Edward began reading aloud while Alexandre and Victor moved on and examined the statues. "Of each holy man and woman, six and six they be, you will pair them with the beast according to the heavens. When the Lord gazes upon your pairs and deems them worthy, the path to salvation will be revealed. Six and six men and women shall not sin six times against the Lord for it is the number of the beast. Each sin sends one farther from the Lord, and on the sixth brimstone and fire will rain upon thee and send thee, and thine house, to Gehenna."

"Fire's gonna rain on us?" one of the crewmen asked, worried.

"Whuts this Gehenna? Is that Hell?" another asked.

The crew began talking amongst themselves and the panic could be clearly seen on some faces. They were trapped in the ark. If the ship caught fire there would be no way to survive.

"Calm, please everyone!" Edward yelled. "Nothing bad will happen as long as we solve this puzzle correctly. We've done this before, we'll do it again." Edward's words eased the minds of the crew. "Now, let's figure this out together." Edward examined the human statues.

From left to right, first six male statues, then six female in a line. Each man was adorned in various style of robes and some holy artefacts like rosaries, Bibles, or crosses, except one who was dressed in armour and held a lance. The women appeared to be nuns with plain clothing covering the head, save two with fancier clothing and crowns. At the base of each statue was an inscription.

Edward read the inscription on the first statue. "Monks under my discipline tried to poison me, but God protected me through miracles, and after this I founded twelve monasteries." Edward chuckled at the notion of monks trying to poison one another.

"He is Saint Benedict," Alexandre stated matter-of-factly.

Edward noticed the Frenchman standing beside the statue. "So, let me guess, you've already figured out how this is solved and won't tell us?"

"*Hélas*, no. I may be intelligent, but I am not a god. Victor and I were able to deduce five of the statues' names, myself three of the five," Alexandre said loudly so Victor could hear, "and only three of which I can tell you where to set. The rest are unknown to me."

"It is rare for you to say that you don't know something," Edward commented, panic setting in. *If Alexandre can't figure this out, what hope do we have?*

Alexandre chuckled. "Despite what many of you think, I am anything but arrogant. I know what I know, and I know what I do not. There is nothing to worry about, *mon Capitaine*. This puzzle, complicated as it is, is designed for pooling of knowledge. *Venir*, see these statues here?" Alexandre pointed to the animal statues behind those of the humans. "What of these does not belong?" Alexandre asked.

Edward scanned the statues. Each was to scale, starting with a rat, then an ox, then tiger, rabbit, and… "Wait, what is this? It appears to be a large snake, but the next statue is a snake." Edward pointed to the statue to the right of the unfamiliar one.

"That is a dragon. A mythical flying lizard. I am sure you recall the English stories such as Beowulf?"

"Yes, I am familiar with dragons, but where are the wings?"

"This is a Chinese dragon, most often depicted without *ailes*."

Edward cocked his brow. "Then what does this mean? How do we pair the statues together?"

"The Chinese Zodiac. The Chinese relate each year with an animal, repeating every twelve years from rat to pig. The statues each relate to a person, a saint most likely due to the five I—"

Victor audibly coughed to Alexandre.

"The five *we* deduced. Depending on the birth year of the person, the statue relates to an animal from the Zodiac. Once we *determiner* what animal they are, we move the statue to these sections here." Alexandre pointed to a barely noticeable wooden square a small distance from each animal statue. The wooden square was coloured differently from the rest of the wood on the ship, but still smooth, with no noticeable indentation. "Placing the statues will be the easy part, the hard part is deciding where."

Edward nodded. "Thus why having more people is better. More knowledge to figure out who each person is and what year they were born. Each one is too obscure for one person, unless they are extremely well travelled and devout. Amongst a group of almost two hundred, it doesn't seem so farfetched." Edward considered the crew milling about, examining the ship and the statues and talking, and noticed several people, including Christina, Herbert, and Nassir, at the entrance to the strange area which took up the back portion of the ark. "Have Anne and William organise people to work on this, I will examine the rest of this ship."

"*Oui, Capitaine*," Alexandre replied.

Edward joined the group gathered at the back. The sectioned wall taking up the back fifth of the Ark was its own oddity. Edward didn't understand the purpose, but if the pedestal was any indication it would not provide a way out in its current state.

Two crewmen began entering the open section. "No, wait!" Edward yelled, stopping them. "It's too dangerous." He led the crewmen away. "We don't want to take any chances."

Edward took a gander into the entrance. Inside was a hallway leading deeper into the ark with a ten-foot clearance. The hallway itself was about a hundred feet long, then turned off to the right with stairs leading up. On the floor, Edward could see the same discoloured wood separating the hallway into ten-square-foot cubes. Each square was part of a larger cube which made up the final four-hundred-foot part of the ark.

"Well, I'm too curious, so I'm going in," Christina declared, walking to the entrance.

Edward grabbed her arm and pulled her back. "That was an order. If previous trials are any indication then there are probably life-threatening traps awaiting any who enter before the puzzle is complete."

"And what if that's not the case? What if there is something in there which could help in solving the puzzle out here?" Christina argued, waving her arms.

"What are you basing this off of? Your assumption is groundless," Edward argued back.

Christina contested everything Edward said and did not accept his answer. The conversation became rather heated until Herbert interjected.

"Stop, children. Stop!" he bellowed. Christina and Edward both glared at Herbert, but he was unfazed. "I feel it is worth exploring further. Perhaps all we need to do is have the courage to enter and the exit will be right around the corner. Perhaps Benjamin means for us to be afraid, while we waste time here. Is that not something he may do?"

Edward frowned, glancing back and forth between Christina and Herbert. "It sounds plausible," he said. Christina jumped and laughed in glee, grinning at her brother coming to her defence. "But, but," Edward repeated with emphasis, "you must take someone with you in case something dangerous lurks beyond those walls."

Christina instinctively turned to her older brother, and he immediately put his hands in the air. "You cannot be serious," he said with a straight face.

"No, of course not. I don't want to carry you around," Christina replied with loving bite only a sister could manage. "Nassir, would you be a gentleman and join me?" Christina linked her arm in Nassir's.

"Certainly. I will not allow any harm to befall you, Christina." Nassir turned to Edward and Herbert. "Is my protection acceptable to you both?"

Herbert and Edward both nodded in assent. Christina smiled from ear to ear and pulled the larger Nassir by the arm into the unknown. Edward glanced at Herbert and they both watched Christina and Nassir as they walked through the hallway.

"So far, so good," Edward said to Herbert as he leaned on the wooden wall.

As if the Devil was listening, a loud click drew Edward's attention to Christina. She was peering at her feet in the middle of the hallway. Edward's heart seized in his chest. He pushed away from the wall and as he was about to run into the entrance, the wall shifted before his eyes and the entrance moved away from him.

Edward backed away from the wall to see what was happening, partially out of fear and partially out of instinct. The entire back section of the ship began moving of its own accord. The entrance previously in the bottom left corner moved back and disappeared. Each ten-foot cube was moving and changing from its original position, and from the noises the cubes behind the wall were moving as well. After a few seconds the wall stopped, and the ship was so quiet one could hear a pin drop.

All eyes were on the back wall. Edward snapped out of his shock, ran to the wall, and pounded on the wood.

"Christina! Nassir!" he yelled as he beat his fist against the grain. "Can you hear me? Are you hurt?" Edward pressed his ear to the wall, but he could hear nothing.

Herbert glanced at the wall with a confused, panicked expression, and followed suit with Edward. He screamed his sister's name and savagely hit the wall. Edward moved to another spot on the wall and held his hand up for Herbert to stop his shouting and banging. "I hear her," Edward said softly. "I hear you, Christina!" he bellowed. "Are you and Nassir safe?"

"Yes, we aren't harmed," Christina replied. "The sections shifted after I stepped on a switch. I think a maze would be the only way to describe what we're seeing in here. There are so many different paths I don't know where to go next."

"Have you moved since the maze changed?"

"No, we thought it best to stay still."

"Try pressing the switch again," Edward yelled.

Herbert grabbed Edward's arm and pulled him away before he could hear anything else. "Are you insane? We don't know what that will do."

"In case you haven't noticed, it's a little late for objections, Herbert. I was against the idea from the beginning, and now she's lost with no way out. Pressing the switch may reverse what happened."

Herbert made no more objections, but still looked displeased. Edward believed he was lashing out because of his choice to let Christina go.

Edward pressed his ear to the wall to listen again. "...ward? I couldn't hear you. Are you sure you want me to press the switch again?" Christina asked.

"Yes, press the switch," Edward commanded.

"Aye, aye."

Edward backed away from the wall and watched as the ten foot cubes began shifting again. Edward wasn't able to follow the movement exactly, but it did seem to be moving opposite to what it had the first time. A few seconds passed with the crew all watching the spectacle. At the end, the entrance returned to the bottom left.

Christina ran out and searched through the gathered crew to find her brother. She rushed to Herbert and embraced him.

Herbert's hands shook as he pulled his sister close. "I feared the worst had happened."

"I'm sorry for worrying you, Herbert. I'm here. I'm safe."

The Voyages of Queen Anne's Revenge

Herbert pushed his sister back and stared her square in the eyes. "I forbid you from going into that maze again. Edward was right, it's too dangerous."

Even Herbert, the sailing master, could not have foreseen the storm unleashed inside Christina at those words. "You forbid me? I am not a child. Both of you do not realise that." Christina looked daggers at both Herbert and Edward. "I am going back in there, regardless of what you want!"

Herbert matched Christina's fury line for line on his face. "And what if you die, hmm? What then?"

"Then at least I would have had some choice in the matter!" Christina yelled. "I know of the arguments you had with Edward each time I have become injured, and I agree with him." Christina turned to Edward. "But you are equally as guilty as Herbert. Neither of you allow me my freedom despite how you venerate the word so. Ever since your accident, Herbert, you unwittingly shackled me with the chains of a child. I know you were hurt by Calico Jack, but when I am hurt it is not Edward's fault." Christina knelt down next to Herbert and the loving gaze of a sister returned to her eyes. "I am not a child who does not know the dangers of gunpowder. I am a grown woman who understands the risks. I will not shame Ochi by cowering in fear when facing our enemies, nor will I let fear of the unknown stop me."

Herbert's eyes welled up with tears. "I don't know what I will do if I lose you. You are all I have left in this world."

Christina shook her head as she touched her brother's leg. "If that is why you are so afraid, then you have nothing to worry about. How many times must you be told, brother? We are your family." Christina gestured to all the crewmen gathered around.

Herbert turned his gaze from the ark's floorboards and into the faces of those staring at him. Many smiled and nodded when they met his eyes. Herbert's gaze eventually landed on Edward, but then he turned away in shame.

"I am sorry, Edward." Herbert opened his mouth to say more, but the no words came out.

"There is nothing to apologise for." Edward lay his hand on Herbert's shoulder, and grinned. "Until you accept us as your family, we will be here. They say you can choose your friends, but you can't choose your family, isn't that right, men?" The crew responded with a holler and some raised fists. Edward chuckled. "You're stuck with us."

Herbert laughed and wiped a tear away. "I wouldn't have it any other way."

After a moment of silence, Edward grabbed the crew's attention. "Alright, Christina, Nassir, be careful." Christina nodded and jogged back to the maze and entered. Soon after the maze shifted again before their eyes. Edward turned his attention back to the crew. "Where are we on the statues?" he asked no one in particular.

"We set the statues we know of, at Alexandre's direction," Jack told Edward, pointing to the five statues standing next to their respected animal companions. "We are about to move one suggested by myself." Jack smiled as he said that part.

"Which one?" Edward asked as he watched ten crewmates lift the heavy statue of a priest.

Jack grinned sheepishly. "Well, the name was inscribed on the statue already. Saint Francis. There are several saints with the same name, so we don't actually know which one it is."

Edward was shocked. "Isn't this dangerous? We can't afford to make mistakes. The engraving on the pedestal mentioned something about six sins and being engulfed in fire, I think you recall."

Jack ran his fingers through his hair. "Well, yes, we know. We have ideas for some of the other statues, but we must start somewhere. I believe this one to be Saint Francis Xavier, born in fifteen-oh-six, which, according to Anne's math, would be the year of the Tiger."

Edward focused on the crew, a few steps from setting the statue down. "I suppose," he agreed, stroking his beard.

The crew dropped the saint's statue next to the Tiger statue and a clicking sounded. At first Edward feared the worst, then his rational mind went through the steps. *Each statue must have clicked before this.* Edward calmed himself with this, but as he glanced at the crew, he could tell something was off. *There was no noise before!*

Another noise started, bringing Edward's attention to the front of the ark, where they had first entered. The wall which first lifted to allow the crew passage to the interior of the ark was now lowering inch by inch.

"Get away from the front of the ark!" Edward yelled, swiping his hand across the air.

The crewmen near the descending wall snapped out of their stupor of curiosity and ran. When the wall was halfway down, Edward could see two large unlit fire pits suspended in the air in the alcove where the wall used to be. When the wall was close to the bottom, Edward noticed the alcove was slanted and covered in a black, tar-like substance. The black liquid spilled over the falling wall and covered it completely, pooling on the floorboards and oozing out towards the middle of the ark and the crew.

The Voyages of Queen Anne's Revenge

When the wall fell flush with the rest of the ship, a mechanism struck flint to steel and created sparks, igniting the two fire pits. After the fire pits were set ablaze, they began descending slowly. Eventually, the fire would reach the bottom of the alcove and, presumably, ignite the black liquid, and in turn the ark.

Edward took charge of the situation before panic took over the crew. "Move the statue off!" he commanded. The men moved the Saint Francis Xavier statue away quickly. After they moved the statue, all eyes were on Edward, waiting for orders. Their survival hinged on Edward's next words, and Edward knew it. "I want all crewmates to split up among the statues. Senior officers will work at taking information on the possible origin of the person depicted by the statue. If you don't know who the person is, or are unsure, move to another group. I want everyone involved in this, no lollygagging. Seven statues, seven groups. Hop to it, men!"

Each crewmate ran to the nearest statue. Anne, William, Jack, Pukuh, Herbert, Alexandre, and Victor each moved to one of the statues, knowing their role without needing to question. They would guide the discussion as well as possible towards finding the solution of who these priests and nuns were and when they were born.

Edward paced back and forth, watching the crew working together, and the slowly falling fire pits some fifty feet away. When he noticed crewmates glancing at the impending doom, he admonished them to stay focused. Individual crewmates shuffled to other groups when they felt they knew nothing about the statue or had no further input to provide their group.

Edward gradually made his way to Alexandre, who simply observed the group discuss amongst themselves, no doubt analysing every word for something worthwhile.

"So, can you tell me what happened back there?" Edward whispered while Alexandre's group were discussing the exploits of female martyrs who were imprisoned.

"We did a test. We had one in seven chances. We were no farther ahead, so I made the call to use Jack's suggestion. Is that *un problème*?" Alexandre asked, brow raised.

"No, but I wish we were in a better position beforehand, maybe had a few more statues figured out before doing a test. Now we have a timer over our heads. How long do you figure we have left?"

Alexandre considered the fire pits, then his sullen eyes examined the angles and the relationship of the pits to the port and starboard walls. "*Cinquante-six* minutes, give or take."

Edward laughed. "Give or take. I enjoy your humble attitude. Always refreshing." Edward patted Alexandre on the back.

"If you ask me, this timer is, for lack of a better term, a godsend. I find that when under threat of death, humans can work more efficiently. Trust me, I've done tests," Alexandre said with a dark grin. "Also, this has brought those previously unhelpful into the fold as *contributeurs*."

Edward glanced at the teams working together. They had adopted frantic expressions, and argued vehemently that their assessment was correct, but all were involved.

"I believe you may be correct. Let us hope this is enough." Edward peered back to the maze behind him, the loud thumping of the shifting cubes telling him Christina was still alive.

Across the next thirty minutes, Edward and the senior crewmates collaborated on the consensus of their groups. The seven debated amongst themselves on whether their group was correct for their statue.

Four statues had riddles about the people they could be, and three had names on them. They were able to make a list of the possible priests and nuns each statue represented, and figured out which combinations would work, but a problem quickly presented itself.

"We're one statue short," Anne said flatly.

Alexandre concurred. "None of the *combinaisons* work with William's statue."

"So, what does it mean? We don't know who that is?" Edward pointed to the statue in question.

"Apparently so," William concluded.

"It matters not, just position the idols," Pukuh chimed in.

Anne sighed. "Pukuh, there are four possible solutions for this. We have fifteen minutes. We may be able to determine this statue's origin by then. According to the text, if we are wrong it will undoubtedly speed the process of our doom."

"What of it?" Pukuh replied, indignant. "Time for talk is over. We must act, or we *will* die."

Anne glanced to the group, and all agreed with Pukuh's suggestion. "Alright, we'll try it your way."

Anne guided the crew in placing another statue. They believed the statue to be Saint Thomas Aquinas, born in the year of the Dog. As the crew moved the holy man's likeness, the fire pit inched ever closer to the pitch-covered wood, looming like the sword of Damocles. One mistake would that sword down, sealing the fate of the *Freedom*'s crew.

Half the crew's eyes were focused on the statue, and the other half on the pits. The priest's statue was plopped down next to the figure of the dog. Those focusing on the pits and those on the statue swapped focus in the seconds after the statue lowered.

The pits kept lowering as normal, and the relief was visible on Edward's face, and the faces around him. Edward glanced at Anne and Pukuh; they both let out sighs.

Anne commanded the crew to move to the next statue. As the statue was set down next to the figure of the snake, Edward unconsciously held his breath, his eyes intent on the fire pit, and his ears listening for a sound he prayed never arrived.

Click

The noise caused Edward's gaze to shift back to the statue. The crewmates who set the statue down aped in shock. The sound of moving metal grinding and clanging echoed beneath the floorboards. Edward followed the noise with his eyes as it travelled all the way to the front of the ark.

The pits fell. Edward watched in horror as the pits sped to the bottom of the alcove. The noise of the iron chain locking filled the room. The pits stopped, swinging back and forth.

"*Deux* minutes," Alexandre counted blandly, filling the void of silence.

Panic gripped the crew of the *Freedom*. Hope was lost in those few seconds, as was order. Each man tried their own way of escape. Most ran to the sides, hacking and shooting at the wood, but none made a dent. Sweat poured from the faces of those men onto the floor of the Ark through their wasted effort.

Anne and the senior officers did their best to quell the squall of voices and calm the pirates, but theirs was also a futile endeavour. Anne and William attempted to reason with some, but it devolved into arguing. Pukuh took a more direct, forceful approach, but one against a mob did not work. Jack's and Herbert's soft-spoken natures were easily overpowered. Alexandre and Victor stood watching, merely observing the chaos.

Edward glanced back and forth at his crew descending into madness, and he'd had his fill. "Enough!" he roared, slamming his fist into the beam and shaking the ark to its core. In a matter of seconds, all eyes were on the captain. "If we die, we die with dignity." Edward stared his men in the eye, then sat down, facing the fire pits.

As Edward's men watched him sit, their hands, held high in defiance, lowered as well. They still had no hope, but they had regained their pride. The crew did not want to bring shame to their captain's name, nor disappoint the one who had given them *Freedom*. The crew gradually joined Edward in sitting.

Anne regarded the men who, so affected by their captain's simple resolve, changed their outlook completely. She joined Edward at the front of the crew.

Anne leaned over to Edward. "How is your hand?" she asked, peering down at the reddish hue forming on the side of his right palm where he'd hit the support beam.

"My hand is fine," Edward replied, pulling his hand close to his chest. Anne took it and wrapped it around hers.

Edward gazed into Anne's eyes, and she into his. Those green eyes of hers captured him as they always did, and, before Edward knew it, he was far away from the ark, and from the impending doom. Edward became lost in Anne's eyes, and she in his.

"I love you, Anne."

Anne smirked. "I know." Edward pushed her playfully. "I love you too, Edward."

The pit reached its destination. The flames grew and filled the alcove with light. In mere seconds the front of the ark was on fire. After overtaking the black pitch the inferno crawled across the floorboards and set the walls ablaze. Smoke filled the room, covering the glass panels of the ceiling. The wood cracked and let out a howl as moisture turned to steam and escaped. The heat intensified as the fire spread, feeding on the wood and air.

The heat and smoke seemed to rob the moisture from the surroundings, and some of the crew began coughing. Edward's throat was scratchy as well, as if he was swallowing ash.

Edward's ears heard all the sounds of the spreading fire, but one sound was missing now. Edward's head spun around to the back of the ship. The moving maze Christina and Nassir entered had stopped after near continuous movement the past hour. Edward glanced at the left corner, and noticed, despite all odds, the maze entrance back in its original position.

"Edward!" a voice sounded from inside the maze.

Edward stood, his brows furrowed. Christina ran out of the maze, followed by Nassir. She was holding something in the palm of her hand.

It cannot be. Edward's eyes opened wide in astonishment.

Christina ran, pushing through the crowd, towards Edward. She now held the object she had found outstretched above her head.

Edward moved back after recovering from his shock. "Hand it to Anne, quickly!" he yelled over the raging fire.

Christina shifted and jumped in front of Anne, shoving a piece of paper into her hands. Anne examined the paper, and soon her expression changed to awe.

"It is a list of years next to the names of animals," Anne said, as she worked everything out in her head. "Everyone on your feet! Lift those statues!"

The crew jumped to the closest statues not already assigned to animals, picking them up of the ground. Anne yelled out directions to each group, pointing as she did. In less than a minute the statues were set.

Edward couldn't hear another click, but he felt a rumbling below his feet. This time the rumbling moved to the back of the ark, towards the maze.

The maze cubes shifted of their own accord, rapidly moving the insides around to another configuration. Edward watched as the entrance moved from one end to the other, then stopped. The back of the ark stopped moving completely.

"Move!" Edward yelled, pointing to the entrance to the maze, or what could be the ship's exit, and their only hope, now.

Edward ran to the entrance, but didn't enter. He stood at the side, watching as his crew entered. Edward yelled for the men to hurry as he spurred them along with a hand on their backs.

When the crew were gone, Edward took one last glimpse at the ark. The roof collapsed at the front, sending wooden planks crashing down. Flames reached the support beam and started climbing.

Edward entered the maze, running through the tunnel. Anne waited at the back, and when she saw him she started off again to the left. Edward turned the corner and saw stairs heading up for the length of two of the ten-foot squares. After Edward climbed the stairs, he flew down another hallway, and around another left turn at the end. The process was repeated around the perimeter of the maze and up.

A deafening crack resounded throughout the ark, stopping Edward in his tracks. In front of him was another set of stairs, but before he could climb, one of the support beams crashed through the nearby wall. The flaming beam broke the wood to splinters with thunder and screeching. It eventually settled in front of the stairs, blocking the way.

Anne appeared in the right corner at the top, the only spot left open in the wake of the beam. "Edward! Are you unharmed?"

"I'm fine, but soon I won't be," Edward replied, eyeing the hellfire through the hole made by the beam. The fire had nearly overtaken the whole ark, and the ship was quickly falling apart.

Anne tried to push herself through the small hole to join Edward, but even her slender body could not fit. Edward moved to the left side, but there wasn't any room to squeeze through either.

"Hang on Edward, I'll be right back." Anne called over some of the crew. "Now lift!" she commanded. "Edward, get ready. We'll attempt lifting the beam to let you through."

Edward positioned himself at the top of the stairs in front of the left side of the beam. He grabbed the side and lifted with all his might to help, but the beam didn't seem to move at all. Edward's body was still healing and weaker than normal.

"We need more bodies. Move in as best you can," Edward could hear Anne say.

Edward lay down on a step and planted his feet into the small opening as best he could. He could hear Anne yell "lift!" and he pushed his feet in tandem with his brothers. After a few seconds of no movement, Anne called for rest, then counted down from three.

"Three."

I will not die here.

"Two."

I'm not done yet.

"One."

"I won't let you win, you hear me you bastard?" Edward yelled.

"Lift!" Anne shouted.

Edward bellowed with rage, pushing the beam with all the strength in him. The pillar inched forward. Edward pushed with his back, the movement of the massive beam feeding him with strength. The pillar moved foot by foot, and with the extra room more people joined in lifting it to save their captain.

"Now, Edward!" Anne yelled.

Edward released his feet from the beam and crawled over to safety. When he was on the other side, the crew dropped the pillar and it fell with a thunderous boom as it smashed through more of the ark.

Anne grabbed Edward's hand and pulled him up. "Move!" Edward commanded between ragged breaths. "And thank you." Edward's afterthought compliment drew more than a few chuckles.

Edward, Anne, and the crew ran through the small hallway, then to another left turn, and up a longer flight of stairs. At the top was an opening to the outside.

Edward emerged from the ark to the bright sun and tropical wind. After his eyes adjusted to the new scenery, he could only see half his crew. He noticed the men descending off the side on rope ladders.

The Voyages of Queen Anne's Revenge

Edward guided the remaining crew to move ahead of himself. The crew swiftly descended the ladders while the fire moved closer like a tiger stalking prey. Edward gazed at the front of the ark, the flames changing it into what could have been a funeral pyre.

Anne and Edward rushed down the hundred-foot ladder on the side of the ark. The heat of the flames licked at them as they moved. As soon as the fire was about to overtake their ladder, the two landed on solid ground. They ran forward, putting a safe distance between them and the death trap before collapsing on the grass.

Edward and Anne breathed heavily from exhaustion, and Edward could hear the crew resting from similar effort.

"I didn't think we would make it," he said.

"Our family is lucky. If any other crew had to face this, I don't think they would have survived."

Edward nodded with a grin. "You may be right... but the crew with a *Pirate Priest* for a captain probably would have done well, right?"

Anne laughed. "Yes, that crew might have fared better."

Edward scanned the crowd of two hundred before resting his eyes on Christina. "Christina!" he shouted, beckoning her over.

Christina turned to Edward's voice, and, after ensuring her brother was unharmed, walked over. "Yes?"

"First off, good job, my dear. You saved us." Christina smiled at the praise. "How did you make it back? The maze must have shifted over a hundred times."

"Well, Nassir and I were running most of the time, but we moved methodically. Each time the maze shifted I memorised where we were, and then if we reached a dead end we went back and tried another route. Eventually we found the paper, and retraced our steps." Christina explained.

Edward was dumbfounded at the explanation. "How could you remember?"

Christina laughed. "I trained myself to remember things. It used to be a game I and my brother would play. We used to see who could remember the most numbers in a random sequence." Christina smirked. "I don't enjoy losing."

"Impressive," Anne remarked. "She is a prodigy." Anne whispered to Edward. "Perhaps we should be training her mind too."

Edward simply nodded in agreement with Anne, he was still in awe of Christina's abilities.

Now that they were out of harm's way, Edward stood and observed the area. The crew was in a field similar to the one before they entered the ark, but surrounded by wooden stakes. Edward could find no discernible exit. Some time had passed since the trial was made, as vegetation had grown over the wood, and the grass was long.

On the left side, the side closest to Bartholomew's group, the wooden stakes appeared different, so Edward examined them.

At the wall, Edward noticed a pedestal similar to the ones they had seen many times before here. Edward noticed no writing, only a switch.

This must to open the way to the next area.

Edward pressed the switch. The ground rumbled and he could feel movement beneath his feet spreading to the wall to his left and in front of him. Suddenly the walls dropped down revealing a whole other area, along with a new danger.

To Edward's left, he could see the crew of the *Fortune* fighting an unknown enemy. The sight made him jump, and he immediately drew his golden blade. His crew were shocked and drew their weapons as well.

Edward's gaze was drawn to an altar in the middle of the two fields. Standing on the altar in the middle of Edward's and Bartholomew's crews, was an accursed man with slicked-back hair and black clothing. He was holding a bloodied Bartholomew by the neck, and he glanced nonchalantly over his shoulder and smiled.

It was Plague.

36. FROM HELL

Blood dripped from Plague's hand onto the grey marbled stone of the altar. The blood of the faithful Bartholomew dripped onto the stone and pooled at his feet.

Edward, his cutlass drawn, ran to the altar and jumped atop. The crew of the *Freedom* rushed to the aid of *Fortune*'s crew. The sounds and smells of battle quickly filled Edward's senses.

"Fitting, is it not? Bartholomew, the Pirate Priest, sacrificed in a place such as this."

"Release him, Plague, it's me you want," Edward commanded as he circled the large surface of the altar.

Edward Russell, known by many names, laughed, sending a chill down Edward's spine. "You know nothing, boy." He dropped Bartholomew, and the Pirate Priest fell in a heap on the marble. Plague slowly drew his weapon, a small dagger. Normally innocuous in the wrong hands, the dagger took on the form of deadly claws in Plague's.

Edward leapt forward and slashed. Plague parried the strike, then punched Edward in the nose. Edward fell backwards, but stayed on his feet. Plague thrust his blade at his abdomen, but Edward smashed his elbow into Plague's hand, nearly knocking the dagger from the assassin's grip.

Plague stopped his advance and adopted a more defensive posture. "You've improved, but methinks you stretched yourself too thin."

Edward breathed heavily, staring intently into Plague's eyes. He pulled his sword close to his chest and held it in both hands. *He's right. I'm not yet fully recovered.*

Pukuh and William both jumped atop the altar beside Edward. "Worry not, Edward, we will handle this. We have business with him."

Pukuh flashed his spear forward in his left hand. "This one owes me an arm."

Plague stood up straight. "You act as if I am the only one here, gentlemen." The man with the slick black hair put his fingers between his teeth and whistled loudly. After a second's delay, two people with masks on joined Plague on the altar. "Leave the one in the middle for me, the other two are yours. If you cannot kill them, at least make yourselves useful and keep them busy."

Without a word, the masked people pulled out Katar, stylised Indian daggers. The daggers had horizontal handles to allow the blade to rest just above the knuckle so they could be punched into the victim. The two rushed Pukuh and William, pushing them back and off the altar, away from Edward.

With Pukuh and William gone, Plague resumed his defensive stance, but pulled out another dagger for his other hand.

Edward assessed his opponent. *Knees bent, low to the ground. No way to unbalance him. One dagger near his face, one around his torso. No way past his defence. If I can distract him, I could gain the upper hand.*

Edward peered over Plague's shoulder, widened his eyes a touch, and nodded. Plague glanced over his shoulder, but no one was there. Edward thrust his cutlass towards Plague's face and the man threw his arms up. Edward changed direction mid-way and swiped at Plague's legs. Edward's double-feint worked and he sliced Plague's thigh open.

Plague ignored the injury, but his eyes flashed with anger. Edward could feel the pressure of those eyes, but he would not run this time. He stared straight into the face of fear.

Plague ran forward, his blades dancing in the air. Edward took each thrust, lunge, slash, and cut and returned them in kind. Plague parried Edward's blows, but every so often he slipped and was sliced on the hands, face, and stomach. Edward was nicked in the forehead, hand, bicep, legs. The two men traded jab for jab, neither one cutting deeper than the surface.

Edward jumped backwards to catch his breath. The blood from his forehead seeped into his left eye, blocking his vision. He wiped away the blood and noticed Plague was also short on breath.

"Maybe *you* are stretched too thin, Plague. Did Bartholomew take the fight out of you?"

Plague stifled his heavy breathing and stood up straight. "Hmph. You are nothing before me." Plague postured with bravado.

The Royal Assassin with a penchant for poison pulled a vial from his pocket. Edward tensed and raised his guard. Plague popped the cork from the vial and took a large sniff from its contents before throwing it to the ground and breaking the bottle.

Edward didn't understand what was happening, but he didn't like it. Plague breathed rapidly, but not from fatigue this time, his eyes widened, and his pupils grew large. Plague threw his daggers away and changed to hand to hand combat.

Whatever had been in the vial changed Plague completely, and with the metamorphosis he regained speed and strength before Edward's eyes.

Plague lowered his body and moved inches in front of Edward, and he didn't have time to react. Plague landed an uppercut and Edward's chin flew up. Plague struck him in the stomach. Edward tensed his stomach and took the blow, then slammed the butt of his cutlass into Plague's head.

Plague punched Edward's right hand and he dropped his cutlass, and the assassin took the drop in his guard to kick him in the side of the knee. Edward dropped to the stone uncontrollably, but twisted and struck Plague in the midsection. Plague doubled over, but dropped his elbow on Edward's head.

Edward was pushed down further to the ground, still on his knee. He gritted his bloodied teeth together and balled his fist. Edward jumped upwards, delivering an uppercut square on Plague's jaw. The man's head whipped backwards, and his eyes went foggy as he began losing consciousness.

Plague forced himself back from the brink, his eyes shooting wide open. The assassin clinched Edward's midsection, fell backwards, and slammed Edward's face into the stone altar.

Edward fell to the ground, his head and body aching. He couldn't rise back up; he was *so* tired. Disoriented too. He pulled his body around as he searched for Plague.

Edward could see the two crews fighting against Plague's crew. First, he noticed Alexandre and Victor fighting back to back. Alexandre used a rapier to cut and thrust into his opponents' vital organs with precision only he could pull off. Victor used a small round shield and curved double-edged blade to parry and slice his opponents.

Next, Edward noticed Nassir and Christina fighting together, and Jack and Herbert attacking from long range. Working together, the two groups were dropping enemies left and right.

In those few flickering seconds of movement, Edward's eyes finally found Plague. He too was overlooking the battlefield, searching for something while he caught his breath. Edward followed Plague's gaze to Anne.

Anne was fighting against Plague's men on the side where the ark was still burning fifty feet away. She directed the crew of the *Freedom* during the battle while firing her favourite rifle and engaging in the occasional swordplay.

Plague pulled out a familiar needle from his pocket.

No! Not Anne! Edward moved his body around and tried to push himself upright. *Damn arms! You're stronger than this.* "Anne! Run!" Edward yelled, but Anne was too far away and the noises of the battle too intense for her to hear. *Damn legs, move!*

Plague set the needle into a crossbow bolt, placed the bolt in a crossbow, and aimed it at Anne.

"Anne!" Edward yelled, but to no avail. He pushed his body with all his might, his face turning red and veins showing from the strain.

Plague pulled the trigger, sending the bolt to Anne at incredible speed, and it struck her in the shoulder. Anne stopped what she was doing and pulled the bolt out of her shoulder, confusion on her face. She turned to the altar. Anne saw Plague and Edward, then she stepped forward, but she collapsed on the ground.

"Anne, God, no!" Edward howled, tears filling his eyes, but still Anne did not answer.

"Mission complete," Edward heard Plague say.

Edward forced himself to his feet, anger driving his muscles. He picked up his cutlass from the altar and approached Plague with lethal intent. Plague turned and picked up his daggers again, ready to kill.

Suddenly, Bartholomew jumped up behind Plague. The big man wrapped his massive arms around Plague's arms and pulled them back to expose the assassin's chest. Then Bartholomew wrapped his legs around Plague's, not allowing him any bit of movement.

Plague struggled against the bonds, but at least for the moment Bartholomew's strength was more than Plague could break. "Hurry, Edward. Kill him!"

Edward pulled the blade back and slashed Plague across the chest. Edward's gritted his teeth, and stared into Plague's eyes. For the first time Edward could see fear in the man's eyes.

Plague broke free from Bartholomew and Edward, and fell forwards to the marble, his shaking hand holding himself up. Blood poured from the open wound. Plague turned himself around and lay back on the raised stone.

Edward approached Plague. He leaned over the body of the man who had haunted them the past months. The man who killed Henry's mother, the man who took Pukuh's arm, and had now poisoned Anne.

Plague coughed blood over the marble, and laughed. He continued to laugh and cough blood as Edward stared at him. Plague was dead, and the man himself knew it, yet he kept laughing.

"William!" Edward beckoned.

William rushed over to Edward's side; he was covered in wounds, but thankfully still alive. Edward lifted his golden blade over Plague's head and stared at William. William nodded and placed his hand over the hilt of the blade.

"Go to Hell," Edward said.

Edward and William slammed the golden cutlass down on Plague's neck, severing his head from his body. The man named Edward Russell, the Plague, one of the Immortal Seven, was finally dead.

Though Plague did not live up to one of his names, those who witnessed his death claimed they could still hear him laughing even after Edward delivered the final blow. He laughed all the way to the grave and beyond.

37. THE SHIP'S NAME

Edward ran like a ship with a storm in its sails. "Stay with me, Anne," he said between breaths. Edward carried her to the *Freedom*, the battle still raging on behind him.

Edward had rushed to Anne's body, calling for Alexandre as he did so. The wooden spikes had dropped, revealing a way out in between the two sides of the trial.

"We need *médecine* from the ship," Alexandre had stated.

Edward had nodded, picked Anne up, and started running with Alexandre closely behind.

Edward ran along the walled path to the entrance they were in not hours before. He rushed around the wooden statue and the pressure plates and into the woods.

Anne's breathing was shallow and she was as pale as a cloud on a summer's day. Her eyes were closed in pain, flickering as the light passed over.

Edward cursed under his rapid breath. *How could I be so foolish? All the signs were there. Plague was never meant for me. I should have seen it sooner.*

"Focus, *Capitaine*," Alexandre commanded, noticing Edward slowing.

"Right," he replied, quickening his feet.

Edward emerged from the forest to see three ships. The *Fortune* on the left, the *Freedom* next to it, and on the right a massive second-rate warship.

Edward could smell gunpowder in the air, and bodies recently sent to the next world littered the beach and water surrounding the ships. The *Freedom* had no marks of battle, but the third ship had many holes across the hull from cannon fire.

"Oi! Is anyone alive?" Edward yelled.

Alexandre pulled on Edward's shoulder, trying to pull him back. The Frenchman held a finger to his lips to force a cautionary silence on the captain.

Before Alexandre could pull Edward back into the forest, a man appeared on the fore of the *Freedom*. "Captain! Praise the heavens you be safe," he said.

Alexandre released the captain and the two ran to the ship. Edward waded through the water and sand, balancing with Anne still in his arms. "What happened, besides the obvious?"

The crewman followed Edward to the side, then dropped the *Freedom*'s jolly boat into the water. "When we saw the warship approachin' those of us leftover from 'ere and the *Fortune* hid in the woods and after theys all left we snuck back and showed the leftovers what-for."

Edward gently laid Anne down in the small boat, but climbed up a rope ladder instead of jumping in. The crewman talking with Edward called others to his aid and pulled the jolly boat back up to the deck.

"Are the boys doing alright?" the crewman asked while pulling hard on the rope. "We saw the enemy head your way, but there were too many for us to stop them."

"All is well, no need to worry yourselves. Bartholomew and I killed their leader, the Plague, and it's only a matter of time before the men finish his crew."

Edward jumped over the railing of the ship as the crew were securing the boat and pulling Anne to the deck. Tala was sniffing Anne and licking her face, trying to wake her. Alexandre was ahead of Edward, running to his medical cabin. Edward took Anne into his arms, and followed the Frenchman to the lower deck.

"What happened to Miss Bonney?" the crewman asked.

"She was poisoned," Edward yelled back before descending the stairs.

Edward took care in transporting Anne down the stairs and the narrow hallway to Alexandre's cabin. She was sweating bullets and mumbling indistinct words Edward couldn't make sense of.

Almost there, Anne. Hold on a bit longer, and Alexandre will save you.

Edward entered the cabin and lay Anne on the table in the middle of the room. At the back of the cabin, Alexandre flew into a frenzy, grabbing a mortar and pestle in one hand and the Mayan plant in the other. He threw the plant in the mortar and crushed the leaves together with the pestle.

"Third shelf, black mushroom. *Vite!*" Alexandre commanded Edward.

Edward jumped to the right side of the room with the various shelves and oddities contained within. He quickly scanned the shelf and found the mushrooms in a glass. Edward removed the glass and handed a mushroom to the surgeon.

"Do you know what poison was used?" Edward asked.

Alexandre dropped the mushroom in the mortar and crushed the plant and it together with some water. "*Oui.* Our man in *noir* was sloppy. I had never seen the poison used on the Mayan devil, so if he used that again our princess would be gone. This is one I have seen before. I did not have enough time to save Henry's mother, but this time…" Alexandre took out a cloth and wrapped the plant and mushroom paste in the centre of the cloth. "Grab the two bottles in the corner." Edward did as commanded and brought the sealed bottles over quickly. "Now smell each of them, *s'il vous plaît.*"

Edward opened the first and took a whiff of the contents. "Smells sweet, but with a hint of rot. Akin to bad wine."

"Close that and try the other."

Edward took the second bottle and repeated the process, trusting Alexandre's process. "Is this vinegar?"

"*Bon,* it is vinegar."

"And the first one?"

"If you wish to kill someone, pour the first liquid on their head." Alexandre smiled devilishly. "We will need it next."

Edward gazed at the bottle with a new appreciation of terror. "Why are they not labelled?"

"Too much work. Now, focus." Alexandre set down a glass and handed Edward the cloth with the plant and mushroom mixture. "Hold this over the glass."

Edward glanced at the liquid Alexandre claimed could kill with a splash, took in a deep breath, and held the cloth over the glass. Edward's eyes were shut tightly and his hands clenched against the glass, his knuckles white in anticipation for the deadly liquid about to be poured near him.

Edward heard some shuffling around him, then nothing. "You may open your eyes," Alexandre said. Edward did as instructed and now saw four wooden clothespins holding the cloth against the glass. "Your dedication to the woman you love is admirable, albeit misplaced. You did not think I would risk pouring the *liquide* over you, did you?"

Edward grinned sheepishly. "No, of course not."

Alexandre gave Edward a knowing glance, then slowly and carefully poured the contents of the first bottle over the cloth. As the liquid passed over the herbs and mushroom it took on a blackish green hue and dripped from the cloth into the glass. Alexandre was meticulous in his preparation, taking his time, which Edward knew was precious in this scenario.

Edward left Alexandre to what he did best and turned to Anne. She was shaking and cold, but her forehead was slick with sweat, like her body was in the throes of a fever.

Edward took Anne's hand and gripped it tightly. "You can make it, Anne. If anyone can beat this, I know you can. If you can hear me, you need to keep fighting a little longer." Edward leaned over and kissed Anne on the forehead before wiping a strand of red hair away.

"*Capitaine*, the vinegar, if you please," Alexandre said over his shoulder.

Edward let go of Anne's hand and grabbed the vinegar bottle, opening it in a single motion. Alexandre held the cloth in his index finger and thumb over the glass.

"When I say now, pour the entire bottle of vinegar over my hands."

Edward cocked his brow. "Why, what are you—"

Alexandre squeezed the cloth together, causing the absorbed liquid to pass through it and over Alexandre's hand. The liquid burned Alexandre's skin as it transferred from the cloth to his hand and down to the glass below. Alexandre shook with the effort to let every drop fall into the glass; his arm convulsed and his eyes widened with pain, but his hands never moved an inch.

Alexandre threw the cloth away and moved his hands to an open area. "Now!" he yelled.

Edward paused for the slightest moment, still in shock from what he'd witnessed. He pulled himself together and dumped the vinegar over Alexandre's hands. The vinegar reacted with the other liquid, providing the surgeon with the needed relief. Edward continued until the whole of the bottle was empty and the room had taken on a smell of sweet vinegar wine, rot, and burning flesh.

"Now, I will need you to make the final *preparation*," Alexandre said, holding his hands in front of him still, showing no sign of pain.

"What do I need to do?"

"Pour a drop into another glass, and fill the rest with water."

"Easy."

Edward took an empty glass and set it on the shelf in front of him. Then, with a shaking hand, he gripped the other glass. Alexandre watch over his shoulder, breathing down his neck.

Edward turned his upper body to face Alexandre. "Do you mind?"

Alexandre backed up a few paces and leaned on the shelf, still watching like a hawk.

Edward took two deep breaths and picked up the glass with the deadly concoction. He gently moved it to the other glass, setting the lip of the first against the edge of the second. Centimetre by slow centimetre Edward tipped the first glass up.

"*Vite*," Alexandre prompted.

Edward closed his eyes in frustration for a moment, then turned to Alexandre. "Stop," he commanded.

Edward turned back to his task, but an idea formed in his head. Edward set the first glass down and pulled a clean cloth from Alexandre's supplies. He took the cloth and dipped the corner into the glass, letting the liquid absorb in. After Edward felt enough liquid was absorbed he positioned the cloth over the second glass, then picked up a clothespin. Edward put the clothespin above the spot on the cloth where the liquid was, then moved the pin down, the pressure pushing the liquid down and out of the cloth. Once a drop fell, Edward removed the cloth and filled the glass with water.

Edward turned to Alexandre, the glass in hand. "Now what?" Edward couldn't be sure, but he believed he saw a small grin on Alexandre's lips.

"Now, you must make her drink."

Edward lifted Anne's head with his left hand while holding the antidote in his right. "Anne, you must drink this. Anne! If you can hear me, I need you to drink this. It will help you."

Edward pushed the glass to Anne's lips. Alexandre dried his burned hands and helped open her mouth. Edward tipped the glass and gradually poured the liquid down Anne's throat.

She coughed, spitting a bit of the liquid out. "Damn," Edward cursed.

"Let her head relax, it will help."

Edward nodded and cradled her head in his elbow. Her mouth naturally opened. Alexandre took the glass from Edward and he took over administering it to Anne.

After a laborious ten minutes, the liquid was gone. Edward gently laid Anne's head back down on the table. She was still sweating and breathing rapidly.

"Now what?" Edward asked.

Alexandre returned his instruments to the shelves. "Now, we wait. The worst is past us. *Se relaxer*, your beloved will live on. Make her comfortable and wait for her to awaken."

Edward nodded, then pulled Alexandre close and embraced him. "Thank you. You saved us all a dozen times over. I know I don't thank you enough for all you've done for our family, and for that I'm sorry." Edward let Alexandre go.

Alexandre smirked. "Careful, *Capitaine*. I may become attached to everyone."

Edward laughed as he picked up Anne from the table. "We both know it's too late for that."

Edward then noticed the audience watching the entire time. He passed by them all, Anne in his arms. The crewmen watched Anne with concern and relief in their eyes. After Edward was outside the room, the crewmen piled into the medical cabin and flooded Alexandre with praise and questions all at once. Edward could see a smile at the corner of Alexandre's lips.

Edward took Anne to the crew cabin and lay her down in their bed in the corner underneath the stairs. He pulled the covers over her, and kissed her on the forehead.

"I won't be long, Anne."

Edward ran back up the stairs of the crew cabin and then up to the top deck. He jumped over the side of the ship and climbed down the rope ladder to the sandy beach below. He ran to the path, but stopped short of entering. The crew of the *Freedom* and *Fortune* were standing in front of Edward. Bartholomew was leading the pack, waving to Edward.

"My boy! Is Anne well?" he asked immediately. His face was bloody, dirt and cuts covering his body, but Bartholomew appeared no worse for wear.

"Yes, she is fine. Alexandre created an antidote for the poison. I trust your return means the battle went smoothly?"

"Aye, God was with us this day. We only battled half of Plague's crew, given the design of this trial, and when providence sent your crew to our aid the numbers were in our favour."

Edward stroked his beard. "So the other half of Plague's crew is stuck behind the ark with no way out then."

"Right you are. Ah, yes, you should be delighted to have this, I presume?" Bartholomew reached into his pocket and pulled out a key.

Edward smiled. "How did you happen upon this?"

"Writing on the front of the altar indicated a need to sacrifice blood. After you left, Plague's blood pooled on the altar and activated it, opening an alcove with the key inside."

Pukuh and William, injured and helping each other walk, trudged over to Edward and Bartholomew.

"Where is Anne?" William asked, concern evident in his eyes.

"She is in the crew cabin, resting. Alexandre made an antidote for her, so she is safe."

William let out a sigh and nodded to Edward in thanks.

Jack and Hank Abbot were next. The two waved to their captains as they passed. Jack was battle worn, but in good spirits considering. He had overheard Edward's mention of Anne being safe.

Christina, Herbert, and Nassir exited the path after Jack and Hank. Christina ran over to Edward, followed by Herbert and Nassir on her heels.

"Is Anne safe?" Christina asked Edward.

Edward laughed, this being the third time he was asked. "Yes, she is well thanks to Alexandre. If you wish to see her, she is in the crew cabin resting."

Christina kissed Edward on the cheek and then ran off to the *Freedom* ahead of her brother. Herbert and Nassir were fatigued, but uninjured. They both nodded to Edward when he glanced over.

The remainder of the crew passed in waves, some more injured than others, and many asked about Anne despite their own worries. Edward answered their questions with a scolding remark to return to the ship and worry about themselves, followed by assuring them Anne was alright.

Victor arrived last, carrying a body slumped over his shoulder, and something in his hand. This time, Edward ran over.

"Did one of our crewmates die, Victor?" Edward asked.

Victor shied away from Edward's eyes as he replied, "No."

"Then, who...?" Edward examined the body, then noticed a severed head in Victor's hand.

"Alexandre wanted the body," Victor said curtly. "Problem?"

Edward stepped aside. "No, no. Continue on."

Edward couldn't help but stare at the head as Victor walked to the ship. Plague still had a smile on his face, and though his eyes had gone glossy and dull already they were no less potent in inspiring fear. Like the eyes of Medusa, Plague could turn even the most hardened man to stone with his gaze.

"Quite the foe, that one. You know him?" Bartholomew asked.

"Yes, we met him a few times on our journey. He was well known by the name Plague, but his true name was Edward Russell. Anne and William believed him to be a Royal Assassin under direct orders from Queen Anne."

"So he was here to assassinate your Anne?" Bartholomew asked. "I don't understand."

"So I take it Anne never told you?" Edward asked, glancing about.

"Tell me what?"

"She's the princess."

Bartholomew laughed. "Princess of what?"

"Denmark and Norway. Anne is the Queen's daughter."

Bartholomew's jaw dropped and his brow cocked. After several protests, and Edward reciting the fact over and over, Bartholomew eventually accepted the truth.

"But why would the Queen want to kill her own daughter?" he asked, not really expecting an answer.

"I do not know. The Queen could feel betrayed after Anne left her again, or she considers Anne a liability. Any number of reasons, really. The two have a poor history, one Anne isn't keen on sharing, but she'll tell me when she's ready, I'm sure." Edward and Bartholomew stood in silence for a moment, letting the sombre talk overtake the moment.

"Let us remove ourselves from this darkness and see your ship opened," Bartholomew said, patting Edward on the shoulder to get him moving.

Edward smacked the key in the palm of his hand thoughtfully. "Not yet. I started this journey of the keys with Anne, and I want to finish it with her. It would not feel right without her."

"Understood. We will wait for her to awaken. Now go back to her, you don't need to attend my sorry self anymore. I can manage."

"One thing before I leave. Half of Plague's crew is still on the island. Could you organise the crews to bring all three ships out to sea? If we don't have to fight them, all the better."

Edward started walking away towards the *Freedom*, but Bartholomew made him turn around with a question. "What are we to do with so large a ship?"

Edward turned, walking backwards. "We're pirates, aren't we?" he asked, his arms spread open. "We sell it."

Bartholomew smiled widely at the young man's boldness. Edward smiled back to his friend, then turned around to join his crew in returning to the *Freedom*, their home.

On the waist, many were resting from the battle and the brush with death in the ark. Edward examined the injured and ensured the crew was doing well. They were in high spirits now that Plague was dead and Anne was safe, despite being battle weary.

Nassir approached Edward, purpose in his eyes. "Captain, I must show you something. I held to this until now, as now the ship is whole."

Edward was confused by Nassir's cryptic talk. *Will he leave the ship again?* "Lead the way."

Nassir first took Edward to the stern. Right beneath the quarterdeck, there was a small square platform with railings on the sides. The location was in the same spot where Nassir had installed a rope for Herbert to climb down instead of having to crawl down the stairs.

"Yes, I've been wondering about this platform. What does it do?"

"I will show you," Nassir said with a grin.

Nassir went to the side of the platform and began pulling on a rope. The platform rose as he pulled, and when he let go it was stationary. Then he pulled another rope and the platform descended again.

"It still requires some testing, and the bow side is not complete, but I thought you would appreciate seeing it."

"Nassir, this is brilliant. This is more than I could have expected. Now Herbert can stay in his wheelchair and travel around the decks. I'm sure Herbert will appreciate that." Edward patted Nassir on the shoulder, and the man smiled.

"That is not all. I have one more surprise."

Next, Nassir took Edward to the bow cabin. The cabin was mainly for storage, and held everything from cannonballs for the top deck to spices which could not fit in the lower cabin. It also had three large twelve-pound cannons for a frontal assault.

Nassir moved to the corner of the room, which held something rather large wrapped in cloth. Edward had no recollection of seeing it before. Nassir unwrapped and revealed the item.

Edward laughed in astonishment. "Nassir, it's beautiful. This is the figurehead you were making, right?"

Nassir nodded and gazed upon his creation with Edward. The wooden figurehead was of a woman with long, flowing curls and piercing eyes wearing a Greek-style robe. The face was akin to Anne, and in the statue's hands were an hourglass and a spear.

"This is not the same statue I was working on before. When you and this ship were taken, I believe the British Navy destroyed the first one I was working on. When I rejoined the crew, I began work on this one. Originally, the likeness was to be of Queen Anne, but later I chose the likeness of our Anne."

"It truly is breathtaking. When next we are at port we will affix it to the bow." Edward stepped closer and stroked the face of the statue. The figurehead was so lifelike in appearance Edward believed the statue would start talking to him.

"Go to her," Nassir said. "This will still be here."

Edward nodded and left the cabin, heading to the lower deck. He passed Alexandre's cabin, which was filled to the brim with injured. Crewmates with lesser injuries were waiting outside. Edward inspected those waiting and peered into the cabin to see Alexandre and Victor hard at work providing care.

The Voyages of Queen Anne's Revenge

Edward continued to the crew cabin and the bed beneath the stairs where Anne was sleeping. William was sitting bedside, talking with Christina and Pukuh, with a few other crewmates listening, and Tala at Christina's side.

At the sound of Edward's footsteps, Tala turned her shaggy head his way. Christina noticed Tala and followed her gaze. "There you are, Edward," she said. "We were trying to figure out why Plague was sent after Anne. I say Plague was a warning for us to stay away from England."

"The Queen would never send the Admiral of the Black as a warning. Anne was the main target, but we were all meant to die." William's arms were folded neatly across his chest.

"We don't know that. If we were targets then why not destroy our ships? If they wanted us all to die they could have done it without even stepping foot on shore," Christina countered, combative as usual.

Edward stepped between her and William. "We can debate this later. For now, Anne needs her rest, which means no yelling. We're setting sail presently, and all of you are needed above."

Christina let out a sigh and strode off with Tala and the other crewmates. Edward watched as they left, leaving him, William, and Anne.

"I need you to take over and have us sailing as soon as possible. I'll stay and watch over Anne."

"Some say setting sail without the captain on deck is a bad omen," William claimed as he rose from his chair.

"If you truly believe that, I am Davy Jones."

"Well, as this ship is not the Flying Dutchman, I will see myself above." William passed Edward, but stopped when he reached the stairs. "Captain?"

"Yes, William?"

William stood straight and saluted. "It is an honour to serve on this ship. And, thank you for saving Anne."

Edward was speechless. All he could do was nod to William, causing the man to leave up the stairs before Edward could wrap his head around what had happened.

Edward sat down at the foot of the bed, and watched Anne as she slept soundly. Her colour was returning and she no longer breathed heavily. She was at peace.

Edward relaxed as the fatigue from the day seeped in. Soon his eyes were closed, and, not long after, he was asleep.

Edward awoke to the sounds of the sea waves lapping the ship. When he opened his eyes he was gazing into the ocean green eyes and ruby red hair on his love, Anne.

"Finally awake?" she asked, chipper as ever.

Edward leaned forward and passionately kissed Anne, embracing her tightly. He held onto her like she was his lifeline in the middle of a storm.

Edward eventually uttered, "I'm sorry."

"Sorry for what, silly?" Anne replied, pulling back to see his eyes, placing a hand on his cheek.

"I almost lost you, and I am to blame."

"Don't ever say that," Anne said forcefully. "It's because of you that I'm still here. You have nothing to be sorry about." Anne smiled and this time she embraced Edward.

After another moment together, Edward pulled away and took something out of his pocket. "Look what Bartholomew found." Edward opened his hand to reveal the final key.

"Have you not opened the final door yet?" Anne asked, her eyes wide.

"No, not y—"

"Well, what are you waiting for?" Anne shuffled herself quickly out of the bed. "The door will not open itself, now will it?" Anne extended her hand to Edward.

Edward smiled and took Anne's hand. Together the two moved up the stairs to the gun deck, heading towards the stern and the last locked door on the ship.

"*Capitaine*," Edward heard behind him. Alexandre was standing at the door to his medical cabin, drying his hands. He had noticed the key in Edward's hand. "See me after you are finished. You as well, Princess. It concerns you both."

Edward was suddenly worried. "Is it urgent?"

"*Non, non.* See me when you are done."

"I am sure I have you to thank for still being alive, Alexandre. I'll give you a proper thanks in a moment."

"I look forward to it. God knows I haven't *enjoyed* enough hugs already," the surgeon said with mock disdain.

Anne laughed, then she and Edward continued walking towards the stern, albeit at a slower pace. He and Anne were starting to gather a crowd. Those resting on the gun deck noticed the key, and Anne, and formed a line behind them. Many also expressed their relief in seeing Anne up and about so soon.

Edward, Anne, and a dozen crewmates stood in front of the large and ornate double doors. Edward stared at the key.

"Well go on, then," Anne encouraged with a grin. The crewmates nearby joined in with her.

Edward lifted the key up to eye level, which at his height meant everyone else was staring up at him. "With this, the game is finally over."

After the weight of Edward's words reached his own heart, he turned around and set the key in the lock. After a deep breath, he turned the key, grabbed the knobs to the doors, and opened the final room.

What met Edward's eyes was the most lavishly decorated room of the *Freedom*. The captain's cabin. *His* cabin.

Red carpet with gilded tassels lined the centre of the floor from front to back. Three gold chandeliers hung from the ceiling in a row, following the path of the carpet. On the side walls several tapestries were hung to keep the room warm, and at the back thick, patterned curtains covered windows to the outside.

Like in the bow cabin, three twelve-pound cannons pointed to the outside. They were on wheels and could easily be turned about in the event the ship was invaded and Edward wanted to make a final stand.

On the left side of the room there was a king-size bed with a wooden bedframe which appeared to be carved from a single piece of oak wood. Silk and cotton sheets with gilded embroidery draped the mattress.

On the right stood a desk of intricate design. It held shelves on the bottom left and right sides, with a chair in the middle. The shelves held anything a captain could want: paper, sea charts, navigation tools, writing instruments, and a few books.

A large round table with chairs was set at the back of the room, similar to the one in the war room above, but smaller and more intimate. This one was meant for entertaining and dining rather than meetings, but it did have a grandiose high-backed chair with red upholstery and gold trim, mirroring the war room.

Edward and the crewmates nearby entered and examined the room more thoroughly. Littered about were small knickknacks like swords, guns, books, chests and a dresser full of extravagant clothes, a statue holding a skull, and bottles of various alcohols of rare vintage.

"This was on the table." Anne held out a piece of paper to Edward.

Edward read the paper. "Congratulations. Signed Benjamin Hornigold." Benjamin's seal, a hunting horn, was beside the signature in gold wax. Edward flipped the paper over, but the other side was blank. He laughed loudly and wiped away a tear. "How anticlimactic."

"Indeed," Anne concurred.

"I think this might change your mind, captain," a crewman said, lifting a heavy medium-sized chest to the table. The crewmate opened the chest with a smile, and gold coins fell out the top.

Edward grabbed one of the coins. The other crewmates' jaws were on the floor, and they too grabbed hold of some of the coins, and tested them.

"Real gold!" one confirmed excitedly.

"There must be a thousand gold pieces in here," Edward said, his shocked expression turning to the widest of smiles.

Edward picked up Anne in his arms and began spinning her around. The crew in the cabin were giddy with excitement at the wealth before them. They embraced and danced with glee.

Anne laughed as Edward spun her in the air. He eventually dropped her back down and kissed her. "I think it might be the gold speaking, but I love you, Anne."

Anne laughed and smacked Edward. "I love you too." She kissed him back.

Edward caught sight of the medical cabin through the open doors of the captain's cabin. He glanced at the crewmen grabbing fistfuls of the gold coins, their eyes in a frenzy.

"Hey, leave the gold in the chest. That's for the whole crew, and rightfully half should go to Bartholomew's crew, so no touching." The crew mumbled cries of dismay, but Edward silenced them, then turned his attention to Anne. "We should see what Alexandre wanted."

"Yes," Anne replied.

Edward and Anne returned to the bow where Alexandre and Victor waited in the cabin. Inside on the table lay the body of Plague, his head lying where it normally would be if attached, but a cloth draped over the face.

"What did you need to tell us, Alexandre?"

"There are *deux* things you needed to see. First, this." Alexandre pulled off the cloth covering Plague's chest. The material made a sickening squish as it caught on coagulated blood and was ripped off. "Notice anything odd?"

Edward inspected Plague's chest, and what he saw didn't make sense. A large wound stretched from the dead man's left shoulder all the way down to his right hip. Opposite to that slash, there was another going from the right shoulder to Plague's left hip. The two cuts made an X in the centre of the assassin's chest.

Edward knew the second wound was from him. "Was this from Bartholomew?" Edward asked, pointing to the first wound.

"*Non*, I inquired, Bartholomew shot Plague here." Alexandre pointed to a bullet hole in Plague's stomach. "But this wound was fresh during your battle. I would estimate within five to ten hours old at the time."

"He fought us with this wound? He must have been weak from blood loss even if he was able to stop the bleeding. That's how I was able to win."

"You must give yourself some credit, Edward," Anne said. Edward cocked his brow. Anne pursed her lips. "Yes, you're right. You would not have won otherwise."

"But who wounded him?" Edward asked.

Alexandre shrugged. "We may never know. They could be dead now because of their fight."

Edward nodded. *If Plague was the one who survived with this wound, I would not wish to be the other person.* "And you say you found something else?"

Alexandre turned around, picked up a piece of paper and passed it to Anne. The paper was worn and flexed. The top of the paper read: "The Daily Courant," and the headline in big bold letters read: "Queen Anne's Daughter Dead."

Anne's knees buckled, but she steadied herself on the table in front of her. Tears formed in her eyes. "This is why she wanted me dead. I am a disgrace to her, Edward." Anne handed the paper to Edward.

Edward read the headline and some of the article. The paper stated how Anne Sofia Stewart, daughter to the Queen, was killed by an unknown group a pirates during a trip to Boston. The date of the paper was almost a year ago, a month after Anne assisted Edward's escape from jail.

"This is her way of telling me I'm disowned." Anne wiped her tears away. "It is better this way, yes. I cut my ties long ago, it's only fitting she make it permanent." Anne began pacing the room. "And, I'm still alive. That is my revenge against her. She can tell herself I am dead, but it will never be true."

Edward, Alexandre, and Victor all focused on Anne, not saying anything. "What? Why are you all staring?"

Edward didn't speak, he simply embraced Anne. At first she stood stock still, shaking, then her arms flew up and gripped Edward's jacket like a vice. She stifled sobs as tears fell on Edward's chest.

After a moment, Victor joined Edward in embracing Anne. He waved for Alexandre to join after he seemed content to stand there. Alexandre sighed and placed his hand on Anne's head. Victor pulled on his shoulder and forced him to join in the embrace.

The three let Anne dry her eyes, their gesture saying more than words ever could. "Thank you," she said meekly.

Victor, Alexandre, and Edward released Anne from their embrace. "There is something I need to tell the crew. Something I've been thinking about for a long time, and now I know the perfect way to go about it." Edward turned to Alexandre and Victor. "Could you two gather the crewmates on the waist?" Alexandre and Victor both nodded and left the cabin.

Edward started to walk away, but Anne stopped him. "Wait, Edward. What do you have to announce?" she asked.

Edward leaned against the edge of the cabin door, his hand on the exit. "The ship's name," he said with a smirk, then he rounded the corner.

Anne jumped forward, trying to catch up to Edward, wiping her eyes. "What do you mean? The ship *has* a name!" she yelled out the cabin door.

Edward was at the stairs. "I'll explain what I mean up top," he yelled back, bounding up the steps.

The salty air filled Edward's nostrils. It became a fine day for sailing. The waves from before they landed were gone, the wind was in their favour, and the sun shone all the harder.

The crew waved and called to their captain as he ran to the quarterdeck where Herbert, Christina, and Tala stood. Anne was on his heels and even more people waved and hollered to her, glad to see her awake.

On the quarterdeck, Edward could see the *Fortune* off the starboard side, and Plague's ship sailing with them off the port side, manned by men from both crews.

"Captain," Herbert said, nodding as Edward approached.

"How fares the sea, Herbert?" Edward asked.

"Smooth sailing, Captain. Winds in our favour. Headed to Bodden Town to unload this cargo, I presume?"

"You presume right, sailing master." Edward smiled.

William joined those on the quarterdeck and spoke words with Anne, ensuring she was well. William knelt, examining her closely. After a few words and nods from Anne, William stood straight and the two joined Edward, Herbert, and Christina at the helm.

"William, could you call the crew together? I have an announcement to make."

The Voyages of Queen Anne's Revenge

"Aye, aye, Captain." William turned to the main deck and yelled for attention.

The crew dropped what they were doing and crowded together near the quarterdeck. Jack and Nassir were on the deck, Pukuh was hanging from a bowline, and Alexandre stood beside Victor, with the remainder of the crew walking up from the lower deck.

"Well, men, I want to start off by saying I am proud of all of you for the courage you displayed back on the island, and for all the times I called upon you to be brave with me.

"Over the course of this journey we've solved deadly puzzles in the underground of not one, but two islands, fought against a Marine Captain who chased us halfway across the Caribbean, saw the unimaginable in the Devil's Triangle, fought a plantation owner, and killed an assassin sent by none other than Queen Anne herself.

"That is more than any crew on these seas could say they've done, and you deserve all the praise. Without you, all this would not be possible, so thank you."

The crew pumped their fists and hollered their appreciation back to their captain.

"And thanks to those efforts, we now have a full ship. The final cabin is opened, but before you view the room I have more to say.

"When I received this ship—some of you may not know the story, but I'll keep it brief for those of you who do—I had a night of wild abandon, with too much to drink, and I used my life savings to buy this warship, when all I wanted to be was a whaler. The man who sold me this ship was named Benjamin Hornigold. He created this ship as a game, and that is what set us on this journey for the keys.

"Little did I know at the time, but because of what he did, he still owned this ship. *Freedom* was his ship, and until I retrieved all the keys, this ship would not truly be mine, as it is now.

"As such, this ship needs a new name," Edward said, placing his hands on the quarterdeck railing.

The crew was confused. "But Captain, why?"

"Simple, gentlemen: We have our *Freedom*. This ship is a symbol for all of us. For some, the ship is our home, our escape, our hope. The name was more than just the name of a ship. *Freedom* was what we sought. Freedom from our former lives, freedom from chains, both literal and figurative. But, the ship is ours now, we are free from our former lives, and we are free from the chains.

"We need a new name, and with that name a renewed purpose."

Edward let the crew murmur amongst themselves, allowing the words to sink in and take root. After the crew talked with each other, they agreed with Edward.

"What's the new name?"

Edward folded his arms. "*Queen Anne's Revenge.*"

Anne's and William's jaws dropped. The crew became louder at the sound of the new name. Confusion was the main theme.

Before the crew could ask more questions, Edward raised his hands to silence them. "The reason why I've chosen *Queen Anne's Revenge* is twofold: Firstly, because the name will be a testament to our victory against Queen Anne and her assassin. This ship will be a constant reminder that despite her actions against us, despite throwing everything she sent against us, we are still here, and we are still alive!" Edward yelled, causing many in the crew to cheer. "Whenever people hear of our exploits, it will be a constant mockery against her and all she stands for.

"And the second reason will be our purpose. Queen Anne's Revenge will be the name the world knows, but to us, the true name of this ship is *Revenge.*

"We have our freedom, so we will avenge those who have had their freedom taken away. Our purpose will be to take *Revenge* for those who can't take it for themselves.

"Slaves, the poor, the imprisoned. We will free them from their chains, and take revenge on those who caged them. Who's with me?"

The crew pumped their fists and chanted together in agreement. They were in a frenzy of excitement so loud that those on the other ships could hear it.

"We are pirates! We will steal *Freedom* back for those who need it, and take *Revenge* on those who think they can take it away," Edward yelled. He raised his fist. "Revenge!"

The ship once known as *Freedom*, owned by Benjamin Hornigold, was now and forever known as *Queen Anne's Revenge*, owned by Edward Thatch, the pirate Blackbeard.

EPILOGUE

One Month Later

The noonday sun shone over the *Queen Anne's Revenge*, the wind cooling the ship and all those gathered on it. The ship drifted in the sea off the coast of Bodden Town. The crew of the *Fortune* mixed on the deck with the crew of the *Queen Anne's Revenge*. Everyone gazed at the quarterdeck, and the ceremony being performed.

On the quarterdeck, Christina stood on the starboard side, and William on the port with Jack behind him playing a light medley with his violin. In the centre, in front of the helm, stood Bartholomew, Edward, and Anne.

"Do you, Edward Thatch, take this woman to be your wife?" Bartholomew asked.

Edward was wearing a white three-piece suit with gold and silver embroidery. He had a white undershirt with a vest and longcoat and the pants went to his knees with white socks pulled up. His beard was in braids and his wavy black hair was slicked back.

"I do," he replied.

"Do you, Anne Bonney, take this man to be your husband?"

Anne wore a stunning white dress with a gold necklace. The dress was embroidered similarly to Edward's suit, with gold along the chest and pearls at various spots. It fit Anne's curves beautifully and had a frilly skirt all the way to her feet. Anne's hair was done up, with her curls spilling out at the front and sides.

"I do," she replied.

The two were wearing rings, simple gold bands made from leftover metal from the forging of Edward's cutlass.

"Then by the power vested in me by the Lord above, I now pronounce you husband and wife. You may kiss the bride."

Edward leaned in and kissed Anne. The crews cheered and threw up their hats in celebration of the union. Edward and Anne, both smiling from ear to ear, turned hand in hand, and gazed at their crew. They lifted their hands together, showing the two wedding bands symbolising their eternal bond.

THE END

ABOUT THE AUTHOR

JEREMY IS CURRENTLY LIVING IN NEW BRUNSWICK, CANADA WITH HIS WIFE HEATHER, AND THEIR TWO CATS, NAVI AND THOR.

Jeremy's first foray into the writing world was during a writing competition called NaNoWriMo, where the goal is to write a certain number of words in the month of November.

After completing the novel he started, and some extensive rewrites, he felt it was worthy of publishing and self-published his first novel, Blackbeard's Freedom in September, 2012.

After writing over ten books under two names, his passion for writing hasn't wavered over the years, and hopes to one day make it his primary career.

Let everyone know what you thought of his novels by leaving a review. He loves getting feedback on his books, and loves to hear from fans of his work.

Want to pirate one of Jeremy's novels? Visit http://www.mcleansnovels.com/free-book-link for a free copy of one of his books.

Printed in Poland
by Amazon Fulfillment
Poland Sp. z o.o., Wrocław

60487802R00201